TESS THORNTON

A MATCH

FOR THE

Cowboy

RIDGEVIEW RANCH

BOOK 4

Library of Congress Number: Pending

First Paperback Edition August, 2022

Cover Art by: GetCovers

Photography and Graphics Courtesy Of: Shutterstock.com, Depositphotos.com, Twenty2 0.com, Elements.envato.com

Editing and Layout by: Eagle Creek Press, Inc.

Printed in the USA

Publisher: Eagle Creek Press,

EAGLE CREEK
PRESS

Contents

For Marty

Chapter One

Gage

Luke's loop shot out like it was on rails, snagging the black steer's horns so clean it was like the ropes had been drawn tight by some invisible force. I grunted, pushing Banner forward with a nudge of my heels, and swung my loop, timing my throw with the steer's back legs.

One... two...

The rope sailed out and snatched both hocks just as Banner slid to a stop. Dust flew up in a fine cloud, coating my lips and making my lungs burn. I let out a satisfied breath, dallying up and feeling the sweet tension of a clean catch humming through the rope in my hands.

"Seven-three!" Luke called, his grin stretched wide as he looked back from his horse, Jester. "Still got it, old man."

"Old man?" I snorted, loosening my dally and letting the steer trot off. "If I'm old, what does that make you? Retirement age?"

Luke laughed, loud and easy. "I've got a house, three kids, and a back that reminds me I'm thirty-one every time I get out of bed. I'm halfway there." He tipped his hat back, the sun catching on his sweat-dampened hairline. "But you? You've got plenty of tread left on those boots, my friend. Best heel side I've roped with all week."

"That's because you've only roped with me," I shot back, wiping a dusty sleeve across my forehead. "Slim pickin's doesn't count as a compliment."

Luke grinned and tossed his loop to Jester's saddle horn. "Yeah, yeah. Take the win where you can."

He was all easy charm these days, the sharp competitive edge we'd shared back in the day mellowed by a wife, a gaggle of kids, and a little more life under his belt. Didn't mean he couldn't still rope circles around most guys at the jackpots, though.

Including me.

I swung Banner around to the back of the pen as the next steer was run in, Jester jogging right alongside us. It felt good to rope again, the kind of good that settled under my skin and got my blood pumping in a way that not much else did these days.

Not that I had a whole lot of time for it anymore. Between holding the ranch together and running enough cattle to keep us above water, fun was a luxury I couldn't afford most of the time. But with things finally starting to look up around the place, I'd let myself give in to Luke's pestering about entering the jackpot this coming weekend. A little roping. A little breathing. I deserved that much, didn't I?

"You're quiet today," Luke said after a beat, pulling his horse to a stop at the edge of the pen. His eyes narrowed in that way they always did when he was trying to pry something out of me. "What's on your mind?"

"Nothing."

Luke snorted. "Yeah, right. You've had that look on your face since you got here. The one where you're thinking too much and telling me too little."

I swiped my hat off and ran a hand through my hair. "It's nothing."

Luke just stared at me, waiting. If there was one thing the man had mastered over the years, it was patience. He didn't push. He didn't prod. He just let the silence do the work for him. Luke Walker, of all people—the yammeringest cowboy I ever knew, and now he was silent as a hilltop sage. Must've been his wife rubbing off on him.

I sighed, shaking my head. "It's just..." I shrugged. "Feels like everything's changing all at once, you know?"

Luke leaned forward on his saddle horn. "That so?"

"Cole's married. Chase and Trent are planning their weddings. Even your brothers have wives and kids now." I shoved my hat back on and gave him a hard look. "What happened? Last I checked, we were all trying to beat the other guy's time, and now half the people I know are handing over rings and arguing about table settings."

Luke chuckled. "It happens quick."

"Yeah, no kidding." I stared out at the pasture, where the steer had trotted off to join the others. "I'm not mad about it or anything. It's just... weird."

"You feel left behind?"

I snorted. "No. I'm not crying into my drink at night about it, if that's what you're asking."

Luke grinned. "Didn't figure you for the pining type."

"I'm not," I said quickly. "I just..." I trailed off, fumbling for the right words. "I don't know. I guess I didn't expect everyone else to settle down so fast. Feels like I blinked, and everything changed."

Luke nodded, like he understood exactly what I was saying. "You'll get used to it. And hey, maybe it's not so bad being the last man standing. You don't have to share your time or your remote."

"Yeah, that's what I'm missing. Control of the TV."

He laughed again, but his expression turned thoughtful as he watched me. "I will say this, though: don't count yourself out, Gage. Life has a funny way of sneaking up on you when you least expect it."

I scoffed. "Yeah, sure."

Luke didn't push it, and I was grateful for that. He just nodded to the steer pen and said, "We running another one, or you need to go back to making money and bossing people around?"

I grinned despite myself. "One more. I need the practice if I'm going to keep up with you this weekend."

Luke tugged his hat lower with a cocky smirk. "You're not gonna keep up with me, but I appreciate the effort."

I flipped him a salute as I pushed Banner into a lope, the rhythm of hooves pounding against dirt settling something in me I hadn't even realized was out of place. Maybe Luke was right. Life was changing all around me, faster than I'd expected. But for now, there was still this—this quiet steadiness, this feeling of doing something right, if only for a little while.

For now, it was enough.

Amber

"THAT'S IT, JESSE. YOU'RE doing great." My voice stayed soft and even—my professional voice, even though I could feel my phone buzzing for the third time in less than ten minutes in my back pocket.

Jesse, a lanky teenager with shaggy brown hair and bright green sneakers, didn't look up. His focus stayed fixed on Jasper's mane as he reached down, tentative and careful, brushing his fingers through the horse's soft forelock.

"This is the best he's done all week," Kate murmured, walking alongside Jasper with the lead rope in her hands. Her voice was low, for my ears only, but I caught the note of pride.

"Yeah, it is." I smiled as Jesse sat straighter in the saddle, his shoulders easing like he was finally finding the rhythm we'd been working on for weeks. "How does that feel, Jesse?"

He shrugged, his expression shy, but I didn't miss the tiny smile tugging at the corner of his mouth. "It's okay, I guess."

"That's better than 'not great,'" I teased gently. "Let's try for a little more movement. Kate, let's pick up the pace—nice and slow, though."

Kate gave me a quick nod, and I fell into step beside Jasper as he moved into a steady walk. Jesse adjusted his balance, his hands twitching nervously toward the saddle horn before he caught himself.

"Good job, Jesse. Trust yourself," I said. "And trust Jasper. He's got you."

The phone buzzed again. I clenched my jaw and ignored it. Gina. I didn't even have to check. It wasn't like my sister to stop at one missed call.

Jasper flicked an ear toward the sound, but Jesse didn't seem to notice. His shoulders were still relaxed, his hands finding a natural rhythm with Jasper's movement. I exhaled slowly. For Jesse, this was a win, and I wasn't going to let anything disrupt that.

When the session finally wrapped up, I helped Jesse dismount while Kate praised him for the progress he'd made. The pride on Jesse's face—small but real—made the buzzing phone worth ignoring. Moments like this were why I did what I did. They reminded me why the therapy center mattered, why it was worth every ounce of stress.

As Kate led Jasper back toward the barn, I finally pulled my phone out of my pocket, my frustration flaring as I saw the missed calls lined up like soldiers. Three calls. Three. And a new voicemail.

I stepped around the corner of the barn and pressed play, bracing myself.

"Amber, it's Gina. Again. Look, I don't know why you're not answering, but I'm at the center now, and they're ready for me to sign the lease papers. Mom and Dad are going to love it here, I promise—it's clean, the staff is friendly, and the community is active. It's perfect for them. But I can't do this without you because of the power of attorney thing. Just call me back, okay? This is important, Amber."

I groaned and rubbed a hand over my eyes. She's signing the lease? Gina wasn't just pushing for assisted living anymore; she was halfway to making it a done deal.

"Everything okay?"

I turned to find Kate coming around the corner, Jasper's bridle looped over her arm and her expression curious but cautious.

I tried to smile, though I could feel how thin it was. "It's fine. Family stuff. Can you finish up here? I need to take this call."

Kate gave me a quick nod. "Go. I've got it."

I shot her a grateful look as I ducked back around the barn, my phone already dialing Gina's number. It rang twice before she picked up.

"Finally," Gina said. "Amber, I—"

"What do you mean you're signing the lease?" I cut in, my voice sharper than I intended.

Gina sighed, the exasperated kind that made me feel like I was the unreasonable one. "I'm not signing it yet. I just said they're ready for me to. It's a formality. I need you to say yes."

"Well, I'm saying no," I shot back. "You don't even know if this is what they want."

"Oh, come on, Amber," Gina said, her tone inching toward condescending. "You know Mom and Dad. They're not going to ask for this, but we both know they need it. This place is perfect for them. They'll have meals cooked for them, cleaning taken care of, round-the-clock care—"

"And do they know you're there trying to get them an apartment?"

There was a beat of silence. "Not yet."

"Gina." My voice dropped.

"They wouldn't come look," she said defensively. "And you know them, Amber. They'll fight it tooth and nail if it's not already a done deal. They don't want to be a burden, but once they see how nice this place is, they'll come around."

"They're not a burden." My voice was low and tight, but it trembled with the kind of anger I didn't have the energy to hide. "And you don't get to decide this for them. We need to talk to them first—"

"And let them say no?" Gina snapped. "What's your plan, Amber? To keep them in that big old house forever? Let Dad fall down the stairs when no one's looking? Mom can barely get around, and you know it. This place is safer. It's better for them."

My chest squeezed. I turned my back to the barn, staring out at the mountains that rose up in the distance. Mom will die if she can't see the mountains. I'd said it once without thinking, but now the thought lodged itself in my chest, painful and unmoving.

"I'll come home this weekend," I said finally. "We can sit down with Mom and Dad and actually talk about this. You don't need to make it a done deal before they've even had a chance to weigh in."

"Amber—"

"No." I cut her off. "I can't talk about this right now. I'm at work, Gina. Working. I can't do this over the phone."

Gina sighed again, but her voice softened, just a little. "Fine. Come home this weekend. But you know I'm right."

I hung up before I said something I'd regret. My phone buzzed again with a text—Gina, sending me a picture of the retirement center's cheerful lobby, complete with potted plants and smiling seniors playing cards at a round table. I shut off my screen and shoved the phone back into my pocket.

I walked back toward the barn, my legs suddenly heavier than they'd been all day. Kate met me halfway, Jasper's coat gleaming from a fresh brush-down.

"Everything okay?" she asked again, her brow furrowed as she studied me.

I forced a smile. "Yeah. Just... my sister. Thanks for finishing up."

Kate nodded slowly, like she knew better than to press me for details. "Anytime."

As I watched her lead Jasper back toward the paddock, my shoulders slumped. I'd promised Gina I'd come home, but even as I said it, doubt crept in like a shadow. What if she's right? What if I'm just being selfish? Sentimental?

Maybe I was holding on too tight to the past. Maybe my parents would be better off somewhere with round-the-clock care and friendly faces. But the thought of them leaving everything—their home, the mountains, the life they'd built—made me feel like I was watching something precious slip through my fingers.

I leaned against the barn wall, staring out at the mountains I knew my mom loved as much as I did.

"They'd hate it," I whispered to no one but myself.

And yet, for the first time, I wondered if I was fighting for them... or for me.

Chapter Two

Amber

"OKAY, NOAH, I WANT you to take a deep breath and let your shoulders relax. Can you do that for me?"

Noah nodded, his face tense as he gripped the saddle horn like it was the only thing keeping him alive. Jasper, the saint of a horse that he was, didn't even flick an ear at the boy's tight grip. He stood steady beneath Noah, patient as ever.

Kate glanced at me from where she held Jasper's lead rope, her expression saying, *He's so close.*

"You're safe up there," I said gently, taking a step closer. "Jasper's got you. And Kate and I are right here. Let's try letting go of the horn—just for a second."

Noah's hands didn't budge. His chest rose and fell in shallow bursts, his breath quick and panicked.

I crouched slightly, making sure I was in his line of sight. "Hey, look at me."

His wide, fearful eyes darted to mine.

"You don't have to let go just yet," I said softly. "How about this instead: loosen your grip. Just a little. Let your fingers rest, and see how that feels."

His knuckles, pale from squeezing so hard, flexed ever so slightly. I caught Kate's grin out of the corner of my eye. Progress.

"You're doing great, Noah. That's all we need for now," I said, keeping my voice even and calm. "Can you feel Jasper breathing? Try to match him."

He stared down at the horse's withers, his little shoulders lifting and falling in rhythm with Jasper's slow, steady breaths.

My phone buzzed in my back pocket. I ignored it. Again.

Kate flicked her eyes toward me, her brow arching, but I shook my head. Gina could wait. Whatever her so-called emergency was, it wasn't going to derail Noah's session.

"Better?" I asked him after a minute.

Noah nodded again, his grip finally easing a little more.

"That's it." Relief bloomed in my chest as I reached out to pat Jasper's neck. "You're doing amazing. Jasper knows you're relaxed, and he's relaxing with you. Isn't that right, buddy?"

Jasper snorted as if on cue, and Noah smiled—a quick flicker, but real. My chest warmed as I glanced at Kate.

"Good. Let's keep breathing, nice and slow."

A truck engine growled to life in the parking lot. My head snapped up at the sound.

The gray truck crawled closer, and I knew exactly who it was before I saw him. Gage Langton, big as life and twice as loud. Of course.

The truck door creaked open, and I heard his boots hit the gravel. My phone buzzed again, and my last thread of patience frayed.

Kate didn't even try to hide her smirk. "Looks like we've got company."

"Great," I muttered under my breath, keeping my voice low enough that Noah wouldn't catch the irritation creeping in.

"Want me to go see what he needs?"

"Yes," I said quickly. "Please get rid of him."

"Wow, tell me how you really feel." She handed me Jasper's lead rope and strolled off toward Gage, who was already ambling toward the barn with that easy, infuriating swagger of his.

"Amber!" Noah's panicked voice yanked my attention back to him.

I shot him what I hoped was a calming smile. "Sorry about that. You're doing great, Noah. Let's see if we can take one hand off the horn. You can keep the other one there—just let one hand rest for a second."

His gaze darted to Jasper's neck again, and for a moment, I thought he might not do it. But then his left hand hesitated, fingers loosening ever so slightly before lifting an inch away.

"There you go!" My voice stayed calm, but I couldn't help the proud grin tugging at my lips. "You've got this."

Kate's laughter floated over from the parking lot, and I clenched my jaw to keep from looking. *Focus, Amber.*

But then Gage's voice rang out, casual and too loud. "Didn't mean to interrupt anything important!"

I took a deep breath, focusing hard on Noah. "Good job. Let's try switching hands now. Put your left hand back on the horn, and let your right one rest. Just like before."

The boy's face crushed into a scowl of concentration, but he did it. Slowly, carefully.

Kate came back a moment later, shaking her head. "He's looking for Chase. Says he needs something for the ranch."

"Of course he does."

"He said to tell you hi."

I didn't bother hiding my groan as I moved to Noah's other side. "One more lap, Noah. You're doing so well."

The boy nodded, his focus shifting back to Jasper. I exhaled slowly, my chest easing just a little as the horse plodded along the rail.

Kate leaned closer, her voice dropping. "He's still watching, by the way."

I didn't look, but I felt Gage's eyes on me like an itch I couldn't scratch. My phone buzzed again, and this time, I couldn't stop the flash of irritation that crossed my face.

"Everything okay?" Kate asked.

"Fine," I said through gritted teeth.

She gave me a look that said she didn't believe me, but thankfully, she didn't press.

We finished the session with Noah in one piece—him beaming with pride, me hanging onto my patience by a thread.

"Thanks, Miss Amber," Noah said as I helped him down from the saddle. His face was flushed, but he looked steady, calmer than when he'd arrived.

"You did amazing today," I told him, crouching so I was at his eye level. "That was all you, Noah. Jasper just followed your lead."

He glanced at the horse, his shy smile growing just a little. "Can I ride him again next time?"

"Absolutely. He'll be waiting for you."

Noah's mom waved from the parking lot, and he ran off to meet her. I leaned against Jasper's shoulder, taking a second to let the moment settle. "Good boy," I said. "You made a difference today, old man."

Kate appeared at my side, already loosening the saddle cinch. "You okay? You've been twitchy ever since Gage showed up. And don't think I didn't notice you pretending your phone wasn't buzzing every two minutes."

I sighed, tugging the reins over Jasper's head and leading him toward the barn. "It's Gina. She's been calling all morning. I know exactly what she wants, and I'm not in the mood for it right now."

"And Gage?" Kate asked, trailing behind with the saddle.

"What about him?"

Kate laughed. "You didn't even look at him."

"Because I was working."

"Sure," she drawled.

I shot her a glare over my shoulder. "What is that supposed to mean?"

"Nothing." Her grin widened. "Just that most people would at least say hi, maybe make polite conversation. You, on the other hand, managed to look like you were personally offended by his existence."

"Not true."

"Uh-huh."

I led Jasper into his stall and rubbed his neck absently, my irritation simmering just under the surface. "He just—he doesn't take anything seriously. You heard him. That whole 'sorry for interrupting' thing? He wasn't sorry at all."

Kate leaned against the stall door, crossing her arms. "You ever think maybe he's just trying to get a rise out of you? You're fun to mess with when you're mad."

"Thanks for pointing that out."

"Anytime."

Jasper nudged my shoulder, and I sighed, giving his neck one last pat. "Anyway, I'm too busy to worry about Gage Langton. Or Gina, for that matter."

Kate tilted her head. "But you *are* worrying about them."

I turned to face her, narrowing my eyes. "Aren't you supposed to be helping me, not psychoanalyzing me?"

"I'm a woman of many talents."

"Go find a new hobby."

She laughed as she pushed off the stall door, heading for the tack room. "You're no fun today. I'll be back to see what's buzzing in your pocket this time."

When she was gone, I let out a long breath and pulled out my phone. Another missed call from Gina. Another text, and another voicemail. "Call me, Amber, it's not funny. This can't wait."

I didn't even open it. Instead, I stuffed the phone back in my pocket and went to grab Jasper's brushes, my hands itching for something to do.

Gage's voice floated through the barn, casual and infuriatingly cheerful as he chatted with Chase a few stalls down. I ground my teeth and focused on brushing Jasper's coat. Just ignore him. He'll leave eventually.

But even as I worked, I couldn't shake the thought of my sister's messages—or the fact that Gage seemed perfectly content to linger where he wasn't wanted.

"Pick your battles, Amber," I muttered under my breath. But right now, it felt like they were all closing in at once.

Gage

"**T**HOUGHT YOU WERE SUPPOSED to be working, Kate. Or is leaning on fences part of the job description now?"

Kate didn't even flinch. Just shot me a look over her shoulder, one eyebrow raised like she'd been waiting for me to show up with that mouth of mine.

"I *am* working," she shot back. "What's your excuse?"

"Borrowing tools," I said, jerking my thumb toward the barn. "Chase said he had that auger I need."

She snorted. "Sure. And you just *happened* to show up during therapy sessions, huh?"

"I don't keep track of your schedule," I said, though I didn't bother pretending I hadn't noticed the familiar chaos around the barn. Horses moving in and out, kids laughing in the distance, the quiet buzz of the ranch humming along like it always did. But I wasn't here for all that. Just the auger.

Right.

Kate's eyes flicked toward the arena, and I followed her gaze. That's when I saw her.

Amber Morris, standing next to a little bay gelding, her hand resting gentle on the horse's neck. She was talking to the kid on his back, her voice low and steady, the kind of voice that smoothed rough edges without trying too hard.

Her hair was pulled back, a few strands stuck to the sweat on her temple, and her shoulders were tight like they always were. I'd seen her around enough to know she didn't have an off switch. She ran full throttle all the time—organized, efficient, like her whole life was a checklist she needed to get through before the sun went down.

I leaned on the fence next to Kate, watching her work, and couldn't help the grin tugging at the corner of my mouth.

"She ever loosen up?" I asked, nodding toward Amber.

Kate laughed under her breath. "Only when you're not around."

"Shame. She's missing out."

"Yeah, I'm sure that's *exactly* what she's thinking."

I chuckled, pushing off the fence. "Where's Chase? I should grab that auger before she starts thinking I'm here just to bother her."

Kate gave me a look that said *you totally are*, but she didn't say it out loud.

I found Chase near the barn, going over some plans with one of the contractors. He waved me over, and we talked tools for a bit, nothing special. I should've left right after. Should've grabbed the auger, thrown it in the truck, and headed back to Ridgeview.

But I didn't.

Instead, I found myself wandering back toward the arena, like I had unfinished business.

Amber was still there, leading a different horse now, with another kid walking beside her who was holding onto the saddle with a shaky kind of pride. She was talking to him, low and calm, like nothing in the world could touch them inside that little bubble.

I leaned against the gate, just casual enough to look like I wasn't trying.

"Didn't mean to throw off your groove there, Amber," I called out, loud enough for her to hear but easy enough to sound innocent. "Didn't realize the stakes were that high for walking a horse in a circle."

Amber stopped mid-step. Didn't even look at me right away. Just let out this slow breath, like she was counting to ten in her head before she turned.

When she did, her eyes narrowed, sharp as the edge of a spade bit.

"Some of us are actually working, Gage. But I wouldn't expect you to recognize that."

I let out a low whistle, pushing off the fence. "Touchy today, aren't we?"

She didn't rise to the bait. Just gave me a tight smile, the kind that looked like she was contemplating about six ways to strangle me. "Some of us don't have time to stand around pretending to be useful."

Ouch.

But I couldn't help the grin that spread across my face. She was fun when she was mad.

"Well, I wouldn't want to keep you from your very important horse circles," I said, tipping my hat as I started toward my truck. "You carry on."

She muttered something under her breath, but I didn't catch it. Probably for the best.

I should've left it at that. Should've driven off and let her stew in whatever mood she'd been in before I showed up. But as I climbed into my truck, I caught one last glimpse of her through the barn doors.

She was talking to the kid's mom now, her face softer, her shoulders relaxed in a way I hadn't seen before. The kid beamed up at her, and she crouched down to his level, saying something that made him laugh.

Huh.

I sat there for a second longer than I needed to, watching her.

She wasn't just all sharp edges and lists after all. There was more there—something steadier, something deeper.

I shook my head, chuckling to myself as I started the truck.

Don't know why you're thinking about it, Langton.

But as I drove back toward Ridgeview, I realized I wasn't thinking about the auger anymore. And that? That was the part that bugged me most.

Chapter Three

Amber

T HE SECOND I STEPPED through the front door, Sir Stumpy came hobbling out of the kitchen like I'd broken some contract with him by staying late.

"I know, I know," I sighed, dropping my bag by the door. "You're starving. Practically wasting away."

The three-legged menace let out an indignant *mrrp* and wove between my ankles, his soft gray tail flicking against my legs. He was mostly fluff and attitude, but I still felt guilty for making him wait.

I headed straight for the kitchen, flicking on the light and grabbing his food bowl from the corner. Sir Stumpy leaped onto the counter while I scooped his kibble, his one front paw landing with a soft thump before he started rubbing his face against my shoulder.

"Off," I muttered, nudging him back down to the floor before setting his bowl in front of him. He dug in like he hadn't eaten in days, purring loud enough to rattle the windows.

At least one of us was satisfied tonight.

I grabbed a pan from the cabinet and turned toward the sink to fill it with water—only to hear the unmistakable drip, drip, drip of my still-leaking faucet.

I closed my eyes. Took a slow breath.

Not tonight.

Flipping the handle, I watched as water gushed out, then slowed to an uneven trickle while a puddle formed around the base. Great. It was worse than before.

I leaned over the sink, tightening the knob with more force than necessary, but the steady dripping continued, each drop needling its way into my already stretched nerves.

Sir Stumpy let out a soft chirp, licking his paw before looking up at me expectantly, like I was going to do something about this.

"You got a wrench hidden somewhere?" I muttered.

He blinked at me.

I grabbed my phone off the counter and did a quick search on how to fix a leaky faucet, scrolling through step-by-step instructions I had no energy to follow.

The screen lit up with an incoming call.

Gina.

Of course.

I groaned and hit the power button to silence it, tossing the phone back onto the counter before turning back to the sink. I did *not* have the patience for another argument tonight.

Sir Stumpy, now full and content, curled up in his usual spot near the window, tail wrapped neatly around his body—the perfect picture of peace. Not. Fair.

I reached for the wrench under the sink, trying to remember the last time I'd actually fixed something without Chase or Trent's help. How hard could it be?

Five minutes later, I had the cabinet doors open, the wrench slipping in my grip as I wrestled with a bolt that refused to budge. Water dripped steadily onto my sleeve, my patience wearing thinner by the second.

My phone rang again.

I didn't even check the screen. "What, Gina?"

"Well, nice to talk to you too," she said, all clipped and businesslike. "Didn't realize I needed an appointment."

I sucked in a slow breath, pressing my back against the cabinet door. "I'm elbow-deep in plumbing, Gina. Can this wait?"

"Not really."

I wiped my sleeve across my forehead. "Of course not."

There was a pause, then a sigh. "Amber, I'm not trying to make your life harder. But the facility needs a decision soon. They can't hold an apartment indefinitely."

I closed my eyes, leaning my head against the counter. "So you want me to say yes just so you can check it off your list?"

"I want you to say yes because it's the right decision," she said, her voice sharpening. "They need more help than we can give them, and this place is perfect. It's got everything—medical care, social activities, security—"

"But do they want it?"

The line went quiet for a minute.

"You know they won't agree unless they feel like it's already decided," she said finally.

"Yeah," I shot back, my jaw tight. "Because they don't want it, Gina."

She huffed out a breath. "I don't understand why you're making this so hard."

Because it is hard. Because the thought of them leaving their home, their land, their mountains—of watching my mom fade in a place that wasn't hers—made my chest feel too tight, like I couldn't get enough air.

I didn't say any of that. Instead, I forced my voice to stay even. "I told you. I'm coming home this weekend. We'll talk about it then."

She let out a slow breath, like she was trying not to slam the phone down like she used to when she was ten. "Fine. But we have to make a decision soon."

"Yeah. I got it."

I hung up before she could say anything else.

The faucet let out a sharp *plink* of water, like it was laughing at me.

Sir Stumpy yawned, completely unbothered by my impending family disaster.

I stared at the wrench in my hand, then at the leak, then dropped it onto the counter with a dull clank.

Dinner could wait. The sink could wait. The only thing I wanted right now was to sit on the couch with my cat and pretend—for just a few minutes—that I didn't have to fix anything at all.

Except... I was starving, and completely out of groceries.

Gage

THE SECOND I STEPPED into the house, I smelled biscuits.

Not the canned kind. The good ones—flaky, golden, the kind that made you reconsider every bad decision you'd ever made just for the chance to be a better man worthy of a second helping.

"Wash your hands before you touch anything," Mom called from the stove, not even looking up.

I smirked, already heading for the sink. "Nice to see you too, Mom."

The kitchen was full, voices overlapping. Cole and Emily sat at the table, their chairs close enough that their knees probably bumped. Trent leaned against the counter, arms crossed, eyes distant, like he was in another world. He was probably chewing on some scheme of Lauren's... or waiting for her to call.

Chase wasn't here yet. Not surprising.

"Hope you're hungry," Mom said, setting a steaming dish on the table. "I made plenty."

"I'm always hungry." I dried my hands on a towel and grabbed a plate. "Can't say the same for Trent, though. He looks like he's contemplating life's deeper questions instead of appreciating that spread."

Trent didn't even blink.

Cole snorted. "Leave him alone. Not all of us have the emotional range of a teaspoon."

I grinned, pulling up a chair. "Hey, I'll have you know I've got layers. Just 'cause I don't sit around pining over some girl like some people doesn't mean—"

"I don't pine," Cole interrupted, throwing a biscuit at me.

I caught it one-handed and took a bite, grinning as I chewed. "Tastes like regret, huh?"

Emily rolled her eyes. "You're impossible."

"Yeah, yeah." I reached for another biscuit. "Where's Chase?"

"Still at White Pines," Mom said, sighing as she sat down. "I swear, that boy works too hard."

Trent finally spoke. "Better than working too little."

The table went quiet for a second.

Mom pressed her lips together like she was debating whether to say something. She went with, "Lauren called earlier."

Trent nodded, pushing food around his plate. "She's still in California, tying up loose ends before she moves back for good. Sounds like she had an argument with her apartment manager about ending the lease."

"You talk about a wedding date yet?" Cole asked, mouth full.

Trent's jaw tightened. "Not yet."

"You better get on that," I said. "Otherwise, you'll end up like Chase, stuck in the will-they-won't-they dance 'til you're too old to remember what you were even waitin' for."

"Thanks for the wisdom, unmarried brother."

I grinned. "Anytime."

The front door creaked open, and Chase walked in, rubbing the back of his neck like he already knew he was late for dinner.

"Before anyone says anything, I know." He dropped into a chair and grabbed a biscuit. "I lost track of time."

"You always lose track of time," Mom said, exasperated.

He just shrugged and took a bite.

Cole leaned back, stretching. "How's construction going?"

"Good. Slow, but good."

Mom set the last dish down and glanced at the empty seat next to Chase. "Where's Kate? I thought she was coming over for dinner."

Chase barely looked up from his plate. "She went home. Helping out with her mom."

Mom nodded approvingly. "That's good of her. Her dad could probably use the break."

Cole nudged me under the table, and I smirked. "Or did she finally realize what she's getting into?"

Chase didn't even look at me. Just stabbed a piece of steak and popped it into his mouth. "You're hilarious."

Cole grinned. "I mean, she's spent years working with horses and kids and stuff. She knows how to handle intense. You, on the other hand..."

Chase shot him a look. "Kate and I are engaged. You're about three months too late for the 'figuring it out' jokes."

"Yeah, but you're still you," I said, stealing the last biscuit before Cole could get to it. "Which means she's probably running cost-benefit analyses every time you leave your socks on the floor."

Emily sighed. "You all talk about relationships like they're a business deal."

"Well," Trent said dryly, finally looking up from his plate, "Gage doesn't talk about relationships at all."

Mom clicked her tongue at that, and I groaned. "Are we really doing this tonight?"

Chase finally cracked a smirk. "Just sit back and take it, man. It's your turn in the hot seat."

Cole pointed at him with a biscuit. "Stay out of it, newly engaged guy. You've got your own problems."

Trent grunted. "Tell me about it."

Mom swatted Chase's hand. "Eat your food."

After dinner, I stepped out onto the porch, letting the cool night air settle against my skin.

Trent followed a few minutes later, zipping up his coat like he meant to stay out here for a while. He leaned against the railing without saying anything, his gaze fixed on the horizon.

"Alright," I said. "Are you gonna mope forever, or just until Lauren gets back?"

Trent exhaled through his nose, shaking his head. "Not in the mood for your jokes, Gage."

I clinked my beer against his. "That bad, huh?"

He didn't answer right away. Just stared out at the land stretching in front of us—the ranch we'd all spent our lives on, the place we were all trying to build into something better.

Finally, he muttered, "It's a lot."

"Yeah?"

Trent nodded and sighed, but not in that stressed out, carrying the world on his shoulders way he used to. More like he was rolling something over in his mind, thinking through all the moving parts.

"The business is taking off," he said. "Which is good. Great, actually. But there's a lot to keep up with—marketing, logistics, making sure we can deliver what we're promising." He exhaled, staring toward the distant tree line. "Lauren's got a dozen ideas a minute, and half of them make me wonder why we didn't do this sooner."

There was something in his voice, something that sounded more focused than before. It wasn't the kind of restless weight he used to carry—it was the kind that came from knowing he was in this for the long haul.

"She's got you thinkin' big," I said.

His mouth quirked. "Guess so."

I nodded toward the pasture. "You still set on putting your place out here?"

"Yeah. Ordered the mobile home last week. Should be here in a couple of months."

I grinned. "Look at you. First one to plant roots."

Trent let out a quiet laugh. "Some roots—a hundred feet from the house we grew up in."

I shrugged. "Someone's gotta stick around. At least you're gettin' out of your old bedroom."

"It's about time, don't you think?"

That part, I didn't doubt. A year ago, he wouldn't have sounded so sure. Now? He had a plan, a future. And for the first time, he was the one who didn't seem restless.

We stood in silence for a while, watching the stars blink to life, the land stretching quiet and endless in front of us.

Eventually, I pushed off the railing. "Better get inside before Mom starts looking at us like we're about to spill our feelings all over the porch."

Trent smirked. "Wouldn't want that."

I left him out there, still looking out at the land like he was searching for something.

Inside, Mom caught my eye as I passed through the kitchen. She didn't say anything, but I could feel the knowing in her stare. Like she saw something in me that I wasn't ready to see myself.

I grabbed another biscuit off the counter and kept walking.

No point in thinking about things that didn't need thinking about.

Gage

T HE FLUORESCENT LIGHTS FLICKERED once before settling into their usual harsh glow, buzzing like an overworked ranch hand on his third cup of coffee. I pulled open the gas station door, stepping into the blessed warmth, and let it swing shut behind me.

Didn't plan on coming into town tonight. But after hanging out by myself in my room long enough to start thinking about things I didn't want to think about, I figured I might as well make myself useful.

Mom had mentioned we were low on coffee and a few other things, and since I wasn't sleeping anytime soon, I'd volunteered. Not that I'd told her that—I just grabbed my keys and left before she could ask questions.

It was late. Past ten. Too late for errands, too early to call it a night. But here I was, hunting down a canister of coffee, maybe a gallon of milk, and a pack of beef jerky like some kind of bachelor stereotype.

The store was mostly empty. An old guy in a camo jacket stood near the register scratching off a lottery ticket, and a tired-looking teenager restocked the chip aisle with the kind of enthusiasm that suggested he'd rather be checking out the backs of his eyelids.

I strode past both of them, heading straight for the cooler in the back. A door slammed behind me.

Didn't think much of it—until I heard the voice.

"Oh, you have *got* to be kidding me."

I turned, slow as ever, just to make sure I wasn't imagining it.

Amber Morris stood near the end of the aisle, gripping a bottle of headache medicine in one hand and looking at me like I was the last thing she needed to deal with tonight.

Grinning, I leaned against the cooler door. "Well, hey there, Doc. You followin' me?"

Amber exhaled hard, tilting her head toward the ceiling like she was asking for patience. "Yes, Gage. I tracked your truck here because I was desperate for a thrilling conversation about—" She gestured vaguely at my hands. "—cheap coffee and processed meat."

I held up the jerky. "High in protein."

"Unbelievable."

She turned on her heel and marched toward the register, and dang if I didn't enjoy watching her storm away.

I grabbed my beer and followed, because I wasn't about to let a prime opportunity go to waste. "Rough night?"

She didn't answer right away, just set the bottle of Advil down on the counter and pulled out her wallet. "I'm fine."

"Right," I drawled, setting my six-pack beside hers. "That's why you're buying headache meds at a gas station at ten o'clock at night."

Amber handed the cashier a ten and ignored me completely. The kid behind the register—maybe eighteen, tops—gave me a nervous glance, like I might start something.

I grinned. "Don't worry, son. She just hates me on principle."

Amber let out a sharp breath. "I don't *hate* you, Gage."

"Strongly dislike, then?"

She grabbed her change and turned, eyes sharp. "I don't have *time* for you."

Something about the way she said it—like time was something she never had enough of, like I was one more thing she couldn't fit into her carefully scheduled life—made me grin wider.

"You should make time," I said, stepping forward to take her place at the register. "I'm delightful."

The cashier scanned my stuff in silence. Probably wise.

Amber let out another one of those long, measured breaths, gripping her paper bag like she was trying to squeeze the top off of it. "Enjoy your—" she squinted at my haul, unimpressed. "—nutritionally questionable choices."

I winked. "Enjoy your headache."

She stomped toward the door. I watched her go.

Didn't mean to. Didn't even realize I was doing it until the bell jingled and she disappeared into the cold.

"That your girlfriend?" the cashier asked.

I huffed a laugh. "Not even close."

But as I grabbed my beer and stepped back into the night, I realized I was still smiling.

Not sure what that meant.

Didn't think too hard about it.

Chapter Four

Amber

S IR STUMPY SAT ON my overnight bag like a furry little tyrant, one
paw neatly tucked under his chest, his yellow eyes blinking slow
and unimpressed.

"You're not coming with me," I told him, reaching for the handle.

He didn't move. Just let out a slow, judgmental *mrrp* and settled in
deeper, like I was going to change my mind if he made things difficult.

I sighed. "You're really not helping."

The faucet in the kitchen gave a slow, mocking plink plink plink,
like it agreed with him.

I shot a glare in its direction. It had been dripping all night, even
though I'd tightened it twice before bed. One more thing I needed to
deal with—just not today.

"Fine, you win." I scooped Stumpy up with one arm and deposited
him onto the couch, where he immediately started grooming himself
like this had all been his idea.

The overnight bag was lighter than it should have been, mostly
because I didn't plan on staying long. Two days, tops. Get in, talk to

my parents, figure out how to shut Gina down without turning it into World War III, and get back before White Pines fell apart without me.

Easy enough.

I slung the bag over my shoulder, grabbed my travel mug from the counter, and headed out the door before I could second-guess anything.

The morning air was crisp, the sun barely up. My truck was covered in a thin layer of frost, and I had to sit there for a few minutes while the defroster did its thing. I should've grabbed a scraper, but I was already running later than I wanted.

By the time I pulled into the Coffee Wagon drive-thru, I could feel my headache creeping in—the early warning sign of a long, exhausting day ahead.

The barista handed me my drink with a too-cheerful smile. "Big bag in the back. Road trip?"

"Yeah," I muttered, taking a sip.

"Where to?"

I hesitated. The question was harmless, but for some reason, I didn't feel like answering. "Just home for the weekend."

She nodded like she understood, but I wasn't sure that even I did.

Home.

Big River Valley was home. The rolling pastures, the smell of horses and leather, the mountain air. The ranch. White Pines.

Missoula was where I grew up, but it didn't feel like home anymore.

The thought stuck with me as I pulled onto the highway, the tires humming against the road. Gina's voice was already in my head, running through every argument she was bound to throw at me. *They need help, Amber. They need real care. You can't just keep pretending they're fine.*

I wasn't pretending.

But as I drove east, toward the life I'd left behind, I couldn't shake the feeling that I wasn't as sure about anything as I wanted to be.

I BARELY HAD TIME to put the truck in park before my mom was opening the front door, her face lighting up in surprise.

"Amber! Honey, what are you doing here?"

I climbed out, forcing a smile. "Thought I'd come home for the weekend."

Her eyes softened, and for a second, I felt guilty for not calling ahead. Then Gina's car came into view in the driveway, and the guilt faded.

I wasn't the only one making surprise visits.

I grabbed my bag from the passenger seat and started toward the porch. The house looked the same as always—modest, clean, the flowerbeds still neatly mulched even in the dead of winter. Inside, I could already hear the hum of the morning news playing at a low volume, the smell of coffee lingering in the air.

Mom pulled me into a hug, her arms warm and familiar. "This is such a nice surprise."

Gina's voice drifted from the kitchen. "Yeah. Real nice."

I sighed and stepped inside, setting my bag by the door. "Hi, Dad."

Dad was at the kitchen table, newspaper folded in front of him, his coffee cup half-empty. He looked up when I walked in, his brow wrinkled as always, and he gave a small nod. "Didn't know you were coming."

"Didn't want to make a big deal out of it."

Gina leaned against the counter, arms crossed, her expression as tight as her clipped ponytail. "Right. Because showing up unannounced isn't a big deal at all."

Mom sighed. "Girls, please."

I ignored Gina and stepped farther inside, eyeing the familiar kitchen. Same cabinets, same coffee pot that had been there since I was a kid. Same mother who was still on her feet, still doing everything herself, despite Gina's claims that she needed more help than we could give her.

Mom motioned toward the coffee pot. "Can I get you some?"

I shook my head. "I grabbed some on the way."

"Of course." She wiped her hands on a dish towel, her smile just a little too bright, too quick. A familiar deflection. "Well, it's good to have you here. I don't remember the last time you stayed more than a night."

Gina arched an eyebrow. "That's because she never does."

I shot her a look. "That's because I work."

"So do I," Gina countered. "And yet, somehow, I find time to show up when it matters."

The words landed like a slap, but I kept my voice level. "Is that what we're doing? Keeping score now?"

Dad cleared his throat. "Enough."

We both went quiet, but she was shooting me a glare that could've melted mom's coffee pot.

Mom, ever the peacemaker, let out a light laugh and smoothed her sweater. "Well, I think it's wonderful that you're here. And you too, Gina." She gave us both a pointed look, the kind only mothers could manage. "Let's not spend the weekend fighting."

I swallowed hard, nodding.

Gina sighed and picked up her coffee, looking like she was biting her tongue.

Mom turned back to me, her expression warm again. "So, what's the occasion?"

I hesitated. *Because Gina is trying to make decisions without you.* Didn't seem like the time to say that yet.

Instead, I shrugged and smiled. "I just wanted to check in."

Mom's smile faltered, but only for a second. "Well, that's sweet of you."

She didn't believe me.

Gina did, though. She shook her head, muttering under her breath. "Here we go."

I ignored her. "Can we sit down? Talk for a bit?"

Dad set his paper aside. "I'm already sitting."

Mom gave him a look, then motioned toward the living room. "Of course, honey. Let's talk."

Gina pushed off the counter, her movements stiff. "Great. Let's."

The four of us moved toward the couch, settling into what was bound to be a conversation none of us actually wanted to have.

And just like that, I knew this was going to be harder than I thought.

T HE CONVERSATION HAD GONE exactly how I expect-
ed—round and round in circles, with Mom dodging the topic, Gina pressing too hard, and Dad barely saying a word.

By the time we finished, nothing was resolved. Mom insisted they were fine, and that Gina was overreacting, while Gina shot me looks that said, *This is why I have to handle things.*

So, now it was late, and I needed air.

I stepped out onto the back porch, my breath rising in faint clouds as I looked out onto the crusty snow covering the yard. The house lights spilled onto the worn wooden steps, the same ones I used to sit on as a kid, kicking my feet and listening to crickets in the summer.

The door creaked behind me. I didn't have to turn to know it was Dad.

He sat down beside me, coffee mug in hand, even though he had to know it was too late for caffeine. Didn't say anything right away. Just stared out at the quiet backyard.

I crossed my arms, tucking my hands under them for warmth. "Didn't think you drank coffee this late."

"Didn't think you came home just to visit."

I let out a slow breath, watching it fog in the cold. "You know why I'm here."

Dad nodded, lifting the mug to his lips. He took a slow sip, then set it down on his knee. "Your mom's stubborn."

I huffed a small laugh. "Yeah. I got that."

He glanced at me sideways, the corner of his mouth twitching. "You didn't exactly miss out on that trait yourself."

I smiled, but it faded fast. "She doesn't want to talk about moving."

"No, she doesn't."

"She won't even consider it."

"No, she won't."

I turned toward him, my frustration rising. "Dad, she's not as steady on her feet anymore. She doesn't ask for help, but she needs it. And what happens if you're not there to catch her?"

He didn't answer right away. Just ran a finger along the rim of his mug.

I sighed, shaking my head. "I know you love this house. I do, too. But Gina's not wrong about everything. You need more support than you're letting on."

Dad nodded, slow and thoughtful. "We do."

That stopped me cold. I blinked. "Wait. What?"

He exhaled, his breath visible in the cold. "We know we need to start thinking about the future, Amber. We're not pretending we're invincible."

I stared at him, thrown. "Then why won't you just say that? Why won't Mom admit it?"

He took another sip of coffee, then set the mug down beside him. "Because if we say it out loud, we have to face what it means."

I swallowed hard, my throat tight. "Which is?"

"That we're getting old. That things are changing." He glanced at me, his expression... tired. "That someday, you and Gina are going to have to make choices we won't get to be part of."

My chest squeezed. "You *are* part of it. That's why I'm here. I don't want Gina making decisions for you."

"She's not," he said simply. "And neither are you."

I frowned. "Then what do you want?"

Dad was quiet for a long time. When he finally spoke, his voice was steady, thoughtful. "It's not about where we live, Amber. It's about how we spend the time we've got left."

Something in my chest twisted.

I stared down at my hands, my knuckles cold. "I just... I don't want you to feel like you have to go. Like we're pushing you out of your own home."

He nodded, understanding. "And we don't want you and Gina fighting over something that isn't yours to fix."

I exhaled slowly. "So, what now?"

He didn't answer right away. Just patted my knee, then stood up, grabbing his mug.

"Go inside," he said, heading for the door. "It's too cold to be out here thinking all night."

And just like that, I had my answer.

They weren't ready to leave.

And I wasn't ready to force them.

Gage

I HAD BANNER LOADED, my rope bag in the passenger seat, and a solid plan for the morning—head to Walker Ranch, rope a few steers, and remind Luke why I was still the better header between the two of us.

Simple.

Or at least, it should've been.

I pulled into the driveway at Walker Ranch, then rolled down the new gravel stretch that led to Luke and Meg's house. I barely had time to shift into park before I realized something was very, very wrong.

Luke's truck was creeping forward across the gravel, engine running, but the way it was moving—uneven, jerky, very not like someone who knew what they were doing—made me pause.

Then I saw the driver.

Lizzy.

Fifteen-year-old Lizzy, sitting high behind the wheel, hands at ten and two like she was on a driver's test.

Luke stood a few feet away, arms crossed, his head tilted like he was already regretting every single one of his life choices.

I rolled down my window. "Walker, what exactly am I looking at?"

Luke exhaled through his nose. "Morning to you too, Langton."

Lizzy braked too hard, and the truck skidded forward on the packed snow, sliding a few extra feet before coming to a lurching stop. She threw it in park and turned, grinning at me through the windshield like she'd just nailed it.

"Hi, Gage!"

Luke muttered, "I fear for my insurance premiums."

I grinned, shutting off my truck and hopping out. "Since when is she learning to drive?"

Lizzy stuck her head out the window before Luke could answer. "Since I have places to go, and Luke is too overprotective to just let me drive into town on my own."

Luke sighed, rubbing the back of his neck. "I am not overprotective. I'm responsible."

Lizzy scoffed. "Luke, you made me practice parking in a hay field for a full week before I even got to touch pavement."

"That's called safety precautions."

I crossed my arms. "And how's she doing?"

Lizzy beamed. "I'm *awesome*."

Luke made a noncommittal grunt, rubbing his jaw. "I mean, she hasn't hit anything today," he admitted.

Lizzy rolled her eyes. "I'm an amazing driver."

"You're a new driver," Luke corrected. "And I don't feel like replacing fence posts if that changes."

"You're still breathing," I noted. "That's something."

Luke shot me a look. "We'll see how long that lasts."

Before I could respond, the front door of the house flew open, and Henry came barreling onto the porch, barefoot, shirtless, and wielding a plastic sword like a knight charging into battle.

"FOR GLORY!" he shrieked, raising his sword above his head.

Right behind him, Josie wailed like her tiny world was ending, her wild curls bouncing as she stomped after her brother, furious about something neither Luke nor I could possibly understand.

Meg followed them out onto the porch, arms crossed, wearing that patient-but-deadly look I'd seen on plenty of wives and mothers over the years.

Luke stiffened immediately.

"Luke," Meg said, voice sweet as honey but sharp as a barbwire fence.

"Yep?" He straightened, all innocence, like he hadn't just been caught actively avoiding whatever was happening inside the house.

"Why is Henry outside half-dressed in the snow, screaming about glory? I didn't even know he *knew* that word."

Luke looked at his son, who was now attempting to climb a snow-covered fence post with one hand while still wielding his sword in the other.

He sighed. "Honestly? I don't know."

I chuckled. "Good to see your leadership skills in full effect."

Luke ignored me, rubbing his hands over his face before crouching down in front of Josie. "Alright, sweetheart. What happened?"

Josie sniffled, her face blotchy and red. "Henry took my pony!"

Henry, still gripping the fence post, yelled over his shoulder, "She wasn't using it!"

Luke sighed again, deeper this time. "Where's the pony now?"

Henry jabbed his sword toward the porch. "Guarding the castle."

I followed the direction of his plastic weapon and spotted a stuffed pink pony sitting upright on the porch railing, covered in snow like it had been there for an unfortunate amount of time.

I smirked. "You are aware that 'castle' is just your mudroom, right?"

Henry scowled at me. "It's a *castle*."

Josie, not to be outdone, turned to me with wide, tragic eyes. "Gage, he *stowe* her!"

I pressed my lips together, trying not to laugh. Pretty sure she meant "stole," but that was one of the cutest things about Josie. She didn't have certain sounds down yet. "That does sound serious."

Luke stood, rubbing his temples. "Henry, give your sister the pony back. Josie, tell Henry thank you."

Josie crossed her arms. Henry huffed but trudged over to retrieve the stuffed pony from its snowy perch. He struck a knee and held it out to her.

"Here," he said, like he was bestowing a royal honor.

Josie snatched it back, but at least she stopped crying. Luke muttered something about needing stronger coffee. I, meanwhile, was wondering what sort of cartoons Henry had been watching. King Arthur or something?

Meg clapped her hands together. "Alright, I have to get going." She leaned in, giving Luke a quick kiss. "Have fun."

Luke's face shifted. "Wait, what?"

Meg was already heading for the truck. "I told you this morning. I have an appointment. Emergency crown replacement. You're on dad duty for the next few hours."

Luke blinked. "I—what?"

Meg smiled sweetly as she slid into the driver's seat. "Love you!"

Luke just stood there, watching her go.

I leaned against the fence, smirking. "So, roping's off, then?"

Luke ran a hand over his face. "Gage, I swear—"

Josie tugged on his jeans. "I'm hungry."

Henry poked him with the plastic sword. "Me too!"

Lizzy strolled past us, completely unfazed by the chaos, and clapped a hand on Luke's shoulder. "I'm going to go hang out with Austin. Good luck."

Luke let out a slow, deep breath. "Yeah. I'm gonna need it."

I laughed, shaking my head. "Well, this has been entertaining, but I think I'll go home and put my horse up."

Luke shot me a glare. "Traitor."

"Hey, you're the one who had kids, buddy." I gave him a mock-sympathetic pat on the back. "Enjoy your day."

I walked off toward my truck, still grinning as Luke got pulled deeper into twin-related negotiations.

But as I climbed into the cab, the grin faded just a little.

Luke looked exhausted, sure, but there wasn't even a hint of doubt in his expression. He might have been drowning in fatherhood, but he wouldn't trade it for anything.

And I...

Well.

I put the truck in drive and headed back toward Ridgeview, pushing that thought away before it could get too comfortable.

Chapter Five

Gage

THE HOUSE WAS TOO quiet.

I flipped through my phone, looking for something—anything—to do. Nothing. I'd already checked on the horses, made a halfhearted attempt at fixing the latch on the back gate, and even considered cleaning up the mudroom before realizing that was a level of boredom I wasn't willing to admit to yet.

I drummed my fingers on the counter.

The problem with Ridgeview Ranch finally turning a corner—actually making money, running smooth for once—was that I had time. And I wasn't used to having time.

My phone buzzed. Luke Walker.

I smirked, answering with, "You lose another kid already?"

"No, they're all accounted for," Luke said dryly. "You wanna come back and watch the game?"

I frowned. "What game?"

A pause.

Then: "Uh. Football?"

I leaned against the counter, biting back a laugh. "Luke. Football season ended last weekend. Don't you remember your team losing?"

Another pause. "There's gotta be something on. Hockey? Motocross? Curling?"

"Curling?" I snorted. "You don't watch curling."

Luke sighed. "Fine. The TV is on, and I need an excuse to sit still for two hours. You in or not?"

I hesitated for about half a second. Then I grabbed my keys.

"Be there in ten."

THE DRIVE BACK TO Walker Ranch was short, but it still felt like an admission of defeat.

I could have found something productive to do. I could have stayed home, tinkered with something in the barn, or even just taken Banner out for a ride. But instead, here I was, pulling back into Luke's driveway because apparently, I didn't actually feel like being alone with my own thoughts today. And I definitely didn't want Mom thinking I had nothing important to do, because that would give her all the wrong ideas.

I walked inside without knocking—Luke's house had never been the kind of place where formalities mattered.

Sure enough, Luke was already parked on the couch, one twin sprawled across his chest, the other snoring softly in the crook of his arm.

The TV was on, but it wasn't football. It was a motocross race.

I stopped just inside the door and crossed my arms. "Luke."

"Hmm?" He barely glanced up.

"You don't even like motocross."

Luke sighed like I was exhausting him by stating facts. "Doesn't matter. Noise is noise."

I smirked. "Right. Because that's what you need. More noise."

Luke shushed me immediately, his grip adjusting around Josie as she stirred. "Don't you dare wake them up. I just got them down."

I lifted my hands in surrender. "Easy, Dad of the Year. I'm not here to start a riot."

Lizzy, who I hadn't even noticed in the corner, snorted from her spot on the armchair, still scrolling on her phone. "You're both old."

Luke didn't even look away from the screen. "You say that now, but one day, you will experience the unique joy of getting a toddler to sleep, only to realize you have to sit in the exact same position for an indeterminate amount of time or risk starting over."

Lizzy wrinkled her nose. "That sounds awful."

Luke nodded, his voice serious. "Oh, it is. Then again... it's also not a bad gig to hold the couch down for an hour."

I dropped onto the couch next to him, shaking my head. "This was your idea, you know. Marriage, kids, the whole settled life thing."

He smirked. "And yet, you're the one who had nothing better to do but come watch it."

I ignored that and nodded at the screen. "So, who are we rooting for?"

Luke shrugged. "I dunno. The guy on the red bike looks confident."

I huffed a laugh. "That's the only criteria?"

Luke lifted a shoulder. "Look, if you want expert commentary, you came to the wrong place. I'm just here for the background noise."

Lizzy rolled her eyes and stood up. "This is lame. I'm going to my room."

"Enjoy your youth," I called after her.

She threw up a half-hearted wave without looking back.

The race continued, engines roaring, dirt flying, the commentators droning on about points and track conditions. I watched for a while, my body finally relaxing into the couch, my mind settling into something quieter. There was a half-eaten popcorn bowl on the coffee table, and I thought about reaching for it, but I was afraid of shifting the cushions and waking a kid.

Luke, though, was watching me instead of the screen.

"You ever miss it?" I asked after a while.

"Miss what?"

I gestured vaguely. "You know. Life before all this."

Luke didn't answer right away. He shifted slightly, adjusting Henry, who had started drooling on his shirt. Finally, he shrugged.

"Nah."

"Not at all?"

He smirked. "You looking for reassurance or permission?"

I scoffed. "Didn't realize I needed either."

Luke side-eyed me, amused but knowing. "Yeah. That's why you came back over here, huh?"

I didn't answer.

We sat in silence, the TV flickering in front of us, the house too quiet now that the chaos had settled.

Finally, Luke nodded at the screen. "Bet you five bucks that guy crashes on the next turn. And they'll flag the guy behind him."

I grunted. "You don't even know the rules."

Luke grinned wider. "Nope. But I know disaster when I see it."

And for some reason, I couldn't shake the feeling that Luke wasn't just talking about motocross.

Amber

"**T**HIS IS A WASTE of time," I muttered as Gina pulled into the parking lot of the assisted living facility.

She shot me a look as she shifted into park. "You agreed to come."

"Only so you'd stop badgering me for five minutes."

Gina sighed, yanking the keys from the ignition. "Amber, just *look* at it. Keep an open mind for once. You act like I'm dragging you into a dungeon, but this place is nice."

I glanced up at the building. It *was* nice—clean, modern, with a wide front porch and cheerful landscaping, even in the dead of winter. The glass doors opened automatically as we approached, revealing a well-lit lobby decorated with homey touches—framed paintings of mountains, a grandfather clock ticking quietly in the corner. It still kind of reminded me of a hospital.

A smiling woman in business casual greeted us. "You must be Amber! Welcome to Evergreen Living. I'm Susan, the director here. Gina has been telling me so much about you."

Gina shook her hand eagerly. "Thanks for making time for us again today."

"Of course," Susan said warmly. "We love giving tours. We're really proud of our community here."

I crossed my arms. *Community*. That was the word places like this always used. Like it made up for the fact that people had to leave their real homes to be here.

Susan launched into her well-rehearsed spiel as she led us down a wide hallway. "Evergreen is designed to be a vibrant, active place where our residents can feel independent while still having the support they need. We have private apartments, chef-prepared meals, and a full activities calendar—bingo nights, yoga, book clubs. A little something for everyone!"

We passed a cozy lounge where a group of elderly women played cards, their laughter spilling into the hall. Farther down, a man sat in a recliner, watching a hockey game, nodding off between plays. A nurse walked by, offering him a friendly pat on the shoulder—probably to make sure he wasn't dead.

I could feel Gina watching me, like she was waiting for me to crack and admit this wasn't the cold, soulless facility I'd imagined.

I didn't crack.

Instead, I turned to her. "Gina, you heard Dad last night. He doesn't want this."

She sighed, exasperated. "Because he doesn't know what's best for them anymore."

I stopped walking. "That's not your call to make."

Susan cleared her throat, kind of awkwardly. "Why don't I show you one of the apartments? That way, you can get a feel for the space."

Gina plastered on a smile. "That would be great."

I forced my jaw to unclench as we followed her into a small but well-furnished one-bedroom apartment. It had a little kitchenette, a comfortable-looking recliner by the window, and—of course—a framed picture of the mountains on the wall.

Like a substitute for the real thing.

Gina turned to me, arms crossed. "You can't tell me this wouldn't be easier for them."

I exhaled, staring out the window. "I'm not saying it wouldn't be easier. I'm saying it's not what they want."

"They don't know what they want, Amber! They say they're fine because they have to! But they're not. You're not here. You don't see it like I do."

I bit back a sharp response, my fingers twitching at my sides. "They're also not senile. They're both still plenty sharp, and we're *not* making this decision for them. End of story."

Gina huffed but didn't argue. Not because she agreed with me—because she knew we'd just keep running in circles.

Susan cleared her throat again, still politely awkward. "Well, why don't I give you a brochure to take home? Just in case your parents want to look it over."

"That'd be great," Gina said, her voice overly chipper.

I stayed silent as we followed her back to the lobby.

The entire drive home was tense, Gina gripping the wheel a little too tightly, me staring out the window, replaying Dad's words from last night. *"It's not about where we live, Amber. It's about how we spend the time we've got left."*

Yeah. They sure didn't want to spend that time in a gussied up hospital. Maybe I'd have to have Mom spell it out in her own words, because so far, she hadn't said much. I didn't know if that was enough to fix this mess. But it was enough for me to know Gina was wrong.

We pulled into the driveway, the house looking just as it always had—familiar, steady. But the second we walked inside, I knew something was off.

The smell hit me first. Coffee grounds. Old food. Trash.

Then I saw the mess.

The kitchen was a disaster. The overturned trash can sat in the middle of the floor, its contents strewn everywhere—shredded paper towels, crumpled napkins, banana peels, half a piece of toast.

And in the middle of the chaos sat Sir Stumpy, licking his one paw like he was proud of himself.

"Stumpy!" I groaned, dropping my bag and stepping over the mess.

That's when I saw Mom, bent over, struggling to pick up the heavier pieces.

My stomach twisted. "Mom! Why didn't you call us?"

She looked up, breathing heavier than I liked. "Oh, it's fine, dear. I've got it."

But she didn't have it. She was struggling, her bad knee wobbling, her balance unsteady.

I rushed to her side, grabbing the trash bag from her hands. "Sit down. I'll clean this up."

Gina didn't say anything.

Not at first.

She just stood there, watching.

Then, in a voice too calm, too certain, she said, "This is exactly what I was talking about."

I stiffened. "Gina—"

"You're *not* here, Amber," she snapped, her voice low but sharp. "You don't see it. You don't *want* to see it."

I clenched my jaw, gripping the edge of the trash can.

Mom waved a hand, dismissive. "Oh, don't make a fuss. It's just a little mess."

But Gina wasn't backing down. "And how many of these 'little messes' do you think she's dealing with while we're not looking?"

I opened my mouth to argue.

Then I closed it.

Because this time, I didn't have an answer. Sure, it wasn't every weekend I brought my menace of a cat home to destroy their house. But cats aren't the only things that can go wrong.

I knelt down, grabbing a handful of crumpled paper towels, and didn't look at Gina again.

But her words stuck anyway.

And I hated that a part of me wondered if she was right.

T HE HOUSE WAS QUIET.

Gina had gone back to her place hours ago, but I couldn't sleep. Not after today. Not after walking through that facility, seeing the trash-strewn kitchen, and hearing Gina's words echo in my head like an accusation I couldn't shake.

I stepped outside, pulling my sweatshirt tighter around me against the cold. The porch light cast a soft glow over the wooden railing, the wind whispering through the trees.

Dad was already out there, sitting in his usual spot with a cup of tea in one hand, the other resting on his knee. He didn't look at me as I sat down next to him. Didn't need to.

"Didn't think you were still up," I said.

He took a slow sip of his tea. "Didn't think you were."

I exhaled, watching my breath fog in the cold air. My eyes drifted across the porch, settling on something near the steps. A small pile of leaves had gathered in the corner, caught against the railing where the wind had pushed them.

It was barely anything. Most people wouldn't notice.

But Mom would have.

She was always sweeping the porch, always keeping things just so. When we were kids, Gina and I used to roll our eyes at how much she fussed over keeping things perfect.

And now there were leaves in the corner. They had to have been there for a couple of months, because the trees had been bare since early November.

I frowned. "Mom hasn't been sweeping out here."

Dad glanced at the leaves like he hadn't even noticed them. "Nah. I was gonna get to it, just forgot."

I didn't say anything right away.

It was a small thing. Just leaves on a porch. But that wasn't the point.

Mom had never let things go like that.

I swallowed. "She's slowing down more than I realized."

Dad nodded, like that wasn't a revelation. "She is."

I hesitated. "So why won't you just—"

"Because we're not helpless, Amber," he said simply, turning to look at me. "Not yet."

The weight of today settled deeper in my chest. I rubbed my hands together, trying to warm them. "I know Gina thinks I don't see it. That I don't want to see it."

Dad studied me for a long moment. "Do you?"

I sighed. "I don't know."

He nodded again, like he expected that answer. "You and Gina both love your mother. You just show it different ways."

I chewed the inside of my cheek. "I just want you to have a choice."

"And Gina just wants us to be taken care of," he said. "Neither of you are wrong. But the choice is still ours to make."

I pressed my lips together, my throat feeling tight. "So what do we do?"

Dad set his mug down and stretched his legs out. "Same thing we've always done. We take it one day at a time."

I didn't argue with him this time.

But as I sat there, staring at the tiny pile of leaves in the corner of the porch, I realized something.

One day at a time was fine. Until one day, it wasn't.

And that was the part I didn't know how to fix.

Chapter Six

Gage

MONDAY MORNING STARTED LIKE most mornings—me rolling out of bed, grabbing coffee, and wondering how long I could get away with "looking busy" before someone roped me into something worthwhile.

Today, that someone was Chase.

"You busy?" he asked, walking up as I leaned against the corral at Ridgeview, watching Trent's latest batch of cattle settle into their feeding pens.

I sipped my coffee. "That depends."

Chase sighed. "On what?"

"On whether this is you actually asking if I'm busy or just pretending to ask so I'll agree to whatever it is you need."

Chase ignored that. "I need a hand at White Pines. We're moving a load of lumber, and Cole's busy training horses."

I arched a brow. "You mean he's busy with Emily."

Chase shot me a look. "Don't start."

I grinned, taking another slow sip. "You sure you need me, or are you just looking for an excuse to boss me around?"

"I don't need an excuse."

Fair enough.

I glanced over at Trent, who was giving instructions to Ethan and Liam on what they were supposed to do when they got home from school. He didn't need me. Not today. And as much as I liked playing up my role as the fun-loving older brother who just happened to be extremely helpful when it suited me, the truth was... I liked staying busy.

"Fine," I said, pushing off the fence. "Guess I'll go play construction worker for the day."

Chase clapped me on the back. "You'll love it."

"Doubtful."

I climbed into my truck and followed him to White Pines.

B Y THE TIME WE pulled in, the morning was already in full swing. Horses being led in the barn aisle, riders warming up in the arena, the steady hammering and clanking of construction echoing from the expansion site.

I parked next to Chase and climbed out, stretching as I took in the scene.

"You still sure you want me here?" I asked. "There's a lot of expensive-looking equipment around. I'd hate to show everyone up with my natural talent."

Chase didn't even dignify that with a response. He just motioned toward a pile of lumber and went to talk to one of his workers.

I was about to head over when I spotted a familiar figure near the arena.

Amber.

She stood next to Kate, watching a client ride one of the therapy horses. Her arms were crossed, her expression serious—*too* serious, even for her.

I had no reason to go over there. None at all.

Did that stop me?

Absolutely not.

I adjusted my hat, made my way over, and leaned against the fence. "Mornin', Doc."

Amber barely looked at me. "I'm not a 'doc,' Gage. Not that you'll remember that."

Kate made a noise in her throat, but she didn't look my way.

I squinted at Amber. "You look like you're thinking too hard. Dangerous habit."

She finally turned. "Says the man who avoids thinking at all costs."

I grinned. "Exactly. That's why I'm still young and full of life."

Amber let out a slow breath and turned back to the arena, clearly not in the mood for my nonsense.

Which, of course, only made me more curious.

I studied her, the tension in her shoulders, the slight crease between her brows. She wasn't usually the lighthearted type, but something was off.

Before I could ask—before I even knew what I wanted to ask—Chase called my name from across the yard.

"Looks like duty calls," I said.

Amber didn't even glance at me. "Don't let me keep you."

I should've let it go. Should've just walked away. Instead, I lingered for half a second longer. "You okay, Morris?"

Amber's jaw tightened, but she didn't look at me. "I'm fine."

That was a lie.

I knew it.

She knew it.

But I also knew I wasn't the person she was going to talk to about whatever was weighing her down.

So I tipped my hat and walked away, the uneasy feeling sticking with me longer than it should have.

Amber

T HE RHYTHMIC SOUND OF hooves against the soft dirt of the arena usually had a calming effect. Today, it barely registered.

I walked alongside Max, a seven-year-old with cerebral palsy, while Kate led Scout, the sturdy gelding carrying him. Max gripped the saddle's handles with small, determined hands, his focus set on keeping his posture straight as Scout moved in a steady, even rhythm.

"Okay, Max," I said, keeping my voice light. "Remember to breathe nice and deep. How's that feel?"

"Good," he said, a little breathless but steady. "Scout's bouncy today."

I smiled. "He's just got some extra energy. But you're doing great."

Max's mom watched from the side of the arena, smiling every time he sat a little taller. This was one of those good sessions, the kind where I could see real progress, where a kid like Max felt stronger, more independent, more capable with every lap around the arena.

I should have been locked in, focused on him.

Instead, my brain kept replaying Gina's words from yesterday. *"You're not here, Amber. You don't see what I see."*

I gritted my teeth and shook off the thought, keeping my attention on Max.

"Alright," I said, "let's practice stopping. Squeeze your legs a little, and tell Scout 'whoa.'"

Max nodded and tightened his thighs against Scout's sides. "Whoa, Scout!"

Scout slowed smoothly, coming to a halt.

"Nice job!" Kate said, patting the horse's neck.

Max grinned, shifting slightly in the saddle. "Can we do it again?"

I smiled. "Of course."

Kate took a step forward, clucking her tongue to get Scout moving again, and Max settled into the rhythm of the ride. I tried to force myself to stay present, but my mind kept drifting.

When we got back to the mounting block at the end of the session, I helped Max dismount. His mom came over, beaming, and gave him a high-five before thanking me.

Max looked up at me. "Can we ride Scout next time, too?"

"Absolutely," I said. "You did great today."

His smile was worth everything.

But the second he and his mom walked away, Kate turned to me, arms crossed, giving me the look.

"Okay," she said. "What's going on?"

I blinked. "What?"

Kate motioned toward the arena. "You were distracted. You're never distracted when you're working."

I sighed, rubbing the back of my neck. "It's just been a long weekend."

Kate's eyes narrowed slightly, reading between the lines. "Everything okay with your parents?"

I hesitated. Kate knew some of what was going on—enough to know Gina and I weren't exactly seeing eye to eye on things. But I wasn't in the mood to rehash it.

"I'm handling it," I said, which wasn't exactly a lie.

Kate studied me for a second longer, then exhaled. "Alright. Just... make sure you actually handle it, okay? Not just pretend it's fine until you explode at the worst possible moment."

I gave her a dry look. "When have I ever done that?"

Kate arched a brow.

Okay. Once.

I sighed. "I'll be fine, okay?"

"Like you were 'fine' when Gage Langton was talking to you? That was weird. On a number of levels."

I frowned. "He's always weird. What's your point?"

"He was being... almost serious. And you didn't threaten to push him into a water trough, so that's weird, too."

I sighed, rubbing my temples. "I don't have the energy for Gage Langton today."

Kate crossed her arms. "Uh-huh. And yet, he definitely noticed something was up with you."

I let out a slow breath, watching Scout flick his tail as he stood patiently near the fence. "I told you. It's just stuff."

Kate studied me, waiting.

I knew that look.

Knew she wasn't going to push, but also knew she wouldn't drop it completely.

I exhaled. "Went home last weekend. Gina's still trying to move Mom and Dad into assisted living. Dragged me to a facility they don't want to move to, trying to make a point. I mean... if it were up to me, maybe we *should* move them. They really are slowing down. Mom had a hard time cleaning up a mess Stumpy made. But like I told Gina, it's *not* up to me... well, *that* turned into another argument."

Kate winced. "That's rough."

I nodded, pressing my fingers to the bridge of my nose. "It's fine. It's just... a lot."

Kate's voice softened. "You sure you don't want to talk about it?"

I shook my head. "Not right now."

She let it go, patting Scout's neck. "Alright. But if you need to, you know where to find me."

I nodded, grateful, but my head was already elsewhere—turning over every conversation from the weekend, every piece of evidence Gina had thrown at me, every tiny thing I wasn't sure I could ignore anymore.

And apparently, I wasn't hiding it as well as I thought.

Because if even Gage Langton could tell something was wrong?

I was in trouble.

Gage

B

Y THE TIME I made it back to Ridgeview, the sun had climbed
high enough to start melting the frost off the fence posts, turning the packed snow in the pastures into a muddy mess.

I parked near the barn, climbed out, and stretched, waiting for that
familiar sense of ease to settle in.

It didn't.

I found Trent out by the cattle pens, clipboard in hand, talking
numbers with one of the twins. He looked up when I walked over,
barely breaking stride in his conversation.

"Everything go alright at White Pines?" he asked, still scanning the
paperwork.

"Depends," I said. "Are you asking if Chase got his lumber moved
or if I got under Amber's skin?"

Trent smirked. "Both."

"Then yes. Very productive morning."

Liam gave a small chuckle before walking off, leaving just the two
of us. Trent finally looked up, adjusting his gloves. "Since when have
you made it your mission to annoy the therapist while she's working?
I thought you thought therapists were all fluff and show, not worth
your trouble."

I shrugged. "Since I said something one day, and she gave me a look
like I'm from another planet. It don't mean nothin'."

"Sure it doesn't." He glanced over at the barn, where Ethan was
pounding on something on the tractor, then back at me. "You stickin'
around?"

That was the plan. Or at least, it should've been.

I glanced at the cattle, at Liam already working the pens, at the
feed already pushed out in the troughs. Everything running smooth.
Without me.

"Looks like you got things handled," I said, not meaning it as anything but an observation.

Trent nodded. "We're in a good rhythm. I'm going to head in and do some invoicing today."

I hesitated. "Need an extra set of hands?"

He studied me for a second, like he was trying to figure out why I was asking. Because the truth was, I didn't usually ask—I just did. But lately, it felt like my role here was... undefined.

"If you're bored, I'm sure I can find something," Trent said.

I huffed. "That's not exactly a glowing endorsement."

He shrugged. "You used to complain when we had too much work. Now you're complaining because there's not enough?"

I scowled. "I'm not complaining."

"Well, if you're looking for something to do, Chase is still working out at White Pines the rest of the week. Could probably use a hand."

That wasn't a bad idea. It was productive. Kept me moving.

But it also meant running into Amber again.

I wasn't opposed to that—exactly—but after this morning, I wasn't sure what to make of the fact that she'd barely snapped back at me. What was the fun in that?

I kicked at a clump of dirt with the toe of my boot. "I'll think about it."

Trent nodded and turned back to his clipboard. The conversation was over.

Because he had things to do.

I, on the other hand, had a whole lot of... nothing.

I leaned against the fence, watching the cattle move through the pens, watching the routine of the ranch continue without me needing to be in the thick of it.

I should have been relieved that things were running well. I should have been happy that Ridgeview was finally on solid ground after years of fighting to keep it afloat.

Instead, I felt like an extra piece in a puzzle that had already been completed.

My phone buzzed in my pocket. I pulled it out and smirked at the name. Luke.

"So, you find a hobby yet, or are you still wandering around aimlessly?"

I shook my head, thumb hovering over the keyboard. I could fire back something smart, something sarcastic.

Instead, I just shoved the phone back in my pocket.

Because the truth was?

I didn't have an answer.

Chapter Seven

Amber

*P*LINK. *PLINK. PLINK.*

I dropped my bag onto the counter and closed my eyes against the relentless sound of the dripping faucet.

It had been leaking for over a week now, and I'd tried to fix it. I'd tightened things, replaced a washer, even consulted the great wisdom of the internet. Nothing worked.

And now, after a long day, it sounded even louder than before.

I tossed my keys into the bowl by the door and marched to the sink. This was the night it ended.

Grabbing the wrench from the drawer, I crouched down and yanked open the cabinet beneath the sink. I could do this. I was a problem solver. I helped people for a living. I was not going to be defeated by a faucet.

I reached in and tightened a connection. The drip slowed.

I held my breath.

Plink.

I exhaled and closed my eyes. "Okay. Fine. Let's try that again."

I twisted another piece, a little more aggressively this time.

Plink.

I twisted harder.

Plink. Plink. Plink.

I smacked the pipe. Because that was definitely a logical solution. The faucet, mocking me now, responded with an even faster drip.

That was it. I was done.

I dropped the wrench with a clatter, grabbed my phone, and called Kate.

She picked up on the second ring. "Uh oh. You never call me after work unless something is on fire."

"This is worse than fire," I said. "My faucet is still leaking."

A pause. "You know, fire is generally considered more dangerous than plumbing issues, right?"

"I can't take another night of this, Kate. I need backup."

Kate, bless her, didn't even hesitate. "Alright. What kind of back-up?"

I rubbed my forehead, already feeling ridiculous. "Someone with tools and muscles. Can I borrow your fiance? If you and Chase come over and fix my sink, I will provide crispy, golden-fried bribes in the form of chicken."

She gasped. "You fried chicken?"

"No. I was going to pick some up at the deli."

Kate snorted. "You're bribing us with food you didn't even cook?"

"I will *procure* it. That counts."

She laughed. "I'll talk to Chase. Hold tight."

I sagged against the counter, relieved. Finally, I could have peace in my own kitchen.

But first, I needed to hold up my end of the deal.

Grabbing my keys, I headed back out, driving the short stretch to the grocery store. The deli section smelled like fried heaven, and I loaded up a box of crispy chicken, some potato wedges, and coleslaw—because I was feeling generous.

Then, because I was a thoughtful person, I grabbed a couple of fancy bottled sodas and a slice of chocolate cake big enough for two people to share. A feast fit for two hardworking, plumbing-savvy people—people who also happened to be pretty decent company over a meal.

I made it back home, arms full, feeling smug about how well this was working out. Chase and Kate would be here any minute. The sink was still dripping, but the cavalry was coming.

I set out plates, lined up the drinks, and even pulled out cloth napkins like I was hosting a proper dinner instead of a plumbing-related bribe. And I let myself believe, for one blissful moment, that this night was actually going to go smoothly.

And then my phone rang again.

Gage

I WAS PERFECTLY CONTENT doing absolutely nothing when my phone rang.

I glanced at the screen. Chase.

I considered letting it go to voicemail, but knowing Chase, he'd just call again. And again. And then text something along the lines of "Pick up or I'm telling Mom you still don't sort your laundry right."

I sighed and answered. "If this is another favor, I'm gonna need a full list of IOUs so I can cash in later."

Chase didn't even acknowledge that. "I need you to go fix Amber's sink."

I blinked. "What?"

"Her kitchen faucet. It's leaking, and she asked me to fix it, but I'm still at White Pines."

I leaned back in my chair. "And this involves me how?"

"Because she's expecting someone, and I can't go."

"Again. How is this my problem?"

There was a pause, and I could hear the smirk in Chase's voice when he said, "She's bribing with fried chicken."

I frowned. "What kind of fried chicken?"

"Golden. Crispy. Still warm, probably."

I sighed, rubbing the back of my neck. "You're lucky I'm hungry."

"You're lucky I just saved you from eating gas station beef jerky for dinner."

I didn't dignify that with a response.

"Just go," Chase said. "It's an easy fix, and you're good at that kind of thing."

"You sending me because of my mechanical skills or because you're secretly hoping I annoy Amber into never asking for help again?"

"A little of both," Chase admitted.

Fair enough.

I grabbed my keys, pulled on my jacket, and headed out, already picturing Amber's face when she opened the door and saw me instead of my very responsible, very professional younger brother.

This was going to be fun.

Amber

I FROZE, STARING AT Kate's name on the screen. I knew before I even answered that this wasn't going to be good news.

"Okay, don't be mad," she said immediately.

I groaned, pressing my fingers to my temple. "Kate—"

"Chase got caught up with something at White Pines. He's not gonna make it."

"Are you kidding me?" I turned to glare at the faucet, which was still dripping like it had won some kind of battle.

"I know, I know," Kate said. "But he got a replacement."

I frowned. "What does that even mean?"

Kate hesitated just a second too long.

And that's when I knew.

"Oh, no," I said. "No, no, *no*. Who did he send?"

Another pause. Then, reluctantly: "Gage."

I closed my eyes, gripping the edge of the counter like it could somehow keep me from falling down. "You can*not* be serious."

"Hey, it's either Gage or no one," Kate said. "Do you want to listen to your sink all night?"

I hated that she had a point.

I groaned. "Fine. But if he makes one single smart remark, I swear—"

"Yeah, yeah," Kate said, clearly amused. "Try not to kill him before he fixes it, alright?"

I hung up and stared at the faucet.

Then at the plates I'd set out.

Then back at the faucet.

Gage Langton was about to be in my house. In my kitchen. Fixing my sink.

And somehow, that felt worse than the faucet leaking.

Gage

TWENTY MINUTES LATER, I knocked on Amber's door.

The exact level of exasperation I was hoping for flashed across her face the second she opened it.

She let out a long, suffering sigh, then deadpanned, "I changed my mind. My faucet is fine."

I grinned. "Too late, Doc. I'm already here."

"I'm not a 'Doc,' and *you're* not a handyman."

I tipped my hat. "Well, I am tonight. I was promised food."

Her eyes narrowed like she was seriously considering slamming the door in my face.

Honestly? Would've been worth it.

Amber let out the deepest sigh I'd ever heard, pinched the bridge of her nose, and stepped aside to let me in. "Perfect. Just perfect," she muttered. "The town yokel."

I strolled into the kitchen, taking my sweet time looking around like I was evaluating a job site. "Nice place you got here."

She shut the door with a little more force than necessary. "Fix the sink and leave, Langton."

"You know," I said, strolling into the kitchen, "most people are a little more grateful when someone comes to fix their plumbing issues."

"You're not most people," she shot back. "And you weren't my first choice."

I tsked. "That hurts, Morris."

She sighed, waving a hand toward the sink. "Just do whatever Chase told you to do, take your chicken, and go home."

I took my time looking around like I was evaluating some complex mechanical problem. The faucet dripped. Once. Twice. A slow, taunting sound.

I glanced at Amber. "You sure you didn't just anger it?"

Her eyes narrowed. "Are you asking if I somehow emotionally wounded my sink?"

I shrugged. "I dunno. You do have a certain energy."

Amber exhaled through her nose, closing her eyes like she was inwardly repeating some soothing mantra to herself, and grabbed the wrench from the counter. "Here. Since you're apparently some kind of miracle worker, go ahead."

I took the wrench from her, inspecting it like I wasn't sure if it was an effective tool or some kind of weapon she was considering using on me.

She was still watching me with suspicion as I crouched down and slid under the sink and shut off the supply line to the faucet. "So," I said, reaching for the connection, "what exactly did you do to make this worse?"

"I did not make it worse."

"Uh-huh. Sure."

"I didn't! I tightened things, replaced a washer, watched a tutorial—"

I snorted. "Let me guess. Some guy in a flannel shirt and a tool belt telling you, 'This one easy trick will fix all your problems!'"

Amber scowled. "He seemed like he knew what he was talking about. Better than a cowboy who doesn't know which end of the wrench to use."

"He was probably standing in a staged kitchen that doesn't even have running water," I said, reaching for the problem connection.

Amber crossed her arms. "Are you claiming you are the actual expert?"

I flashed her a grin from under the sink. "Well, I am currently the one fixing your plumbing, aren't I?"

She muttered something under her breath that I was pretty sure wasn't a compliment.

I twisted the fitting, immediately feeling why she hadn't been able to fix it.

Ah. There it was. The actual problem.

One of the seals had shifted, letting water sneak through even though everything was technically tightened. Not a big deal—if you knew what to look for.

I pulled back and wiped my hands on a rag. "Yeah, you weren't gonna fix this with a YouTube tutorial, Morris."

Amber sighed, exasperated. "Why not?"

"Because your seal slipped, and the threads aren't catching right. You tighten it too much without fixing that first, and you just make it worse."

She threw her hands in the air. "So that's why it kept leaking!"

"Yep." I reached into my back pocket and pulled out a roll of plumber's tape.

She eyed it suspiciously. "Where did that even come from?"

"My truck. I come prepared, Morris. Unlike some people."

She rolled her eyes so hard, I thought she might hurt herself.

"Alright, stand back, let the professional work," I said, enjoying this way too much.

She muttered something about how I was *not* a professional, but stepped aside.

I wrapped the threads in a fresh layer of tape, made sure the seal was lined up right, and tightened everything down the correct way this time. A couple of quick adjustments, turn the water back on, and—

No more dripping.

I got out from under the sink and turned the water on and off at the faucet for good measure. No leaks. "There. Now you can suffer in peace without the sound of your sink mocking you."

Amber crouched next to me, inspecting the pipes, like she needed to see with her own eyes that I wasn't lying.

"You actually fixed it," she said, almost reluctantly.

"Told you I would." I wiped my hands off and leaned back against the cabinet, completely at ease in her kitchen.

Amber, on the other hand, looked supremely annoyed.

Not because the faucet was fixed—because *I* was the one who did it.

"Don't look so thrilled, Doc," I teased. "You could at least pretend to be grateful."

Amber pushed up to her feet and grabbed a plate of fried chicken. "Here's your payment. Now go away."

I picked up a drumstick and took a slow, deliberate bite, dragging this moment out just because I could.

"You know," I said, licking a bit of grease off my thumb, "for someone who prides herself on fixing things, you sure needed my help tonight."

Amber pointed the serving fork at me. "Get. Out."

I grinned, snagging one more piece of chicken for the road, and strolled toward the door like I had all the time in the world.

"See you later, Doc."

Amber groaned so loudly, it was probably heard in the next county.

And honestly? That almost made the whole trip worth it.

Amber

THE SECOND GAGE SHUT the door behind him, I dropped my head back and let out a long, long sigh.

The faucet wasn't dripping anymore.

But somehow, Gage Langton's presence still lingered in my kitchen, like an unwanted aftertaste.

I turned back to the counter, arms crossed, scowling at the empty plate where he'd shamelessly stolen a second piece of chicken.

He was ridiculous. Completely insufferable.

And yet, I was standing here, still annoyed, replaying the entire interaction in my head like I needed more reasons to be irritated.

I picked up my drink and took a sip, hoping that focusing on something normal would clear my head. Instead, I caught sight of the wrench sitting on the counter.

The same wrench I'd spent a ridiculous amount of time fighting with last night.

The same wrench Gage had used for all of two minutes before magically fixing my sink like it was the easiest thing in the world.

I grabbed it and shoved it back into the drawer with a slam. Then I turned on the faucet.

Water ran smoothly. No leak.

I shut it off.

Silence.

It was fixed.

And I should have been relieved.

But instead, I stood there, arms crossed, frustrated for an entirely different reason.

Because now, every time I looked at my kitchen sink, I'd think about Gage Langton.

Smirking at me. Calling me "Doc." Getting way too comfortable in my space.

I scowled at the faucet like it had set this whole thing up on purpose.

Then I picked up my dinner, marched into the living room, and flipped on the TV loud enough to drown out any lingering thoughts about a certain cowboy handyman.

It almost worked.

Chapter Eight

Gage

T HE SUN HAD BARELY burned off the morning frost when
I stepped outside, stretching as I took in the quiet hum of
Ridgeview waking up.

Ethan was already out in the equipment shed, half-buried under
the hood of an old tractor, muttering to himself. I leaned against the
doorframe, sipping my coffee. "You talkin' to yourself, or tryin' to
convince that tractor to run on pure stubbornness?"

Ethan didn't even flinch. "Bit of both."

I smirked. "How's that workin' out for you?"

He sat up, wiping grease on a rag. "Needs a new belt. I can replace
it easy once Trent orders the part."

His confidence wasn't misplaced—Ethan was good at this stuff.
Kid had a natural knack for engines, mechanics, fixing things most
people would give up on.

"You ever think about doin' this full-time?" I asked, nodding toward the tractor.

Ethan shrugged, grabbing a wrench. "Yeah. Maybe. Dunno yet."

I knew that tone. The 'I want it, but I'm not sure if it's mine to take' tone.

"Huh. Better go get cleaned up. Bus'll be here in about fifteen miutes, and I ain't driving your bum to class again today because you 'forgot' what time it was."

Behind us, just outside the barn, a soft whoosh of rope cutting through the cold morning air caught my attention. I turned, already knowing who it was.

Liam must have finished his chores already, because he was cleaned up, wearing his non-barn-stained coat and boots. He stood near the practice dummy in the yard, twirling a loop—not in a showy way, but careful, focused. He wasn't just messing around—he was trying.

I watched for a second, waiting. If he wanted help, he'd ask.

But he didn't.

Instead, he just set up another loop and swung it at the dummy's horns.

Missed.

He exhaled, adjusted his grip, and tried again.

Still missed.

I didn't say anything, just took another slow sip of coffee. Liam wasn't frustrated. Just focused. Determined.

Ethan caught me watching and smirked. "You gonna help him, or you just gonna stand there like some kind of cowboy statue?"

I ignored him and walked over. "You gonna keep missing, or you gonna ask for pointers?"

Liam startled slightly but covered it fast, masking the flicker of nerves with a smirk. "I was gettin' there."

I crossed my arms. "Sure you were."

Liam shifted his weight, clearly debating if he actually wanted help or if he wanted to figure it out on his own.

I made it easier for him.

"You ever roped from a horse?" I asked, nodding toward Hickory, who was poking his head over his stall.

Liam shook his head. "Not yet."

"Huh. He's good. I saw him back in his glory days."

I almost suggested that we could saddle up after he got home from school so I could show him some stuff, but then I thought about the time of year, the snow-covered pastures, the frozen dirt in the arena. Not that that woulda stopped me, but... well, heck, it was cold out. And he'd have homework later, right?

"Tell you what. Maybe some afternoon or on Saturday or somethin', I'll take you over to Walker Ranch, let you rope with Luke and Dusty in their indoor arena."

Liam's grip on the rope tightened. "For real?"

"Nah, I just like danglin' opportunities in front of people for fun. Yes, for real!"

Liam huffed a quiet laugh, but there was something behind his expression that wasn't just excitement. It was relief.

Like he hadn't expected to be included or thought of.

Huh.

Well, we had a few minutes before the bus showed up. I walked closer and took the rope from his hands. "Start here. Keep your elbow up." I spun the loop once, easy and controlled. "You don't muscle it. Feel it."

Liam nodded, watching closely. When I handed the rope back, he tried again—and this time, he didn't miss.

It wasn't perfect. But it was progress.

Liam exhaled, grinning. "Alright. That felt kinda good."

"Told ya."

Ethan clapped sarcastically. "Congrats. You're officially less terrible."

Liam made a gesture Mom woulda skinned him for, if she'd seen it, but he was grinning.

I rolled my eyes. "Alright, you two, let's at least pretend to be civilized. Better get ready for the bus."

Amber

T HE BREAK ROOM AT White Pines smelled like coffee and leftover chili. I sat at the table, picking at last night's fried chicken, while Kate stirred sugar into her tea.

Kate glanced at my plate and smirked. "So, how'd it go with Gage fixing your sink? He came, right?"

I stabbed a piece of chicken with my fork. "Oh, you don't get to act innocent. This was your fault."

Kate grinned unapologetically. "It was Chase's fault first."

"You could have warned me!"

"And miss the sheer joy of imagining your face when you opened the door? No chance."

I scowled. "I was expecting a responsible adult. Instead, I got him standing there, grinning like he'd just won the lottery."

Kate actually wiped tears from her eyes. "I should have paid to see that."

"You should have," I said, waving my fork. "And since you didn't, you missed out on extra fried chicken."

Kate straightened. "Wait, how much extra are we talking?"

"Enough that I had leftovers for lunch today and probably all week. And I had dessert, too. But since you sent Gage instead of coming yourself, I'm eating it all without you."

Kate gasped. "Amber. That's cruel."

I grinned and took a slow, exaggerated bite of my chicken. "Actions have consequences, Kate."

She shook her head, laughing. "You're ridiculous."

The door swung open, and Morgan stepped in, balancing a stack of client sheets. "Hey, guys. Thought I'd drop these off before I forget."

Kate reached for the papers. "Thanks. Who do we have this afternoon?"

Morgan flipped through the top sheet. "Let's see... Kate, you've got the Branson boy and Mrs. Lindholm. You can handle them without Amber's oversight, I think. Amber, you're with Ellie again."

I nodded. Ellie was one of my regular clients, a quiet teenager with cerebral palsy who'd been making incredible progress.

Morgan set the papers down and leaned against the counter. "So what's got Kate looking so offended?"

Kate pointed at my plate. "She's hoarding dessert from me."

Morgan laughed. "Cold. Never trust someone who doesn't share the sweets."

"Thank you!" Kate cried.

I rolled my eyes. "It's not hoarding. It's justice."

Morgan shook her head. "You two are impossible." She grabbed a coffee pod and popped it into the machine.

Kate took a sip of her tea. "I'd crash your place tonight to make you share some of that leftover dessert, but Chase told me this morning that Lauren's coming back today. Trent's having a welcome-home dinner for her at the ranch."

I set my fork down. "Wait. Lauren's back already?"

Kate nodded. "Yep, I guess she was able to get everything squared away earlier than she thought. And knowing Trent, this dinner is probably going to turn into full-blown wedding planning. He's ready to keep Lauren in town for good."

I shot her a sideways glance. "You guys were engaged first. You're gonna let them beat you to the altar?"

Kate snickered. "No way. But Chase is a detail guy—one of my favorite things about the man. He's got a spreadsheet, and we must complete the spreadsheet."

I groaned. "You're kidding me. That sounds like you're walking straight into wedding chaos tonight. And on purpose!"

Kate grinned. "What can I say? I like my fiancé."

Morgan grinned. "Speaking of wedding stuff, have you guys decided anything yet? Dresses? Colors?"

Kate made a face. "Sort of. Lauren and I are still trying to coordinate."

That got my attention. "Wait. Coordinate? As in...?"

Kate froze.

Morgan narrowed her eyes. "Oh no. What did you do?"

Kate hesitated. Then, reluctantly: "We... *might* be considering a double wedding. It's way cheaper if we only have to rent one facility, one set of tuxes..."

I gasped, delighted. "You have to do it."

Kate groaned. "I knew you'd say that."

Morgan clapped her hands. "That's amazing."

"It's insane," Kate corrected. "It started as a joke, but then Trent and Lauren were like, 'Hey, maybe that's not a terrible idea,' and now I'm stuck trying to figure out if we're actually doing this."

I couldn't stop grinning. "This is the best thing I've ever heard."

Kate pointed at me. "Do not encourage this."

Morgan ignored her. "Okay, but like... logistically, it makes sense. One venue. One guest list. One set of decorations. Boom. Done."

"Exactly!" I said. "It's efficient."

Kate groaned and dropped her head onto the table. "Why are you like this?"

I shrugged, still way too entertained.

Morgan grabbed her coffee. "Anyway, I'll see you guys later. Try not to bully Kate into anything crazy."

"No promises," I said as she left.

Kate lifted her head and sighed. "I cannot believe my life choices have led me here."

"You don't want to do a double wedding?" I asked. "Seriously. I can understand, you know—you only get one of these, in theory. It's okay if you don't want to share it."

"Oh it's not that at all. I love Lauren, and Chase's whole family is incredible. I was just thinking of keeping it... less. If I had my way, we'd do what Luke and Kelli Walker did and just hit the courthouse. Boom, done. It's not that I *mind* all the... bigness. I just don't want to have to be the one to think about it and plan it."

I smirked. "Well, sounds like there are plenty of others to do what you don't want to do yourself. That's what you get for signing up to join the Langton family."

Kate rolled her eyes but didn't argue.

She took another sip of her tea, then gave me a knowing look. "So. Back to Gage."

I groaned. "We were past that."

"No, no. We are circling back."

I stabbed the last bite of chicken. "He's just annoying."

Kate raised an eyebrow. "Yeah? 'Cause he never used to bother you."

I sighed, already regretting this conversation. "Yeah. Back when he didn't even know I existed."

Kate's smile widened. "Oh, this is good."

I scowled. "It is not good."

She leaned forward. "So what changed?"

I hesitated. Because I knew what changed.

A couple of months ago, back when Chase and Kate were still just dancing around their feelings, I'd been in the barn, organizing tack, when I overheard Gage running his mouth.

He and Chase had been fixing something—probably a fence, maybe a truck, definitely not their maturity levels—and Gage, with his usual smugness, had said, "You know it's happening, right? You and Kate. Might as well stop pretending."

Chase had muttered something grumpy in response, and I, feeling particularly bold that day, had cut in from across the barn.

"Yeah, Gage. Guess you're just an expert at seeing these things coming, huh?"

He'd glanced over, eyebrow raised, because I almost never jumped into their conversations.

And then, for reasons I still don't understand, I'd added—jokingly, because it was absurd— "Don't act like he's so blind, because most people would say you and I are *way* more likely to get together than Gage and Kate."

I'd meant it sarcastically. Ironically.

Gage's response?

A lazy smirk and the most obnoxious wink I'd ever seen.

"Not sure you could handle me, Doc."

That was the moment.

The moment he became insufferable.

Ever since then?

Every single time he saw me, he'd made a point to needle, tease, and generally act like a walking, talking nuisance.

And the worst part?

It worked.

Kate was crying laughing before I even finished telling her. "No, way. You did not say that to him! *You?* I can't believe it!"

I threw my napkin at her. "It's not funny."

"Oh, it absolutely is." She wiped her eyes. "Amber. He likes teasing you."

"I know."

Kate grinned. "Because he likes you."

I froze.

Then scoffed. "No. No way."

Kate shrugged, way too smug. "Believe what you want."

I finished my drink and stood. "I am leaving this conversation immediately."

Kate just laughed.

And as I walked out, I ignored the tiny, nagging thought in the back of my mind.

Because if Gage was really just teasing me to get a reaction...

Why was it working?

Gage

I SHOULD'VE KNOWN THIS was a trap.

Dinner at Ridgeview was usually loud, busy, and full of good food—which made it tolerable.

Tonight?

Not tolerable.

Because tonight, wedding talk had officially taken over.

I sat at the far end of the table, fork in hand, regret in my soul, while my entire family debated the logistics of a wedding I had zero stake in.

Lauren, freshly back in town, was going over details with Kate, Emily, and my mother. Dresses, colors, flowers, venues. Things I had no opinion on but was apparently required to listen to, anyway.

Trent, the groom in question, was taking it seriously, which made sense, because Trent takes everything seriously.

Chase, on the other hand, was sitting beside Kate, chewing his food with the blank, exhausted expression of a man who had fully accepted his fate. Or one who had made careful plans that were already being scrapped in favor of chaos.

Cole was trying to be helpful. I was trying to disappear into my steak.

"Trent," Lauren said, pointing her fork at him, "if we're doing this double wedding thing, we need to lock down the venue this week."

I froze mid-bite.

Double wedding?

I glanced at Chase. "What's this about a double wedding?"

Chase sighed. "It started as a joke."

Kate stabbed a piece of chicken. "And then Trent and Lauren said maybe it wasn't a bad idea."

Lauren shrugged. "Two weddings, same family, close together—it makes sense."

"I guess," I muttered, finally understanding why tonight felt like a trap.

Mom smiled. "It'll be beautiful."

I looked around the table. Nobody was panicking but me.

Even Ethan and Liam, sitting near the end, weren't reacting much. Then again, Ethan was already done eating and halfway to an escape.

He set his fork down. "Alright, I'm gonna check on that tractor."

"Be back inside by nine," Mom reminded him.

Ethan nodded and made a smooth getaway.

Liam, still finishing his food, wasn't so lucky. He glanced at Ethan's empty chair, then at his plate, hesitating like he wasn't sure if he was allowed to leave, too.

I sighed, pushing back from the table.

"C'mon, kid," I said, nodding toward the door. "Let's rope a little."

Liam blinked. "Now?"

I smirked. "You wanna sit here and listen to centerpiece discussions?"

Liam's chair scraped back so fast it almost fell over.

"Thought so," I muttered, following him outside.

THE SECOND LIAM AND I stepped outside, the cold hit fast, sharp, and bracing. Not brutal, but enough to remind me it was still February. The yard was packed with a mix of frozen mud and snow, the porch light throwing long shadows across it.

Liam shoved his hands into his coat pockets. "Not that I'm complaining, but you sure you wanna rope now?"

I smirked, grabbing two ropes off the fence post where I'd left them earlier. "You wanna go back inside?"

Liam didn't even hesitate. "Nope."

"Didn't think so."

I handed him a rope, then nodded toward the practice dummy, a worn plastic steer head mounted on a set of wooden sawhorses. Liam exhaled, focused, and coiled the rope over his hand.

"Alright," I said, stepping back. "Let's see what you got."

He took a deep breath, swung his loop, and let it fly. It missed, landing just shy of the horns. Liam muttered something under his breath and reset.

This time, the rope hit clean, but slid off before he could pull it tight.

I nodded. "Closer."

Liam huffed, adjusting his grip. "Didn't feel closer."

"Yeah, well, you're not far off, either." I gestured for him to go again. "Keep your elbow up this time."

Liam nodded, rolling his shoulders. He was determined, I'd give him that.

He swung again—and this time, the rope hit true, tightening around the horns. Liam grinned, exhaling like he'd just won a championship.

I slugged him lightly in the shoulder. "There it is."

He uncoiled the rope, shaking off the tightness in his shoulders, but something about the way he kept shifting his weight told me his mind wasn't just on roping.

"Something on your mind?"

Liam shrugged, rolling his loop up slowly. "Not really."

I eyed him. "That's what people say when they definitely got something on their mind."

Liam coiled the rope in his hands, slower than before. Then, almost offhanded, he said, "D'you think there's even a point in me learning this?"

I frowned. "What?"

He kept his eyes on the rope. "I mean, it's not like I'm gonna be here forever."

The words landed like a slap to the back of my head. I straightened. "What're you talking about?"

Liam shrugged, too casual. "Just—" He flicked the end of the rope toward the dummy. "I can't exactly take this with me when I go."

I stared at him, my stomach tightening. *When I go.*

Like it was already decided.

Like he wasn't even considering the possibility of staying.

Liam tossed his loop again, not even trying to catch this time. Just moving. Filling space.

"Once I graduate, foster care's done. Ethan and I are on our own." He gave a small, forced chuckle. "Guess I gotta start figuring out what that means."

I didn't say anything. Because I hadn't thought about this. Not really.

I mean, sure—I knew he and Ethan were almost eighteen. I knew the system technically cut them loose after that.

But they were Langtons now. They were ours.

So why the heck was Liam talking like he was already packing his bags?

I opened my mouth—to say what, I wasn't sure. But Liam kept going, voice quieter now.

"And Hickory... I mean, I know he's not mine." He hesitated, rubbing the lead rope draped over the fence. "Not like I'd have somewhere to keep him. And you all can't keep feedin' him for nothing—he's no good on the ranch, really. He'll probably have to go somewhere else."

And there it was.

This wasn't just about roping. It wasn't just about where he'd go.

It was about what he'd leave behind.

I exhaled, shoving my hands in my pockets, rolling through what to say. I wasn't Trent. I wasn't good at big-picture, serious talks.

But I knew one thing.

Liam wasn't going anywhere.

At least, not unless he decided to.

I nudged the rope with my boot. "If you don't wanna practice, just say so. But don't give me that 'no point' nonsense."

Liam looked up, brows furrowed. "It's not nonsense."

"Yeah, it is." I tossed him the rope again. "You're here now. Hickory's yours now. You wanna get better at roping? Then rope."

Liam caught the rope automatically, holding it tight like he wasn't sure if he believed me.

I nodded toward the dummy. "Go on. Let's see it."

Liam swallowed, rolling his shoulders back. Then he swung—and caught the horns clean.

"See? You belong here more than you think."

Liam exhaled, the tension in his shoulders finally easing. And as I watched him reset his loop, I knew this wasn't the last time we were gonna have this conversation.

Not even close.

Chapter Nine

Amber

I SHOULD'VE IGNORED THE call.

The second Gina's name flashed on my screen, I knew exactly how this was going to go. But I answered anyway. Because if I didn't, she'd just keep calling.

"What now?" I said, already bracing.

"Oh good," Gina said dryly. "You're actually picking up today."

I rubbed my temple. "I just saw you last weekend. What could possibly be urgent?"

"We need to figure this out," she snapped. "Mom and Dad can't keep living like this."

I bit my tongue, forcing myself not to react right away. Because Gina always talked like she was dealing with a crisis. Like our parents were on the brink of collapse instead of two perfectly functional adults who were just... getting older.

"I am not driving back again this weekend, Gina."

She let out an exasperated breath. "Amber, you are being impossible."

"No, I'm setting a boundary," I shot back. "That's different."

Gina steamrolled right past it. "So what's your plan, then? Just keep pretending they don't need help?"

My fingers tightened around the coffee cup in my hand. "I never said that."

"Then tell me what you're actually gonna do."

I opened my mouth—and came up blank.

Because the truth was, I didn't have an answer yet.

Gina was quiet for a second—I could imagine that dirty scowl she always got when she was stewing and trying to make me agree with her. Then she sighed. Deeply. The kind of sigh that said she was officially done with me.

"That's what I thought," she muttered. Then she hung up.

I stared at my phone, frustration curling tight in my chest. Fantastic. Just fantastic.

I set my cup down with a little more force than necessary. If Gina wasn't going to listen, I needed to talk to someone who would.

I tapped my mom's number and lifted the phone to my ear.

"Amber, honey!" Mom answered, cheerful as ever. "How's my girl?"

I forced a smile into my voice. "Good, Mom. Just checking in."

"Oh, we're good. Your dad had that mole on his cheek removed yesterday, and he's been walking around here acting like a pirate with a patch on his face."

I giggled. Yeah, that sounded like dad. "How bad was it?"

"Psssh," Mom scoffed. "Hardly anything. He doesn't even need that bandage anymore but he thinks it's funny. Oh, did Sir Stumpy, like his tuna?"

She'd been sending me home with cans of tuna every time I visited, claiming they were about to expire, but I knew full well she kept a stack in her pantry just for him, for whenever I made it home for a weekend. I smiled despite myself. "Mom, he's a cat. Of course he liked the tuna."

"Good, he deserves it," she said. "He's missing a leg, you know."

I sighed. "Yes, I do know that, considering he lives with me."

She made a thoughtful noise. "Maybe I'll send more next time. Poor thing."

I shook my head, knowing full well Sir Stumpy was currently sprawled across my couch, living his absolute best life.

"So, how's work? I bet things are really moving over there now, huh?" Mom said, her voice warm. "I remember when you barely had enough space for everything. I remember your boss... Morgan, right? She was hoping to build a new viewing area when we were there a few years ago."

I hesitated, then sighed. "Mom, we didn't just expand. It's a whole new facility now, and even this one is being expanded."

"Right, right," she said vaguely. "But still, same place, just bigger."

"No. Completely different place. Up the mountain. Brand new barns, arenas, therapy spaces—built specifically for the program instead of trying to cram everything into an old ranch layout."

"Mmm," Mom said, the kind of noise that told me she was nodding along but not really picturing it.

And that's when it hit me. She had no real idea what White Pines had become. And who would be prouder to see it than my mom, who had been the one to suggest Equine Therapy for me as a career in the first place?

I tapped my fingers against my desk. "You should come see it sometime."

That got her attention. "Oh! That would be wonderful!"

And just like that, I made a terrible mistake.

"Well... what if you and Dad came to visit? I don't know if you're free—"

A gasp. Like I'd just offered her front-row seats to the biggest concert of the year.

"Oh! That would be wonderful! What about this weekend? I could come—"

Before I could even finish the thought, I heard my dad's voice in the background.

"We're goin' where?"

"Amber invited us to visit!" Mom called out.

A clatter. More movement. Then my dad picked up the other line, his voice bright and full of excitement. "Well, heck yeah, we'll come! I'll dust off the old Winnebago, and we'll be there soon."

Oh no.

I sat up straight. "Dad, that thing hasn't moved in three years. Let me come pick you up."

He chuckled, unfazed. "Runs just fine. I started it last fall just to make sure. Just needs an oil change, flush the anti-freeze out of the water lines, and it'll be good to go."

I was already picturing the thing breaking down on some remote stretch of mountain highway.

"Or maybe a major tune-up," I muttered.

Mom wasn't listening. She was already making plans.

"Oh, I'll pack up a few meals so we don't have to stop too much. What do you think? A lasagna? A pot roast? Maybe some sandwiches for the road? Amber, you always liked my chicken salad, right? That's not really a winter food, though. Maybe I'll make a casserole and freeze some servings."

"Hey, Amber," Dad asked, "you got a hose hookup in your driveway? And a 110 electrical plug-in? I can't remember from last time."

I buried my face in my hands. "Yes, Dad, it's still there. But really, you can stay in my house. I have an extra bedroom, and I can come pick you—"

"Oh, I'll need to make the bed out there," Mom said. "I pulled the sheets off to wash them... wait, that was a while back. Honey, did we take it to Yellowstone last year when we went with Bill and Vi?"

"No, no, we got a hotel—one of those fancy places at the base of the mountain," he replied. "Remember the French Toast breakfasts?"

"Oh, that's right. So, I think I need to get fresh sheets out there. Amber, honey, should we bring lots of blankets? How cold is it there now?"

I sighed. "Cold, Mom. About like it is at your house."

"Well, maybe I won't de-winterize the rig until we get there," Dad said. "Hate to have the pipes freeze over the pass. I'll get the oil changed this afternoon, and we'll head out tomorrow morning, first thing."

This was happening.

There was nothing I could do to stop it.

My parents were coming. In a twenty-four-foot rolling disaster on wheels.

And all I could do was pray they actually made it.

I JUST NEEDED ONE thing.

A simple errand. A quick in and out.

But the second I stepped into the feed store, I felt it. That prickle at the back of my neck. Like I was being watched. Which could only mean one thing.

Gage Langton was here.

I sighed before I even spotted him. But sure enough, there he was, over by the stacked grain bags, all relaxed confidence and zero urgency, like he had nowhere better to be.

Which made one of us.

I immediately considered turning around. I'd had exactly enough Langton interaction for one week, thank you very much. But before I could even take a step back toward the door—

"Well, look who it is."

I closed my eyes briefly, then opened them again. Yep. Still there.

I pasted on the world's least enthusiastic smile. "You again?"

Gage grinned, leaning against a stack of alfalfa pellets like he had all the time in the world.

"I live here, Morris. Get used to it."

I muttered something deeply uncharitable under my breath and headed for the shelves, determined to get my horse treats and leave.

But, because the universe hated me, Gage followed. "Everything alright?" he asked, too casually.

I didn't answer.

Because if I did, I'd start talking about Gina, and my parents, and the fact that my dad was probably at that very moment prepping a twenty-four-foot deathtrap for a four-hour mountain drive.

And Gage Langton did not need to know about that.

But, because I hesitated for half a second too long, he grinned. "Ah," he said knowingly. "Sister drama. That explains the storm cloud over your head. Kate said something about your sister gettin' up in your business."

I stopped, grabbed the closest bag of peppermint treats, and shot him a glare. "Would you like to get involved?" I asked sweetly. "Because I'd be thrilled to redirect her calls to you."

He chuckled. "Tempting. But I prefer my family drama second-hand."

I exhaled, shaking my head. "Then maybe don't ask next time."

He didn't move out of my way. Just kept watching me, too perceptive for my liking.

"So what's the latest?" Gage asked, too casually. "She still trying to bug you about stuff?"

I stiffened.

Because *how* did he know that?

My eyes narrowed. "Where'd you hear that?"

Gage shrugged. "Kate mentioned something."

I exhaled sharply, irritation flaring. Of course he did. "Great," I muttered. "So now my personal business is just Langton family gossip?"

Gage grinned like that was the most entertaining thing I could have said. "Oh, absolutely."

I scowled. "That wasn't a compliment."

"Didn't take it as one."

"What the heck did Kate tell you? That little gossip, I'll..."

"Okay, wait," he said, holding his hands up. "She didn't go blabbin', don't blame her. I was walkin' by the other day when she was talkin' to Morgan and Morgan asked about your parents and your sister. Kate didn't even seem to know much."

"That's because she doesn't! Because it's not her business, or anyone else's business."

"Right." He dipped his cowboy hat in a sharp nod. "You tell 'em, Doc."

I rolled my eyes. "If you don't stop calling me that..."

"Sure, Amber." He shrugged and made himself more comfortable against the stack of alfalfa pellets. "So, what's really eatin' you today?

You've got that 'out to get the world' look on your face, so somethin's up."

I sighed. Good grief, Gage was good at being annoying.

But I had to say something, because he was not going to leave me alone until I spilled the tea. And because if I didn't vent to someone, I was going to snap and scream into a hay bale. Might as well be the guy whose good opinion I didn't give two straws about.

"My sister wants me to come back this weekend," I muttered, tossing the bag of treats into my basket. "I was just there last weekend, and I said no."

Gage tilted his head. "And that's a problem because...?"

"Oh, man. Where do I start?" I crossed my arms. "My sister wants to put my parents in a home, and they don't want to go. There, are you happy? You know all the gossip now, more than Kate."

His eyebrows raised so much they pushed up his hat. "Huh. Well, just tell her no."

I huffed. "Saying no to Gina is like telling a dog not to chase a rabbit. It just makes her double down."

"Sounds exhausting."

"You have no idea."

Gage leaned a little closer, studying me. "So what are you gonna do?"

I sighed. "I already did something."

He raised an eyebrow, and something on the back of my neck shivered. You know that feeling you get when doom is approaching? It feels a lot like that.

I shifted the basket in my hands, avoiding his gaze. "I invited my parents to visit."

A pause. Then, very dryly— "You what?"

I groaned. "I didn't mean for it to happen, okay? It just—came out."

He blinked. "So they're actually coming?"

I muttered, "...In the Winnebago. Tomorrow. If they don't roll down the mountainside first."

Silence. Then Gage barked out a laugh so loud the guy behind the counter turned to look.

I whipped around, glaring. "It's not funny."

"Oh, it's hilarious."

"No, it's a disaster waiting to happen."

Gage grinned, shaking his head. "Oh, come on, Doc. Have a little faith in your old man."

"He hasn't driven that thing in years." I crossed my arms. "You do know what mountain highways are like, right? Hairpin turns, cliffs, runaway truck ramps—"

"I know," he said easily. "I also know guys don't just forget how to handle a rig just because there's a little snow on the roof. He'll be fine."

I shook my head. "You don't get it. The last time he drove that thing, I followed him, and he almost hit a deer and two mailboxes before we even got out of town."

Gage winced, but still looked far too amused. "Okay. That's... not ideal."

"No, it is not."

He shrugged. "You could always drive out there, pick 'em up yourself."

I rolled my eyes. "I already offered. *You* try telling a grown man that he's not allowed to drive his own vehicle."

"Seems like something you'd try."

I threw my hands in the air. "I can't win with you!"

"Nope," he said cheerfully.

I groaned and turned toward the checkout counter.

But before I could walk away, Gage's voice lost some of its teasing edge.

"Seriously, though," he said. "You worried about them, or just worried about what happens after?"

I stopped mid-step. Because that was the real problem, wasn't it? This wasn't just about one road trip.

It was about where this was all leading.

I swallowed, then shook my head. "Doesn't matter. They're coming, either way."

Gage watched me for a second, then nodded. "Guess you better stock up on coffee, then."

I huffed. "And possibly Valium."

He grinned. "You have fun with that."

I turned toward the register, ignoring the way my stomach twisted.

Because Gage Langton, of all people, had just put words to a fear I hadn't let myself say out loud yet.

And I didn't like that at all.

Gage

I CLIMBED INTO MY truck and shut the door, but I didn't start it right away. Instead, I sat there, fingers drumming against the steering wheel, watching through the windshield as people moved in and out of the feed store.

A minute later, Amber walked out.

She wasn't storming, exactly. But there was a tightness in her shoulders, a set to her jaw that said her brain was still chewing on something.

I huffed a quiet laugh to myself. Yeah, I'd definitely rattled her.

Didn't mean to, exactly.

Didn't *not* mean to, either.

I watched as she loaded her bag into the passenger seat of her SUV, pausing for a second like she was trying to shake something off.

Her folks were coming. In an old Winnebago.

And based on the way she talked about it, that was a bigger deal than she wanted to admit.

I realized then that I didn't even know where her parents lived. I knew plenty of things about Amber Morris—that she took her work seriously, that she had a sharp mind and an even sharper mouth when I got under her skin. That her house had an absolutely terrible faucet, and her three-legged cat had better table manners than I did.

But I didn't know where she was from. Didn't know what her folks were like.

And I didn't know why I was suddenly curious about it.

Amber got into her SUV, pulling out of the lot without noticing me, and I shook my head, finally starting my own truck.

No point thinking on it. I had chores waiting at home, and I always did my best thinking when I had work to do.

Chapter Ten

Gage

THE NEW WING OF the White Pines barn was finally coming together.

After months of planning, building, adjusting, and Chase arguing with at least three different subcontractors, we were down to the final touches. Which was why, this morning, I was following Chase and the building inspector around, pretending to care about load-bearing walls and fire exits.

The inspector—a gruff, no-nonsense guy named Samuels—was walking through the space, clipboard in hand, muttering things to himself while Chase answered questions.

I wasn't much help. Mostly just existing in case Chase needed an extra pair of hands. Which was fine by me.

I leaned against a freshly installed stall door, watching Chase's phone vibrate in his pocket for the third time in five minutes.

"Your pocket's about to catch fire," I told him.

Chase sighed, pulling it out. Another text. He read it, thumbed out a quick reply, and shoved the phone back in his pocket.

I raised an eyebrow. "Kate?"

"And Mom," he muttered.

I grinned. "Lemme guess. Wedding stuff?"

Chase made a noise somewhere between a grunt and a groan.

Samuels interrupted before I could push further.

"This wing's fully climate-controlled, right?" he asked, eyeing the insulated ceiling.

Chase nodded, shifting gears instantly. "Yep. Temperature and humidity regulation. The therapy horses need consistent conditions, and some of our clients are medically fragile, so we went all in on keeping the space comfortable year-round."

Samuels made an approving noise, scribbling something on his clipboard.

While he inspected the electrical panel, I nudged Chase. "So? What's the verdict? You overwhelmed yet?"

Chase exhaled sharply. "I just wanna be married. Get it over with."

I stopped short. Because for all my teasing, I hadn't expected him to actually say that.

"Wow," I said. "Romantic."

Chase scowled. "That's not how I meant it."

I crossed my arms. "That's how it sounded."

He rolled his shoulders back, frustrated. "Look, the planning is fine, Kate's doing great, having fun with it, everything's great. I just... I don't need all the extra stuff. I don't care about what color the napkins are or what kind of flowers go on the tables. I just want to marry her."

I nodded slowly. And before I could stop myself, I said, "Don't take it for granted."

Chase paused mid-step. "What?"

I shifted my weight, vaguely uncomfortable. "I'm just saying—maybe don't act like all the extra stuff doesn't matter. Maybe it's not just for you."

Chase's eyes narrowed. "Where is this coming from?"

I shrugged, glancing toward the stall door. Then, before I even knew I was going to say it—

"Marshall Walker told me something once," I muttered.

Chase blinked. "Marshall? What's he got to do with anything?"

I shrugged. "Couple-three years back, at Luke and Audrey's wedding. Marshall and Kelli got married sometime before that at the courthouse after, like, a two-day engagement, remember that?"

Chase tilted his head. "Yeah, I think so."

"Well, that day, Marshall said something to me." I hesitated, rolling my shoulder. "Said he never regretted it—not for a minute—but when they were sitting there at the wedding, watching Audrey walk down the aisle and Luke was all teary-eyed like a big sop, he leaned over to me and muttered, 'I'd have paid good money to have a memory like that of Kelli walking toward me in some big white fluffy dress.'"

I didn't know why I remembered it.

Didn't know why I was even bringing it up.

Chase stared at me, eyebrows raised. "You're telling me you've been sitting on that for three *years?*"

I shrugged. "Didn't know I remembered it either. Not 'til you were talking just now."

Chase let out a slow breath, rubbing his jaw. "Well, if you ain't the biggest sentimental blowhard I ever heard of."

"Not me. It was Marshall who said it."

Chase barked a laugh, but before he could make fun of me more, Samuels cleared his throat. "Walk me through the plumbing system. I assume you followed all the new codes?"

Chase blinked, snapping back into work mode. "Yeah. PEX piping, everything's insulated, pressure's solid—"

I tuned them out, still half-stuck on my own words.

Because, apparently, I'd been walking around with that conversation buried in my brain for years, and I had no idea why it had decided to surface now.

I walked through the open barn doors, just in time to see Amber's SUV pulling out of the parking lot, and kind of in a hurry.

I frowned, glancing at my watch. 10:30. Too early for lunch.

Which meant... what? Family stuff?

Probably.

I watched until her taillights disappeared down the long driveway... popping up now and again over the hill, then finally down onto the road. Then I shook my head, exhaled, and forced my focus back to work. Because none of that was my business.

Even if, for some reason, I was dying to know where she was going.

Amber

I HAD THIRTY MINUTES before the Winnebago from Hell rolled into my driveway.

Thirty.

Not nearly enough time to prepare for the inevitable disaster, but plenty of time to work myself into a full-blown meltdown. I grabbed the dish towel from the sink and wiped down the counters for the third time. Not because they were dirty—they weren't—but because I needed to do something with my hands before I lost my mind.

Sir Stumpy watched from the couch, his tail flicking lazily. I turned, pointing the towel at him. "You think this is funny, don't you?"

He blinked. Slow. Unbothered.

I checked my phone for the millionth time. No new texts. Which meant they were still on the road, and there had been no mechanical failures.

Yet.

I tapped out a quick message. "How's the Winnebago running?"

A minute later, Dad replied.

> *Great! Only a little smoke when I started it up. Cleared right out.*

I froze mid-wipe.

I read it again.

Then I dropped my forehead against the counter.

Sir Stumpy let out a judgmental little chirp.

"Don't start with me," I muttered.

The phone buzzed again. This time, it was Mom.

> *Just realized we forgot the lasagna! Oh well, I'll cook at your house!* :)

I sat up so fast I nearly knocked the soap dispenser off the sink. *No, no, no.*

Mom's version of "cooking" meant taking over my entire kitchen. Every pot, every pan, flour on every surface.

And if she was cooking, she'd make enough to feed us for a week. Way past the little weekend visit I originally imagined. A sudden prickle of fear raced over my skin.

I mean... not that I didn't *want* them around. But I had a job! I couldn't babysit my parents. I texted back.

How long are you staying?

No response.

Just three little dots appearing. Disappearing. Appearing again.

I stared at the screen, waiting, bracing. And then nothing. She probably typed something and forgot to hit Send.

Sir Stumpy stretched, yawned, then hopped down and limped toward his food bowl. And suddenly, I had a horrifying thought.

I gasped. "Did I buy enough tuna?"

Because if not, Mom would go to the store, and if Mom went to the store, she would buy another twelve cans "just in case." Along with half the remaining shelves in the store.

I grabbed my keys, half-ready to run out and stock up before she got the chance—

A sound outside.

Not just any sound.

The unmistakable deep, rattling rumble of an ancient motorhome struggling its way down my driveway.

I froze, eyes wide.

Sir Stumpy looked up from his bowl. Let out a single chirp. Like he knew his free Tuna Dispenser was about to pull up.

I swallowed hard.

Showtime.

Gage

I WASN'T *PLANNING* TO drive by Amber's place.

Not really.

I was just taking the scenic route home. Which happened to go past her road. And I happened to slow down slightly as I got closer.

For reasons.

Completely unrelated to the fact that Amber left work early, and I was dying of curiosity. But as I rounded the bend, I spotted it. And dear Lord, I was not prepared.

A Winnebago.

A big, lumbering, ancient beast of a thing—the kind that looked like it had rolled straight out of 1983 and hadn't received a single upgrade since. It was trundling up Amber's driveway, bouncing over the uneven gravel, listing slightly to one side like a ship taking on water.

I slowed to a stop just in time to witness the whole masterpiece.

One of the side mirrors was held on with duct tape. The engine gave a final wheeze as it came to a stop, and something let out a concerning hiss.

I squinted. Was that... steam? Smoke? Hard to say.

But the best part?

Amber stood on the porch, arms crossed, looking like she was preparing for battle.

I grinned, shifting into park. Because I wasn't about to miss this.

Her dad hopped out first, grinning like he'd just piloted a luxury yacht instead of whatever this was.

Amber's arms tightened across her chest.

"Made good time!" her dad announced, slapping the side of the Winnebago. The whole thing wobbled ominously.

Amber winced.

Her mom climbed down next, already talking.

"The drive was gorgeous. Oh, and I thought of something on the way—I'll need to borrow your biggest pot for the soup tonight."

Amber's expression didn't change. "Mom, how long are you staying?"

Her mom waved a hand. "Oh, we'll see! We're in no rush."

Amber's eye twitched.

I bit the inside of my cheek to keep from laughing. Because this was the best entertainment I'd had all week.

Amber dragged a hand down her face. "Please tell me everything went okay with the drive."

Her dad waved her off. "Oh yeah! No major issues. Started right up."

"Dad."

He hesitated. "...Might need to check the brakes, though."

Amber's mouth fell open. "The *brakes?!*"

Her mom patted his arm. "Oh, don't worry, honey. He knew they were soft before we left."

Amber looked like she was about to self-destruct on the spot.

I couldn't help it.

I laughed.

Out loud.

Amber's head snapped in my direction like she was just realizing I was there. Her eyes narrowed dangerously.

I grinned and gave her a lazy wave from the truck.

She looked seconds away from throwing something at me. Which just made this even funnier.

Her dad noticed me then, eyes lighting up like he just found a new audience.

"Well, hey there! You must be a friend of Amber's!"

Amber closed her eyes briefly. "Dad, no."

"Oh, come on, now," he said, striding toward my truck like we were about to have a full conversation. "You gotta let me meet the neighbors. What's your name, son?"

I bit back another laugh, then tipped my hat. "Gage Langton, sir. And I'm not a neighbor. I live up at Ridgeview Ranch. Just driving home."

Amber made a pointing gesture back toward the highway, and even I couldn't mistake her meaning. But I wasn't about to leave yet.

Her dad grinned. "Langton? Any relation to Chase? Amber told me about him, I think. He's been doing the work over at White Pines, right?"

"Yes, sir. He's my brother."

Her dad nodded, looking delighted. "Good man! Heard great things about his work." He clapped a hand to his chest. "Bob Morris. Nice to meet you."

Amber muttered something I couldn't hear, but was probably unkind.

Her dad glanced back at her, then leaned in slightly. "She always this friendly?"

I smirked. "Oh, absolutely."

Amber threw her hands in the air and walked inside.

Her mom sighed fondly. "Poor thing's a little high-strung sometimes."

Bob grinned at me. "You sticking around for supper, Gage?"

"NO, HE IS NOT!" Amber shouted from inside.

I chuckled, pushing my hat back. "Appreciate the offer, sir, but I should probably let y'all get settled."

Bob nodded easily. "Another time, then."

Amber reappeared in the doorway. "Dad, stop inviting strangers to dinner."

"Aw, come on, honey," he said. "He's not a stranger."

Amber looked me dead in the eyes. Then she pointed toward the road again. "Leave."

I grinned, throwing the truck into reverse. And as I backed out, I swore I could hear her dad chuckling to himself.

Chapter Eleven

Amber

I LOVED MY PARENTS.

I really did.

But having them here meant I was constantly on high alert.

Because unlike when *I* visited *them*, where I could come and go as I pleased, here, they had no one else to entertain them. Which meant I felt responsible.

Which meant stress.

Which meant I was currently watching my mother unpack an entire grocery store's worth of food onto my kitchen counters while my dad opened random cabinets like he'd never been in a house before.

"Mom, we can just go get a burger for lunch. There's a great place—"

She waved a hand, already rearranging my spice rack. "Oh, I have sandwich stuff in the motor home. Tell your dad to go bring it in."

I exhaled slowly, forcing patience. Sir Stumpy sat on the kitchen table, watching the entire ordeal with the detached amusement of a ruler surveying his kingdom.

Dad, meanwhile, was in his own world, poking around my cabinets. "Where's your coffee?" he asked. "I brought my French press. Hey, don't you get ants, keeping your sugar in this ceramic thing instead of Tupperware?"

I blinked. "No, I don't have ants, and my coffee maker's literally right there."

"Yeah, but I like my French press," he said, grabbing his bag of coffee like he was about to change my life.

I sighed and let him do whatever he was going to do. Maybe caffeine would slow him down.

Maybe it would make him worse.

Too early to tell.

Mom finished organizing my spices—wrong, by the way—and turned back to me, smiling warmly. "Oh, honey, you still haven't showed me where you keep your soup pot."

I froze. Then slowly turned to face her.

"...Mom," I said carefully, hoping my voice sounded excited rather than fearful, "exactly *how* long are you planning to stay?"

She made a thoughtful noise. "Oh, a few days, a week—"

"A week?"

"Amber," she chided. "We live in Missoula! If we're driving four hours through the mountains, we're going to make it worth the trip."

I pressed my fingers to my temple. "Well," I said, trying to salvage my sanity, "at least you'll get to see White Pines while you're here. We'll go tomorrow."

Her eyes lit up. "Oh, yes! I can't wait! It'll be so good to see how much it's grown."

I opened my mouth to correct her again, but before I could get a word in, she tilted her head, frowning slightly. "Honey," she said. "Who was that nice young man outside?"

I blinked. "What?"

"The one in the truck."

I stared at her.

"...Gage?"

She snapped her fingers. "Yes! Gage. He was very polite. Kind of cute, too."

I let out a slow, controlled breath. "Mom. No."

"No, what?"

"No... whatever you're thinking."

She gave me her best innocent expression. "I wasn't thinking anything."

Dad, who was now wrestling with my coffee maker, called over his shoulder. "Oh, she's thinking something."

Mom shushed him. "I was just making conversation."

I groaned.

Because if my mother was noticing Gage Langton, that meant she was going to have opinions.

And I was going to lose my mind.

Gage

I WASN'T EXPECTING TO see Amber's parents again so soon.

But the second I stepped out of the barn at White Pines the next morning, there they were. The Winnebago Survivors, standing in the parking lot, looking fresh and cheerful like they hadn't just conquered the mountain highways in a vehicle that belonged in a museum.

Amber was already out of the car, smoothing a hand down her black embroidered "White Pines Staff" coat, looking like she was trying to exude patience. Her eyes narrowed when she spotted me.

I grinned and tipped my hat.

And that's when Bob saw me. "Hey! Gage, right?"

Amber closed her eyes briefly. Probably wishing for a trapdoor to swallow her into the earth.

Bob strode toward me, grinning like we were old friends.

"Yes, sir," I said easily. "Good to see you again."

Bob clapped a hand on my shoulder, nodding toward the barn. "So, you work out here too?"

Amber muttered, "No, he just loiters."

I laughed it off. "I'm a little of everything. I help run the ranch with my brothers, help Chase up here when he needs an extra hand. This project is going to be done in another month or so, so I guess I'll be back to full-time cowboying unless Chase digs up another construction project."

Bob nodded like this was deeply fascinating information, and her mom joined us, beaming. I hadn't caught her name yet. "Oh, it's just so nice to see friendly faces. Everyone here seems so kind."

Amber cleared her throat, clearly desperate to regain control of the conversation. "Yep. Well, we're all here. Let's head inside, Mom."

Bob, completely ignoring her, pointed to a corral full of rescue horses across the driveway. "So, Gage—tell me something."

I glanced at Amber. She looked seconds away from panic.

I turned back to Bob. "Sir?"

Bob squinted at me like he was sizing me up. "How's your rope work?"

I blinked. Not what I expected.

Amber rolled her eyes. "Dad."

"What?" Bob said. "It's an important skill. Full time cowboy, he's gotta know his way around a loop."

I grinned. "I do all right."

"You know, back in my day—"

"Oh, my word," Amber muttered. "Dad, Morgan is waiting for us inside. She canceled appointments so she could make time to give you a special tour. We—"

Bob ignored her completely. "—I used to throw a loop every now and then. Not for real work, just for fun. Haven't done it in years, though."

I raised a brow. "You wanna try?"

Amber's head snapped toward me, eyes wide, as if to say, "*Do not encourage him.*"

Bob perked up. "Oh, I don't know about today, but maybe one of these days."

Amber exhaled slowly. "Come on, Dad," she said, shooting me a warning glance, "before anyone starts roping anything, let's go inside."

Bob and his wife smiled happily and followed her.

Amber lingered for half a second, glaring at me.

I smirked. "You okay, Morris? You look tense."

She pointed a finger at me. "If you turn my father into a cowboy again, I will end you."

I chuckled. "Not my fault if it's still in his blood."

She groaned, then turned and stomped inside.

And I followed, grinning the whole way. I hadn't planned to be part of this little family tour. But I wasn't about to leave now.

Not when Bob Morris clearly had stories to tell.

Amber

I LOVED MY PARENTS. I really did.

But I had reached my limit.

We'd been at White Pines for almost an hour now. An hour.

An hour of Mom stopping every two minutes to admire something. An hour of Dad asking a million questions about the barn design, the horses, and roping—always roping. An hour of watching Gage charm his way right into my father's good graces, which was probably the most stressful part of all.

And now?

Now, I had finally, finally managed to get Mom talking to Morgan and Kate about the sorts of therapies we offered, and Dad talking to Chase about the expansion, and I had a minute to breathe.

I slipped away, leaning against the fence just outside the barn, letting the cool air settle my nerves. I had barely taken two deep breaths when I heard boots on gravel.

I closed my eyes briefly, already knowing who it was.

"Surviving?" Gage asked.

I exhaled. "Barely."

He chuckled, leaning next to me. "Didn't know you were so bad at hosting."

I shot him a look. "It's not that I don't want them here. It's just... a lot."

He nodded, surprisingly quiet.

And maybe it was the exhaustion. Maybe it was the fact that I'd been trying so hard to hold everything together.

But before I could stop myself, I muttered, "I don't know what's worse. That Gina wants to shove them in a retirement home, or that part of me is scared they actually need it."

I regretted saying it immediately. Because I hadn't let myself think that. Hadn't let myself say it.

But now it was out there.

And worse? Gage didn't even look surprised.

He was just watching me. Really watching.

I shook my head, forcing a laugh. "You must think I'm a mess."

He shrugged. "No. I think you care."

Something about the way he said it made my chest squeeze. I turned back to the barn, swallowing hard. "Doesn't feel like caring. Feels like failing."

Gage was quiet for a long moment. Then, voice low, he said, "If you didn't care, you wouldn't be out here stressing about it."

I hated that that made sense.

Hated that it helped.

I sighed, rubbing my arms against the chill through my thin sweater. "You ever feel like nothing you do is enough?"

He huffed a quiet laugh. "I'm the oldest of four boys. What do you think?"

I glanced up at him. He wasn't looking at me—just staring out at the field with a look that could have spanned a thousand miles.

It had to be the exhaustion. That must be it, because why else would I just stand there and gaze at Gage Langton while he looked all philosophical? Had to be the exhaustion.

Then I heard my dad's voice from inside. "Amber! Come here a second!"

I closed my eyes, braced myself, and turned to go.

Gage tipped his hat, back to his usual grin. "Go get 'em, Morris."

I muttered something about praying for my own patience and walked inside.

#

A^{MBER}

#

Day Three: I woke up to the smell of coffee.

Which was good.

And the distinct scent of something burning.

Which was bad.

I shot upright, heart pounding. A second later, I heard frantic clicking from the kitchen, followed by my dad's voice.

"It's fine! Just a little extra crispy."

I threw off my blankets, and all but sprinted down the hall. The scene that awaited me? My dad fanning smoke away from the toaster.

My mom, completely unbothered, setting the table like this was a perfectly normal Saturday morning. Sir Stumpy, perched on the counter, presiding over an empty can of tuna and licking his one front paw with his usual air of feline superiority.

I leaned against the doorway, catching my breath. "What... are you doing?"

Dad turned, grinning. "Making breakfast!"

I stared at the blackened remains of what used to be toast. "By setting off my smoke alarm?"

"Oh, that won't happen. I already took the battery out," he said, gesturing toward the detector on the counter.

I closed my eyes briefly.

Mom set a plate down. "Sit, honey! We've got toast, eggs, and your dad made coffee."

I eyed the coffee suspiciously. "With what?"

"French press," Dad said proudly, holding it up like it was the secret to life itself.

I exhaled. "Dad. I own a coffee maker."

"Yeah, but this is better."

"Okay. Sure. Fine. Whatever."

I sat down at the table, fully prepared to accept my fate.

Mom passed me a plate, then smiled like she was about to say something casual. "Oh, Bob wants to fix the Winnebago later. There was smoke or something."

I froze mid-reach for the butter. Then I slowly looked up. "...What?"

Dad waved a hand. "It's making a little noise, but I'm sure I can fix it."

I set my fork down with deliberate slowness. "Dad," I said, keeping my voice as even as possible. "The last time you fixed something, you nearly set the shed on fire."

"That was an electrical issue," he corrected. "This is just an engine thing."

"And that's better?"

"It's completely different."

"Dad, I know a mechanic. Several, in fact, I'll make a call and—"

Mom cut in, smiling. "Oh, Amber, don't worry so much. He just needs to check a few things."

"I *am* worried."

Sir Stumpy let out a small chirp, clearly siding with me.

Dad ignored all of us and took a triumphant sip of his coffee.

Mom patted my hand. "Try your toast, sweetheart."

I stared at the charred rectangle on my plate, my soul slowly leaving my body.

If the Winnebago survived the day, it would be a miracle.

Gage

I WAS SITTING AT the ranch, halfway through my second cup of coffee, when my phone rang. I didn't recognize the number. I almost ignored it, like I ignore all unknown calls.

Almost.

I don't know why, but I set my mug down and answered, expecting maybe a contractor or a wrong number. What I got instead was—

"Gage! Good morning, son!"

I blinked.

...Bob Morris?

I sat forward in my chair. "Uh. Morning?"

Bob sounded downright cheerful. "Hope I didn't wake ya!"

"I'm a rancher, Bob. I've been up for four hours already," I said slowly. "...How did you get my number?"

"Oh, ran into your brother Chase at the gas station this morning. Nice guy. He gave it to me."

I processed that for a second. Bob Morris had run into Chase, asked for my phone number, and Chase just... gave it to him? Sounded to me like a had a brother to pummel.

I was still wrapping my head around that when I heard Amber's voice in the background.

"Dad? Who are you talking to?"

Bob called over his shoulder. "Gage Langton!"

A pause.

Then Amber, much closer to the phone now, voice full of shock: "*How* do you have Gage Langton's phone number?"

"I just told Gage that, didn't you hear? Ran into your buddy Chase, the one working on White Pines up there. Great guy. We had a whole conversation."

I grinned, imagining Amber's face.

There was a scuffle on the other end of the line. Then, suddenly, Amber was directly into the receiver. "Gage."

I bit back a laugh. "Morning, Morris."

"Do *not* entertain him," she hissed.

"Honey, that's rude," her dad protested.

"Gage, whatever my dad is asking—say no."

I leaned back in my chair, grinning at the ceiling. "Oh, I don't know," I said lazily. "I haven't even heard the offer yet."

Amber made a strangled noise.

Bob cheerfully cut back in. "Oh, it's nothing big! Just a little extra set of hands while I check a few things under the hood."

Amber groaned. I could practically hear her rubbing her temples. "Dad," she said slowly, like she was trying to de-escalate a hostage situation, "we talked about this. The Winnebago does not need you 'checking' things. I'll call a mechanic—someone with tools and a lift, who doesn't have a bad back."

Bob scoffed. "Amber, honey, it's just making a little noise. It's probably nothing, but I just want to have a look."

"Dad—"

He kept going. "And I figured, who better to call than a Langton boy? Ranchers can fix anything with baling twine."

I laughed. "Can't argue with that logic."

Amber groaned again. "Gage..."

I stretched, enjoying this a little too much. "Sorry, Doc," I said, all casual. "Looks like I've been recruited."

Amber made an outright frustrated sound. "Dad, stop roping innocent people into your projects."

"Now, Amber, that's not fair—he's agreeing."

"I haven't agreed yet," I said, just to see what would happen.

"Then don't," she blurted immediately.

"Come on, son, it'll be quick," her dad protested.

"Dad!"

I laughed outright. Because I had absolutely no idea what I'd just gotten myself into. But judging by Amber's sheer level of distress?

It was going to be great.

Chapter Twelve

Gage

I WASN'T SURE WHAT I expected when I pulled into Amber's driveway. But the second I parked, I was greeted by the sight of Bob Morris already striding toward my truck like I was his long-lost son.

Amber stood on the porch, arms crossed, looking like she was already regretting ever admitting to her dad that she knew me. I climbed out of the truck, grinning.

"Mornin', Morris," I said. "You look thrilled to see me."

Amber's glare intensified. "I need you to know this is a mistake."

Bob clapped a hand on my shoulder before I could respond. "Gage! Good to see you, son!" He turned and pointed proudly at the Winnebago like it was some kind of prized racehorse. "Here she is."

I took one look at the thing.

It was definitely not a racehorse.

It was still listing slightly to one side, and I was pretty sure something was leaking underneath.

I rocked back on my heels, nodding slowly. "She's a beaut."

Bob grinned. "That's what I said! A little older, maybe, but still runs fine, and what do we need with anything fancy? It's got a bed and a fridge and air conditioning for what whole week of the summer when it's hot enough to bother with."

Amber made a sound that was one part exasperation, one part suppressed scream.

I bit back a laugh. "So, what exactly are we dealing with?" I asked, walking over for a closer look.

"Well, see, it started with a little whump-whump-whump noise when we were coming down the pass, but then it evened out. Thought it was just the road, you know? But then, right before we hit town, it did this chug-a-chug thing, and I had to tap the brakes a little harder than usual. Not a lot harder, just enough to make me go, 'Hmm.'"

Amber, from behind us: "Dad. Please stop making noises."

Bob ignored her. "Then, when we pulled into the driveway, I swear I heard a little hiss-pop—but only for a second. Could be nothing! But could also be something."

I nodded seriously, because I was not about to stop this train. "A hiss-pop is definitely somethin' we should check out. What's your gut tellin' you?"

Bob tapped his chin. "Hard to say. But back in my day, we didn't ignore a good hiss-pop."

Amber groaned, dragging a hand down her face. "I need you both to stop saying hiss-pop."

Bob grinned. "See? She's worried, too."

I bit back a laugh and leaned down, checking for leaks. "Alright," I said, straightening. "Let's take a look under the hood."

Bob clapped his hands together, pleased. "Atta boy."

Amber groaned even louder.

And I was pretty sure this was the most fun Bob had had in a while.

I POPPED THE HOOD, half-expecting a small animal to jump out.

Nothing did. Which meant things were already going better than I thought they would.

Bob peered in, rubbing his hands together like we were about to perform high-stakes surgery. "Alright," he said. "What do you think?"

I grabbed a rag from my back pocket, checking the fluids first. "Well, your oil's fine. No leaks I can see." I stepped back, eyeing the engine. "Might just be some buildup on the fuel line. And the brakes..."

I opened the driver door of the little Class C and climbed in behind the wheel, then pressed down on the pedal experimentally. It gave way too easily.

Bob frowned. "That bad?"

I looked at him. "You drove four hours on these?"

Bob waved a hand. "Had to press down a little harder than usual, but I made it, didn't I?"

"You made it," Amber said, appearing suddenly beside him with a fresh cup of coffee. "The rest of us are still processing the trauma."

Bob chuckled, but I caught the way his hands settled on his hips, the quiet little nod he gave.

Because he knew.

Maybe he wouldn't say it outright, but he wasn't as stubborn as Amber made him out to be.

He just wasn't ready to admit it yet.

I got out of the cab and rolled my shoulders, reaching for the toolbox he'd brought out. "I can tighten up the brake line, might buy you some time. But if you're serious about taking this thing back through the mountains, you'll wanna get it looked at for real. We got a friend, Jess Walker who's a real sharp diesel mechanic, and I bet this would be a cinch for her."

Bob nodded again. "Appreciate it, son."

And there was something about the way he said it—simple, casual, like it was just a fact. Something about the way he stood next to me, watching the work like he used to *be* the guy fixing things and just hadn't done it in a while.

I exhaled, bending down to tighten the line, trying not to think about *my* dad.

Because that's what this felt like. Working on an old rig, shooting the breeze while hands stayed busy—it felt like standing in the shop with my own father, watching him tinker with something that wasn't technically broken but could "use a little attention."

I hadn't thought about those moments in a long time.

Didn't like to.

But here it was, sneaking up on me anyway.

I pushed the thought away, but it stayed at the edges of my mind, settling somewhere deep.

Amber's voice snapped me out of it as she leaned over my shoulder. A lot closer than she probably realized, because I could feel her coat brushing the back of mine. "How's it looking?"

I turned around, wiping my hands on the rag. "Well, I tightened the line, checked the fuel system, and made sure nothing was about to explode. Which means—" I tapped the hood. "—she'll probably survive the weekend."

Amber sighed, half in relief, half in pure exhaustion.

Bob grinned like I just gave him a clean bill of health. "Knew I called the right guy."

And weirdly? That meant something.

I wasn't used to hearing that.

Didn't expect to like the way it felt.

But I did.

Amber

I HADN'T SAID A word in the last fifteen minutes. Because for the first time since this whole thing started, I didn't need to intervene. I just... watched.

Watched Gage keeping my dad busy but not in a condescending way.

Watched him steer the project without making my dad feel useless.

Watched my dad having fun.

And, worst of all—

Watched Gage actually be helpful.

Which was not at all what I had prepared for. I had expected chaos. I had expected smirking and teasing and maybe some well-meaning destruction.

I had not expected him to take the whole thing seriously.

But he was.

Gage had his hat pushed back, listening to my dad's commentary like it actually mattered. And my dad?

He looked happy.

Like this was exactly the kind of thing he missed doing. Like he hadn't even realized how much he missed it until now. Something in my chest unclenched. I let out a slow breath and walked down the steps, finally closing the distance.

Gage caught the movement, glanced up from where he was wiping his hands on a rag. I hesitated. Then sighed.

"…Thanks."

He raised an eyebrow. "That word painful to say?"

I scowled. "I will take it back."

His grin was infuriatingly smug. "Nah, I think I'll hold onto it."

I crossed my arms, but my irritation felt half-hearted now. And then—the worst thing happened.

He smiled.

Not his usual teasing smirk. Not that cocky, bet-I'm-gonna-get-a-reaction grin.

A *real* smile.

Easy. Familiar. A little bit devastating.

And for some awful reason, my brain decided to acknowledge that. I immediately turned toward the house, muttering, "I have things to do."

Behind me, Gage chuckled.

"Don't panic, Morris. It's not illegal to have a good time."

I didn't dignify that with an answer.

Because the last thing I needed was Gage Langton knowing he'd just thrown me completely off balance.

Gage

A MBER MAY HAVE GONE back inside, but Bob and I weren't done. We were standing next to the Winnebago, wrapping up the last few things, when Bob let out a satisfied sigh.

"Well," he said, clapping his hands together. "That was a good morning's work."

I grinned. "Not bad at all."

Bob nodded, clearly pleased. "You know, Gage, you remind me of a fella I used to work with back in the day. Knew his way around a wrench, didn't talk much, but got things done."

I chuckled. "Guess that's better than reminding you of the guy who set your brakes on fire."

Bob laughed. "Oh, that was Gary. Man was a menace with a socket wrench."

"Oh, then no worries. I barely know which one to use. When in doubt, get a bigger hammer—that's what my dad always said."

Bob's grin got even wider as he gave the Winnebago one last pat. "I've done that a time or two, myself. Appreciate the help, son."

And there it was again. That simple, easy way he said it—like it was just a fact. Like it was assumed I'd be there to help. Which was weird, because... well, isn't that what real sons are for? Or sons-in-law? I was nothing but a guy who got under his daughter's skin from time to time.

But he kept saying it, and that feeling settled somewhere deep. I wasn't sure what to do with it. So I just nodded, adjusting my hat. "Anytime, sir."

Bob grinned. "Alright, let's get some lunch. Amber! You got food in there?"

From inside the house, there was a brief pause. Then Amber stepped into the doorway, expression carefully neutral, arms crossed like she was already bracing for whatever came next.

Her eyes landed on me, sharp and assessing.

I grinned.

Bob leaned in slightly, voice low. "She's a little too serious sometimes, huh?"

"You have no idea."

Amber exhaled slowly, like she was gathering patience. Then, after a beat, she opened the door wider. "Fine. Come eat."

Bob grinned, clapping me on the shoulder. "See? Knew she liked you."

Amber gave him a look, then turned and disappeared inside. Bob laughed.

I followed, still grinning. Because whether she wanted to admit it or not—I was growing on her.

Amber

I HAD MADE A lot of mistakes in my life.

But letting my dad and Gage Langton spend the morning together?

This might be my worst one yet.

I stood in the kitchen, watching in growing horror as Gage made himself at home at my table. Dad was talking up a storm, clearly thrilled with his new best friend. Mom, of course, was delighted with another mouth to feed.

"Oh, I'm so glad you're staying for lunch, Gage!" she said, setting a plate in front of him. "Amber, honey, grab the iced tea, would you?"

I narrowed my eyes. "You don't even drink iced tea."

"But you do. I bought some this morning," Mom said cheerfully.

I sighed and grabbed the pitcher from the fridge. Meanwhile, Dad was elbow-deep in conversation with Gage.

"I tell you what, son," Dad said, reaching for a roll. "Not every guy would take time out of his day to help an old man with his Winnebago."

Gage grinned, completely at ease. "Oh, I don't know. Free entertainment and mechanical work? Pretty good deal."

Dad laughed, clearly charmed. "See? I like a guy who likes keeping his hands busy."

I glared at Gage as I set the iced tea down. He gave me that infuriating cowboy smile.

And, unfortunately, I noticed it. Again.

I sat down, pointedly ignoring him, and focused on my food.

But the betrayal wasn't over yet. Because the next thing I knew, Mom was giving me a very *particular* look.

A look I knew way too well.

The matchmaker look.

Oh, no.

Absolutely not.

I set my fork down and said, "No."

Gage raised a brow. "No, what?"

Mom waved a hand. "Oh, don't mind her, sweetheart."

Sweetheart?!

I picked my fork back up and stabbed at my pulled pork with unnecessary force.

Dad, oblivious to my suffering, turned back to Gage. "So, son, you always planned to work the ranch?"

And just like that, the mood changed. Gage's easy grin faltered—just barely.

But I saw it.

And for some reason, that made me pay attention. Gage shifted his weight, rolling his shoulder like the question didn't quite sit right.

"Didn't really plan much of anything," he admitted. "Ranch was always just... there. Figured I'd help out wherever I was needed. Work with my brothers, whatever they're doing, keep the ranch running, look after my mom and the foster kids."

Bob nodded thoughtfully. "That's how life goes sometimes, huh? You fall into a rhythm before you even realize it."

Gage hummed in agreement, but his expression had faded to something... thoughtful. And something about that—about him not immediately cracking a joke or brushing it off—sat in my mind.

And before I could stop myself, I said, "Does that bother you?"

His gaze flicked to mine. I didn't expect him to actually answer. But he did.

He shrugged. "Sometimes."

Something in the way he said it caught me off guard. Like he hadn't meant to say it out loud. Like he'd only just realized it himself.

A beat of silence passed.

Then, like clockwork, Dad saved him.

"Well," Dad said, spreading butter on his roll. "Far as I can tell, you're dang good at what you do."

Gage grinned—just like that, back to easy confidence. "Well, I appreciate that, sir."

And the moment was gone.

Mom sighed happily, sipping her tea. "Isn't this nice, Amber?"

I gave her a flat look.

She just smiled.

Gage reached for a biscuit and said casually, "Y'know, this might be the best meal I've had all week."

Bob laughed. "That right?"

"Oh yeah." Gage leaned back in his chair, looking at me. "My mom's a great cook, but she's been doing taxes—she does all the books for the ranch, you know—and we've been fending for ourselves this week. These pulled pork sandwiches are a sight better than the cold turkey cuts we've been livin' on at home. Guess I've got you to thank for that, huh, Morris?"

I narrowed my eyes.

He smiled. Easy. Charming. Infuriatingly cute.

I took a slow sip of my iced tea.

And plotted his demise.

Chapter Thirteen

Gage

THE SECOND I WALKED into the house, I knew I'd made a mistake.

The kitchen table was full of people, full of noise, and—most horrifying of all—full of wedding talk. I hesitated in the doorway, considering my options.

Could I back out before anyone noticed me? Maybe just turn around and—

"Gage!"

Nope. Too late.

Mom beamed at me from her seat at the head of the table, where she was surrounded by Kate, Lauren, and what looked like an entire encyclopedia of wedding plans.

"You're just in time," she said cheerfully. "We were talking about the double wedding."

I exhaled slowly. "Fantastic."

Trent tightened his arm around Lauren and shot me a grin. "Don't worry. You won't have to do anything except show up."

"That's still asking a lot."

Lauren laughed, elbowing Trent. "See? Told you he'd say that."

I grabbed a glass from the cabinet, filling it with water, trying to ignore the way Chase looked way too comfortable in the middle of all this.

"You're really going through with this double wedding thing, huh?" I asked.

Kate nodded enthusiastically. "It makes sense! We're all family now, anyway."

I took a sip of water, mulling that over. A year ago, none of this was even a thought. Cole still had a chip on his shoulder and a grudge about the pretty blonde who could out-ride and out-show him. Chase was still daydreaming about being an architect and totally clueless about the girl with the dark brown eyes that followed him everywhere he went. And Trent was the hardworking cowboy on weekdays who spent his weekends rotating through rodeo girls like a sampler platter.

Now? The Langton boys were dropping like flies.

"March fifteenth," Mom said, flipping through what looked like a color-coded calendar. "That gives us exactly four weeks."

I choked on my water. "Four weeks?"

Chase shrugged. "Why wait any longer?"

"Yeah," Lauren said, smiling at Trent. "We're ready. No reason to drag it out."

I narrowed my eyes. "And you're all sure about this?"

Trent raised a brow. "You think I'd go through with a wedding if I wasn't?"

"Fair point."

Mom sighed happily, clearly loving every second of this. "Oh, and tomorrow's Valentine's Day, so we're making reservations at The Timberline."

Chase grinned at Kate. "Perfect."

"Timberline?" I scrunched up my face. "That the ski lodge up the mountain? Who goes there?"

Mom gave me a long-suffering look. "People who want something different from the tavern."

"Well, what's wrong with Beaufort's? And what do you mean, *'we're'* making reservations. Like... all of you together? For Valentine's Day?"

Mom shrugged. "They all decided they wanted to have one big dinner. Instead of everyone trying to make individual reservations at the same restaurant and sitting at adjoining tables, pretending to ignore each other, they decided on this. What do you think, want to be my plus one?" Mom grinned mischievously.

I chugged down a huge gulp of my water. "Mom..."

"Unless you have other plans," she said quickly. "You should do that instead."

Kate giggled. "You're just mad because you'll be the only one at the table without a date."

I lifted my empty glass. "And yet, somehow, I'll survive."

Mom laughed. "Oh, I don't know, sweetheart. Maybe it's time for you to find someone special."

I took another slow sip of water.

Not touching that one.

Cole grinned. "Careful, Ma. You start pushing, and he'll dig his boots in just for spite."

I pointed my glass at him. "Finally, someone in this family gets me."

Liam and Ethan wandered into the kitchen then, both eyeing the table like they were trying to decide if they wanted to get involved.

Ethan took one look at the wedding planning mess and turned right back around.

Liam hesitated. Then, after a moment, he stepped outside instead.

I frowned.

That was... new.

I FOUND LIAM ROPING the dummy just past the porch, his hat
pulled low like he didn't want to be bothered.

Didn't stop me, though.

"Thought you hated practicing alone," I said, stepping down onto
the packed snow.

Liam didn't look up. "Ethan is playing with that stupid tractor
again."

I leaned against the railing, watching him swing the rope. He'd been
getting better lately. His aim was sharper, his confidence stronger. But
tonight? His usual rhythm was off.

Something was bugging him.

"You worried about something?"

Liam hesitated mid-loop, then shook his head. "No."

I raised a brow. "Wanna try that again?"

Liam sighed and finally looked at me.

Liam tossed the rope at the dummy again, but this time, he missed
completely.

He stood there for a second, jaw tight, eyes locked on the empty
loop.

Then, voice flat, he said, "Social worker came by today."

I stilled. That was new. "Yeah?"

He shrugged. "Talked to your mom—didn't really talk to us. Just
checking in. Making sure everything's still 'on track.'"

I didn't like the sound of that. "For what?"

Liam let out a short, dry laugh. "April first."

I frowned. "What happens on April first?"

He twirled the rope once in his hand, forcing a grin. "Our birthday. April Fool's Day."

Oh. I hadn't been thinking about how close that actually was. Hadn't realized how fast the clock was running down for them.

Liam shook his head. "It's kind of fitting, isn't it? Spend most of our lives bouncing from place to place, just to age out on a joke holiday."

I exhaled slowly, crossing my arms. "You and Ethan talk about this?"

Liam rolled his shoulders. "Not really. He's doing his thing, pretending it's all fine. I figured I'd try that too, but..." He huffed a humorless laugh. "Turns out, I suck at it."

I didn't have an answer for that.

Because what could I say? I hadn't even realized how little time they had left. Hadn't thought about what came next for them.

"You still have to graduate, right?" I ventured. There, that pushed the looming deadline out another couple of months.

He shrugged. "Yeah. Nora promised she'd keep us in school... I guess. But legally, we don't have to."

"Liam, you have to graduate. Don't ask me why, 'cause I don't know. You just.... You gotta get your diploma."

Liam must've caught the look on my face because he forced another fake grin and muttered, "Whatever. I guess I'll stick around for that, but the rest... Just trying not to think about it too much."

I nodded, but the thought wasn't going anywhere. Now that it was out there, I wasn't sure how to *stop* thinking about it. I didn't have an answer for him.

Because honestly? I wasn't even sure what *I* was doing half the time, let alone what a pair of foster kids who were never loved by anyone before ought to do with their lives.

But one thing I did know was that that kid deserved better than spending every night worrying about what was coming next. If anyone in this world besides his twin brother cared about him, would have his back.

I stepped forward, picked up the rope he'd dropped, and tossed it back to him. "Come on. Show me a clean shot before we freeze out here."

Liam eyed me, like he knew exactly what I was doing.

But after a moment, he sighed, adjusted his grip, and got back to work.

And I watched, the thought settling deep—Liam wasn't the only one who needed to figure some things out.

Amber

I WAS *NOT* WATCHING Gage Langton.

I was grabbing coffee and pastries for my parents before heading to work. That was it.

The fact that he just so happened to be in the café at the same time? Completely irrelevant.

...Except he wasn't alone.

I stood at the counter, waiting for my order, when I spotted him near the back, talking to a woman.

I had never seen her before.

She was pretty. Long dark hair, easy smile. And she looked comfortable with him.

Which meant they knew each other.

Which meant I was still watching.

Which was absolutely not necessary.

I dragged my gaze back to the barista, who was ringing me up like I wasn't having a minor internal crisis.

It didn't matter who Gage was talking to. He was probably just flirting—because of course he was.

And I didn't care.

I did *not* care.

I reached for my coffee, determined to leave before—

"Mornin', Morris."

Oh, for the love of—

I turned, schooling my expression into one of polite indifference.

Gage was standing entirely too close, coffee in one hand, grinning a smile bright enough to light up the whole town.

Like he'd been expecting me to see him.

"I wasn't stalking you," I said immediately.

His grin widened. "Didn't say you were."

I narrowed my eyes. "You were thinking it."

"I mean..." He lifted a shoulder. "It *is* Valentine's Day. If you wanted to see me first thing in the morning, just say so."

I exhaled, forcing myself not to react.

"Trust me," I said flatly. "You were *not* the first thing I wanted to see today."

"Second?"

I grabbed my bag of pastries. "Not even top five."

He chuckled, taking a slow sip of his coffee, like he had all the time in the world. And just like that, I was irritated again.

Not because he was here.

Not because he was grinning at me like we had some kind of inside joke.

But because I was still paying attention.

And I was way too aware of the way other people were looking at him—how natural and easy he was in any setting. How the woman he'd been talking to was still watching him.

I cleared my throat, snapping myself out of it.

"Anyway," I said briskly, "some of us actually have jobs to get to."

He tipped his hat, all lazy charm. "Have a good one, Doc."

I huffed. "Not a doctor."

He just grinned and took another sip of his coffee.

I spun on my heel and walked out.

And definitely did not look back.

Gage

I WAS MINDING MY own business.

For once.

I had just swung by White Pines to check in with Chase, fully intending to be in and out. But before I could even make it to the barn, I heard—

"Gage! You got plans tonight?"

I turned to find Bob Morris walking toward me, grinning like we were already in the middle of a conversation. Which, as far as I knew, we weren't.

I frowned. "Uh... no?"

Bob clapped a hand on my shoulder like I just gave him the best news of his life. "Well, that settles it! You should take Amber out."

I blinked. "I should what?"

"It's Valentine's Day!" he said, like that explained everything. "A young guy like you shouldn't be sitting at home alone."

I opened my mouth. Closed it. Opened it again. "...Sir, you can't just throw out ideas like that with no warning."

Bob laughed. "Why not? Makes sense, doesn't it?"

No. No, it absolutely did not.

And I was about to tell him that—politely—when I heard the worst possible sound at the worst possible time.

Amber.

"Excuse me?"

I turned just as she stepped around the barn, arms crossed, expression deadly.

Bob, completely unfazed, grinned at her. "Gage here was just telling me he's free tonight."

Amber's eyes narrowed. "Oh, was he?"

I could have clarified. I could have easily shut this down. But where was the fun in that?

I crossed my arms, grinning. "Yeah, Morris. What do you say? Romantic dinner?"

Her death glare intensified.

Bob looked entirely too pleased. "See? That's the spirit!"

"I have work," Amber seethed through gritted teeth.

I shrugged. "Shame. Guess you'll just have to pine after me from afar."

Amber made a noise that I was pretty sure was not fit for polite company.

Bob patted me on the back. "I like you, son."

I grinned. "I like me too."

Amber turned on her heel, muttering something about needing to rethink her entire life, and disappeared inside.

Bob chuckled. "Pick her up at six? She'll be waiting for you."

I wasn't sure about that.

But I did know one thing—

She was absolutely plotting my murder now.

And I was absolutely enjoying every second of it.

Amber

I DIDN'T WANT TO talk about it.

I didn't want to think about it.

But unfortunately, my mother did not share those feelings.

"Oh, Amber," she said, sounding absolutely delighted. "A Valentine's date! I knew you'd find someone last minute."

I stared at her. "It's not a date."

My dad chuckled from his recliner. "That's what your mom said to me on our first date, too."

I groaned, and wished, for like the dozenth time, I'd taken that job in Alaska. The one that seemed so far from civilization that I wondered how they even had clients, let alone horses. Why, *why* did I have to come to Big River Valley?

My mom ignored me entirely, bustling around the kitchen like she had something to celebrate. "Oh, we should've known something was going on! Bob, did you notice the way she's been talking about Gage?"

Bob perked up. "Oh, yeah. Lots of 'Gage is annoying. Gage is impossible. Gage is ruining my life.' That's the good stuff. Means she likes him."

I turned toward my father. "I don't say that."

"No, but you think it."

"Dad, there's nothing there! Do *not* encourage this."

He winked. "Already did."

I let my forehead drop to the table.

Mom just sighed happily, getting herself a cup of tea. "Oh, I just love Valentine's Day."

That got my attention. I lifted my head. "Wait. You guys always do something, don't you?"

Dad grinned. "Of course we do."

Mom waved a hand. "It's nothing fancy, just a little tradition we started years ago."

I narrowed my eyes. "...What kind of tradition?"

She smiled, all soft and giddy, like a little girl. "Every year, we write each other a love letter and read them out loud. But we have to write them like bad poetry. The cornier, the better."

Dad chuckled. "Your mother once rhymed 'marriage' with 'extra cheese on a sandwich.'"

Mom sniffed. "And yet, you still swooned."

I blinked.

Dad shrugged. "It's the effort that counts."

That alone was enough to make me question everything I thought I knew about my parents. But then Mom grinned at Dad, eyes sparkling like a twelve-year-old girl swooning over her first cute boy. "Oh, tell her about the year we rented the Mustang."

I frowned. "...What?"

Dad let out a low whistle, leaning back in his chair like he was reliving a core memory. "Valentine's Day, 1989. We drove by a rental place, saw a candy apple red Mustang, and thought, hey, that looks fun."

"Dad. Please tell me you didn't."

Mom laughed. "Oh, we absolutely did."

Dad grinned. "Took it straight into the mountains."

I sputtered. "In February?"

Mom waved a hand. "Oh, the roads weren't that bad."

"Well, not all of them," Dad said. "We only bottomed out on that one corner... you remember that, sweetheart? We slid a little into a snow bank and that nice young couple pulled us out?"

I dropped my face into my hands. "You were *those* people."

"I like to think of us as romantics with a sense of adventure," Mom giggled.

Dad nudged her. "You mean idiots with no survival instincts."

She laughed. "That too!"

I lifted my head, still trying to process. "And you lived?"

Dad grinned. "Survived and made it home with an intact rental deposit."

I shook my head, fully reevaluating everything I thought I knew about my responsible, level-headed parents.

Mom just sighed happily, like she was reliving the best day of her life. "Oh, it was wonderful. The car was completely impractical. The roads were awful. And the whole time, we were singing along to the radio and passing a notebook back and forth, writing our terrible poems."

Dad chuckled. "And occasionally praying we wouldn't skid off the road."

I shook my head, my eyes glazing over. "I am never letting you lecture me about responsible decisions again."

Dad grinned. "Oh, sweetheart. We stopped trying to give you responsible advice years ago."

Mom winked. "We just like watching you struggle."

I had no idea what to do with this information. My parents, who had been together for literal decades, were still writing each other terrible love poems and reminiscing about how they almost went over a cliff together.

It was corny.

It was adorable.

And it was exactly why they weren't ready to let go of their independence.

I swallowed, pushing that thought away before it could settle too deep.

Mom turned back to me. "Anyway, while you're out with Gage, we'll be here, enjoying our evening. Right, handsome?" She grinned at Dad and wiggled her eyebrows.

I stood up so fast my chair almost fell over. "Okay, and that's where we stop talking."

Mom laughed. "Oh, honey, don't be so uptight."

Dad chuckled. "Let her go, Joyce. She's gotta get ready for her date."

I spun around. "It's not a date!"

Mom just smiled, sipping her tea. "Mmm-hmm."

I STARED AT MY closet.

Then at my reflection.

Then back at my closet.

I had no idea how to dress for this. Where were we going? What were we doing? I had exactly zero details.

I knew how to dress for work.

I knew how to dress for errands.

I even knew how to dress for an actual, pre-planned date.

But this?

This was Gage Langton ambushing me into a Valentine's outing because my father has no sense of boundaries.

I sighed and settled on something safe—dark jeans, a sweater, boots. Comfortable. Casual. Like I wasn't overthinking this.

I pulled my hair into a loose ponytail, gave myself a final, deeply unamused look in the mirror, and walked back into the living room.

Right on cue, a knock sounded at the door.

Mom beamed. "Ooh, he's punctual. That means he's responsible."

"Or it means he likes her," Dad suggested.

I rolled my eyes and opened the door.

And there he was.

Gage Langton, leaning against the doorframe like he had all the time in the world. Hat tipped back. That lazy cowboy smile firmly in place.

And, worst of all—he looked good.

Too good.

He took me in, from head to toe, and grinned. "Nice sweater, Morris. You dressing up for me?"

I stepped outside and slammed the door behind me before my parents could say something horrifying.

Gage chuckled, offering his arm. "Shall we?"

I didn't take it. But I walked beside him, anyway.

Chapter Fourteen

Amber

G AGE'S TRUCK RUMBLED TO life, headlights cutting through the cold February night. I folded my arms, staring out the window as we passed through town, bracing myself for whatever ridiculous plans he had in store.

Then we drove right past Beaufort's.

The nicest restaurant in town. The one every Valentine's couple was going to tonight.

I turned my head. "Uh. Gage?"

He flicked on his turn signal. "Yeah?"

"We just passed the only remotely decent place in town."

"Yep."

I waited.

That was it?

"...So, we're not going there?"

Gage grinned. "Nah. Too predictable."

Predictable.

Right. Because when a woman is forced into a Valentine's dinner against her will, the real problem is that it's too predictable.

I sighed and sat back, watching as we pulled into the parking lot of... the tavern?

The tavern.

Not a restaurant. Not even a diner.

A tavern.

The kind of place where the floors were permanently coated in peanut shells and sawdust. Where the smell of grilled burgers fought for dominance with the scent of beer. Where the only decorations were taxidermy and neon beer signs.

Gage killed the engine and looked over at me, clearly waiting for a reaction.

I gave him one. A long, slow blink.

"This," I said, gesturing vaguely toward the establishment, "is your Valentine's date idea?"

"Hey, you wanted non-romantic. At least, I figured you did."

"And you took that as a challenge?"

His grin widened. "C'mon, Morris. Give it a chance."

What choice did I have?

I sighed and stepped out of the truck, pulling my coat tighter around me as we walked inside.

The place was exactly like every other tavern in every other small town across the rural landscape. Dim lighting, basketball playing on the TV over the bar, a few old ranchers hunched over their drinks like they'd been here since noon. The waitress at the front barely glanced up from her notepad. "Sit wherever."

Gage tipped his hat and led the way to a booth in the corner.

I slid onto the seat, shaking my head. "You know, every other couple in town is at least pretending to make an effort tonight."

Gage leaned back, completely unbothered. "Yeah, and I bet half of them are faking it."

I frowned. "Faking what?"

He gestured vaguely. "The whole thing. Flowers, candlelight, forced romance. Most of them are probably checking the clock, waiting for it to be over."

I hesitated.

Because... he wasn't completely wrong.

I'd heard enough complaints from friends over the years about awkward Valentine's dates that felt more like obligations than anything special.

But that didn't mean he was *right*, either.

"So, what you're saying," I said, propping my elbows on the table, "is that this—" I gestured to our very unromantic setting. "—is better than a nice dinner?"

He grinned. "I'm saying this is honest."

I narrowed my eyes. "That's a very convenient way of saying 'low effort.'"

The waitress walked over, pen poised. "What'll it be?"

Gage didn't even hesitate. "Nachos."

I sighed and handed my menu back to the waitress without opening it. "Same." At least the nachos here were good.

I exhaled, leaning back against the booth, watching my "date" as his grin widened. I couldn't decide if he was actually as entertained by this as he seemed or if he was just trying to get a reaction out of me.

Either way, I wasn't about to let him win.

I folded my arms. "Fine. You got me here. Now what?"

"How's your aim?"

I frowned. "My what?"

He tipped his head toward the back of the tavern. Where an old dartboard was nailed to the wall. A slow smile spread across his face.

"I think it's time we settle something, Morris."

Gage

A MBER FOLLOWED ME TOWARD the dartboard, arms crossed, already looking skeptical. "I don't play darts," she informed me.

"That's what makes this fun."

She sighed, like she was already thinking about printing a picture of my face and hanging it in front of the dartboard.

Too late to back down now. I grabbed the darts off the ledge, rolling one between my fingers.

"We'll go best of three," I said, lining up my shot. "Winner gets bragging rights."

Amber arched a brow. "That's it? No stakes?"

"Didn't figure you'd want to embarrass yourself that badly."

She narrowed her eyes. "Wow. You're really confident about this."

I threw the first dart. It landed cleanly near the center—just off the bullseye.

Amber gave a single, unimpressed nod. "Not bad."

I tossed the next one. Another solid shot. I turned back to her, grinning. "Still want to back out?"

She tilted her head like she was considering it. Then took the last dart from my hand.

Stepped up. Lined up her shot.

And absolutely nailed the bullseye.

I froze.

Amber, without a shred of humility, turned back to me and deadpanned, "Huh. Beginner's luck."

I stared at the board. Then at her. Then back at the board.

"...Excuse me?"

She shrugged, walking over to retrieve the dart. "Guess I'm just naturally talented."

I squinted. "You've played before."

She smiled—too innocently. "Nope."

She was lying.

Had to be.

Because there was no way she just walked up to the dartboard, first try, no warmup, and hit a bullseye.

I crossed my arms. "Do it again."

Amber rolled her eyes. "Fine."

She lined up another shot.

And hit the bullseye.

Again.

I exhaled slowly. "This is some kind of trick."

She smiled sweetly. "I did tell you I don't play darts."

I narrowed my eyes. "Uh-huh. And what, exactly, do you play?"

She smirked. "Archery. Back in college."

I stared.

She tilted her head. "Something wrong?"

I dragged a hand down my face. "Morris, I swear—"

Amber grinned like she had just won the lottery. "Aren't you the one who wanted to settle something?"

I muttered something under my breath that was probably not fit for polite company.

She took another shot—didn't even bother lining it up properly this time—and still landed a solid hit near the center.

This woman.

This absolute menace of a woman.

Amber sighed dramatically. "So what were you saying about bragging rights?"

I rolled my shoulders. "Best of five."

She arched a brow. "I thought it was best of three?"

I grabbed another dart. "Well, now it's best of five."

Amber laughed.

Actually laughed.

And somehow, that was worse than her winning.

Because now, I wanted her to do that again.

Amber

THE NACHOS ARRIVED PILED high with cheese, jalapeños, and entirely too much sour cream. And honestly? I was starving. I grabbed a chip and took a bite, still ridiculously pleased with myself over the darts game.

Across the table, Gage leaned back in the booth, watching me with that easy, cryptic expression that made me wonder if he actually had any real feelings, or just liked to pretend.

I raised a brow. "You're taking that loss really well."

"You think this is me taking it well?"

I shrugged. "You haven't demanded a rematch yet."

"Oh, I'm absolutely demanding a rematch." He reached for a chip. "I just gotta get over the embarrassment first."

I snorted. "I thought you were shameless."

"I thought I was, too." He crunched into his nacho. "Turns out, getting annihilated by a therapist with an archery hobby is a humbling experience."

I grinned, popping another chip into my mouth.

We ate in comfortable silence for a minute.

Which, honestly, was new.

Gage wasn't a silent person. He was always talking, teasing, keeping the conversation on his terms. But right now? He was just *here*.

And I had to admit—I didn't mind that.

I picked at my napkin. "Can I ask you something?"

He wiped his hands off on a paper towel. "You can try."

I smirked. "Why'd you start teasing me?"

Gage raised a brow. "Teasing you?"

"Yes, teasing me. You didn't even know I existed until a few months ago, and then suddenly, you made it your life's mission to be a constant source of annoyance."

He chuckled, but there was something thoughtful behind it.

I tilted my head. "Well?"

He rubbed the back of his neck, looking oddly reluctant. "I dunno. I guess..."

He trailed off.

I waited.

Finally, he sighed. "I guess I was curious."

I blinked. "Curious?"

"Yeah." He met my gaze. "I really hadn't noticed you before. But then I did. And you just seemed... different."

Different. What a compliment.

I picked up another chip, turning that over in my head. "I could say the same about you," I said. "Except I had noticed you before. Just never thought you took anything seriously."

He huffed a quiet laugh. "Yeah? What gave you that impression?"

I shrugged. "I don't know. You just seemed like the guy who was always goofing off. I've never heard of you dating anyone. You're not married. What's your deal?"

He went quiet for a second.

I watched him, waiting.

But he didn't answer.

I sighed and went back to eating my nachos.

Then, just when I was about to let it go, he spoke.

Soft. Measured. Like he was still figuring it out himself.

"I do take things seriously," he said.

I stopped chewing.

Waited.

He exhaled slowly, rolling a chip between his fingers. "When my dad died, I was in my early twenties," he said. "And I figured—okay. This is it. Time to step up."

I frowned, listening. He glanced at me, then back down at his plate.

"Thing is... nobody needed me to," he said. "Trent was better at handling the cattle side of things. Chase had the machinery and buildings covered. Cole managed the horses. I was there. I worked. I did my part. But I wasn't needed to be the guy in charge of anything."

Something tightened in my chest. The big brother burden... I could understand that. I was the big sister, after all.

"So I guess," he continued, voice a little quieter, "without meaning to, I just became the one who floats."

He lifted his gaze to mine.

"And it stuck."

I didn't know what to say to that. So I just chewed my nacho, thinking. Then I swallowed and said the first thing that felt right.

"That was probably humble of you."

Gage snorted. "Yeah, that's me. Humble."

"I'm serious." I leaned forward. "You could've fought for a bigger role, but you didn't. You let the people with the right skills use them. That's... a leadership trait, you know."

He arched a skeptical brow. "So now I'm a leader?"

I nodded, gesturing with my chip. "A good leader doesn't take over all the jobs. He floats, making sure everything's running and removing obstacles so other people can succeed."

He tilted his head, thinking that over.

I shrugged. "Sounds to me like you're filling your dad's shoes better than you thought."

For the first time since this conversation started, Gage looked... surprised. Like he hadn't considered that before. I watched as he sat back, crossing his arms, turning the idea over in his mind.

Finally, he nodded. Slowly.

"...Never thought of it that way," he admitted. "But now that I do, I guess that's exactly what I should be doing. I'm available for all of them. But there's probably stuff I could do better."

I smiled. "Sounds like a plan."

And then he smiled back.

But not his usual cocky, teasing grin.

A real one. The kind that hit differently.

The kind that made me slip.

Because for a second—just a second—I forgot to be annoyed by him.

Gage

A MBER LEANED BACK IN her seat, finally looking relaxed. The nachos were half gone.

The tavern had settled into its usual low buzz—ranch hands swapping stories at the bar, the occasional clink of pool balls in the background.

And for once, we weren't bickering.

I rested an arm on the table, watching her. "So, what's your deal?"

Amber blinked. "Excuse me?"

I smirked. "You know. Never married, never dated. No secret boyfriends? You hiding some tragic love story?"

She huffed a soft laugh, shaking her head. "No tragic love story."

I raised a brow. "Not even one?"

She sighed, picking at a napkin. "It's simple, really. I grew up with a perfect love story. And if I couldn't have that... I didn't want to settle for less."

That got my attention. I sat forward. "Your parents?"

Amber nodded.

I leaned back in my seat, grinning. "Alright. What's their deal, anyway?"

She snorted. "Their deal is that they met at eighteen, married by twenty, and have been obnoxiously happy ever since."

I chuckled. "Sounds familiar."

She raised a brow.

I shrugged. "My folks were the same way."

Amber considered that, then nodded. "I guess we're both cursed with good examples."

"That's why you don't date? Because the bar's too high?"

She shrugged. "More or less."

I watched her for a second, thinking. "And now you're the one taking care of them."

Amber's face softened. "...Yeah."

She didn't sound bitter. Didn't sound like she resented it. But there was some weight behind that single word.

The kind of weight that meant it was a whole lot more complicated than she let on.

I took a sip of my drink, then set it down. "So, what's the actual plan?"

Amber sighed. "If I had a solid one, I'd be a lot less stressed."

I leaned back. "Well, let's figure one out."

She shot me a look. "Gage, I have spent months trying to figure this out. You are not going to solve it in one night over nachos."

I grinned. "Bet I can give you a better idea than your sister."

That got a real laugh. "Good luck."

"Alright. Hit me with the problems."

Amber exhaled, but I could tell she was actually considering it. "My sister wants them in a retirement community. I get it—they are starting to need a little help. Just a little security, in case something happens. But it's wrong for them. They don't want it, and I know it would kill my mom's spirit. So the other option is... me."

I nodded. "So, keep 'em with you. What's stopping you?"

Amber sighed. "For one, they'd need more space. And privacy."

I leaned forward. "An addition to your house?"

She shook her head. "I thought about it. But that's expensive. And time-consuming. And I'm not sure how much sense it makes to renovate my whole home for a temporary solution."

I nodded. Fair. I took another chip, chewing thoughtfully. "Guest house?"

Amber smiled just a little. "I actually love that idea. But again—expensive. And where would I put it? My property's not that big."

I exhaled, thinking. "Tiny home?"

Amber tilted her head. "Maybe. But I'd still have to buy land for it if I wanted them to have their own space."

I frowned. "Their house is probably paid off, right?"

She nodded.

"So why not sell it and use the money to build something new?"

Amber hesitated. I could tell she'd thought about it before. But she didn't like where her mind was going.

Finally, she said, "It's not just a house. It's *their* house. They built a life there."

I nodded slowly.

Now I got it.

This wasn't just about logistics.

It was about letting go.

She exhaled. "That's why I keep running into dead ends. No matter what I come up with, there's always some obstacle. And I hate that my sister is pushing for the thing that's easiest instead of what's right."

I sat back, watching her. She had that same fierce determination in her eyes that I'd seen before—when she talked about her work.

Amber Morris wasn't the type to walk away from a problem. Even if it wasn't hers to carry.

I drummed my fingers against the table. "So what do they want?"

Amber chewed the inside of her cheek.

Then, after a second, she huffed a small laugh.

"They want to be together. That's all they've ever wanted."

I didn't say anything right away. Because suddenly, I got it.

All of it.

The weight she carried. The pressure to get it right. The reason she never settled for anything less than a fairy tale.

Because she'd already seen what real love looked like.

And now? She wasn't just chasing it for herself. She was fighting to protect it for them.

I leaned forward, resting my forearms on the table. "Well. You'll figure it out."

She gave me a small, tired smile.

"I don't know, Gage," she said quietly. "Some things don't have perfect solutions."

"Maybe not. But you don't seem like the kind of person who backs down when things aren't perfect."

Amber blinked.

And then she smiled.

For real.

And I felt something shift.

Something small. Something that made me a little too aware of how close we were sitting.

Amber shook her head, but there was no edge in it anymore. Then, still smiling, she reached for another chip and crunched with a teasing grin that warmed me all the way to my backbone.

And for the first time all night...

I was the one thrown off balance.

Chapter Fifteen

Amber

WE LEFT THE TAVERN still talking. Still easier than I ever expected it to be.

The conversation at dinner had been... different. *Real.*

And I wasn't ready to pick it apart yet.

So instead, I let myself relax into the quiet as Gage drove, the road stretching dark and empty ahead of us. For a few minutes, neither of us spoke.

The only sound was the radio, turned low. Some old country song hummed in the background, the kind my dad would sing off-key while tinkering with something in the garage.

It felt... comfortable.

Which was dangerous.

Because I had no idea how we got here. How he went from being the guy who lived to push my buttons...

To being someone I could actually talk to.

And worse—someone I might want to *keep* talking to.

I turned to sneak a glance at him. Gage looked completely at ease. Like he wasn't thinking about the fact that we had just spent an entire evening together, with zero fights, zero disasters, and an alarming number of moments that had felt dangerously close to nice.

He caught me looking, and I immediately snapped my gaze forward.

"Morris. Were you just staring at me?"

I scoffed. "No."

"You were definitely staring."

"I was *thinking*."

"Oh, so now I'm inspiring?"

I rolled my eyes. "Yeah. I was just sitting here marveling at the fact that you made it through an entire meal without making a mess."

He patted his chest. "It's called restraint."

I snorted. "You don't have that."

"Don't I?"

I gave him a look. "Gage. You tried to stack the nachos into a cheese tower just to see how high you could get before it collapsed."

He nodded solemnly. "An experiment in structural integrity. You wouldn't understand."

I huffed a laugh, shaking my head.

There it was.

That natural, ridiculous rhythm that had become alarmingly familiar.

Back to teasing.

Back to bouncing off each other like we always did.

Back to safer territory.

And then—my phone buzzed. I pulled it out, glanced at the screen, and sighed. Of coruse, it was my mom. She probably wanted to ask how my "date" went before she went to bed.

Could you grab some tuna
for Sir Stumpy? He's out.

I rolled my eyes and put my phone away. No way was I dignifying that right now. But then it buzzed again.

He's very upset.

I bet he was. Mom had packed at least a pound on my three-legged cat in the last five days. He had gone through an entire tower of tuna cans. I grimaced and typed an answer.

He does not need more,
Mom. He's too fat now.

But he keeps poking me with
his little paw. He's so sad.

I sighed and shook my head, typing back.

No.

One last buzz.

His tummy just growled.
Please don't make him suf-
fer.

I groaned, rubbing my temple.

Gage, clearly still riding the high of humiliating himself at darts, leaned in slightly. "What's wrong? Did I ruin you for all other men?"

I exhaled slowly. "That would require me to be impressed by you in the first place."

Gage grinned. "You keep telling yourself that, Morris."

I ignored him and texted my mom back.

I'll get some tomorrow.

But he's out NOW.

He knows I'm texting you.
I can tell. He knows you've
betrayed him.

I sighed.

Gage, still watching me like he knew he was about to be entertained, smirked. "Alright. What's up?"

I stared at the screen.

Then at him.

Then back at the screen.

Finally, I muttered, "My cat is apparently staging a hunger strike."

His face scrunched. "Huh?"

"My mom. She's got him so spoiled on tuna that he doesn't believe in regular cat food anymore. Apparently he's eaten all the tuna in the house already."

Gage perked up. "Oh, we're stopping, then."

I frowned. "No, we are not."

"Yeah, we are."

"Gage—"

Too late.

Gage

T HE FLUORESCENT LIGHTS BUZZED overhead, humming with the same enthusiasm as a half-asleep ranch hand on his third cup of coffee.

Amber, true to form, went straight for the canned food aisle.

I did not. Because where was the fun in that?

Instead, I veered toward the sad little Valentine's Day clearance display near the front of the store. Half-price chocolates. Wilted roses. A selection of stuffed animals that looked like they'd lived hard lives.

And that was when I saw him.

A hideous, pink, wide-eyed bear.

Its fur was too bright, its face slightly lopsided, and it had a stitched-on heart that read "HUG ME" in a font that looked vaguely desperate.

It was perfect.

I plucked it off the shelf and marched toward Amber, holding it out. "Here," I said. "For you."

She didn't even glance up. "Absolutely not."

I grinned and wiggled its little arms. "But he loves you."

Amber grabbed a can of tuna without looking at me. "I have enough problems, thanks."

"That's cold, Morris. He was ready to commit."

She didn't dignify that with a response. So I set the bear down on the nearest shelf—facing the aisle, like it was judging her.

She turned just in time to see it and paused mid-step. Then shook her head. "You're ridiculous."

I smirked. "Ridiculously thoughtful, yeah."

She muttered something under her breath and headed to the register.

But I wasn't done yet. I scanned the impulse-buy shelves, looking for one last thing to cement my victory.

Then I spotted it.

A clearance bag of pink, heart-shaped marshmallows.

Perfect.

I grabbed it and plopped it onto the conveyor belt. Amber eyed the bag, frowning. "Pink hearts? You don't look like the type."

I shrugged. "They're not for me."

She hesitated. Then narrowed her eyes. "...Then who are they for?"

I grabbed the bag and gave it a thoughtful shake. "I dunno. Maybe I'll hand 'em out. Brighten someone's night."

Amber gave me a slow blink. "You are *not* about to go around spreading Valentine's cheer like some elf who forgot what month it is."

I smirked. "Aren't I?"

She huffed. "No. Because that's weird."

I tore the bag open.

Amber's eyes widened. "Gage—"

I grabbed a handful of marshmallows and tossed one at her. It bounced off her arm and hit the floor.

She gasped. "Did you just—"

Another one. Right at her shoulder. Amber snapped up a marshmallow and threw it back at me. It hit my hat and rolled into the next aisle.

The older guy stocking shelves gave us a long, confused look.

Amber froze. "Sorry. We'll pick it up."

I grinned, tipped my hat at him, and popped another marshmallow into my mouth. The guy sighed and went back to stacking soup cans like he hadn't just witnessed the most embarrassing moment of Amber Morris's life.

Amber hissed. "You are an actual menace."

I held out a marshmallow. "Truce?"

She narrowed her eyes. "You're going to throw it at me."

I scoffed. "Morris. That would be childish."

She didn't move. I gave her my best, most innocent look.

Amber sighed, took the marshmallow... and immediately threw it at my chest.

I caught it before it hit the floor and smirked. "Nice try."

She grunted. "I hate you."

"No, you don't."

Amber grabbed her can of tuna and marched toward the checkout, spine straight, steps determined. Like she could physically escape my nonsense.

She could not.

I followed, still popping marshmallows like I was the picture of innocence.

The cashier—a teenager who looked like he wanted to be anywhere but here—gave Amber a bored look.

"Find everything okay?"

Amber sighed. "Unfortunately."

I casually tossed one last marshmallow onto the conveyor belt next to her tuna.

Amber's eyes snapped to it.

Then to me.

Then back to the marshmallow.

She picked it up slowly, like she was debating the consequences of throwing it at my face in front of a witness.

I gave her a completely innocent, nothing-to-see-here smile.

The cashier rang it up, anyway.

Amber stared.

Then turned back to me so, so slowly.

"Gage," she said, in the exact tone of a woman questioning every choice that led her here.

I grinned.

She exhaled sharply, grabbed the bag, and stuffed it into mine.

"If I have to suffer," she muttered, "so do you."

I chuckled, grabbed the bag, and held the door open for her.

And just like that—

I'd won.

But, judging by the way her lips twitched as she walked past me, maybe she had, too.

Amber

WE STEPPED OUTSIDE THE market, the air crisp and quiet. For the first time all night, Gage wasn't talking.

Neither was I.

The town was mostly shuttered for the night, the glow from the streetlights casting long shadows over the parking lot. Gage unlocked the truck, but we didn't get in right away. He just stood next to me, hands in his pockets, looking... thoughtful.

I glanced at him. "So... was this everything you hoped for?"

"'Hope' is a strong word for something I had no say in. Neither did you, remember?"

"Alright. How about 'expected'?"

He smiled. "Well, I did get to witness you proving your dominion at darts."

I huffed. "I didn't rub your nose in it."

"You were smug."

I shrugged. "You were wrong."

He chuckled, watching me a little too closely. Like he was considering something.

Like he was debating a next move.

And suddenly, everything felt different. The cold wasn't as sharp. The quiet wasn't as empty. And I was far too aware of the space between us.

Or rather, how little of it there was.

He shifted slightly, and for half a second, I thought—

Oh.

Oh, no.

Was he about to—

I should step back.

I should say something.

I should—

He reached out.

My breath hitched.

And then—

He handed me the bag of marshmallows.

I blinked.

"What?"

Gage's expression didn't change. "For Sir Stumpy."

I just... stared.

My brain, which had just braced itself for a completely different scenario, took an extra beat to catch up.

Finally, I managed, "My cat does not eat marshmallows."

Gage grinned. "No, but you'll be forced to keep them in your house. And every time you see them, you'll think of me."

I opened my mouth.

Closed it.

Then narrowed my eyes. "...You are diabolical."

He grinned. "I know."

T HE DRIVE BACK WAS quieter than I expected.

Not awkward. Just... comfortable.

Gage had the radio turned low, some old country song humming through the speakers, and I let myself stare out the window, watching the streetlights flicker past.

It felt like the night should've been over. Like I should've been exhausted. But I wasn't.

Not really.

I blamed the ridiculous amount of laughing I'd done.

And Gage. Obviously.

I shifted in my seat, stealing a glance at him. He looked like he belonged there—one hand on the wheel, the other resting easy on the console, completely at home in his own skin.

Like this had been just another night for him.

Like he hadn't just spent the last two hours dragging me into his brand of chaos.

Like this hadn't been, in some small, twisted way, kind of perfect.

I swallowed and turned my gaze back out the window, ignoring the warmth creeping up my neck.

Gage pulled into my driveway a few minutes later, the headlights sweeping over the old Winnebago.

The house was dark. My parents were probably already in bed, sleeping off their night of bad poetry. I unbuckled and grabbed the grocery bag. "Thanks for the ride."

Gage leaned back in his seat, watching me with an expression I didn't trust.

I narrowed my eyes. "What?"

He nodded toward the bag. "Don't forget to put those marshmallows somewhere important."

I groaned. "Gage—"

"Oh, and take a picture when you do."

"Absolutely not."

"And make sure you send me that picture. I'll hold you to that."

I paused my escape and gave him a thoughtful look. "You know, maybe I could, if I had your number."

Gage shrugged. "Get it from your dad. He'll be calling me tomorrow anyway, I bet."

He was so impossible. And so... I don't know. Sometimes when he said something unexpected like that, it made me want to poke him back. Dig under the surface, make him talk.

Instead, I just sighed, pushing open the door. "Goodnight, Gage."

"Night, Morris."

I stepped out, closing the door behind me. But as I walked up to the house, I could still feel him watching me.

I didn't look back.

But I was definitely still smiling when I walked inside.

Chapter Sixteen

Amber

MY PHONE RANG JUST as I was finishing up paperwork. I sighed. Of course, it was Gina.

For a second, I considered ignoring it. I could pretend I was too busy, let it go to voicemail, and deal with it later.

But I already knew what this was about.

I pressed accept and braced myself. "Hey, Gina."

"Have you seen the forecast?"

No hello. No preamble. Just instant stress.

I pushed my paperwork aside and dropped my pen in the cup. "For what?"

"The pass, Amber. The mountain pass."

I glanced at my computer screen, frowning. "No, why?"

"There's a storm coming," Gina said, voice clipped. "They're saying it'll hit by the weekend. You need to get Mom and Dad on the road before it snows them in."

I closed my eyes, exhaling. I knew this conversation was coming. But I still wasn't ready for it.

"They've been there over a week," Gina pressed. "It's time."

It's time.

I glanced at the calendar. She wasn't wrong. They'd already been here several days longer than I originally expected.

But the thought of them leaving... settled wrong.

"They're fine here," I said.

"For now," Gina shot back. "But what if the storm is bad? What if the roads are a mess? Do you really want them trying to drive that giant RV through the mountains in the middle of a blizzard?"

I gritted my teeth. "I never said that."

"Then don't stall. They need to go before the storm hits."

I bit the inside of my cheek. Because I wasn't stalling.

...Was I?

"I'll talk to them," I finally said.

Gina sighed, like she could already tell I was hesitant. "You're making this harder than it needs to be."

Something flared in my chest. "*I'm* making it harder?"

Gina huffed. "Yes, Amber. You didn't want them moving in with you. Fine. But you can't just let them keep pushing this back indefinitely."

I exhaled sharply. "No one's pushing anything back. If a storm hits, they can stay a little longer. They've got a place to stay, they've got their privacy. They're safe here. It's not a big deal, Gina. No reason to stress about it."

"No reason to stress?" She scoffed. "That motorhome is probably moldy and gross. You want them sleeping in that thing for weeks?"

I opened my mouth to argue. Then hesitated. Because... I'd wondered the same thing at first.

When they pulled into my driveway last week, I half-expected the musty smell of neglect to hit me when I stepped inside. But it never came.

I crossed my arms. "It's not moldy. I was shocked too, but Mom kept everything super clean and dry on the inside, and Dad parked it under cover. It seems fine to me."

"Amber, you don't know that," Gina pushed.

"Maybe not," I admitted. "But I also don't think kicking them out in a rush is the answer."

Silence.

The kind that meant Gina was holding something back.

I frowned. "What?"

More silence.

Then a long, slow exhale. "I have a hold on a room," Gina finally admitted.

My stomach dropped. "*What?*"

"The assisted living place," she said, voice tight. "They had a unit available, so I put down a deposit. But they have to claim it by the end of the month or we lose it."

My pulse spiked.

"You—" I sucked in a sharp breath. "You *what?*"

"It was the right thing to do," Gina insisted. "I couldn't just sit around and wait for them to come to their senses. This is their best option."

"You had no right to do that!" I snapped.

Gina groaned. "Amber, I—"

"No," I cut in, anger creeping into my voice. "You didn't talk to them. You didn't ask. You just... decided for them."

"Because they *won't* decide!" she snapped back. "You know them. They'll keep saying they're fine until something forces their hand. And by then, what if they don't have choices left?"

I closed my eyes, pressing my fingers to my temple. I understood her logic. But that didn't make it right.

"If you lose your deposit, that's on you. No one forced you to do that."

Gina was quiet for a long moment. Then, finally, she muttered, "You're impossible."

I exhaled slowly. "I'll talk to them, Gina. But I won't push them into something they don't want."

Gina let out a bitter laugh. "Then you better hope they actually tell you what they want, Amber."

And before I could say anything else, she hung up. I lowered my phone slowly.

Because that was the problem, wasn't it? Mom and Dad hadn't made any firm decisions. Were adamantly refusing to do so. They'd just... let things unfold.

And maybe Gina was right.

Maybe they really were waiting until they had no other choice.

I rubbed a hand down my face, feeling suddenly exhausted.

Gage

T HE HORSES WERE FED, the morning chores were done, and I was still thinking about that conversation with Amber last night.

Leadership.

She'd said it like it was something I already had. Like it was something I should have been using all along.

I wasn't used to thinking that way.

I worked hard. I pitched in wherever I was needed. But that wasn't the same as taking ownership of something.

And for the first time, I was starting to think maybe I wanted to. I just didn't know what that looked like. I mulled it over as I stepped into the house, the smell of coffee hanging thick in the air.

Mom was at the kitchen table, a fresh cup in her hands, staring out the window like she was a thousand miles away.

I leaned against the counter. "How was last night?"

She blinked, pulled from her thoughts, and turned to me with a small smile. "Oh, it was lovely. The Timberline was beautiful, as always."

"Anyone make a scene? I mean, I guess we already got the proposals out of the way, so nobody got down on one knee for Valentine's Day, right?"

Mom chuckled. "No, your brothers managed to behave themselves." She took a sip of coffee. "We missed you."

I shrugged, pushing a hand through my hair. "Well, I wasn't bored."

Her brows lifted slightly. I could see the assumption forming.

"Right. I'm sure you found something to do."

Bingo. She probably figured I'd gone out with Luke Walker or one of my other ranching buddies. Maybe ended up at the tavern, maybe caught a game somewhere.

I didn't correct her.

Because if I told her I'd spent the evening playing darts with Amber Morris and buying marshmallows just to mess with her, she'd have questions.

Ones I didn't know how to answer.

I exhaled, grabbing a mug and pouring myself some coffee. Then, after a beat, I said, "You're thinking about Dad."

Mom blinked, surprised.

Then she smiled, soft and a little wistful. "I always do." Mom set her mug down and sighed. "It's worse on nights like last night."

I looked at her, waiting. "Yeah?"

She smiled to herself. "Your father hated dressing up, you know. But he did it for me. And every single time we went somewhere fancy, he'd do something to make me laugh." She shook her head, eyes shining. "One year, we were at The Timberline, and he—"

She laughed, covering her mouth for a second, like she wasn't sure she should say it.

I raised a brow. "What?"

She exhaled. "He smuggled a flask in."

I barked out a laugh. "No way."

She nodded, laughing too. "He swore the drinks were overpriced and that he could make a better Old Fashioned himself."

That sounded exactly like something my dad would do.

Mom sighed, shaking her head. "I miss him all the time. But some nights? I miss him in a way that feels fresh. Like he just walked out the door and I'm waiting for him to come back in."

Something pulled tight in my chest. I didn't know what to say to that.

So I didn't say anything.

Mom gave me a small smile. "You remind me of him, you know."

I blinked. "Me?"

She nodded. "More than any of your brothers. I see him when you walk in the door, wearing his old hat."

I frowned. "It's just the hat."

"No... it's the way you wear it."

I scoffed. "I'm the least like him of any of us. Chase has his detail-oriented streak. Trent has his passion for the stock. Cole has his way with the horses. What do I have?"

She studied me for a long moment, like she wasn't sure how to put it into words. Then she reached across the table, tapped her fingers against my wrist. "You have the part of him that made people feel safe."

I swallowed.

Mom smiled, squeezing my hand. "Your dad didn't always need to be in charge. He didn't need to be the loudest or the one out front. But he made people feel steady. Like no matter what happened, he'd be there."

I sat back, rolling that over in my head. Because that... didn't sound like me.

I wasn't steady.

I wasn't the guy people counted on.

...*Was* I?

I cleared my throat. "So what you're saying is, I should start charging Trent for emotional labor."

Mom laughed, shaking her head. "That's not what I'm saying."

I grinned. "Too late. I think I could make a real business out of it."

She rolled her eyes but smiled.

And maybe she thought I was joking.

But as I walked out of the kitchen, I was still thinking about what she said.

Because maybe... just maybe...

She was right.

Amber

MOM HUMMED AS SHE dried the last dish and set it on the counter, her movements slow and easy. Dad was still sitting at the table, picking at the last few bites of pie, acting like he had all the time in the world.

And for the past twenty minutes, I had been sitting across from him, trying to force myself to say it.

To tell them it was time to leave. But I couldn't seem to make my mouth work.

Because the truth was... I didn't want them to.

Which made no sense.

I had spent the last week stressing, over-managing, making sure they weren't overdoing it, making sure they were comfortable. I had been exhausted trying to balance work and taking care of them.

And now that Gina was saying it was time, I should have felt relieved.

So why did it feel like I was handing them over to something I couldn't control?

I swallowed and set my fork down.

Mom immediately noticed.

"Something wrong, sweetheart?"

Dad paused mid-bite, glancing between us.

I forced myself to smile. "No, I just—" I exhaled. "Gina called today."

Mom and Dad exchanged a look. The kind that meant they already knew where this was going.

Dad leaned back in his chair, crossing his arms. "And?"

"She saw the weather forecast. There's a storm coming. She's worried about you getting stuck here if you don't leave before it hits."

Dad shrugged, completely unfazed. "So we wait out the storm. Not like we got anywhere to be."

Mom gave him a look. "Bob."

He raised a brow. "What? It's true."

Mom sighed, then turned back to me.

"She's probably right," she admitted. "It's a long drive, and we should do it while the roads are still clear."

I nodded. Because I agreed—she was talking sense.

But it still sat wrong.

Dad watched me for a second, then gave me a crooked smile.

"What, you gonna miss us already?"

I huffed a laugh. "You've been here for over a week, Dad."

"Yeah, and I still haven't finished that fence project with your cowboy friend," he mused. "Might have to stick around a little longer."

"What fence project?"

"Your back yard," Dad said, as if it were the most obvious thing in the world. "How will you ever keep a dog in the yard with all those holes in the fence?"

"Dad, I don't have a dog, and I'm not planning on getting one."

He grinned, lifting his coffee cup. "Plans change, sweetheart. Your fence is falling down. Let your old man fix it for you, eh?"

I chuckled. "Maybe you should wait for summer, at least."

Dad glanced at mom and acted like he was considering it. "Deal. But you tell Gage he's got the first week of June booked, got it?"

I rolled my eyes, but Mom just smiled.

"We'll come back," she promised.

And I believed her.

But still...

I looked at my plate, suddenly not that hungry anymore.

Gage

T HE SUN WAS SINKING behind the ridge by the time I found
Ethan and Liam, wrapping up the evening chores. They were
in the feed room, stacking bags of grain, working in that silent rhythm
they'd developed over the last few months—one grabbing, the other
shifting, both moving like they'd done it a thousand times before.

I stood in the doorway for a second, just watching.

They'd both grown since they'd come here.

Liam had filling-out muscles now, no longer just a wiry kid. Ethan
carried himself with the kind of confidence that came from knowing
his place in the world which was a far cry from the shifty, "serial-killer"
vibes he gave off the first day he walked into our house.

They'd fallen into the routine here, found a place. We didn't have
to tell them much now, and even Ethan didn't complain when he had
to pull his weight. This ranch had become a home to them.

But something about the way they were moving today—silent, a
little tense—made me wonder. I finally pushed off the doorframe and
walked in. "You two need another hand?"

Liam didn't look up. "We got it."

Ethan grunted his agreement, shifting another bag into place.

I leaned against the nearest post, crossing my arms. "Figured I'd
check in."

Liam stretched his back, rolling his shoulders. "Oh, yeah? What's the occasion?"

I raised a brow. "Do I need one?"

Neither of them answered. Which, in itself, said a lot.

I watched for another minute, then asked, "Everything alright?"

Ethan wiped his hands on his jeans. "Yeah."

Liam hesitated. Then shrugged. "Sure."

I frowned. Too casual.

I watched him as he grabbed another bag of grain, shoving it onto the pile with a little too much force. "You're thinking about graduation," I guessed.

Liam didn't look at me. Didn't answer right away. But his silence was loud enough.

Ethan exhaled. "Liam thinks we should move to Twin Falls and get jobs. That way we could share a place."

Liam shot me a look, like he expected me to counter the idea. "What? It makes sense."

"Does it?" I asked, keeping my voice neutral.

Liam grabbed another bag, talking as he worked. "It's not like we can just keep hanging around here forever."

"Who said you had to leave?" I asked.

Liam finally stopped moving.

Ethan did too.

For the first time, neither of them had a quick answer.

I let out a slow breath. "You two are part of this family. You know that, right?"

Liam frowned. "Yeah, but—"

"No 'but.'" I shook my head. "You don't age out of family. Not this one."

The words sat there, heavy. Liam swallowed, looking down at his boots.

Ethan crossed his arms, his jaw tight. "We've heard that before."

I understood what he meant. Plenty of people had told them they mattered. That they were wanted. Right up until they weren't.

"I mean it," I said simply.

Liam exhaled sharply, rubbing the back of his neck. "We don't want to be a burden."

I huffed. "You think you're the only ones pulling your weight around here?"

Ethan's mouth twitched, like he almost wanted to smile.

Liam's shoulders relaxed—just a little.

I shrugged. "I don't have it all figured out. But you two? You've got a place here as long as you want one. You need a job? Three squares? Buddy, you're in the right place. Nobody here's any better than you."

Liam hesitated.

Then, softer this time, he asked, "And if we don't know what we want?"

I shrugged. "Then you figure it out."

Silence.

Then I added, "And in the meantime, you've got a home. It's not just me talkin', either. Mom'd cry her eyes out if you guys left."

Ethan blinked. "She would not."

"Don't make me prove it. I hate it when my mom cries. I'll go drag you back from wherever you wander off to just so you can hug her and make her stop."

Liam let out a breath he'd probably been holding for months, and a hesitant grin fought to break free on his face. Ethan finally relaxed his arms and glanced at his brother, then back at me. And smiled.

I nodded toward the house. "Come on. Mom's making chili."

Liam blinked. "That's it?"

I grinned. "What, you want me to write up a formal invitation?"

Liam huffed a quiet laugh, shaking his head. Ethan still looked like he had a million things running through his brain.

But he didn't argue.

He just grabbed his gloves, tossed Liam a look, and followed me out.

Chapter Seventeen

Gage

I WAS IN THE shop, wiping the last bit of grease off my hands, when Chase walked in.

He had his phone in one hand, a to-go coffee in the other, looking like a guy who was already running behind schedule. He nodded toward me. "You free for a few hours?"

I raised an eyebrow. "That depends. What's broken?"

Chase huffed a laugh, setting his coffee on the workbench. "Nothing. Just figured I'd see if you wanted to ride out to White Pines."

I tossed the rag onto the counter. "You need me for something?"

"Nah, just checking in on the new HVAC system before the snow hits. Thought you might want to come."

I leaned against the workbench, studying him. Something about the way he said that felt pointed. I grabbed a wrench, turning it over in my hands. "What's really going on?"

Chase scratched the back of his head. "Ran into Bob at the gas station this morning. He said they're heading out tomorrow."

I stopped fidgeting.

Right.

Of course, they were leaving. That had been the plan all along. But somehow, I hadn't let myself think about it.

Chase must've noticed something in my expression because he gave me a look. "Did you forget they weren't staying forever?"

I shook my head. "No."

But I didn't like it. Bob had been a presence this past week. He reminded me a little of my own dad—the kind of man who'd rather be "fixing" something than sitting still, even if he ended up breaking it worse than it was to begin with. The kind of man who made himself useful even when no one asked him to.

And now, just like that, he was packing up and heading out.

Chase took a sip of coffee. "You gonna stop by and say goodbye?"

I shrugged. "They're not dying, Chase."

"No, but you'd regret it if you didn't. He really likes you. Talked about you a lot."

I let out a slow breath, turning that over in my head. I wasn't usually one for goodbyes. Not because I didn't care, but because I never knew what to say.

What was I supposed to do? Walk up, shake Bob's hand, and say 'Nice knowing you?'

Didn't seem like enough.

But not saying anything felt worse.

Chase tipped his coffee toward me. "You coming or not?"

I thought about it for another second. Then grabbed my hat. "Yeah. I'm coming."

B Y THE TIME I got to White Pines, Amber was working.

I found her out in the main arena, leading a session with a teenage boy and a steady old gelding. I didn't interrupt. Just leaned against the fence, watching.

Amber had that calm, steady presence she always carried when she worked. She spoke softly but firmly, guiding the boy through each movement, nodding when he got something right, adjusting when he didn't.

It was... impressive.

I'd seen her frustrated, annoyed, practically vibrating with stress. But here? She was different. More in control. More at ease.

Like this was the one place she didn't have to second-guess herself.

I leaned against the top rail. "Did you hypnotize this kid?"

Amber's head snapped up.

For a second, she looked startled—like she hadn't noticed me standing there.

Then she narrowed her eyes. "That's not how therapy works, Gage."

"Are you sure? Because that kid looks one step away from levitating."

The boy in question gave me a confused look.

Amber sighed, exasperated. "Ignore him, Travis."

Travis nodded, looking relieved.

I chuckled. "I'm not that distracting, am I?"

Amber shot me a look.

I grinned.

Then, without thinking, I added, "You're almost done, right? Thought I'd stop by before heading over to your place."

She blinked. "Why?"

I shrugged. "Your dad's leaving soon. Figured I'd help him out with the Winnebago, make sure it's road-ready. I'm actually kind of worried about those brakes, and last night when I was there, I saw a puddle of something underneath the front end. Should at least check it out."

Amber stared at me for a beat too long. Like she was trying to figure out what my angle was. Finally, she exhaled. "I'll call Jess Walker. You don't have to do that."

"I know."

She frowned.

I held her gaze, waiting for the fight that was probably coming. But instead, she just... nodded. Like maybe she was too tired to argue with me today.

She turned back to Travis, signaling the end of their session. "Alright, that's it for today. You did great."

Travis smiled. "Thanks, Miss Amber."

Amber helped him dismount, giving him a few last pointers before his mom waved him over.

Then, finally, she turned back to me. Her expression was still carefully unreadable. But today, I noticed something.

A little wrinkle at the corner of her mouth. A bit of warmth in her eyes that hadn't been there before.

Maybe she didn't hate me as much as she pretended to.

"What?"

Amber shook her head. "Nothing."

"You looked like you were having a thought."

She crossed her arms. "I have lots of thoughts."

"Any of them about how great I am?"

"Oh, yeah. Humblest guy in town, that's you."

I laughed. "You know, it'd be easier to stay humble if I saw a bit more of you."

Her eyes narrowed, and she tipped her head in a dangerous form of curiosity. "I'm almost afraid to ask, but... why?"

"Because you've spotted just about all my flaws, but you still talk to me, anyway."

She blinked, her mouth dropping open slightly.

Then, before she could answer, I pushed off the fence and started walking toward the truck.

"See you in a bit, Amber."

She didn't react.

Didn't stiffen. Didn't correct me.

And that's when I knew.

She hadn't even noticed.

Amber

T HE WINNEBAGO WASN'T GOING to fix itself.

Which, unfortunately, meant Dad was determined to fix it *him*self.

Gage was right about the puddle under the engine compartment. It had a greenish sheen and seemed to be coming from everywhere. That was bad, right? But Dad just shrugged and said it was probably some coolant or something, no big deal.

I sighed, watching him from the front porch, arms crossed as he bent over the engine compartment, muttering to himself. I wasn't worried about his ability to get it running. Well... it would be more fair to say I was *less* concerned about that than I was about him pushing himself too hard, doing too much, trying to prove he could still handle things.

Which was why I'd been keeping an eye on him all afternoon.

And why, when Gage didn't show up right away, I'd figured he wasn't coming. Not because he was unreliable—Gage wasn't that guy. But because I half-expected him to forget, get sidetracked with ranch stuff, or just decide this wasn't his problem.

So when I stepped off the porch, ready to intervene, and spotted him walking up the driveway, toolbox in hand, I... paused.

Because there he was.

Like it was the most natural thing in the world.

Dad straightened, clapping Gage on the shoulder. "Told you she'd be hovering."

I blinked. "You're here."

Gage glanced at me, looking completely at ease. "Said I would be. Don't sound so surprised, Amber."

I frowned.

Something about the way he said my name felt... different.

Not teasing. Not smug. Just... easy. Like he'd been saying it forever.

And somehow, I hadn't even noticed.

Before I could overthink it, Dad turned back to the engine. "Told him I was giving it a once-over before we hit the road, and he figured he'd pick up a few quarts of oil for me. Got some brake fluid, too, I see."

I crossed my arms, narrowing my eyes at Gage. "You figured?"

He shrugged. "Seemed like the neighborly thing to do."

I eyed the supplies he'd set on the folding table Dad had brought out to the driveway as a workbench—motor oil, brake fluid, even a new set of wiper blades.

I arched a brow. "You stopping by to help, or trying to overhaul the whole rig?"

Gage grinned. "Just figured if I was already at the auto shop, might as well get what he needed."

"I told you, sweetheart. He's a fine assistant."

I snorted. "We'll see about that."

Gage chuckled, setting his toolbox down. "You hear that, Bob? She doubts my mechanical expertise."

Dad patted his shoulder. "Well, let's prove her wrong."

I sighed, shifting my weight. "If he makes anything worse, I'm blaming you both."

Neither of them looked concerned. Dad turned back to the engine, giving Gage a rundown of what he'd already checked. I lingered, watching them fall into an easy rhythm.

Dad had always been the kind of guy who didn't like to be fussed over. I knew that.

But something about the way he and Gage worked side by side, trading tools, swapping theories, figuring things out together—felt...

Good. Like Dad was enjoying this. Like he felt useful.

Like he wasn't just someone we had to take care of.

I swallowed down the sudden lump in my throat and turned back toward the house.

Gage's voice stopped me. "Where you going?"

I glanced over my shoulder. "I have things to do."

Dad shot me a look. "Come on, Amber. Grab us some drinks and sit for a bit."

I hesitated. Because this whole thing felt *too*.. normal.

Gage being here. Helping my dad. Talking to me like we weren't constantly at odds.

I should've been irritated.

Instead, I found myself walking back inside, grabbing a few iced teas from the fridge, and bringing them out before I could overthink it.

Dad took one with a nod of thanks.

Gage took his with a lopsided smile. "See? She likes me."

I scoffed, handing him the bottle. "Don't make me regret it."

He just winked, untwisted the cap for a big swig, and went right back to work.

And for the first time in... maybe ever, I let myself sit back and watch. And I let myself admit—just to myself—that maybe...

This wasn't so bad.

Gage

THE WINNEBAGO RUMBLED TO life, that old eighties engine sounding deep and throaty, the way Bob had promised it would. I stepped back, wiping my hands on a rag, watching as he tested the throttle, listening carefully to every sound like a man who knew his machine inside and out.

Bob grinned, pleased. "Like a dream."

"How about the brakes?" I asked. I was a *lot* more worried about the brakes.

"Aw, good to go. Hey, what do you think of—"

Amber's mom appeared on the porch, drying her hands on a dish towel. "Dinner's ready!"

Bob cut the engine, looking over at me. "Well, duty calls. You stayin'?"

I hesitated. Not because I didn't want to stay, but because... it wasn't my place.

Amber must've sensed that because she answered before I could. "He's got his own dinner waiting at home."

"Shame. Would've loved to have you."

"Well, thank you, sir, but Amber's right. I've got plenty to do at home."

Bob just grinned, then clapped a hand on my shoulder. "Thanks for your help. You're a good man, son."

Something lodged in my throat... like a knot or something. I couldn't say anything back—not because I didn't appreciate it. But because... I hadn't expected it.

I wasn't his kid.

I wasn't even really part of their world.

But here he was, offering something simple, solid—like I'd earned it just by being here.

I swallowed, adjusting my hat. "You take care out there."

Bob nodded and headed inside, leaving just me and Amber in the fading light.

For a second, neither of us said anything.

The sky was shifting, warm oranges fading to dusky purples, the first stars just barely starting to show.

Amber stood there, arms crossed, but not in a defensive way. More like she was trying to hold something in.

I shifted my weight. "You alright?"

She let out a slow breath, watching the last streaks of light slip behind the mountains.

"Yeah," she said softly. "I just... I think I'm gonna miss having them here."

The way she said it—quiet, a little raw—well, it did... something to me. Like that thing they say happens to a guy when the woman he loves is hurt or sad. That feeling that you would move heaven and earth to fix it, but there was nothing here to fix.

And anyway, Amber and I weren't... well, we weren't.

I swallowed and, since I didn't know what else to say, I just said, "I know."

And for some reason, that was all I needed to say.

Amber turned, studying me for a long moment. Like she was seeing me in a way she hadn't before. I wasn't sure what she was looking for.

But whatever it was, she must've found it.

Because instead of brushing me off—instead of making a joke, or rolling her eyes, or shoving me away like she usually did—she just... smiled at me.

For a second, it felt like she'd gone soft. Like maybe, if I took a step forward—if I touched her hand, or tilted my head just enough—she wouldn't stop me.

But then she blinked, breaking the moment, and looked away.

I let out a slow breath, then tipped my hat. "See you around, Amber."

She didn't correct me. Didn't argue.

Didn't pretend like she hadn't felt that... *something*... too.

She just stood there, watching as I walked back to my truck.

And that's when I knew.

I didn't like walking away from her.

Amber

THE WINNEBAGO BACKFIRED WHEN Dad started it up, sending a small puff of exhaust into the crisp morning air. I stood on the porch, arms crossed, watching as Dad checked his mirrors like they were about to embark on an expedition to the Arctic.

Mom fussed over something in the passenger seat, probably making sure they had snacks within reach. They were ready to go.

And I was not ready to let them.

I sighed, stepping off the porch and down the front walk. "You guys have everything?"

Mom popped her head out the window, her gray curls bouncing. "You put the sandwiches in the fridge like I told you, right?"

I smiled. "Yes, Mom."

"And you'll make sure Sir Stumpy gets his tuna?"

"I always do."

Dad leaned out the driver's side window, grinning. "You're gonna miss us, aren't you?"

I snorted. "Not for a minute. I'll finally get my quiet house back."

Mom just smiled knowingly. "I bet you'll have *plenty* of company."

Dad chuckled. "Alright, sweetheart. Be good."

I took a deep breath, bracing myself. I'd spent the past week telling myself that I wasn't going to cry when they left. That I was an adult, perfectly capable of handling an empty house.

But when Mom leaned a little further out the window, soft eyes studying me like she was memorizing my face, my throat tightened.

"Love you, baby girl," she said softly.

I cleared my throat. "Love you, too."

Dad put the RV in reverse, rolling forward exactly three feet before I squinted at the bumper—

And saw the long-expired tags.

My stomach dropped. "Dad—wait!"

He hit the brakes so fast the RV rocked slightly. "What? What's wrong?"

I pointed. "Your registration expired five years ago!"

Dad blinked. Then grinned. "Guess we'll be driving the speed limit, then."

I pressed my fingers to my temple. "Dad—"

"Love you, sweetheart!"

And before I could argue or drag him to the DMV myself, the RV pulled onto the road and headed toward the highway.

I stood there, watching them go, arms crossed, already picturing the phone call I'd get later when they inevitably got pulled over.

But despite my exasperation, I smiled.

Because for all the worry, all the uncertainty, all the back-and-forth with Gina...

They were happy.

And that was all I wanted.

I took a deep breath, exhaled, then turned back toward the house.

The quiet was going to take some getting used to.

Chapter Eighteen

Amber

THE HOUSE WAS TOO quiet.

Not in a peaceful way.

Not in the *Ahh, finally some space to breathe* way I'd imagined.

Just... quiet.

The kind that sank into the walls, settled in the air, felt bigger than it should.

I stood in the middle of my kitchen, staring at the clean countertops—no travel mugs, no half-eaten plates of toast, no Mom bustling around asking where I kept the honey or Dad brewing coffee in his special doohicky.

Sir Stumpy flicked his tail from his perch on the windowsill, watching me with his usual unimpressed stare. And yeah, he had an empty can of tuna that he'd batted into view, just to make sure I saw it.

"Well," I muttered, leaning on the counter. "Guess it's just you and me now."

He yawned.

Which was fair.

Because I was being ridiculous. I'd known they were leaving. I'd been fine with it. But as I picked up my keys and headed to White Pines, that stupid empty feeling followed me.

I THREW MYSELF INTO work.

If I kept moving, kept busy, I wouldn't have time to think about an empty driveway and a too-quiet kitchen.

By mid-morning, I'd gone through patient files, adjusted schedules, and reorganized the entire supply closet just for something to do.

I was halfway through stacking a pile of paperwork onto Morgan's desk when Kate leaned against the doorframe, arms crossed.

"I thought you were looking forward to things getting back to normal," she said.

I glanced up, caught off-guard.

"I was."

Kate raised an eyebrow.

I sighed, setting the paperwork down. "I *am*."

She didn't say anything. Just gave me that *look*. The one that said she wasn't buying it.

I crossed my arms. "What?"

"Nothing."

I narrowed my eyes. "That was not a 'nothing' look."

She shrugged. "It's just funny, that's all."

"What's funny?"

"You. Acting like you don't miss them already."

I scoffed. "I'm fine."

Kate nodded slowly. "Sure. That's why you've been reorganizing the same stack of paperwork for the past ten minutes."

I glanced down.

Okay. So maybe I had.

I exhaled. "I was looking forward to things getting back to normal. It's just... weird. First day stuff. That's all."

Kate softened. "You got used to having them around."

I nodded. That was it, exactly. For all my worries, all my frustrations about what came next, the past week had been...

Nice.

Even the chaos. Even the little arguments. Even the way Gage kept showing up.

Especially the way Gage kept showing up.

I frowned, quickly shoving that thought aside.

Kate tilted her head. "You okay?"

I forced a smile. "Yeah."

And maybe, if I said it enough, I'd actually believe it.

Gage

THE LATE AFTERNOON SUN stretched long across the snow-covered pastures, turning the landscape into a glowing mix of blue shadows and golden light. I stood in the doorway of the shop, wiping my hands on a rag, watching the ranch shift and settle around me.

Everything felt in motion lately.

New plans. New futures.

And somehow, I was standing still.

Inside the house, I could hear low conversation. My brothers were gathered in the kitchen, tossing around living arrangements and logistics over cups of coffee, while Lauren and Emily helped Mom with dinner.

Even the kitchen table felt crowded these days.

Trent's mobile home was officially happening. They'd cleared a spot near the south pasture and were laying the foundation this week. He and Lauren would have their own space, their own little house, but they'd still be here, still be part of the ranch.

Cole and Emily were settled in their rental at White Pines for now, and from the way Emily talked about it, they were happy there. I snorted. Horse trainers—they were an even crazier breed than cattle ranchers. They'd live on the moon, so long as there were horses there. Pretty sure they'd be happy anywhere they were together.

Chase and Kate were the ones still figuring it out.

I stepped inside, making my way to the kitchen just as Chase set his coffee down with a decisive thud.

"I talked to Kate's dad," he said. "They're not against the idea."

Mom glanced up from the stove. "Of adding on to the house?"

Chase nodded. "They don't want to move, and I get that. But they're already struggling to keep up with everything. If we build a small addition—something designed for her mom's needs—then Kate and I can take over the mortgage and keep them in a space that works for everyone."

Trent leaned back in his chair, rubbing his jaw. "Zoning isn't an issue?"

Chase shook his head. "Not as far as I can tell. I looked into it—so did Kate. We'd need permits, obviously, but it should work. And we can be around to help, because you know Kate. She won't leave her dad to take care of her mom alone."

Mom turned the burner down, stirring something. "It's a big project."

Chase exhaled. "I know."

But he wasn't backing down. He was building a future. One that had space for Kate's family.

One that would allow them to move forward without leaving anyone behind.

My stomach tightened.

Because suddenly, I was thinking about Amber.

About the way she'd probably stood in her driveway this morning, watching her parents pull away. Back to a house they probably couldn't keep up on their own for much longer, and the ever-present prospect of a group home they weren't interested in. But Amber was right—what were their options?

She didn't have room to add on to her house. Heck, her parents weren't even sure they were ready to leave Montana, anyway, so that was probably out.

But her mom...

Her mom loved seeing the mountains.

I stared out the window, past the snow-dusted fencelines, to where the peaks rose sharp and steady against the sky.

Maybe the view wasn't the problem.

Maybe the problem was that Amber didn't know where home was supposed to be anymore.

I didn't let myself follow that thought too far.

Instead, I turned back to the room, shifting my focus. Ethan and Liam were sitting a little apart from the rest of us. Not excluded, not yammering with everyone else. Just... unsure.

Like they weren't quite sure how they fit into the conversation.

Trent must've noticed too, because he turned toward them. "You two aren't saying much."

Liam glanced at Ethan, like he wasn't sure if he should answer.

Ethan cleared his throat. "Not much to say."

Chase frowned. "You're part of this too, you know."

Ethan gave a tight-lipped smile. "We know."

But I could see it—the hesitation.

They'd heard us.

Heard us talking about houses and futures and where everyone fit.

And even though I'd told them they belonged here, I wasn't sure they believed it yet. Because no one else had really said it.

I crossed my arms, leaning against the counter. "Mom, how long do you think it'll take to get the new mobile home set up?"

She glanced up. "A couple of months, I'd guess. Why?"

I shrugged. "Just thinking out loud."

I let the words sit for a minute, then turned toward Ethan and Liam. "You two ever talk about what you want?"

Ethan's brows lifted slightly. "What do you mean?"

"For after graduation."

Liam looked at the table. "We're figuring it out."

I nodded. "Alright. Let's figure it out here, then."

They both froze.

Ethan blinked. "You mean... stay?"

I shrugged. "I meant what I said the other day. You're part of this family. That means we plan for you just like we plan for everyone else. The bunk house is working fine for now. You got your privacy and somplace clean and warm and all your own. But it *is* kind of cramped, and maybe you don't wanna be roomies forever."

Liam swallowed, eyes darting between me and the rest of the table.

Trent nodded. "He's right. If you want to stay, we'll figure it out."

Mom smiled, setting the spoon down. "We want you here."

Ethan sat back in his chair, still processing.

Liam's fingers tapped restlessly on the table, like his brain was spinning through every possible scenario. Finally, he let out a slow breath. "What if we're not sure?"

Trent shrugged. "Then you take your time."

Liam swallowed. "And what if we mess up?"

I leaned forward. "Then you fix it. And we'll be here to knock your heads straight again."

Another long silence.

Then Ethan exhaled, something loosening in his posture.

Liam picked at the edge of his sleeve, thinking.

And for the first time, I saw it—the idea settling in.

Like maybe, just maybe...

They were allowed to believe it.

Amber

T HE HOUSE WAS FREEZING.

Not just a little cold. Not the "Oh, I should've worn thicker socks" kind of cold. The "I can see my breath in the air" kind of cold.

I stood in the entryway, still wearing my coat, glaring at the thermostat like I could melt it with heat vision. Heat vision would have come in pretty handy about now.

I turned the dial up.

Nothing.

I flicked the little "heat" switch off, then back on.

Still nothing.

Sir Stumpy padded into the room, sniffed the air, then promptly turned and stalked back toward the living room, as if I was responsible for the arctic blast creeping through the walls.

"Don't look at me like that," I muttered, already moving toward the breaker box.

Maybe it had tripped. I'd be surprised if Dad's motorhome plugged in in the driveway didn't short half my house out.

I flipped the switch.

The heater did not roar to life.

I flipped it off and on again.

Still nothing.

I cupped my hands around my mouth to blow warm air on them, forcing myself to stay calm. There had to be an answer. A reason my house was turning into a walk-in freezer.

I grabbed my phone, Googled every troubleshooting tip I could find, and tried all of them.

Reset the system.

Checked the pilot light.

Tried the breaker one more time, just for good measure.

Nothing.

I let out a slow breath, stepping back.

Okay.

Fine.

This was not an emergency. I could handle this. I just needed help. I scrolled through my contacts, found Kate's name, and hit call.

She answered on the third ring. "Hey! What's up?"

I exhaled. "I need to borrow Chase again."

Kate paused. "What happened?"

"My heater's out," I admitted, trying to keep the frustration out of my voice. "I've tried everything, but I can't get it running."

Kate sighed, but not at me.

At the timing.

I could already tell.

I frowned. "What's going on?"

"We're at my parents' house," she said, voice softer now. "Talking through some big decisions."

I winced.

I should've known. Chase and Kate had a lot on their plate right now. She'd told me some things over lunch today, and... well, it sounded amazing, but only if everyone was satisfied with the solution, and it sounded like that hung on the line right now. I didn't need to be adding to it with my dumb heating problem.

"I'm sorry," I backpedaled. "Forget I called."

"Amber—"

"No, seriously. It's fine. I'll figure it out."

Kate was quiet for a second.

Then she said, too casually, "You could call Gage."

I scowled. "Absolutely not."

Kate laughed. "It was just a suggestion."

"A bad one," I muttered.

Kate sighed again. "Okay, fine. I get it. I'll tell Chase later, and he can stop by tomorrow if you still need help."

I nodded, even though she couldn't see me. "Thanks. Sorry for bothering you."

"You're never a bother, Amber," she said, warm and sincere. "But I also think you're about to call Gage."

I snorted. "No, I'm not."

"Mm-hmm. Sure you're not."

"I'm hanging up now."

Kate laughed. "Tell him I said hi."

I ended the call. Then I stood in my freezing house, arms crossed, staring at my phone like it was the enemy.

I could just deal with the cold.

Pile on some extra blankets. Wait it out.

I was *not* calling Gage.

Not happening.

No way.

Two minutes later, I was calling Gage.

G AGE ANSWERED ON THE first ring. And somehow, I just *knew* he was grinning.

"Amber Morris," he drawled, his voice full of smug amusement. "This is a surprise."

I closed my eyes, pinching the bridge of my nose. "Don't start."

"Start what?"

I exhaled. "Gage—"

"Now, let me guess," he continued, clearly enjoying himself. "You just happened to be thinking about me, couldn't resist the urge to hear my voice, and—"

"My heater's out."

Silence.

Then, way too cheerfully, he said, "Oh, that's even better."

I groaned. "Are you going to help me or not?"

"Of course," he said easily. "I'd never leave a lady freezing."

I rolled my eyes. "Spare me the cowboy charm."

He chuckled. "Be there in ten."

G AGE SHOWED UP EXACTLY ten minutes later, toolbox in hand and a look on his face that would probably melt any woman's heart. If she didn't already know what a massive pain he was.

He stepped inside, glancing around like he was assessing the situation. "Well, well. Back so soon."

I crossed my arms. "I didn't invite you."

He arched a brow. "Pretty sure you did."

I sighed. "Just fix my heater. Please."

Gage grinned and headed toward the unit.

I followed, hugging my arms against the cold. "It just stopped working when I was at work today. I tried everything."

Gage crouched down, popping open the panel. "Breaker?"

"Checked."

"Thermostat?"

"Double-checked."

He hummed, inspecting the wiring. "Pilot light?"

"Relit it twice."

"Huh."

I watched as he poked around, testing connections, then suddenly stopped.

Stared.

Then slowly, very slowly, turned his head toward me.

I frowned. "What?"

He said nothing.

Just reached into the panel and pulled out a very, very obviously disconnected wire.

My stomach dropped.

Gage held it up, smirking. "You sure you checked everything?"

I blinked.

Then blinked again.

Because that...

That was *so* obvious.

Painfully, embarrassingly, I-should-have-seen-it-immediately obvious.

But I hadn't.

Because I wasn't the kind of person who checked wires.

But my dad?

Oh, he was.

My eyes widened. "No."

Gage bit back a laugh. "Oh, yes."

I pressed my fingers to my temple, groaning. "He sabotaged me."

Gage grinned. "You gotta give the man credit. That's commitment."

I dropped my hand and glared at the ceiling. Of course, my parents were still trying to set me up.

Of course, my dad would deliberately break something just so I'd have to call someone for help.

And of course, he'd choose Gage.

I groaned again. "I am going to kill him."

Gage chuckled, reattaching the wire like it was the easiest thing in the world. He flicked the switch, and the heater roared to life. Warm air poured through the vents.

Gage rocked back on his heels, wiping his hands on his jeans. "Well, I don't want to disappoint your parents, so..."

I arched a brow, but my voice wasn't as steady as I wanted it to be. "So?"

His signature grin softened just enough to make my stomach twist.

Gage was always teasing. Always pushing. Always throwing some smug, offhanded comment my way like it was nothing.

But this?

This *wasn't* nothing.

He was looking at me differently now. Not like I was a challenge to be needled or a puzzle to be solved. Just... like I was a woman he wanted.

And he was giving me the choice.

"So," he said, watching me a little too closely. "Can I kiss you?"

The question was simple. Straightforward.

But the way he said it—low, warm, careful—sent something unexpected through me. I hesitated, my heart picking up a step.

Not because I didn't want him to.

But because, for the first time, I realized I kind of did.

That realization sent a flicker of panic through me.

This was *Gage*.

The same Gage who spent half his time making my life difficult.

The same Gage who grinned like the world was one big joke, and yet somehow, had still spent the past week quietly helping my dad like it was no big deal.

And now he was standing way too close in my freezing kitchen, watching me with an expression I wasn't entirely sure how to process.

I should have overthought it. I should have come up with all the reasons why this was a bad idea.

But instead, I just... stood there. Smiling like a teenager looking at her first cowboy.

My body felt weirdly weightless, my pulse doing something annoying beneath my ribs.

I forced a smirk, hoping he wouldn't notice the way my fingers curled into the hem of my sweater. "Wouldn't be the worst thing that ever happened to me."

His mouth tipped into something amused. A breath of a laugh, a shift in his stance.

Then, slowly, deliberately, he stepped closer.

I stayed rooted in place, but something in me went very, very still.

Not tense. Not nervous.

Just... waiting.

Gage didn't reach for me right away. Instead, he studied me like he was making sure I wouldn't bolt. Like he was giving me every opportunity to tell him no.

But I didn't.

And when his fingers finally brushed the side of my face, the warmth of his touch sent a quiet shiver down my spine.

I swallowed hard, staring up at him. Everything in my brain was a mess of static. The heater was finally working, but somehow, the room felt warmer for an entirely different reason.

My pulse jumped when he tipped his head just slightly, his thumb skimming lightly along my jaw.

And for the first time in a long time, I wasn't thinking at all.

I was just waiting.

Waiting to see what it would feel like when Gage Langton finally kissed me.

And, Heaven help me...

I was pretty sure I wanted to find out.

Chapter Nineteen

Amber

THE FIRST THING I noticed when I woke up was how warm my house was.

Which shouldn't have been a surprise, considering the heater was finally working again. But somehow, it was. Because the last time I stood in this room, Gage Langton was standing in it, too.

And he kissed me.

The memory hit like a slow, creeping heat. The way he'd looked at me—not teasing, not smug. Just... hopeful.

The way he'd stepped closer, giving me every opportunity to back away.

The way I hadn't.

I let out a long breath, pressing my palms into my mattress. Okay. I needed to get up. I needed coffee.

Sir Stumpy chose that moment to jump onto my chest, glaring down at me with zero patience. I groaned. "You're judging me, aren't you?"

He let out a sharp *mrrp*, which was probably cat for yes, obviously.

I sighed, shoving back the blankets. "Fine, I'm up."

He leaped off me and trotted toward the kitchen, his tail flicking like he'd won some kind of battle. And just like that, I had no excuse to keep lying in bed, overanalyzing the fact that Gage Langton kissed me last night, and why I'd enjoyed it.

Except that I absolutely *was* still overanalyzing it.

T HROWING MYSELF INTO WORK was the best way to avoid feelings.

So that's what I did.

Lessons. Paperwork. A meeting with Morgan about scheduling next week's therapy sessions. Everything was moving, everything was fine.

Except for the part where I wasn't.

Because even though I'd managed to distract myself for a couple of hours, eventually, I sat down in the breakroom just long enough to catch my breath.

And that's when Kate walked in.

She barely made it three steps before pausing mid-motion, eyes narrowing as she studied me.

I froze, suddenly hyper-aware that I was sitting there with zero distractions to hide behind.

Kate crossed her arms, her expression knowing. "You're acting weird."

I snorted. "I am not acting weird."

She lifted a brow. "Amber, you reorganized the supply closet twice last week, and today you're avoiding eye contact."

I forced myself to hold her gaze. "I am not avoiding eye contact."

"You just blinked aggressively while saying that."

I groaned, rubbing my forehead. "I didn't blink aggressively."

Kate grabbed a bottle of water from the fridge, still watching me. "Come on, you're a therapist, for crying out loud! It was you who taught me everything I know about reading people. Something happened."

I hesitated.

Because technically...

Yes.

Something *had* happened.

But was it really a thing?

Or was it just one of those fleeting, temporary moments that didn't actually mean anything?

I wasn't sure.

And until I was, I wasn't talking about it.

I forced a sigh, standing up. "I have work to do."

Kate followed me with her eyes. "You're dodging."

"Am not."

She took a slow sip of water. "So if I asked what you were doing last night, you'd tell me?"

I paused.

For exactly half a second too long.

Kate's eyes widened slightly. "Oh my gosh, the heater. You did call a cowboy."

I grabbed my notebook off the counter and started backing out of the room. "I have things to do."

Kate was grinning now. "You have secrets."

"I do not."

She gasped. "Is he a good kisser?"

I nearly tripped. "What?"

She burst out laughing. "Relax, I'm kidding."

I muttered something under my breath that probably wasn't appropriate, and escaped down the hall before she could grill me any further.

And for the rest of the day, I made extra sure to stay busy.

Gage

I HAD EXACTLY ONE goal this morning. Do *not* think about Amber Morris.

It should've been easy.

The project at White Pines might be winding down, but Ridgeview was gearing up for calving season, which meant there was plenty to keep me busy. Feed to haul, supplies to check, equipment to service—zero reason for my brain to be wandering elsewhere.

And yet...

I stood outside the barn, stacking feed bags in the back of the truck, and somehow, instead of thinking about cows or schedules or the fact that I still hadn't eaten breakfast, my brain was stuck on last night.

On her.

Amber.

Standing in her kitchen, arms crossed, throwing me that skeptical look.

The way she blinked exactly three times when I asked if I could kiss her.

The way she hesitated, like maybe she was thinking about saying yes.

I tossed another bag of feed onto the stack, maybe with a little too much force. This was *not* what I needed to be doing today.

Focus, Langton.

"Did you even sleep last night?"

I turned.

Liam stood in the doorway, one brow lifted.

I frowned. "What?"

"That's my job. What gives? You don't do my jobs."

I snorted. "Maybe I do."

Liam just shook his head, walking over and hopping onto the tailgate. "You're still takin' me to Walker Ranch this weekend, right?"

"Yeah, we're going." I tightened the straps securing the feed bags. "Luke's expecting us."

Liam grinned, the kind of easy, excited smile that didn't happen often with him. Kid was getting better at letting his guard down.

"That's good," he said, swinging his feet. "Maybe I won't suck so bad this time."

I rolled my eyes. "You didn't suck last time."

He huffed. "Tell that to the steer I completely missed."

"Steers don't care."

Liam smirked. "No, but Luke did."

I chuckled. "Luke gives everyone crap. You should hear the way he talks to me."

Liam studied me for a second. "Yeah, but you don't let it bother you."

I shrugged. "You think I always had thick skin?"

Liam didn't answer. Which meant he didn't know what to say. Because he was still figuring that out for himself, I guess. Still deciding what kind of person he wanted to be.

I reached over, nudging his shoulder. "You got nothin' to prove, Liam. You'll get better just by putting in the time. And hey—don't tell Luke I said this, but Hickory's faster'n' that fat old stud of his."

Liam laughed. "No, he's not."

"Okay, well, no, he's not. But he's steady. That's what you need—a good, solid partner. Something you can trust while you figure out what's next."

He nodded slowly. Then narrowed his eyes in a way that kids have a tendency to do when they think they're about to say something smart. "Yeah... a partner. So... who's your partner?"

Why that little... I knew, I *knew* he wasn't talking about a horse now. I cuffed him in the shoulder. "We'll talk about that later."

Liam just shot me a cocky grin. "Okay."

The barn door swung open again, and Ethan walked in, looking about as unimpressed as ever.

"Are we actually working today," he asked, "or are you two just sittin' around, getting philosophical?"

Liam flipped him off.

I sighed. "Alright, you two. Knock it off and grab the next load, or I'll have to make you sit in the horse trough for bad language."

"I didn't say anything," Liam protested.

"Ever hear of sign language? Well, I got a sign for you." I held up my hand in a big "L" shape. "No more of that crap now, y'hear? Or I'll have to tell Luke you can't heel for him because I broke your hand off."

Liam looked a little shamefaced... sort of. But he also snickered as he said, "Sorry, Gage."

"Good enough. Better finish your chores." I turned back to the truck, hands on my hips, exhaling slowly.

Trying really hard not to think about how, when Liam asked who I had for a "partner," I didn't have an answer.

Amber

I BARELY HAD TIME to sit down with my lunch before my phone buzzed on the breakroom table.

Gina.

I stared at the screen, debating. I could ignore it. Let it go to voicemail. Pretend I was too busy.

Except I knew how this would go. She'd just keep calling.

With a sigh, I grabbed my phone and answered. "Hey."

"Finally." Gina let out a breath, already impatient. "I've been trying to catch you all morning."

"I've been working all morning. I can't answer my phone in the middle of a session."

She made a noncommittal noise. "So, have you finally convinced Mom and Dad to be reasonable?"

My appetite vanished.

I pinched the bridge of my nose. "Gina—"

"No, really," she pressed, already ramping up. "They've had their fun. They saw you, did the whole road trip thing, and now it's time to get serious."

I gritted my teeth. "If by 'serious,' you mean forcing them into a situation they don't want, then no."

Gina sighed like I was being difficult on purpose. "Amber, we don't have time to keep waiting on them to make the right choice."

I frowned. "Waiting on them?"

"You know what I mean."

I did.

And I didn't like it.

I shoved my half-eaten sandwich aside, sitting up straighter. "Gina, they're not toddlers who need to be told what to do."

She scoffed. "You think I don't know that?"

"I think you're talking about them like they don't get a say in their own lives."

Silence.

Then, more measured, Gina said, "I am thinking about the long-term."

"So am I."

Gina huffed. "Then why are you making this so hard?"

I almost laughed. *I* was the one making this hard? "You put down a deposit on that place without asking them."

"Because they wouldn't have considered it otherwise."

"Maybe because they don't want it."

"Look, you're the one who has power of attorney. You can make this happen if it's in their best interest."

"That's not exactly how that works."

Gina's voice softened—just a little. "Amber, we have to be realistic."

I rubbed my temple. "Oh, so now we're being realistic? Because you were the one acting like putting them in a home was some magical, perfect solution."

"It's not a home," Gina snapped. "It's an independent living community. It's nice, Amber. They'd have friends, activities, support."

"They have support."

"In Montana?"

I flinched.

Because, fine. That was a fair point.

But I wasn't ready to admit it.

Gina sighed. "Look, I know you don't want to hear this, but keeping them in that house isn't practical. And playing road trip in a motorhome isn't a solution. Did you hear that Dad slid past a stop sign on the way into town? Almost hit a guy?"

I swallowed. "No. Was the other car okay?"

"He wasn't in a car. He was on the sidewalk! Amber, they had *no* business driving that thing. Have you seen the tags?"

I gritted my teeth. "I saw, Gina, and while I appreciate all the... the difficulties, I'm also not budging on this. It's not your decision to make, and I'm not going to force it."

"Yeah?" Gina's voice rose. "Well, someone has to make one, because they sure aren't."

The words hit deep. Because they weren't entirely wrong.

Mom and Dad were dodging this conversation as much as we were.

And I was letting them.

But still—

"If you lose your deposit, that's on you," I said, steady, final. "Not me. Not them."

Gina exhaled sharply. "Fine. But if they end up needing it later, don't come crying to me when there's no room left."

The call ended.

I set my phone down on the table, pressing my palms against my face. Because, honestly? I didn't know if Gina was wrong.

And that was the worst part.

Gage

I HAD ZERO PLANS to talk about Amber Morris today.

None.

I was just driving back from town, minding my own business, when my phone rang.

A little prickle raced over my scalp as I glanced at the screen. Maybe it was...

Luke Walker.

I considered letting it go to voicemail.

Because Luke? Luke had a way of seeing things before I was ready to admit them.

And I wasn't in the mood for it today.

But if I ignored the call, he'd just keep trying.

So with a sigh, I answered. "Walker?"

"Langton."

I smirked. He always said my name like it was a challenge. "What's up?"

"Just checking in," Luke said easily. "You still bringing Liam over this weekend?"

"Yeah. He's looking forward to it."

"Good. Dusty'll be there too. We'll get some solid runs in."

"Sounds like a plan."

There was a pause.

A long one.

And right when I started to get suspicious, Luke said, "So, are you finally gonna admit it?"

I frowned. "Admit what?"

"That you've got it bad."

I sighed, rubbing my temple. *Here we go.*

"Walker—"

Luke chuckled. "Gage, you ever notice how you only call me 'Walker' when you're trying to avoid a conversation?"

I scowled at the road. "I do not."

"You absolutely do."

I took a slow breath. Changed the subject. "Calving season's coming up. You all set over there?"

Luke ignored me completely.

"So, Amber Morris, huh?"

I rolled my eyes. "I don't know what you're talking about."

"Oh, come on." He sounded entirely too amused. "You think I haven't noticed the way you've been acting lately?"

"I've been acting exactly the same."

"Right." His voice was all skepticism. "You know, Audrey told me something interesting the other day."

I braced myself.

Because if Luke's wife was involved, I was doomed. The Walker women were a force to be reckoned with—all five of them. Six, if you included Morgan... Amber's boss. Who saw *everything*.

I wanted to slam my head on the steering wheel.

"Yeah, so Meg said Kate told her that Amber's been weird lately. And then I thought about how you've been weird lately. And then I thought... huh. That's interesting."

I sighed. "Do you have a point?"

"My point is," Luke drawled, "it's always the ones who say they're not the marrying type."

"I never said that."

"No, but you've always been the guy who doesn't take things too seriously."

"Untrue," I said flatly.

"Really? What's the longest relationship you've ever been in?"

I gripped the steering wheel. "This is a stupid conversation."

Luke laughed. "I'll take that as 'not long enough to count.'"

I ground my teeth. "Luke—"

"You like her."

"Didn't say that."

"You didn't have to."

I pulled into Ridgeview's long gravel driveway, exhaling sharply. "Look, I don't know what you want me to say."

"How about the truth?"

"I don't know what the truth is."

And that shut him up.

At least for a second.

Because even I wasn't expecting to say that.

But it was the truth.

I had no idea what I was doing.

I had no idea what Amber was thinking.

And for the first time in my life, I wasn't trying to be charming or teasing or easygoing about it.

Because it didn't feel like that kind of thing.

It felt... bigger.

Luke let out a slow breath. "Well, damn."

I ran a hand over my face. "Yeah."

Another pause.

Then, lighter this time, he said, "Just don't fight it, cowboy."

I huffed. "I gotta go."

Luke chuckled. "See you this weekend."

The call ended.

I sat there for a second, gripping the wheel.

Because maybe Luke had a point.

But I still had no idea what I was supposed to do about it.

Amber

B Y THE TIME WORK wrapped up, I was running on a dangerous mix of frustration, exhaustion, and exactly three cups of coffee.

Between Gina's phone call, an afternoon full of therapy sessions, and Kate's increasingly suspicious looks, I was officially done.

So when I finally stepped outside, ready to get in my truck and go home, the absolute last thing I expected was to see Gage Langton pulling into the White Pines parking lot.

I stopped mid-step, brow furrowing.

Gage slowed his truck, then rolled down the window, resting an arm on the door like he had all the time in the world.

"Didn't expect to see you still here."

I crossed my arms. "Didn't expect to see you at all."

His signature grin appeared, lazy and easy. "You wound me, Morris."

I narrowed my eyes. "Did you just stop by to annoy me, or is there a real reason you're here?"

Gage cut the engine, pushed open his door, and climbed out like he belonged there.

"Needed to check in with Chase about some of the finishing work on the new barn wing," he said, like that wasn't *at all* suspicious.

I arched a brow. "That's it?"

"That's it." He shut the truck door, then leaned against it, watching me.

I should have walked away.

I should have gone straight to my truck, driven home, and left whatever weird, lingering tension from last night behind.

But instead, I hesitated.

Gage's gaze flicked over my face. "You alright?"

It was casual. Easy. Like he was asking just to ask.

But for some reason, I believed he actually cared about the answer.

I shifted, fingers tapping against my thigh. "Just a long day."

"Yeah?" He studied me for a second, then tilted his head. "That why you look ready to set something on fire?"

I blinked. "Excuse me?"

He shrugged, completely unfazed. "You've got your murder expression on."

"My what?"

"You know. The one where you stare into the distance like you're plotting someone's untimely demise."

I exhaled through my nose, equal parts exasperated and amused. "I do not have a murder expression."

Gage smirked. "Mmm. Debatable."

I fought the urge to roll my eyes, but the teasing pulled something loose in my chest.

I sighed, adjusting the strap of my bag. "It's just... family stuff."

Gage nodded, like he already knew. "Gina?"

Of course, he remembered.

I let out a breath. "She called today. I guess Dad nearly creamed a pedestrian with that motorhome of his."

"I warned him about those brakes."

I scrubbed my face with my palms. "I just... I don't know, we *have* to do something. Gina's right about that. Maybe not tomorrow, maybe not even next year, but she's right that they need more help than I can give them from here or she can give them from Bozeman. But it has to be something *they* want, too, and I have no idea what they'll agree to."

Gage didn't say anything right away.

Didn't jump in with a quick fix or a solution.

He just... listened.

Finally, he said, "That's a tough spot."

And it wasn't much. But it was enough.

Because everyone else in my life had an opinion. Kate thought I should stick to my guns. My mom wanted to avoid the conversation entirely. Gina wanted control.

But Gage?

Gage just let me be tired.

Something in my chest unraveled.

I glanced at him. "You ever deal with something like this?"

He considered that, leaning back against his truck, eyes flicking up toward the mountains.

"Not exactly," he admitted. "But when Dad died, everything kinda shifted. Mom went from raising us to depending on us. And none of us were real sure how to handle that."

I watched him, surprised by the honesty. Gage didn't usually talk about his dad. And definitely not what it had been like to lose him.

He exhaled, running a hand over his jaw. "No right answers, Doc."

I didn't even bother correcting the nickname this time. I just nod-ded, letting that rattle around my head for a minute.

Because maybe he was right. Maybe there weren't any right answers. Just the ones we could live with.

And somehow, that helped.

I adjusted my bag on my shoulder. "I should get home."

Gage nodded, pushing off his truck. "Don't plot anything too nefarious."

I snorted. "No promises."

And for the first time all day, I actually smiled.

Chapter Twenty

Gage

THE FIRST TIME I asked Ethan if he wanted to come roping, he barely looked up from his coffee and muttered something about having better things to do. So when I walked outside this morning to see both twins loading up in my truck, I was more than a little surprised.

"Didn't think you were coming," I said, tossing a saddle into the bed.

Ethan shrugged, adjusting his cap. "Didn't have anything better to do."

Liam scoffed. "You literally said yesterday that roping is stupid."

Ethan climbed into the passenger seat without looking back. "Yeah, well, if I stay here, Chase'll make me muck the outside pens. Might as well watch you guys."

I chuckled, shaking my head. "Glad to have you, kid."

Liam muttered something under his breath about "wasting a perfectly good day on something he doesn't even care about," but I ignored him and climbed in.

Banner and Hickory were already secured in the trailer, saddles packed, ropes coiled neatly in the backseat. We had everything we needed. Including, apparently, an extra twin.

I started the truck. "Let's get to Walker Ranch before Luke starts thinking I forgot how to drive."

Liam snorted. "Pretty sure he already thinks that."

Ethan smirked, staring out the window. "Sounds like a smart man."

Fifteen minutes in, Liam finally gave in to the tension I could practically feel radiating off him. "Alright," he muttered. "What's the deal?"

Ethan didn't look away from the passing landscape. "What deal?"

"You. Being here."

Ethan shrugged. "It's not illegal, is it?"

Liam's jaw tightened. "You don't even like roping."

Ethan still didn't look over. "Don't hate it."

Liam made a noise that was very much not believing him.

"Maybe I just wanted to hang out with Cole," Ethan said. "He'll be there, too."

Liam snorted. "Oh, sure. That makes sense."

Ethan shot him a look. "You got a problem with that?"

"You don't even like Cole."

"I don't dislike him."

"You called him 'sunshine cowboy' last week."

"And was I wrong? Dude never stops smiling. It's weird."

Liam groaned. "Not everyone is miserable, you know!"

I chuckled, shaking my head. "Ethan, you ever considered professional instigating as a career?"

Ethan grinned. "They pay for that?"

"If they don't, they should."

The teasing faded after a while, and silence settled in the truck. Not an awkward silence. Not even a tired one.

It was "thinking too hard" quiet.

I knew that kind of quiet.

I reached for a water bottle from the console and held it out. "Drink."

Liam gave me a look but took it, anyway. "I'm not thirsty."

I shrugged. "Yeah, well, hydration makes you smarter. Might help you not suck at roping."

Ethan huffed a quiet laugh from the back seat. Liam scowled but twisted the cap off, taking a sip.

"I don't suck," he muttered.

I shot him a look. "You sure about that?"

He rolled the bottle between his hands, avoiding my gaze. Then, just barely loud enough to hear—"I just don't wanna embarrass myself."

Something about the way he said it made my grip tighten on the wheel. I let the words sit between us for a second before speaking. "You ever watch a baby colt try to stand up?"

Liam frowned. "What?"

"They're a mess. All legs. Wobbling, slipping, face-planting left and right."

Liam blinked. "This is incredibly motivating, Gage. Really."

I fought a grin. "Point is, they don't quit. They keep getting back up. Over and over until they figure it out."

Liam let out a breath, staring out the window. "Yeah. Well. They don't have anyone to prove themselves to."

"Neither do you." I nudged the brim of my hat up. "Just yourself."

He didn't answer, but I could see the wheels turning.

And Ethan?

He hadn't said a word. Just watched the whole exchange from the back seat, quiet but focused—like he was filing it all away for later. I had a feeling both of them were.

Good.

Because today wasn't just about roping. It was about learning how to stand back up.

As soon as we pulled up, Luke and Dusty were already in the barn aisle, saddling horses. We could see them from the parking area, just finishing up. Luke tugged his cinch tight on Two Bits and dropped his stirrup, then led his horse to the door to give me one of his corny looks.

"Took you long enough," he said as I popped the truck door open.

I grabbed my hat out of the truck. "Traffic was terrible."

Luke snorted. "Yeah, I'm sure those three cars you passed were real trouble."

Dusty appeared beside Luke, leading that pretty gray mare he was so proud of, and waved. "Brought both of 'em, huh?"

Liam grabbed his gear from the back. "Ethan just wants to bother Cole."

Ethan shrugged. "Gotta have goals."

Luke chuckled, glancing at me. "You got your hands full, Langton."

I grinned. "Tell me somethin' I don't know."

W ALKER RANCH HAD ONE of the best indoor roping setups in the county. Solid footing. Good lighting. Nice chutes and your pick of fresh cattle. It was the kind of place that made a guy want to practice ten days a week, whether he needed it or not.

I swung into Banner's saddle and pointed, nodding toward Luke and Dusty. "Well, boys, you ready to teach some young blood?"

Luke shook out his loop. "That depends. Are they teachable?"

Ethan snorted. "That depends. Are you good at teaching?"

Luke arched a brow. "You got a lot of mouth for someone who doesn't even have a horse yet."

Ethan shrugged. "Maybe I'll just stand here and judge."

Before Luke could come up with something smart to say, Cole walked over from the barn, a lead rope in hand. "Hey," he greeted, tipping his hat to me before turning to Ethan. "Figured you might need something to ride."

Ethan blinked, caught off guard. "Oh."

Cole handed him the reins. "This is Maverick. Solid head horse. Smooth ride, he'll put you right where you need to be."

Ethan hesitated, then took the reins, running a hand down the gelding's neck. "He's huge."

Cole grinned. "Yeah, he's a big boy. But he's got a brain."

Luke made an experimental swing with his loop—showing off *just* a little. "Think you can handle that, sunshine?"

Ethan shot him a flat look. "I don't make promises."

Cole just chuckled. "Cody said to try him out today, see if you like him. No pressure."

Ethan nodded slowly, still looking at Maverick like he wasn't sure how this had happened.

I glanced at Cole. "Appreciate it, little brother."

Cole shrugged. "No problem. I got a couple of cutters to exercise today, so I'm off. You guys need anything, just holler." He wandered back toward the barn, leaving us to it.

And just like that, both twins had a horse under them. Whether they felt like they belonged... well, that was up to them.

W E SPENT THE FIRST half-hour warming up, letting the horses stretch out. Liam was focused, adjusting Hickory's stride, finding his balance. He was starting to get a good feel for riding. Definitely one of those kids who liked to try to figure it out on his own before asking for help. I respected that. But I also liked that he was starting to learn when to ask—that showed smarts.

Ethan was... well, he was adjusting.

"Your stirrups feel alright?" I asked as we rode side by side.

Ethan glanced down, shifting his weight. "They feel like stirrups."

Luke, who had absolutely zero chill, rode up next to us and grinned. "Need a booster seat, kid?"

Ethan stared at him. "I'm taller than you."

"You sure about that? Step down off that mammoth and look me in the eye, we'll find out."

Ethan opened his mouth. Closed it. Then just shook his head. "This was a mistake."

I laughed, watching as Maverick started to relax under him. "You look fine."

Ethan exhaled. "Yeah, well, I feel weird."

"That's normal."

Ethan arched a brow. "You saying you used to be bad at this?"

I smirked. "Nah. Just saying you are."

Ethan rolled his eyes. I'd hoped he'd crack a grin, like he usually did when I dished it back at him, but his hands were still white-knuckle gripped and I wasn't sure when the last time was that he took a breath.

"Look," I told him, "Luke and Dusty, Cole and Trent—all of us grew up in the saddle. Not a one of us can even remember the first time our daddies hoisted us on the back of some old nag and sent us out to push steers. You can't compare your first ride to mine. But just 'cause we had a head start don't mean you can't catch up. It's not a contest. Not even about ego."

"Then what's it about?" he asked me, staring at me without blinking.

Crap. I didn't have an answer yet. The rest sounded so darn smart that I hadn't thought that far ahead. I cleared my throat to buy a few seconds.

"It's about... I guess today is about having fun."

He finally blinked. Like he'd never thought of something that frivolous before—or, rather, had never been given permission to have fun without having to steal the pleasure despite what others told him to do.

"Are you breathing?" I asked. "Because you turning purple and falling out of the saddle might put a damper on our day."

Finally, finally, he cracked a faint smile. "I got it," he muttered. But his smile got a little wider, and I caught the way his shoulders relaxed.

We ran drills first. Dummy work. Swinging the rope. Footwork. All the basics that the boys never knew before, but it wasn't just for them. Basics make a decent roper into a consistent roper.

Once Luke was satisfied, we moved on to live cattle.

Liam missed his first run.

Then his second.

His third was worse than the first two combined, the loop catching air and landing nowhere near the steer's legs.

By the fourth miss, his grip on the rope was white-knuckled.

I pulled up next to him, keeping my voice easy. "Breathe, kid."

Liam exhaled sharply. "I *am* breathing."

From across the arena, Luke called, "Doesn't look like it."

Liam shot him a glare. "Maybe I don't need live commentary."

Luke chuckled. "Let it float. Don't force it."

Liam muttered something I didn't catch, but shook out his rope, rolling his shoulders. The frustration was still there, but he nodded for the next steer.

This time, his loop hit clean. It wasn't perfect, but it held.

I grinned. "There we go."

Liam let out a breath, finally relaxing. Then we ran it again.

And this time? He didn't miss.

Meanwhile, Ethan was off to the side, working on his own loops with the borrowed horse Cole had set him up with. Unlike Liam, he had no muscle memory for this. No instinct for the rhythm of swinging a rope and delivering it clean.

The first time he threw, the loop hit the dirt a full three feet behind the steer.

The second time, he overcompensated, jerking his arm too hard, and nearly smacked himself in the face when the rope snapped back.

Luke rode up beside him, watching for a second before tilting his head. "Alright, hop down."

Ethan frowned. "What?"

"Get off your horse." Luke swung a leg over and landed lightly on the ground. "Let's go back to square one."

Ethan hesitated, but obeyed.

From my vantage point, I saw Luke take him over to the dummy, breaking down the movement in slow, easy steps.

"Your hand's too tight," Luke murmured, adjusting his grip. "Relax your wrist. It's not a hammer; it's a whip."

Ethan tried again. The loop still wasn't great—but it was better.

Luke nodded. "There you go."

A few more reps, a few more small corrections, and by the time Ethan mounted back up, he wasn't holding the rope like it was some foreign object. And on his next run?

He caught.

It wasn't smooth, it wasn't fast—but it was something.

Luke gave an approving nod. "Not bad for a first-timer."

Ethan's grin was small but real. "Thanks."

As we were wrapping up for the day, I caught movement near the entrance of the arena. A familiar figure strolled inside, boots dusted, hat settled low against the late afternoon light.

Blake Walker.

A legend in his time—one of the best ropers I'd ever seen back when I was a wide-eyed five-year-old kid that my dad dragged along to the roping arena. Blake and my dad used to be just about unbeatable, and Luke and I grew up in their shadow with our little kid lariats and stick horses.

Blake didn't rope anymore, not officially, not since his body started reminding him he wasn't twenty-five anymore. But that didn't mean he wasn't still part of it. He still kept up with the sport. Still watched. Still had something to offer.

Luke spotted him first and tipped his hat. "What's up, old man?"

Blake snorted. "Meryl made a pie and told me to take a break before I got underfoot."

Luke grinned. "Translation: She kicked you out so she could bake in peace."

"Something like that."

His gaze shifted, landing on Ethan, who was still sitting on Maverick, coiling his rope, quiet and thoughtful.

Blake crossed the arena toward him, adjusting his hat as he stopped beside Ethan's stirrup. He gave Maverick a once-over, then flicked a glance up at Ethan. "You look like you're thinking too hard."

Ethan straightened instinctively, gripping his reins a little tighter. "I—"

Blake shook his head. "Don't."

Ethan frowned. "Don't what?"

Blake reached up and ran a hand over Maverick's neck, his voice easy, steady. "Overthink it."

Ethan swallowed.

Blake nodded toward the rope in Ethan's hand. "Roping's got feel to it. Muscle memory. You practice right, and your hands'll start knowing what to do before your brain catches up." He gave Ethan a pointed look. "That's the trouble with thinking too much. It gets in the way of doing."

Ethan hesitated, glancing down at his loop. "So I just... throw and hope for the best?"

Blake huffed a quiet laugh. "No. You throw, knowing you're gonna miss sometimes." He rested a hand against Maverick's shoulder. "A good roper doesn't waste time wondering if he belongs in the box. He just rides in, nods for the steer, and handles what comes next."

Ethan didn't answer right away. But something shifted in his expression.

Blake gave the saddle a solid pat. "Maverick'll take care of you. Let him do his job, and you do yours."

Ethan nodded. "Yes, sir."

Blake tipped his hat. "Keep at it, kid."

And just like that, he wandered off, leaning against the rails to watch.

It was casual. Offhand.

But the way Ethan straightened in the saddle told me it landed exactly the way Blake meant it to. No big speech. No drawn-out explanation.

Just a quiet, solid truth.

I exhaled, watching Blake as he settled into his usual place at the edge of things. Still present. Still engaged. Still part of the life he'd built here, even though he didn't step into the box anymore.

That was something I'd always admired about the man. The way he still invested in the next generation, even when he didn't have to.

And man, Ethan and Liam needed people like that, just as much as Blake Walker still needed to feel... needed.

And then, like the biggest light bulb ever went off in my head. Just like... Amber's parents still needed to feel needed.

Because it wasn't just about where people lived. It was about having a place where they could still give something back.

And suddenly, just as clear and steady as if it had been waiting for me to catch up—

I knew exactly what Amber needed to hear.

Amber

W HITE PINES DIDN'T TECHNICALLY have work today. But when you ran a full-scale equine therapy program, there was always something that needed doing.

Today? That meant bodywork.

A chiropractor and an equine massage therapist were making the rounds, adjusting joints, loosening tight muscles, and generally making our hardworking therapy horses feel their best.

The horses loved it. And so did we. Because after the past few weeks, we needed a day that felt light.

Morgan stretched her arms overhead, rolling out her shoulders with a groan. "I swear, I want to come back in my next life as a therapy horse. Full retirement with health and dental benefits. Regular massages. No stress. No notes."

Emily huffed a laugh. "Sounds better than being a rancher, that's for sure."

Kate snorted, shifting her weight against the stall door. "Or a contractor's fiancée."

Emily's smile faltered. "Oh no. What did Chase do now?"

Kate waved her off. "Not Chase. Trent. Lauren texted me last night and said they started picking out countertops for their kitchen." She paused, giving us a knowing look. "Guess how long that lasted before it turned into a full-blown debate about which kind of stone has the best resale value."

Morgan let out a low whistle. "Oh, he would."

Kate laughed. "Lauren knew what she was getting into."

Emily sighed, shaking her head. "She really did."

The four of us turned to watch as one of our geldings—Ranger—let out a deep, contented sigh, his lower lip sagging as the massage therapist worked over his loins.

Kate leaned against the stall door, shaking her head. "I can't believe how much they relax for this."

Morgan chuckled. "It's the ultimate spa day. No stress. No schedules. Just getting pampered."

I smiled, watching as Ranger practically melted under the therapist's hands. "Speaking of…" I turned toward the others. "When do we get our turn?"

Morgan arched a brow. "You volunteering to go first?"

I pretended to consider it, then shook my head. "Absolutely not. I'd rather let Kate take the lead on this one."

Kate laughed. "Not happening. I still have battle wounds from the last time we all did a self-care day."

Emily raised a hand. "That was not my fault. You were the one who insisted on the DIY face masks."

"They were supposed to be soothing," Kate muttered.

Morgan snickered. "And instead, you walked around looking like a tomato for three days."

Kate sighed, but she was laughing, too.

For the first time in weeks, the air felt light.

And we needed that.

B Y THE TIME WE finished with the last horse, the barn was quiet, peaceful—almost too peaceful.

So naturally, we did the only logical thing.

We made ridiculous, over-the-top coffees and acted like idiots.

Morgan stretched as she leaned against the counter, checking her watch. "I should probably get going soon. Kelli's got the kids, but I don't want to take advantage of her. Four toddlers is a lot."

Her phone buzzed before she could move, and she glanced at the screen before grinning. "Speak of the devil! Never mind. Cody's picking them up."

Kate saluted with her coffee cup. "So, you do get a spa day."

Morgan snorted, then disappeared into the tack room. A second later, she emerged, holding a handheld massage gun like it was a sacred artifact. "Alright. Who's first?"

Kate and Emily immediately pointed at me.

I sighed. "I walked into that, didn't I?"

Morgan grinned. "Absolutely."

Before I could even pull off my puffy vest, she cranked the massage gun to full power and pressed it into my shoulder.

I yelped, nearly dropping my coffee. "Morgan! What is that?"

Morgan laughed. "Relax! It's good for you."

Kate took a long, dramatic sip of her caramel latte. "I don't know, Amber. You have been kinda tense lately."

Emily smirked. "Yeah. What's that about?"

I shot her a look. "Oh, I don't know. Maybe because my sister is still fighting me about my parents. Or because my heat went out, and I had to call Gage Langton for help."

Kate perked up instantly. "Oh, yeah. Let's talk about that."

I groaned. "Absolutely not."

Morgan pressed the massage gun into my other shoulder. I flinched, then resigned myself to my fate. It actually felt pretty good after I breathed through the first shock.

And that was when Morgan, ever the instigator, casually mentioned, "You know... Cody told me the Walker boys were all giving Gage a hard time the other day."

Emily grinned. "Oh, yeah. Cole said Luke was merciless."

Kate's eyes lit up. "Wait, what? What did they say?"

Morgan shrugged innocently. "Oh, you know. Just casual conversation about how Gage suddenly seems to be in town a lot more these days."

Emily grinned. "I think Luke might have called him 'domesticated.'"

Kate nearly spit out her coffee. "No way."

Morgan nodded solemnly. "Oh, yes."

I groaned, burying my face in my hands. "This is exactly why I didn't want to tell you people."

Emily smirked. "You love us."

Kate wiggled her eyebrows. "You know who else might be loving something?"

I pointed my cup at her. "I swear—"

Morgan cranked the massage gun up one more notch and pressed it back into my other shoulder, making me squawk.

Kate giggled. Emily snorted her coffee. Morgan grinned in satisfaction.

And just like that, the conversation shifted back to regular stuff. But not before I caught Kate exchanging a knowing look with Emily.

And not before I realized that, for the first time, the mention of Gage Langton didn't make my stomach twist in frustration.

It made my heart do something else entirely.

Chapter Twenty-One

Amber

B Y THE TIME I got home, I was officially relaxed. A full day of easy barn work, coffee, and ridiculous girl talk had done its job.

Even Sir Stumpy seemed more agreeable than usual, curling up beside me on the couch instead of launching himself into a dramatic flop across my laptop keyboard. I tucked my feet under a blanket, grabbed my phone, and dialed.

Dad picked up on the second ring. "Hey, sweetheart!"

I smiled. "Hey, Dad. Just checking in."

"Good timing," he said, sounding even more cheerful than usual. "I just got off the phone with your friend, Gage."

I froze.

Sir Stumpy protested loudly as I suddenly sat straight up, dislodging him from his spot.

"...What?"

Dad chuckled. "Yeah, he called me up, said they had some roping videos from today and thought I'd like to see 'em."

I blinked. "Gage Langton called you?"

"Sure did. Sent over the videos, too. Good stuff. That Liam kid's got a good swing—needs to work on his timing, but he'll get there."

I stared at absolutely nothing, trying to process this. Gage Langton—professional menace, expert teaser, and unwelcome free handyman—had just called up my dad for no reason other than wanting to share something with him.

I shook my head, leaning back against the couch. "That's... surprising."

Dad chuckled. "He's a good kid."

I made a noncommittal noise. "He's... something."

I heard some shuffling on the other end, and then Mom's voice came through the line. "Amber! Did you eat those leftovers I left you?"

I blinked. "Uh. Some of them?"

"They'll go bad if you don't freeze them," she warned. "You do *not* want tuna casserole going bad in your fridge."

I smiled. "I know, Mom."

"Do you?"

I laughed, shaking my head. "Yes."

"Alright." There was a pause. "Did your dad tell you he got rid of the motorhome?"

The words didn't register right away. I blinked. "...Wait. What?"

Dad's voice came back on. "Yep. Sold it yesterday."

I sat up again, and Sir Stumpy gave up trying to find a place on my lap. He stalked off, his tail quirked into an angry question mark. But my cat was the least of my concerns. "Why would you sell the motorhome?"

Dad made a vague noise. "Ah, thing was old. Got terrible fuel mileage. Fridge went out on the way home, so I figured, what's the point?"

I frowned. "You loved that motorhome."

"Eh."

Eh?

This was the man who had refused to sell it when Gina had spent six months trying to convince him it was 'too impractical to keep.' And now, suddenly, he was getting rid of it?

I shook my head. "You're not making sense."

"Some young guy wanted it. Gave me five hundred bucks. Figured I'd let someone else get some use out of it."

I opened my mouth. Closed it.

Mom's voice came back on the line. "Alright, honey, my oven timer just went off. I'm going to finish getting dinner on. Love you."

Dad chimed in, "Ooh, dinner. Never been late for that in my life. Love you, sweetheart."

"Love you too," I said automatically.

The line clicked off.

And I was left sitting in silence, staring at my phone. Sir Stumpy made a disgruntled noise and reclaimed his spot on my lap, clearly unimpressed with the abrupt movement earlier.

I absently scratched behind his ears, still trying to process everything.

Gage had called my dad.

My dad had sold his motorhome. I stared at my phone for a full minute. Then I did the only logical thing.

I called Gage.

It rang twice before he picked up. "Well, well." His voice came through the speaker, slow and smug. "To what do I owe the honor, Doc?"

I huffed. "Don't call me that."

He chuckled. "Alright, Amber. What's up?"

I hesitated. Because now that I had him on the line, I didn't actually know how to start this conversation. I shifted on the couch, disturbing Sir Stumpy, who grumbled and flopped onto the floor in protest.

"I just got off the phone with my dad," I said finally.

Gage made a humming noise. "That so?"

"Yes. And he told me something... interesting."

"Mm."

"He said you called him."

Gage was silent for half a beat. Then: "Yeah."

I blinked. "*Yeah?*"

"Yeah," he repeated, like it was the most normal thing in the world. "Figured he'd like to see some roping from today."

I stared at the ceiling. "You figured."

"Uh-huh."

"...Since when do you and my dad have casual phone calls?"

Gage laughed. "Since today, I guess."

I shook my head, trying to wrap my mind around this. "You really just... sent him videos?"

"Yeah. We were talking about Liam trying to practice the other day, and I figured he'd get a kick out of seeing how he's coming along."

I exhaled slowly. Because somehow, the idea of Gage Langton going out of his way to make my dad feel included was...

I didn't even know.

Unexpected. Sweet.

Dangerously sweet.

"Alright," I said, pulling myself together. "That's not even the biggest shocker of the day."

"Oh?"

"My dad also sold the motorhome."

This time, Gage wasn't the least bit surprised. "Yeah, he said that."

I narrowed my eyes. "Wait. You knew?"

He exhaled, amused. "Yeah. Remember, I talked to him earlier. Is it supposed to be a secret?"

I gaped. "I—What? You just seem so casual about it."

He chuckled. "I wasn't when he told me. I was about as confused as you are right now."

I ran a hand through my hair. "So let me get this straight. He sold the motorhome, chatted to you about it, and didn't even tell me until I called him just now?"

Gage paused. "You sound like he went out of his way to offend you or something."

"I... that's not the point. He loved that thing, Gage."

"I know."

"He wouldn't let Gina talk him into selling it, but some random guy with five hundred bucks shows up and suddenly it's gone?"

"Yep."

I shook my head. "That doesn't make any sense."

Gage's voice softened. "Maybe it does."

I frowned. "How?"

"Maybe he's letting go of the old plan to make room for a new one."

I went still. Because something about the way he said it sank deep.

Maybe Gage was right.

Maybe my dad was realizing something I hadn't. That he wasn't stubbornly clinging to the past. Maybe he was making room for the future, whatever that was.

I didn't know what to say. For once in my life, I just... sat there. Thinking.

Gage must have picked up on it, because he didn't make any comments. Didn't tease. Just let the line go quiet.

And for some reason, it wasn't awkward.

It felt easy.

Finally, I whispered, "Maybe you're right."

Gage hummed. "That's gotta sting."

I huffed a soft laugh. "A little."

He chuckled. "Well, don't worry. I won't rub it in. Yet."

I rolled my eyes.

And yet, I was still smiling.

WHITE PINES WAS QUIET today.

Not completely quiet—there was always something happening on a ranch—but the usual buzz of lessons and therapy sessions was absent. After an entire morning spent double-checking feed orders and reviewing therapy schedules for the next month, I was ready to get out of my office.

I stepped outside, stretching my arms overhead, breathing in the crisp February air.

And that's when I saw him.

Gage Langton.

Leaning against a fence post like he had nowhere else to be, talking to Chase and helping him load some tools in his truck.

I hadn't seen him in over a week. I mean... yes, I'd talked to him on the phone two days ago about my parents. Even had a text from him the next day, like he was checking in. That was weird. Sweet, but weird.

But I hadn't actually seen him in person. Not since...

Well.

Not since he'd kissed me.

My stomach churned uneasily as I walked toward the barn. How could it not be weird now? Would he be different? Would I? Could we just... pretend it didn't happen?

I squared my shoulders, forcing my expression into something neutral. The last thing I needed was for the people I worked with—or worse, Gage—to read too much into my hesitation.

Gage was the first one to see me. His head lifted, his easy, familiar smile appearing like it had never left. Like nothing between us had changed. Like he had no idea how much time I'd spent overthinking this exact moment.

"Look who finally decided to get some fresh air," he said, tipping his hat.

Chase glanced up from where he was inspecting the fence. "She's been buried in paperwork all morning."

"Some of us have real jobs," I informed him with a grin.

Gage leaned against the post, his cheesy smile widening. "Hey, moving cows around and fixing broken fences is a real job."

"Mm-hmm."

His gaze lingered on me—not teasing, not smug. Just... easy. Comfortable.

Like I was no longer the girl he tried to provoke for the fun of it. I was just part of his life now.

And that... that suited me fine, too.

B Y THE TIME I got home, I was feeling... lighter. Which, given the way things had been lately, was a rare sensation. Maybe it was the fresh air. A good day at work—some great sessions today, the kind that make me love my job all over again.

Or maybe it was Gage acting normal when I wasn't sure he was even capable of it.

Either way, I wasn't ready for my phone to ring the second I stepped inside. I glanced at the screen.

Gina.

I sighed, answering before I could talk myself out of it. "Hey."

"Amber." Her voice was tight. Frustrated. Tired.

I sucked in a breath. *Here we go.*

"Mom and Dad are still acting like they're on vacation," Gina said, bypassing all pleasantries. "I just got off the phone with Mom, and she said they've been busy."

I blinked. "Busy doing what?"

"Apparently, Dad's been helping one of the neighbors with some project, and Mom joined some kind of... quilting group?"

I snorted. "That sounds exactly like them."

Gina wasn't amused. "Amber, Mom slipped on the porch yesterday—there was ice, and she couldn't catch herself. Dad wasn't even home, and she had to call the neighbor. Thank goodness *he* was home. He took her to the urgent care and she has a contusion on her arm that's black all the way to her shoulder."

I blinked. Of course, they didn't tell me this. "Is she okay otherwise?"

"Yeah, I guess. Look, they can't keep going on like this. They're filling their time with stupid things instead of facing reality."

I sighed. "They're not ignoring reality, Gina," I said, keeping my voice calm. "They're just figuring it out in their own way."

Gina exhaled sharply. "We don't have time for them to 'figure it out.' Mom got lucky this time. What happens when something actually happens?"

I bit my lip. Because that question had been nagging me, too. I sat down on the couch, running a hand through my hair.

"Okay," I said finally. "What do you actually want?"

Gina was quiet for a second.

Then she sighed. "I want them to be somewhere safe. Somewhere they have access to care, to people looking out for them."

I nodded, even though she couldn't see me. "Alright," I said. "What if we ask them what they want? Nail them down, make them answer this time. Not just where they think they *should* be, but what would actually make them happy? Maybe we could hire some in-home help so they could stay where they are. Someone to look after them, help them with the maintenance, be there in case they fall..."

Gina hesitated, like she couldn't believe her ears. Because for the first time, I wasn't just pushing back. I was trying to meet her halfway.

"...Okay," she said cautiously. "They might go for that. I could live with that. But what if we can't find someone? You can't just hire any old person off the street."

"Well, we'll just have to talk that over when we get there. We have to talk to Mom and Dad about it first."

A beat of silence. Then, Gina let out a slow breath.

"Alright," she muttered. "But you're the one who has to ask them."

I smiled. "Deal."

T HE PAST TEN DAYS had been steady. Which, after the roller-coaster of the last month, felt like an improvement.

Gina and I had finally stopped fighting long enough to start making progress. My parents were still living their lives their way. They didn't want someone living with them full time, and we hadn't really come up with any other great answers, but at least now, we were all talking.

And Gage...

Well. He was still around.

Not every day. Not all the time, but a lot. I seemed to run into him when I really needed to smile, and I'm not sure how that worked, because it wasn't like we planned it.

All the ranches around were swept up into calving season, and Ridgeview was no exception. It had him running nonstop, and I was pretty busy at White Pines.

But we still texted most evenings. He still sent videos to Dad. And occasionally, he'd pick up the phone to ask me some random question or just tattle on some nonsense my parents were up to before going back to whatever cowboy things he was doing.

Which was fine.

Really.

Because I *wasn't* thinking about him.

Not at all.

Definitely not.

"A MBER, PLEASE TELL ME you can help."

Kate barely looked up from the massive list in her hands as I stepped into her kitchen, which was currently covered in wedding chaos.

Fabric swatches. Seating charts. Stacks of RSVP cards.

Lauren was flipping through a binder, muttering something about chair rentals. I took one look at the mess and seriously considered backing out the door.

Kate must have sensed it, because she grabbed my wrist before I could escape.

"Nope. You're here now. You're helping."

I sighed, setting my purse down. "How bad is it?"

Lauren snorted. "Let's just say if I hear the phrase 'rustic elegance' one more time, I'm eloping."

Kate shot her a look. "Not funny. I'm *not* getting married by Elvis."

Lauren grinned. "I hear Gene Simmons is an option now."

Kate slapped her notebook closed. "No. And the Denny's wedding is a no, too, before you bring it up."

I laughed and crossed my arms. "Okay, Vegas is off the table. You gotta stick it out, Lauren. What's left?"

Kate made a face. "Finalizing guest seating, double-checking the menu, and... well..." She hesitated.

Lauren coughed. "The groomsmen."

I blinked. "What about them?"

Kate sighed. "They're a disaster."

Before I could ask how, exactly, the groomsmen were a disaster, Kate's front door opened. And in walked the last person I expected to see.

Gage.

Carrying a notebook.

Looking completely unbothered by the chaos.

I stared. "What are you doing here?"

He tipped his hat. "Evening, ladies."

Lauren grinned. "He's here because Trent and Chase don't have time to wrangle the guys, so guess who volunteered?"

I blinked.

Gage?

M   r   .

I-go-wherever-I'm-needed-but-don't-make-me-in-charge-of-anything Langton?

Kate handed him a list. "All the groomsmen are birthing cows this month, and not a single one of them has gone for a tux fitting. Serves us right for planning a March wedding. We need to know who can actually be here and when."

Gage flipped through the list. "Alright. I'll get it sorted."

I raised a brow. "Since when do you do wedding logistics?"

"Since my brothers decided to get married at the same time."

Lauren laughed. "You should've seen him at the cake tasting. Most efficient decision-making I've ever witnessed."

Kate sighed dreamily. "Because someone actually understands time management."

Gage shot me a smug look. "No, because I know what good frosting should taste like."

I rolled my eyes, but I was still watching him. Because I wasn't sure what to make of this.

Gage Langton. Wedding coordinator. What universe was this?

I grabbed a pen and a fresh sheet of paper. "Alright. If we're going to do this, we need a real game plan."

Kate nodded, jumping in immediately. "We need to confirm the groomsmen's schedules, figure out the final count for the rehearsal dinner, and—"

"Wait," Gage interrupted, looking at my list. "You do logistics?"

I frowned. "I run a therapy center. Of course, I do logistics."

His grin softened just slightly. And for a split second, it felt like we weren't in a room full of wedding chaos.

Like it was just him and me.

Kate didn't miss it. She nudged Lauren, who immediately looked down but did a terrible job of hiding that smirk.

Gage didn't even notice.

He just tapped his pen on the notebook, back to business.

But I was still sitting there, looking at him, my stomach doing something I refused to analyze.

Gage

BY THE TIME WE finished wrangling wedding details into something resembling a plan, it was well past dark.

I didn't mind. Not really. Because for once, I actually felt useful.

Not just another set of hands, floating wherever I was needed. But part of something bigger. The guy solving problems, clearing the way for other people to do what they needed to do.

And I hadn't missed the way Amber kept watching me tonight. Like she was figuring something out. And I was in no hurry to stop her.

Kate and Lauren were still arguing about floral arrangements when Amber grabbed her jacket and headed for the door.

I didn't think about it. Just followed.

"Need me to walk you to your truck?"

She glanced up with a playful smile. "Because the mean streets of Kate's driveway are so dangerous?"

I shrugged. "Never know. Some rogue wedding planner might try to rope you into another task."

Amber huffed a laugh. "Good point."

We stepped outside, the air crisp and cool. I glanced at her out of the corner of my eye. She looked tired—but in a good way. Like someone who had done a full day's work and didn't regret any of it.

Her breath came out in a soft puff of white. And for once, she wasn't filling the silence with words. Just walking beside me, like it was the most natural thing in the world.

She stopped at her truck, keys in hand, unlocking it.

I didn't move.

Didn't say anything.

Because I wasn't ready to leave yet.

And neither was she.

Her fingers lingered on the door handle, hesitating. The night was quiet around us—just the faint rustle of pine boughs in the breeze, the soft shuffle of horses moving in the paddock. The sky stretched out dark and endless overhead, stars scattered like someone had tossed them there just for us.

She finally spoke, her voice softer than before. "You've been busy."

I nodded. "Calving season."

She nodded too, like she already knew. And she probably did. Because we talked now.

Not just when we "happened" to see each other. Not just when we had a reason.

Amber shifted, her weight moving from one foot to the other. It wasn't nerves. Just... something unspoken hanging between us.

I rubbed the back of my neck. "You know, technically I lost a bet tonight."

She lifted an eyebrow. "Technically?"

"Well, I talked to Luke earlier and he... well, you know Luke. He makes assumptions. He bet five bucks you wouldn't let me kiss you again, but since I never asked, it kind of feels like I lost by default."

She rolled her eyes, but there was a quiet smile behind it. "That's a stretch."

I grinned. "Nah. I think you owe me a rematch."

"A rematch? Are we talking about kissing, because that sounds more like you're talking about darts again."

I lifted a shoulder. "I'll take what I can get. What do you say?"

She hummed like she was considering it. "Maybe."

I stepped closer, just enough that I could see the glint of amusement in her eyes.

"I'll take a maybe."

Amber exhaled a small laugh, shaking her head, but she didn't pull away.

Didn't move at all.

And neither did I.

Not until I reached up, tucking a loose strand of hair behind her ear.

She didn't flinch.

So I leaned in, just enough to press the gentlest kiss to her lips.

Not teasing. Not playful.

Just something real, something solid. Something *us*.

When I pulled back, she looked at me for a long moment, then shook her head with the ghost of a smile.

"You really can't stand losing, can you?"

I grinned. "Not to you."

Amber rolled her eyes again—but this time, I didn't miss the way her fingers curled a little tighter around her keys, like she was holding onto something she didn't quite want to let go of yet.

Neither did I.

But for now...

"Goodnight, Amber."

She hesitated, then—softer than before—"Goodnight, Gage."

And leaving her there felt just a little bit harder every single time I did it.

Chapter Twenty-Two

Amber

THE WEDDING RECEPTION WAS over, and both happy couples were on their way to their honeymoons, racing off to catch their evening flights. The church hall, which had been buzzing with people and music all afternoon, had settled into quiet cleanup mode.

I stacked another set of chairs, pausing to stretch my arms behind my back. Across the room, Gage was wrangling table linens into a bin, talking with Audrey and Luke Walker about something that must have been mildly entertaining, judging by the wide grin on his face.

Because, of course, he was the kind of guy who made a point of having fun during cleanup. It was actually... kind of cute. I rolled my eyes and went back to collecting stray cups and plates.

Most of the family had already left. Calving season, naturally—my conservative estimate of the wedding guests was that at least eighty percent of them had some sort of cattle-induced crisis happening at home by the time they got there. The rest, even those who didn't have cows dropping calves, still had chores to finish before turning in for the night.

Which left... us. The stragglers. A mix of friends and family who either felt guilty leaving a mess or just weren't ready to call it a day yet.

I wasn't sure which category I fell into. I just knew I wasn't in a hurry to go home. And, apparently, neither was Gage.

Morgan looked around at the rest of us as she dropped a handful of plastic cups into the trash. "Y'all sticking around forever," she said, smirking, "or are you actually gonna go enjoy what's left of the day?"

Gage stretched, rolling his shoulders. "Not a bad idea." He glanced at me. "You got plans?"

I blinked. "Not really."

"Good," he said easily, grabbing his jacket.

I frowned. "Good... why?"

Gage just grinned. "Let's do something."

Amber

I THOUGHT GAGE MEANT getting food. Maybe a drive to nowhere in particular. Something simple. Something normal.

I was wrong.

Because instead of heading toward the diner—or literally any place that made sense—Gage turned onto Main, coasting past the closed shops, past anyplace that resembled entertainment or dining or even sight seeing. We weren't going to my house... we weren't going to his.

"Mind telling me what we're doing?" I finally had to ask.

He shot me a grin. "I'm figuring it out."

I sighed, leaning my head back against the seat. "This is why I don't do spontaneous."

Gage chuckled. "That's a shame. Spontaneous is where all the best stories come from. Remember the Great Dart Showdown? You think I planned that? But I got a story to tell all the guys, didn't I?"

"And what story would that be? Are you actually admitting you got beat by a girl?"

"A really *good-looking* girl," Gage corrected. "That's a badge of honor."

I snorted. "Now I know you're lying." But secretly... I was blushing.

The sun had started its slow descent, casting long shadows over the fields, painting the snowy mountains in soft golds and purples. I let my head rest against the window, watching the scenery blur past.

It was... nice.

Easy.

And even though I wasn't the spur-of-the-moment kind of person, I had to admit—this felt good. Just being here. Just driving. Just talking.

We fell into conversation about the wedding—laughing over how Trent had been more nervous than Lauren, how Chase had managed to step on Kate's dress twice before they even got down the aisle.

"I thought for sure she was going to murder him," I said, shaking my head.

Gage chuckled. "She was real close. I saw it in her eyes. And did you see how nervous Trent was?"

I nodded. "You'd think a guy who helps birth calves in snowstorms wouldn't sweat saying 'I do.'"

"Yeah, well, have you met Lauren? She was a little intimidating today."

I smiled, remembering Lauren's fierce, let's-get-this-done attitude while getting ready. "A little?"

Gage rolled his eyes at me in a "tell-the-truth" sort of expression.

I laughed. "Okay, a lot. She means business, that woman, in everything she does. I say Trent's a lucky guy."

Gage huffed a silent little laugh and adjusted his grip on the wheel. "Yeah. He is."

I smiled, glancing out the window again— and that's when I saw it.

The car.

Not just any car. A candy apple red sports car.

I sat up straighter. "No way."

Gage shot me a quick look. "What?"

I pointed. "That car."

He followed my gaze, frowning slightly as we passed the lot.

"What about it?"

I twisted in my seat to keep looking. "My parents rented one just like that, for Valentine's day back before I was born. Just for fun."

His brows lifted. "Seriously?"

"Yeah. But you know, that was from some big rental place out of Missoula or Bozeman. But this—" I turned forward again, shaking my head. "—what is this thing doing *here?*"

"Good question," he said. "Not like we get much call for car rentals in this town anyway, let alone fancy ones like that."

I stared out the window at the thing. "That place usually only has like, five cars. All boring, because the only people who rent them are people whose car is in the shop. So how did that end up here?"

Gage didn't say anything. He just slowed the truck.

And before I even realized what he was doing—

He turned into the lot.

I blinked. "Gage."

"We're renting it."

I stared. "What?"

His grin was pure mischief. "Come on, Amber. Let's be sponta-neous."

T HE SECOND WE PULLED out of town, I knew this was a mis-take.

Not because it was reckless. Not because of the icy backroads or the fact that we had nowhere in particular to be.

But because I was having *fun*.

The kind of fun that made me forget to be cautious. The kind that made my laughter come easy, unguarded. The kind that made me glance over at Gage, the icy March wind ruffling his hair under that worn-out ball cap, and want to stay in this moment a little longer.

The road stretched ahead, dark asphalt cutting through the white-dusted hills, the mountains rising in the distance like quiet sentinels against the evening sky. The last light of the day burned gold on the peaks, streaks of pink and orange melting into deep blue. It was the kind of winter evening that felt untouched, like we were the only two people left in the world.

I rolled down the window without thinking, letting the sharp, cold air whip into the car. It stung my cheeks, tangled in my hair, but it felt good. Clean. A deep breath I hadn't realized I needed.

Gage glanced over, his lips twitching. "See? Told you this was a good idea."

I shook my head, turning my face into the wind for a moment before rolling the window back up. "This is completely reckless."

His grip on the wheel was easy, relaxed, like he wasn't driving a completely impractical rental car through backroads covered in hard-packed snow. "You call it reckless. I call it necessary."

I turned to look at him, eyebrows raised. "Necessary?"

He nodded, eyes still on the road. "Absolutely. Like I said, the best memories come from the stuff that probably wasn't a great idea."

I scoffed. "You mean bad ideas?"

"*Terrible* ideas," he corrected, flashing me a grin.

I exhaled, shaking my head, but I didn't argue. Because maybe he had a point. Maybe the best memories weren't planned. Maybe they just *happened*.

W E DROVE FOR A while. Not aimlessly, but not with any real destination, either. Just letting the Mustang eat up the miles, the steady hum of the engine filling the quiet between us. Snow-dusted pines blurred past, broken up by open valleys and stretches of frozen creeks reflecting the last of the evening light.

Gage had one hand on the wheel, the other resting easily on the gearshift, completely at home behind the wheel of a car he didn't own, on a road he probably hadn't planned to take. He didn't check a map or second-guess himself. He just drove.

And for once, I didn't ask where we were going.

That felt... new.

Because normally, I needed to know the plan. I needed structure, direction. I needed certainty.

But with him?

For some reason, I just trusted it.

Eventually, he turned off onto a narrow side road, winding up into the hills. The slushy pavement gave way to gravel, and then to muddy dirt roads, the tires spinning a little as the Mustang climbed higher.

I glanced over. "Where are we going?"

He grinned but didn't answer.

I frowned, crossing my arms. "I'm assuming you have a plan?"

"Not a plan." He nodded toward the windshield. "Just a view." A few seconds later, he slowed and pulled into a turnout.

I turned my head—and felt my breath catch.

Below us, the land stretched for miles, rolling out in an endless patchwork of white and gold. Frozen rivers cut through the valleys, reflecting the last of the evening sun. The mountains beyond stood tall, their peaks glowing pink against the deepening blue of the sky. The air felt different up here—cleaner, quieter, untouched.

I'd lived here for five years. I'd seen plenty of beautiful places.

But something about this—about today, about Gage sitting next to me—felt different.

I exhaled, glancing at him. "How'd you find this place?"

He shrugged, draping an arm over the steering wheel. "Been coming here for a while. Just whenever I needed space."

I studied him for a second, trying to picture it. Gage Langton, usually in the thick of things, always surrounded by family, out here alone with nothing but the sky and the mountains.

For some reason, it was hard to imagine.

Or maybe... it wasn't.

For a while, we just sat there. Not talking. Just watching.

Then, out of nowhere, Gage asked, "Did you ever think about getting married?"

I blinked.

Of all the things I thought he might say, that was not one of them.

I hesitated. Then shrugged. "Yeah. I guess."

His voice was casual. "What stopped you?"

I thought about that for a second. Then sighed. "I never wanted to settle for something that wasn't real, and I never found anything that was."

Gage turned his head slightly, watching me. "And now?"

I frowned. "Now, I don't know."

He didn't say anything right away. Just sat there, fingers drumming lightly against the wheel. When he finally spoke, his voice was quieter than before.

"You ever think maybe what your parents have wasn't luck?"

I turned to him, brows knitting. "What do you mean?"

"Maybe it wasn't about finding the perfect person." He exhaled, watching the horizon. "Maybe it was about choosing them. Every day."

I stared at him. Because that was…

A really good point.

And it was coming from *Gage*.

The wind picked up outside, rattling through the trees. I shivered, pulling my jacket tighter around me.

Gage noticed. Without a word, he reached behind his seat, grabbed his coat, and held it out.

I hesitated. "Aren't you cold?"

He shrugged. "I'll survive."

Something about the way he said it—so casual, so certain—made my chest feel tight.

I took the coat. Pulled it around me. And for some reason, that small act of kindness felt bigger than it should have.

We didn't talk after that.

Didn't need to.

We just sat there, looking out over the world.

For the first time, I stopped thinking. Stopped calculating. Stopped bracing myself for whatever came next.

I just let myself be here. In this ridiculous red Mustang. On an aimless drive through the mountains.

With Gage.

And to my own surprise... I didn't mind it. Not even a little.

W E DIDN'T STAY AT the overlook long. The sun was already dipping below the mountains, and the cold was creeping in, turning my breath into little white clouds. We didn't talk about it—we were just both ready to go at the same time.

Gage pulled the Mustang back onto the road, and pointed it back down the mountain. We didn't turn on the radio. Didn't fill the silence with unnecessary words. The air between us had shifted—not in a big, dramatic way, but in a way I could feel.

Like a string had been pulled just a little tighter.

I curled into his jacket, the scent of leather and something warm and familiar settling around me. I should have given it back.

I didn't.

About halfway home, Gage finally broke the silence.

"So... what do we call this?"

I glanced at him. "Call what?"

He smiled, but it wasn't his usual teasing kind.

"This. Us."

My stomach did something weird. Because what even *was* this?

A date? No.

A... whatever came before a date?

I sighed. "I don't know."

Gage nodded, like that was a fair answer. Then, after a second—

"Do we need to call it anything?"

I hesitated. Then shook my head. "No."

And for some reason, that was okay.

The town lights came into view, glowing softly against the deep blue of twilight. The streets were mostly quiet, the after-dinner lull settling in, leaving just the occasional car rolling past.

Gage pulled into my driveway, idling in the quiet. I reached for the door handle, but something made me pause. I turned back to him.

And I wasn't sure what I was expecting.

A cocky remark?

A casual see you around?

But he just smiled at me. Like this thing between us—whatever it was—didn't need to be rushed or defined right now. It just *was*.

And maybe that was enough.

Still, when I started to step out, Gage shifted, leaning in slightly. Not enough to make a big deal out of it. Just enough to give me the option to meet him there.

So I did.

It wasn't a long kiss.

It wasn't urgent, or dramatic, or anything out of a movie.

It was just... nice.

Nice enough that when we pulled back, I found myself smiling a little, still wrapped in his jacket, still tucked into the moment.

Gage brushed his thumb over my knuckles, like he wasn't quite ready to let go, either. Then he exhaled, his mouth curving into something amused.

"So... friends who have kissed three times?"

I arched a brow. "That's what you're calling us?"

He shrugged. "Not that I'm counting."

I huffed a laugh and stepped out of the car, closing the door behind me. And as I walked up my porch, I still didn't know what this was.

But I knew I liked it.

Chapter Twenty-Three

Gage

I TIPPED MY HAT lower against the wind, breath fogging in the cold. The sky stretched wide and endless above us, the stars sharp against the black. If I weren't so dang tired, I might've appreciated it. But at least it wasn't raining.

Instead, I was half-frozen, knee-deep in mud, and staring at a stubborn heifer who seemed determined to drag this out as long as possible. At least I had Cole to lend me a hand this week, with Trent and Chase both still off honeymooning.

Cole exhaled hard, rubbing his hands together for warmth. "She's making us work for it."

"She's making herself work for it," I muttered, shifting my weight.

Most of our heifers this year were doing well enough on their own, but this one... Cole saw it coming, said this one would have a bad time, and he was right. She'd gone down an hour ago, contractions slow and dragging, and now the calf's hooves had finally started showing—but that was it. Just another contraction. Another long pause.

Cole crouched beside her, jaw tight. "She's in a bad spot. We need to move her."

He wasn't wrong. She'd picked the lowest dip in the pasture and her head was down in it, the ground slick and uneven. Bad for birthing. Bad for us.

"Gage, get the rope."

I didn't argue. Just grabbed the lariat from my saddle, coiling it in my hands as I stepped forward. The heifer's sides heaved as she shifted, her eyes flicking toward me in wary exhaustion.

"Easy, girl," I murmured, moving slow. Looping the rope gently around her back legs, careful not to spook her. Then I went back to my horse, mounted up, and dallied my rope.

She grunted, nostrils flaring, but she didn't fight. Good.

Cole stepped back and nodded. "Alright. Pull slow."

I backed my horse up, easing the tension just enough to coax her out of the worst of the dip. She resisted at first, grunting, shifting, making us work for every inch.

But finally—finally—she moved.

Right to where we needed her.

Cole was on his knees beside her the second she stopped, steady hands checking the calf's position.

"She's still got time," he said, exhaling. "But not much."

Translation: If this didn't happen soon, we'd have to step in with the calving chains. We waited, breath fogging the air.

The heifer groaned, body tensing with another contraction. Then another. And then—

The calf slid free.

A wet, shivering, wobbly little thing, hitting the ground with a soft thud. The heifer turned, immediately licking her calf clean, instinct kicking in without hesitation.

Cole checked his watch. "Took her long enough."

"She was probably enjoying the show," I muttered, wiping my hands on my jeans.

Cole chuckled, shaking his head. "Alright. Let's move on."

Move on. Right, because we had four more that looked close, in a herd of fifty that could go "soon." I ran a hand down my face, exhaustion settling in deep.

This was only the first night for us. We'd gotten a later start on calving season this year, but now that it had kicked in, we had weeks of this ahead.

I pulled out my phone, checking the time. 3:27 AM. And before I could stop myself, I checked my messages.

Nothing.

Not that I expected anything.

Amber wasn't exactly waiting by the phone.

But still...

I kind of wished she was.

Amber

I SHOULD'VE BEEN ENJOYING the quiet.

For weeks, it had been nothing but chaos—wedding planning, back-to-back therapy sessions, my parents visiting. Every day had been packed from morning to night, and if I wasn't dealing with a client or my sister, I was putting out some kind of fire somewhere else.

Now? White Pines had finally settled. The therapy horses were back in their normal rotation, the schedule was steady, and my evenings were my own again.

It should have been a relief.

Except... it felt *too* quiet.

I hadn't noticed it at first. I'd kept busy, throwing myself into work, making sure the transition back to normal went smoothly. But this morning, as I was grooming one of our geldings in the barn aisle, the silence felt like a wet blanket, smothering me in a way I couldn't quite explain.

I gave myself a shake. I was probably just adjusting. Things had been hectic for so long, my brain wasn't used to the lull yet.

That was all.

Morgan tossed a brush onto the workbench. "I'm heading up to the house to spell my husband on kid duty. He was out all night helping with calving at Walker Ranch, so he's beat."

I glanced up, grateful for the distraction. "Yeah?"

She nodded. "Luke called him in late. I guess it's a rough start to the season. Cold snaps. A few hard deliveries. He didn't roll in until almost sunrise."

I ran a hand absently down the gelding's neck, my mind catching on her words. *Calving season.*

I hadn't really thought about it.

But now that I did...

Ridgeview was probably in the thick of it, too.

I frowned slightly, adjusting the brush in my grip. "Bet the Langtons are running on fumes, then."

Morgan chuckled, shaking her head. "No 'bet'. All the ranches are this time of year." She zipped her coat, but her eyes flicked to me again, a little too knowing. "I haven't seen Gage around lately."

My hand stilled for half a second before I forced myself to keep moving.

Because she was right.

I hadn't seen Gage around either. Not at the feed store. Not at White Pines. Not anywhere.

And I'd only just realized why.

I cleared my throat, keeping my voice casual. "Yeah, well. He's probably got his hands full."

Morgan hummed like she didn't quite believe me, but she let it go.

I finished up with the gelding, took my time putting my tack away, and then—without thinking—grabbed my phone the second I stepped into the break room.

I had one notification from Gina—just reminders about upcoming doctor appointments for Mom and Dad. Nice to be kept in the loop, but I wasn't exactly critical to the event.

Nothing from Gage.

Not that I expected anything.

But still.

I tapped my fingers on the table, my phone resting face-up in front of me. Then, before I could talk myself out of it, I sent a message.

Surviving over there?

I set my phone down, crossed my arms, and stared at the screen.

One minute.

Two.

Three.

Then, just as I was about to shove my phone back into my pocket—

Three little dots appeared.

Gage

I DROPPED ONTO THE bunkhouse couch with a groan, every muscle in my body protesting the movement.

Everything ached. Not the good kind of ache—the satisfying, well-earned kind after a long day. No, this was the miserable, bone-deep kind that made a man question all of his life choices.

My back hurt. My knees hurt. My hands were raw from the cold.

And I was pretty sure I had frostbite on at least two toes.

For the first time in days, I had a few free hours. No cows in active labor. No emergency vet calls. Just a quiet house, a warm meal waiting in the kitchen, and a couch with my name on it.

I let my eyes drift closed, soaking in the silence.

Then the door swung open, bringing a gust of cold air and two familiar voices.

Ethan and Liam stomped inside, shaking off the last of the cold. Ethan tossed his gloves on the counter. "Barn's quiet for now."

Liam yawned, rolling out his shoulders. "Might have a few go tonight, but Nora says we're good for the next few hours."

I grunted in acknowledgment, too tired to do much more.

Liam eyed me. "You look like you died already."

I curled my lip without moving.

He grinned, grabbing a water bottle from the fridge. "You gonna eat?"

"Too tired."

A new voice—one that carried a whole lot more authority—cut through the room. "You're *not* too tired to eat, Gage."

I cracked one eye open to find Mom standing in the doorway, arms crossed.

I sighed, pushing myself up. "I could be."

She wasn't buying it. "Eat first," she said. "Then you can collapse. I'm not cleaning the kitchen again tonight when you finally decide to graze from the cupboards."

Fine. I'd eat now.

I grabbed a plate from the counter, shuffled to the table, and sank into the chair with a groan. The warmth of the food seeped into my cold fingers as I picked up my fork.

Ethan and Liam sat across from me, both scrolling through their phones between bites. Mom had settled near the stove, keeping an ear on the conversation while she sipped her coffee.

I pulled my own phone out without thinking, scrolling past a few junk messages. A couple texts from Chase about equipment maintenance.

One from Luke:

You alive?

I snorted and texted back.

Barely. You?

I died a week ago, but my
wife told me I had to watch
the twins or birth calves. So I
went back out with the cows.

I chuckled and was thinking of thumbing back another response when another text landed. From Amber.

Surviving over there?

I blinked. My fingers hovered over the keyboard for a second longer than necessary before I finally typed a response.

Barely. Entertaining offers
to be put out of my misery.

Three dots appeared almost immediately.

I charge by the hour. Ex-
pensive rates.

I huffed a quiet laugh, shaking my head.
Liam glanced up. "Something funny?"
I kept my face neutral. "Nothing."
But it wasn't nothing.
It was *her*.
And for the first time in days, I didn't feel quite so exhausted.

I WASN'T SURE HOW many days had passed since I'd last gotten a full night's sleep. Time had blurred together in the chaos of calving season—one long stretch of late nights, cold mornings, and wading through knee-deep mud to help stubborn cows bring their babies into the world.

The only reason I even knew what day it was?

Trent and Chase were finally back.

Their honeymoons were over, their wives had officially moved in—even though that particular arrangment was only temporary. Even Cole was putting in some extra hours here for the season, so for a while, at least, the Langton brothers were all back at Ridgeview, which meant at least some of the workload was shifting off my shoulders.

Didn't mean I wasn't still running on fumes.

But at least now I had a chance to sit down, kick my boots off, and breathe.

I sat at the kitchen table, my plate of food half-eaten, my muscles aching so bad I barely cared that I was starving.

Across from me, Trent scrolled his phone, catching up on whatever he'd missed while he was off enjoying his newlywed bliss.

I was too tired to be bitter about it.

"Mom said you've been up to your ears in calving while I was gone," he said, not looking up.

"Good to have you back," I muttered, rubbing my eyes.

He huffed a laugh, setting his phone down. "You look like someone dragged you behind the tractor and forgot to hang you out to dry."

"Thanks," I deadpanned.

Cole walked in from outside, shaking snow off his jacket. "He's right, though. You need sleep."

I grunted, slumping back in my chair. "I need a new career."

Trent smirked, grabbing his coffee. "Thinkin' of finally running off to Vegas? Maybe start a lounge act?"

I shot him a glare. "More like thinking of hiring a ranch hand so I don't die out here."

Cole chuckled, grabbing a plate of food. Trent took a sip of coffee, watching me over the rim of his mug. "You could always marry rich."

I snorted. "You volunteering to fund my early retirement?"

He shook his head. "Nah. But you could always find yourself a sugar mama."

Cole coughed to cover a laugh. "You are spending a lot of time in town lately."

I didn't bite. Didn't even look at them. Because I already knew exactly what they were getting at.

Amber.

Which was not a conversation I was willing to have right now. Instead, I grabbed my phone from the table and flipped it over.

No new messages.

I tried not to be annoyed by that. Tried not to let my thoughts drift back to our last conversation. The teasing texts. The easy back-and-forth.

And then, right as I was about to put my phone down—

A new message popped up.

Finally getting some sleep?

I blinked. Then huffed a laugh.

Trent frowned. "Something funny?"

I shook my head, typing a quick reply.

> *What is this sleep word you speak of?*

> *Incredible. You should try it.*

> *Yeah, but then I might not wake up for a month. What do you think? Worth it?*

A pause. Then—

> *Debatable.*

I exhaled, some of the exhaustion lifting just a little. I didn't realize I was still grinning until Trent leaned back in his chair, watching me with way too much interest.

"You're awful smiley for a guy who claims to be on death's door."

I scowled, locking my phone and shoving it into my pocket. "You're awful nosy for a guy who just got back from his honeymoon."

He just smirked, shaking his head.

I ignored him. Except... For some reason, just texting wasn't enough. Not tonight. Not after the week I'd had.

And before I could talk myself out of it, I pulled my phone back out— and hit call.

The line barely rang once before she picked up.

"Didn't think I'd hear from you anytime this decade," Amber said. No hello, no hesitation.

I grinned, leaning back in my chair. "Miss me, Doc?"

She scoffed. "You sound half-dead."

I ran a hand down my face. "Not far off."

"Did you at least eat something?"

I glanced at my half-finished plate, pushing it away. "Tried."

"That's not the same thing."

"You checking in on me?"

"Someone has to."

I chuckled. "Good thing I've got you, then."

There was a small pause. Then, quieter—"Yeah. Guess so."

I closed my eyes, letting my head rest against the chair. She didn't fill the silence with meaningless chatter. Didn't push for me to talk if I didn't want to.

She just was there, and that was pretty nice.

"Long day?" she asked after a moment.

"Long week."

She sighed. "I bet."

I could hear movement on her end. Then a quiet thump—probably her cat jumping onto the couch.

"You working tomorrow?" I asked.

Amber yawned. "Of course. White Pines doesn't stop."

"Neither do cows."

"Yeah, well. Maybe *you* should."

I cracked one eye open. "You offering to run the ranch for me?"

She huffed a laugh. "Sure. How hard can it be?"

I grinned. "I'll have you castrating calves by noon."

Amber made a strangled noise. "Okay, never mind."

I chuckled, letting my eyes close again. "You're real fun to mess with, Morris."

She didn't argue. Just sighed, the sound softer than before. "You should get some sleep," she murmured.

I should have.

But instead, I found myself hesitating. Then I said, "Thanks for texting and checking in."

Amber was quiet for half a second longer than normal.

Then—"Yeah?"

"Yeah," I admitted, rubbing my jaw. "Made me feel... I don't know. Normal, I guess."

She didn't say anything right away.

But when she did, her voice was softer.

"Good," she said simply. "'Night, Gage."

Chapter Twenty-Four

Amber

T HE MORNING HAD STARTED off like any other—quiet, predictable, the way I liked it. I settled into my desk at White
Pines, my coffee warm in my hands, the scent curling around me like
a promise of an easy day. There was nothing urgent on my schedule,
nothing chaotic looming over me. Just paperwork, a few calls, and
maybe, if I was lucky, a slow afternoon with the horses.

Then my phone rang.

I sighed, glancing at the screen. *Gina.*

For half a second, I considered letting it go to voicemail. Things had
been better between us lately. No more fighting about Mom and Dad.
No more sharp words and simmering tension. I didn't want to break
the streak.

So I answered.

"Hey, Gina."

"Hey!" she said, her voice unusually bright, almost bubbly. *Too*
bright. Immediately, I felt an ulcer coming on.

"They're all settled in! Everything went so smoothly. I just left, and
they're already making friends—it's honestly such a relief."

I frowned, my fingers tightening around my coffee cup.

"...What?"

Gina let out a small laugh, like I'd just missed an obvious joke. "Mom and Dad. They moved in on Monday."

The words barely registered.

Moved in?

Monday!

That was three days ago.

I blinked at the calendar on my desk as if seeing the date would somehow make it make sense. *Three days*. And no one had told me.

My grip slipped on the desk as I tried to process it. "They... they moved in?"

"Yeah!" Gina said, her tone still light and casual, like this wasn't news. Like this wasn't something that should have warranted a call, a text, anything. "It was so easy. They got everything unpacked the first day, and they've already had dinner with two different couples. I really think they're going to be happy here."

The coffee in my cup had gone cold. Or maybe I just couldn't feel the warmth anymore. My ears were ringing—not with shock, not even with anger, just... emptiness.

"When were you going to tell me?" I asked, my voice too steady, too even.

There was a pause. Just for a second. Then Gina exhaled. "I figured Dad would have. They didn't call you?"

Something inside me cracked, because of course. *Of course*. Because apparently, I wasn't even worth a phone call anymore.

I swallowed hard, pushing down the sudden lump in my throat. "And... they're happy?"

Gina let out a breath, like she was relieved I wasn't arguing. "Yeah! Well—" There was another pause, the first hesitation in her otherwise cheerful voice. "You know how Mom is. She's still adjusting. But that's normal."

I squeezed my eyes shut.

Still adjusting.

That was the easiest way to say something wasn't right without actually saying it.

I suddenly felt cold. Like all the warmth in the morning had drained out, leaving me sitting there, hollow and frigid.

"Amber," Gina said, softer now, "this is what they wanted. They made the decision. It's good for them. It's good for all of us."

I didn't answer.

Because I didn't believe her.

And suddenly, I needed to hear it for myself.

T HE SECOND I HUNG up with Gina, I stabbed my dad's number into my phone. My hands were shaking, but I wasn't sure if it was anger or something worse.

The dial tone barely rang once before he picked up, cheerful as ever. "Hey, sweetheart! What's up?"

I squeezed my eyes shut, steadying my breath. *Act normal. Don't go in angry. Just get answers.*

I forced my voice to stay light. "Hey, Dad. Just checking in."

"Oh, we're good," he said, his tone easy, like he had all the time in the world. "Your mom got a new recipe for apple pie today and she's been making everyone taste it. Personally, I like her old recipe better, but don't tell her that. She'll just make more to prove me wrong."

Despite everything, I huffed a small laugh. That sounded like Mom. "Is she okay?"

"She's fine. Got her hair done today. Man, I had no idea they had a hairdresser's in this joint. And a nail place, too. Crazy!"

I nodded, even though he couldn't see me.

For a second, neither of us spoke.

Then I exhaled, bracing myself. "So... you moved."

A hesitation. Just for a second.

Then, "Yeah, we did."

Like it was nothing.

I pressed my fingers against my temple, trying to keep my voice steady. "When were you going to tell me?"

Dad let out a breath, the kind that said he was choosing his words carefully. "Didn't seem like there was much to say. We just packed up and came over."

"Without a word?"

"Now, now, don't be dramatic," he chuckled. "You knew we were thinking about it."

Thinking about it?

My stomach twisted. "Yeah, Dad. Thinking about it. I didn't realize we skipped straight to doing it without telling me."

Dad sighed, the sound edged with patience, like he was explaining something simple to someone making it complicated. "Sweetheart, we didn't want to make a big deal about it. It was just time."

That word—*time*—felt like a slap.

Like it had been some natural, inevitable shift. Like I was overreacting for even asking.

I swallowed hard. "Gina said you're already settling in." My voice was too tight.

"Oh, yeah." Dad sounded too cheerful. "People here are real nice. Good folks."

I waited.

Nothing.

"And Mom?"

"She's doing great."

I blinked. "...That's it?"

"What else is there to say?"

Everything.

But he wasn't going to tell me.

I tried to keep my voice even. "How's the apartment?"

"Oh, it's good," Dad said easily. "Cozy."

I frowned. Cozy?

"Sure."

That wasn't an answer.

"Do you have a nice view?"

A pause. Too long.

"Well... not the mountains, exactly, but we see plenty of trees."

I clenched my jaw.

Mom *loved* the mountains. She needed them.

And he wasn't saying she was happy. Just that she was "doing great." I knew a deflection when I heard one.

Dad cleared his throat. "So, how's work? Everything good at White Pines?"

I stared at my desk, my nails digging into my palm.

I could push him. Demand real answers. But I already knew what would happen.

He'd wave it off. Tell me not to worry. That they were fine.

I wasn't going to get the truth.

I swallowed, forcing my voice to sound normal. "Yeah, work's good."

"Glad to hear it. Hey, it's lunch time, and I gotta get your mom down to the cafeteria.

Another pause.

And just like that, the conversation was over.

"Okay, Dad. Bye." I sighed and ended the call.

Then immediately pulled up my contacts.

Because there was one more person I needed to talk to.

I pressed Gage's name.

T HE PHONE BARELY HAD a chance to ring before Gage picked up.

"Everything okay?"

His voice was easy, casual. Like he had no idea my world had just flipped over.

I stared out the window, my pulse thrumming beneath my skin. "My parents moved."

Silence.

A second too long.

I turned away from my desk, pacing. "They moved, Gage. Three days ago. They packed up and left and didn't even call me."

Still nothing.

That silence was an answer in itself.

I exhaled sharply. "I had to hear it from Gina. Three days after the fact. Three! They just—left the house they swore they'd die in. No call.

No text. Nothing." My voice wavered, so I bit down, hard, forcing it steady. "Who does that?"

Gage cleared his throat. "Amber—"

I dragged a hand down my face. "And Gina—good grief, Gina was acting like this was fine. Like I should have just assumed this would happen and not be surprised."

Gage still didn't speak.

I let out another breath, frustration pressing at my ribs. "And Mom— Mom is 'adjusting.' That's what Gina said. Which is the same thing as saying she's not adjusting, but we're all supposed to pretend she is so no one has to feel bad about it."

Gage made a low noise, like he understood exactly what that meant.

And suddenly, I felt stupid. Maybe I had called him at a bad time. Maybe I'd dragged him into something he didn't need to be in.

I took a slow breath. "I—I'm sorry, I shouldn't have just dumped all that on you. I didn't even ask if this was a bad time."

There was a pause. Then, softer than before—"Now's fine."

"I just... I don't even know what to think. Why wouldn't they at least call me? I never said I was against the idea of them moving. What I was against was them being forced. But now, it seems like they did it behind my back!"

"Amber..."

That was all it took.

My stomach dropped. I turned back toward the window, gripping my phone tighter. "You don't sound very surprised by all this."

Gage exhaled. "Your dad called me last week."

I blinked, caught off guard. "What? Why?"

"He was getting rid of some stuff before the move. Their house closed and he was posting some tools and junk for sale. Asked if I knew an easy way to fix a riding lawnmower that didn't... ride... anymore."

A sharp, bitter laugh pushed past my lips. "A riding lawnmower"

Gage sighed. "Yeah."

I let out a breath, shaking my head. "I don't—I don't understand. You knew?"

"Yeah," he said quietly.

I pinched the bridge of my nose, trying to push back the pounding headache forming there. "And you didn't tell me?"

"Not my place. They were going to call you themselves."

"Were they?" I snapped. "Because it kinda feels like they weren't. And anyway, why wouldn't you say something? We *talked* every day last week!"

Gage hesitated. "He asked me not to."

A sharp, stinging pressure settled behind my eyes. *Of course* he had. Because he knew I would've argued.

I pulled in a slow, shaky breath, forcing myself to stay calm. "So, what? You just kept it from me?"

He sighed. "Amber, you were the one who said their decisions had to be theirs. That their wishes needed to be respected."

His words hit hard. Because he was right. This was *exactly* what I had said.

But it still felt like a betrayal.

I turned away from the window, pacing across the office. "They sold their house—the house I grew up in, Gage! They didn't even tell me *after* they moved! I had to hear it from Gina."

"They didn't want to worry you. Look, I'm not saying I agree with it, but they knew how you felt. They'd made up their minds, and didn't want to argue or make you feel like you failed them or something. I think they wanted to prove they were okay before you jumped in on this."

I shook my head, swallowing against the lump rising in my throat. "I need to go."

"Amber—"

But I didn't let him finish. I just hung up. Because I wasn't ready to hear whatever came next.

And for the first time in weeks, I didn't want to talk to him anymore.

AFTER MY PARENTS BRUSHED off the conversation like their move was the most normal, natural thing in the world, and my... I don't know, was Gage my boyfriend?—whatever he was, he'd made me feel like the biggest idiot in the world. And I barely had time to process it all before my phone rang again.

Gina.

I debated ignoring it.

But if I didn't answer, she'd just keep calling, and I wasn't in the mood for that. I swiped to accept the call, pressing the phone to my ear.

She didn't even give me a chance to speak. "Amber," she said carefully, "I swear, I didn't know."

I let out a slow breath, leaning back in my chair. "You really didn't push them?"

A scoff. "Are you serious? Of course not. I swear, I had completely dropped it."

I still didn't answer.

Because I wasn't sure I believed her.

But then she sighed. "Honestly? I didn't think they'd ever do it."

I frowned. "...What?"

"I mean, think about it," Gina said. "I've been pushing for this for months, and they dug in their heels every time. I thought they'd never leave that house."

My grip tightened on the phone.

But they had.

Without a fight.

Without telling me.

"I really thought you talked them into it," I muttered.

Gina let out a sharp laugh, but it was hollow. "Amber, if I had talked them into it, don't you think I'd be calling to rub it in your face?"

That stopped me.

Because... yeah. She would.

But before I could respond, she sighed again, sounding tired. Regretful.

"I just got off the phone with them," she admitted. "I thought—" She stopped, exhaling sharply. "I thought they told you. I really did."

Something sharp twisted in my chest.

She hadn't known. She truly, honestly believed they'd included me in this decision. And they hadn't.

I ran a hand through my hair. "Then why now?"

A pause.

Then Gina spoke, quieter this time. "I don't know. Maybe they finally just saw reason."

Maybe.

Or maybe something happened to scare them into it.

Because our parents didn't make major life decisions without talking to us. At least, they never had before.

I stared at the window, the ache in my chest settling deep. "I guess if they're happy, that's all that matters."

Gina hesitated. Then, softer than before, she said, "Yeah."

But neither of us sounded convinced.

Gage

I WAS IN THE middle of spreading hay when my phone rang.

I pulled it from my jacket pocket, glancing at the screen.

Bob Morris.

I frowned, brushing the dust off my gloves before answering. "Hey, Bob."

Bob let out a breath, slow and measured. "Hey, son. Hope I'm not catching you at a bad time."

I tossed another flake of hay into the feeder, shifting the phone to my other ear. "Not at all. What's up?"

Bob hesitated. Just for a second, but long enough to make me pause.

Then he exhaled. "I think I owe you an apology."

I frowned. "For what?"

A tired chuckle. "I think I put you in the doghouse with my daughter."

That made me huff a short, dry laugh. "Yeah, you might've done that."

Bob sighed. "I didn't mean for that to happen, Gage. I didn't think—" He hesitated, like he wasn't sure how to explain. "I just needed a sounding board. Someone outside the family to talk to while we were figuring things out. I figured you'd understand."

I leaned against the fence, shifting my weight. "I do."

"I didn't realize Amber would take it so hard." His voice softened, like he wasn't just talking to me, but working through it himself. "I thought maybe she'd be relieved we made the decision without dragging her into it."

"You know she just wanted to be included, right?"

He sighed again. "I know that now."

I waited, giving him space to say whatever else he needed to.

Bob cleared his throat. "The truth is, this wasn't just about the long-term, or Gina's pushing, or anything else. We had a bit of a scare right after we got home from Amber's place."

I frowned. "What happened?"

Bob hesitated, and I could hear him take a slow, steadying breath. "It was bad, Gage," he admitted finally. "Sherri blacked out."

I stilled, gripping the top rail of the fence a little tighter. "What?"

Bob exhaled. "I was out in the garage. She was inside, just making coffee. Next thing I knew, I walked in and found her on the floor." His voice dropped, like the memory still rattled him. "She was out cold, Gage. Not just dizzy—out."

A cold knot formed in my chest. "How long?"

"Couple minutes, maybe? Felt like forever." He let out a humorless laugh. "By the time I got to her, she was starting to come around, but she was confused. Disoriented." His voice went tight. "She didn't even remember falling."

I muttered a curse under my breath. "You take her in?"

"Of course. I got her to the doctor that afternoon. They ran tests, checked her heart, ruled out a stroke." He sighed, the weight of it all settling into his voice. "Said it was low blood pressure. Could've been dehydration. Could've been standing up too fast. Could've been nothing at all."

"But it didn't feel like nothing," I guessed.

"No." His voice was quiet now. "It felt like a sign."

I chewed on that for a second. Amber's parents hadn't left their home because they wanted to. They'd left because, for the first time in their lives, they were afraid to stay.

"I didn't tell Amber because... I didn't want her to feel like she had to fix it. She's always been that way, you know? Always the one trying to keep us safe. I just—" He exhaled. "I wanted to handle it."

I rubbed a hand over my jaw, processing.

Amber was going to lose her mind when she found out.

And she *would* find out.

I shifted, staring out over the frozen pasture. "You know she's gonna hear this from me, right? Assuming she's still talking to me."

Bob sighed. "I know."

"She's gonna be pissed."

He let out a tired chuckle. "Yeah. But better at me than her mom."

I didn't argue.

But I also wasn't sure how to fix this.

"Just... go easy on her," Bob said, almost like a plea. "She's got a good heart, Gage. She just doesn't always know where to put all that fight."

I let out a slow breath, nodding to myself.

I knew exactly what he meant.

Chapter Twenty-Five

Amber

B IZ STOOD LAZILY BESIDE Walter, his big buckskin head drooping like he had not a single care in the world. Which, to be fair, he didn't. Walter scratched his shoulder with exaggerated enthusiasm, and Biz leaned into it with a dramatic sigh, clearly in absolute heaven.

"Look at this handsome boy," Walter crooned. "Now *this* is a real horse."

Kate adjusted the lead rope. "Yeah, yeah, Walter, we know you love Biz more than all of us combined."

Walter didn't even try to deny it. "Can you blame me? Biz never nags me about doing my exercises."

Kate burst out laughing. "That's because he has better things to do."

I exhaled loudly, biting back a groan. This was supposed to be a mobility therapy session, not a casual catch-up between Walter and his favorite horse.

"Walter," I said, forcing patience, "you have exercises for a reason."

He waved a dismissive hand, still scratching Biz like a lapdog. "Yeah, yeah. Strength, mobility, balance. I know the drill, Boss."

Kate barely stifled a chuckle. "Oh, you do listen."

Walter winked at her. "Only when you're talking, sweetheart."

That was it. I turned to Kate, glaring. "Would you stop encouraging him?"

Kate was outright grinning now. "I'm not encouraging him, I'm just having a great time."

Walter sighed dramatically, finally letting go of Biz. "Finally, someone appreciates my charm."

I crossed my arms. "Kate, if he refuses to do his therapy because you're too busy letting him flirt with you, you can do the paperwork explaining why his session didn't meet its objectives."

Kate held up her hands in mock surrender. "Alright, alright, I'll behave. Hear that old man? I'll have to call my husband in here if you keep flirting with me."

"Call him. I wanna shake his hand, because I've never seen you smiling so much. Married life looks good on you, kid."

She grinned back up at him. "Thanks, Walter. Now, better cooperate before Amber fires me."

Walter patted his prosthetic leg like it was a good dog. "I'll be good. I promise." He let Kate help him adjust his stance, then finally—finally—started his usual mobility exercises.

The session was moving, but not fast enough for my liking. Walter wasn't even trying to concentrate. He kept glancing over at Kate like she was the best thing to happen to this barn, grinning like a schoolboy.

"So," Walter said, carefully stepping forward, his prosthetic making a soft clunk against the barn floor, "honeymoon was fun?"

Kate smiled, soft and real. "Yeah. Short, but fun. That's what I get for marrying into a ranching family."

Walter nodded, satisfied. "That Chase fella's a good one. I like him."

Kate grinned. "Glad to hear it, since it's a little late to change my mind."

Walter laughed. "See? That's why you're my favorite."

I exhaled sharply, crossing my arms. "Walter, you're supposed to be focusing on walking, not giving Kate a marriage review."

Walter smiled like I was amusing him. "Sorry, Boss. A man's gotta enjoy his morning."

I sighed. "And a man's gotta do his therapy, Walter."

Walter let out a suffering sigh. "Fine, fine. Let's get this over with before you start taking away my snacks too."

Kate grinned. "She might. She's been real strict lately."

Walter clucked his tongue. "That's no good. No good at all."

I didn't dignify that with a response.

For a few blissful minutes, Walter actually focused. He did his balancing work, stopped talking, and put some real effort in. And then—because he clearly couldn't help himself—he sighed.

"You know, Doc, you gotta loosen up."

I frowned. "Excuse me?"

"You're too in your own head these days. You've always been kind of quiet and serious, but lately, it's like you're carrying around a whole second person on your shoulders."

I stiffened. "I'm fine, Walter."

Walter chuckled. "Mmm-hmm. And I'm a ballerina."

Kate snorted. "I'd pay to see that."

Walter grinned. "You and everybody else."

I exhaled, trying not to take the bait. "Walter, your balance—"

"My balance is fine," he said, patting his prosthetic again. "Can't exactly fall on this one. It's sturdier than the other."

I wanted to groan.

Walter gave me a knowing look. "You know what your problem is, Doc?"

I gave him a flat look. "Oh, please, enlighten me."

Walter just grinned. "You're always trying to steer the horse before you've even got a saddle on."

I blinked. "What?"

Walter gestured at Biz, who flicked his ears in our direction. "You don't just grab a horse and expect him to go exactly where you want right off the bat. You gotta let him settle. Gotta feel it out." He shot me a pointed look. "You can't control everything, Amber."

I didn't answer.

Because I didn't like not having control.

Walter sighed, finally finishing his last step. "Look, Doc, I know you. You're one of the good ones. But you gotta let go a little. Life's too short to try and micromanage it all."

My throat felt tight, and I had to clear it before I could speak.

Kate nudged me lightly. "That was... surprisingly deep."

Walter smirked. "I contain multitudes."

Kate chuckled, but I just nodded absently.

Because Walter had said a lot more than he realized.

Gage

THE EARLY AFTERNOON SUN hung low, casting long shadows over Ridgeview's main pasture. A dozen steers shifted restlessly in the sorting pen, their heavy bodies shuffling in the dirt as we prepped them for transport.

I gripped the edge of the fence, scanning the herd, barely hearing the hum of activity around me. Trent stood by the trailer, checking tags against his clipboard while Ethan and Liam wrangled the next few head toward the loading chute. Everything was running smoothly.

Or, at least, *they* were running smoothly.

I wasn't.

Because my mind was a thousand miles away.

Or more accurately, about fifteen miles away—at White Pines, with a certain woman who had taken up way too much real estate in my head.

I didn't even realize I was zoning out until Trent whistled sharply.

"Gage!"

I blinked, snapping my attention back to the present.

Trent gave me a pointed look. "Think you could stop daydreaming long enough to help?"

I sighed, rubbing the back of my neck. "Yeah. Sorry."

I climbed into the trailer, moving toward the steers already settled inside, checking that they were properly secured for the haul. The trailer rocked slightly as another steer stepped up the ramp behind me, Liam guiding it with practiced ease.

Trent leaned against the open gate, arms crossed, watching me like I was an uncooperative ranch hand instead of his older brother.

"Alright," he said, too casually. "Who is she?"

I frowned. "What?"

"You're distracted as all get-out, and last time I checked, calving season's not romantic enough to put that look on a man's face."

I rolled my eyes. "Trent—"

He held up a hand. "Don't even try to tell me it's nothing. You've been dragging your knuckles all morning, and now you're staring off into the fields like you're composing poetry."

Ethan, who had just stepped up beside us, snorted. "That would explain why he forgot to lock the back gate on the first trailer."

I shot him a look. "It was one time."

Liam smirked. "Today."

Trent exhaled, shaking his head. "Okay, seriously. What's going on?"

I leaned against the side of the trailer, trying to find an answer that didn't make me sound like an idiot.

Because the truth was?

I was distracted.

And it was because of Amber.

I couldn't get her out of my head. Not the way she'd looked at me after our drive in that ridiculous Mustang. Not the way her voice softened when she talked about her parents, her eyes full of worry. Not the way she'd fit against me when I'd kissed her—

I cleared my throat, pushing off the trailer. "I'm just thinking."

Trent raised a brow. "Dangerous habit."

I ignored him, stepping aside as Liam guided another steer into the trailer. "Lauren's new campaign is working, huh?"

Trent let it slide, turning his attention back to the clipboard. "Yeah. Orders picked up again this week. We're on track to move more beef this quarter than we expected."

I nodded, pretending to focus on the cattle. "That's good."

Trent didn't look convinced. "It is good. But you're clearly not thinking about beef, so just spit it out."

I hesitated.

Then, against my better judgment, I sighed. "Amber's parents moved into the assisted living place."

Trent frowned. "Isn't that what her sister wanted?"

"Yeah," I said. "But not Amber."

Trent rubbed his jaw. "And what about them? Are they happy?"

I exhaled. "Bob says they are."

Trent's brow lifted slightly. "But?"

I hesitated.

Because that was the problem.

I wanted to believe Bob. Wanted to take him at his word. But something about the whole thing wasn't sitting right.

Trent must have read something on my face, because his expression shifted. "You don't think they really wanted this, do you?"

I shook my head. "I think... I think they thought it was the right call. But I'm not sure it feels like home for them."

Trent was quiet for a moment.

Then he looked at me, his gaze sharper than before. "And this is just about her parents?"

I frowned. "What do you mean?"

Trent smirked. "You keep saying them, but it sure sounds like you're thinking about her."

I sighed. "She's upset, Trent. They didn't even tell her."

Trent nodded slowly. "And that's bothering you because...?"

Because I couldn't stand seeing her hurt.

Because every time I thought about how she'd sounded on the phone—angry, betrayed, lost—I wanted to fix it.

Because I liked her. A lot.

I just didn't know what the heck to do about it.

Trent watched me for a beat longer, then just shook his head, amused. "Man. I never thought I'd see the day."

I shot him a look. "What's that supposed to mean?"

He grinned. "The great Gage Langton, finally caught up over a woman."

I rolled my eyes. "Get back to work, Trent."

He chuckled, giving me a slap on the shoulder before turning toward the cab of the truck.

I sighed, glancing back out at the open fields before climbing in behind him.

Amber

I SAT AT MY desk, staring at the open spreadsheet in front of me. Numbers blurred together, words lost all meaning. I had emails to answer, schedules to finalize, a dozen things demanding my attention.

And yet, I couldn't focus.

Because my parents had moved.

They were settled.

And somehow, nothing about that felt settled to me.

I picked up my phone and scrolled through my call history, my thumb hovering over Mom.

They sounded happy when I talked to them. They said all the right things. So why did I feel like I was waiting for the other shoe to drop?

I exhaled sharply, then hit call.

The line rang twice before she picked up.

"Oh, sweetheart! Twice in one day? We're spoiled."

I forced a smile, even though she couldn't see it. "Just checking in."

She launched straight into details—how the weather was nice enough today to sit outside for a while, how she met a woman down the hall who used to teach music, how there was a book club she might join if she could find something she actually wanted to read.

It was all perfectly normal.

Too normal.

I listened, nodding in all the right places, waiting for something—anything—that would tell me she was really happy. That this wasn't just her putting on a show.

I didn't hear it.

"Dad around?" I asked carefully.

"Of course! Hold on."

There was a muffled shuffle as she passed the phone over.

Then his voice came through, warm and easy. "Hey, kiddo!"

I smiled faintly. "Hey, Dad."

"Everything good up there in cowboy country?"

I leaned back in my chair, staring at the ceiling. "Can't complain."

"That's good, that's good. I was just telling your mom, they've got a game night in the common room every week. We went last night—broke out the old Scrabble board. I'm pretty sure the guy sitting across from me was making up half the words he played, but I wasn't about to argue. Seemed real proud of himself."

I huffed a quiet laugh. "Did you at least beat him?"

"Pfft. Of course."

I shook my head, relaxing slightly.

It all sounded... fine.

But that was the problem.

It *sounded* fine.

Like a story he had rehearsed. Like a script.

He told me what they were doing. But not how they felt about it.

It didn't sound like *them*.

"Everything else going okay?" I asked, treading carefully.

"Yeah, yeah, everything's great," Dad said easily. "People here are real nice. Good folks."

There it was again. That easy, practiced answer. The same words he'd used when I asked before.

I wanted to push. Needed to push. But if I did, he'd just brush it off. Tell me not to worry.

I swallowed back my frustration and exhaled slowly. "Well... alright. Just wanted to check in."

"Appreciate it, sweetheart. You take care, okay?"

I nodded, even though he couldn't see me. "Yeah. You too."

I ended the call and let my phone rest against my desk, my fingers still curled around it.

They said they were fine.

They sounded fine.

So why didn't I believe them?

I ran my thumb absently over the screen, scrolling to the name I didn't want to admit I was looking for.

Gage.

The last time I called him, I'd barely let him speak. Hadn't given him a chance to explain.

And now?

Now I wasn't sure I was ready to hear that maybe—just maybe—I was the one who got it wrong.

I hesitated for a long moment.

Then I set my phone down.

And tried to pretend that everything was fine.

Even though I knew it wasn't.

Gage

T HE CATTLE WERE SETTLED for now, calves tucked against their mamas, breathing little clouds of steam into the cold February air. The morning had been busy, but the pace had finally slowed, giving me a rare stretch of quiet.

I should've been focused on Ridgeview. On the fences that needed mending, the feed schedule, the dozen little things that actually required my attention.

But my head wasn't on the job.

It was back at my phone, where I hadn't heard from Amber in days.

Bob's words kept circling my mind.

We had a scare.

She fell.

It made us realize we can't keep doing this alone.

The longer I thought about it, the less okay I was with it. I got why Bob hadn't told Amber—because I knew what it meant for a man like him to admit that he couldn't do it anymore. That he needed help. But Amber deserved to know. And when she found out?

It was going to wreck her. And I didn't want her to find that out when she was alone.

Near the barn, I spotted Liam and Ethan checking a fence line, heads bent together in easy conversation. They'd been talking about the future lately. Ethan had started looking into trade schools. Liam was still figuring it out.

But for the first time, they actually had options. A future. A home. A place.

And I was pretty proud of that. I felt like my family… like *I* had been some part of that for them—putting options before them they never saw before. And it made me think about the things my mom had said to me. The things Amber said to me.

My place was to help people feel safe. To grow, or even to break, if they needed to. And I figured that right now, Amber could use a bit of that safe feeling, if only I dared call her.

I pulled my gloves tighter, shoving my hands into my pockets. I could've reached out. I wanted to. But after the way we left things, I wasn't sure she was ready to hear from me yet.

Chapter Twenty-Six

Amber

T HE HOUSE WAS QUIET. Too quiet.

Sir Stumpy was curled up beside me on the couch, a solid, warm weight against my leg. The TV flickered in the background, low volume, casting shadows across the room. It was some show I wasn't really watching, something to fill the space. Normally, this was my favorite time of day—when the world settled, when I could just be alone with a book or a mug of tea and not have to answer to anyone.

But tonight... it wasn't enough.

I tapped my fingers against my mug, staring at the swirling tea leaves at the bottom.

Because no matter how much I tried to shove the thought away, Gage Langton kept pushing his way back in.

He was everywhere lately. In my dad's voice when he talked about the videos Gage had sent. In Kate's knowing glances when she mentioned Ridgeview. In the way my own thoughts lingered longer than they should, replaying conversations I shouldn't still be thinking about.

Because Gage wasn't just teasing anymore.

And worse... I wasn't just resisting anymore.

I pulled my legs up under me, adjusting the blanket, scowling at my own ridiculousness.

This—whatever *this* was—felt dangerous. Like something that could upend the way I'd carefully built my life.

I liked my life. I liked knowing where I stood. I liked that my heart wasn't tangled up in someone else's choices, that I didn't have to wonder if I was someone's *maybe*.

And Gage Langton was a *maybe* kind of man.

At least, that's what I'd told myself.

So why couldn't I stop thinking about him?

I let out a breath, dragging my gaze to the coffee table.

My phone sat there, face-up. Waiting.

I wasn't going to text him.

I wasn't.

I—

I grabbed my phone.

Before I could stop myself, I opened our messages.

This is a mistake.

A huge, massive mistake.

And I did it anyway.

Hey. You around?

I stared at the screen, my thumb hovering over the keyboard, my breath caught somewhere between regret and anticipation.

For a split second—just a split second—I considered deleting it.

But before I could, the three little dots popped up.

For you? Always.

My stomach did something annoying and traitorous, something warm and weightless.

That... wasn't teasing.

That wasn't Gage, the insufferable cowboy.

That was just him. Honest. Easy.

And somehow, that was so much worse.

I tossed the blanket off my legs, nearly knocking Sir Stumpy to the floor. He grumbled in protest, then jumped down and stalked off toward his food bowl.

I barely noticed, because I was already moving.

Already grabbing my keys.

Already stepping into my boots, hauling on my coat, stuffing my phone into my pocket.

I didn't overthink it.

Didn't make a pros and cons list.

I just got in my truck and drove.

Because for the first time in weeks, I actually knew what I wanted.

And it was waiting for me at Ridgeview.

Gage

THE SOUND OF HER truck rolling up Ridgeview's long driveway sent a jolt of something sharp and immediate through my chest.

It wasn't just the rumble of an engine. It wasn't just the creaking of the old gate as it opened for the truck. It was her.

And she hadn't called first. Just that one random text with no follow-up. I'd been starting to think she'd texted me by accident, meaning to send the message to someone else.

But now, fifteen minutes later, here she was.

I pulled off my gloves, stuffing them into my back pocket as the headlights swept across the yard. No questions. Just Amber, stepping out of the cab, hands shoved into her coat pockets like she wasn't sure what to do with them.

Her breath curled in the cold air, cheeks pink from the drive. She hesitated, just for a second, like she was debating whether this was a mistake.

I leaned against the fence, keeping my voice easy. "Didn't expect to see you tonight."

Her eyes flicked to mine, and something in them made my chest tighten. She looked different.

Not the usual Amber—the woman who was always in control, always with a plan.

No, this Amber looked... like she wasn't sure where she stood anymore. Like she was figuring this out as she went.

"I texted," she said.

I raised an eyebrow. "Oh. Is that what that was? A warning?"

She exhaled, not quite a sigh. "I don't really know why I came."

Her gaze darted away, shoulders tense, fingers flexing inside her coat pockets like she needed something to hold on to.

Amber Morris was never nervous. But right now, she looked at me like she'd stepped into something bigger than she'd planned for.

And if she had, I wasn't about to let her regret it.

I pushed off the fence, taking a slow step forward. "Want to come inside?"

She hesitated again, a moment of indecision playing across her face. Then, finally, she nodded.

That was all I needed.

But instead of heading toward the house, I led her into the barn.

The air inside was warmer, the scent of hay and horses wrapping around us. A few heads lifted in curiosity, ears twitching, tails flicking in the dim light. Amber reached out, running her hand down the nearest horse's mane, fingers smoothing through the strands like she was grounding herself.

Her shoulders eased—just a little.

"You're not going to make this easy on me, are you?"

The teasing edge in her voice wasn't sharp. It wasn't the usual armor she wore when she wanted to keep people at a distance.

This was different.

I tilted my head. "Make what easy?"

She shot me a look. "You know what."

I did.

But I wanted her to say it.

She traced absentminded circles against the horse's coat, her fingers lingering there. Then, finally, she let out a slow breath.

"You were just honoring my dad's wishes, weren't you?"

It wasn't quite a question. More like a realization.

I leaned against the stall door, my voice steady. "I'd do the same for you."

Her hand stilled.

Slowly, she turned to face me. She studied me, like she was trying to fit a puzzle piece into place.

Her lips parted, something flickering behind her eyes.

And for the first time since she'd stepped out of that truck... she didn't look like she wanted to run.

"...What about *your* wishes?" she asked softly. "What do you want, Gage Langton?"

I took a slow breath. Because for the first time, the answer was so easy.

I held her gaze.

"You."

She went still.

Then, before I could second-guess it, before she could come up with a reason to step back, I closed the space between us, reaching for her the way I'd been wanting to for weeks.

She stiffened. Just for a second.

And then, she leaned in.

The kiss was slow, unhurried. The kind of kiss that erased distance, that rewrote every sharp-edged moment between us into something softer.

The kind that made everything else—the cold, the past, the way we'd spent months at odds—fade into nothing.

When I finally pulled back, her eyes fluttered open, her breath mingling with mine in the quiet barn.

I brushed my thumb against her jaw. "Guess that makes four times."

She blinked, still looking a little dazed. "...Four?"

I grinned. "Kisses, Amber. But who's counting?"

Her lips parted like she wanted to argue. Then she shook her head, huffed a soft, breathy laugh, and whispered, "Make that five."

Amber

"T HERE'S SOMETHING I NEED to tell you."

I tensed, fingers curling into the lapel of his jacket. "What is it?"

He hesitated, like he was weighing his words. Then, carefully, "The reason *why*. I guess your mom had a fall."

I shook my head, trying to process. "Gina already told me. It was on the porch, right? She slipped on some ice—"

Gage's jaw tightened. "No. That was a different fall."

The words landed like a punch. I blinked, struggling to make sense of them.

His hands stayed steady on my shoulders, holding me together. "This one was inside. Your dad was outside working on something, and she blacked out in the kitchen."

I blinked. *No, no...*

"She hit the floor hard," he continued. "Scared the daylights out of your dad. By the time he got inside, she was disoriented. Shaky. Took her a while to get her bearings."

I covered my mouth with my hand, my heart hammering against my ribs. "Why—" My voice cracked. I swallowed and tried again. "Why didn't they tell me?"

Gage exhaled, his fingers flexing slightly against my waist before settling again. "They didn't want you to worry."

I let out a sharp laugh, but it didn't sound like me. It was hollow. Disbelieving. "That worked out great."

He let me have that moment, just watching as I tried to gather myself. I turned away, swiping at the tear that slipped down my cheek. I wasn't going to cry.

I *wasn't*.

But the more I thought about it—about my mom, alone on the kitchen floor, about my dad rushing in too late, about how they must have looked at each other and known, without saying a word, that it was time...

I couldn't stop another tear from slipping free.

A rough chuckle rumbled in Gage's chest, and before I could react, his thumb brushed against my cheek, catching it.

I jerked my gaze to his, startled by the tenderness in the gesture.

His lips tugged at the corner, his voice low. "This time, I told your dad I wasn't keeping it from you."

I swallowed hard. "So why am I hearing it from you instead of them?"

Gage sighed, shaking his head slightly. "I think... I think your dad *wanted* me to be the one to tell you."

I frowned. "Why?"

He smoothed a hand down my arm, his touch steady, deliberate. "Because he didn't want you to hear it over the phone. He figured if you were upset, you'd need someone here."

I thought about that for a second. And, against my will, a breathy, broken laugh escaped me. "He set me up. Again."

Gage's lips twitched, his thumb still lingering on my cheek. "Seems that way."

I shook my head. "Of course, he did. It's his M.O."

Because that was my dad. Taking care of me, even when I didn't ask him to.

Even when *I* was the one who was supposed to be taking care of *him*.

I exhaled slowly, letting my hand drop, letting Gage's warmth pull me back from the tangle of emotions twisting inside me.

I met his gaze. "And you? You were just gonna... let me show up here and fall apart on you?"

His voice was soft. "Only if you needed to."

I stared at him.

Because somehow, that was exactly the answer I needed to hear.

And before I could second-guess it—before I could let the weight of everything else pull me back into my own head—I closed the space between us, pressing my forehead lightly against his chest.

For once, I didn't have to hold everything together. Not while his arms were holding me.

Gage

AMBER WAS STILL CURLED against my chest, her breathing slow and uneven, when her stomach growled so loudly it startled the both of us.

For a second, she froze.

Then, before I could stop myself, a chuckle slipped out.

She groaned and buried her face against me. "I hate everything."

I grinned. "Well, that seems dramatic."

She swatted at my arm but didn't move.

I dipped my head toward hers. "You know, I was just thinking to myself, 'Man, this moment could really use a loud, undignified stomach noise.' And here you go, delivering."

Amber huffed a quiet laugh against my shirt, and something inside me settled.

That was what I wanted.

Not just to hold her while she let herself break—but to be the one who made her laugh after.

I ran a hand down her back, slow and steady. "Come inside."

She sighed. "Gage—"

"You need food, Doc."

She tipped her head back, leveling me with a look. "You ever gonna stop calling me that?"

I pretended to consider it. "Probably not. Makes you sound smarter than me, which we both know you already are."

Amber sighed again, but this time, I saw the corner of her mouth twitch.

Yeah. That was better.

I took her hand, threading my fingers through hers, and didn't give her time to argue before leading her toward the house.

The door was unlocked—because of course it was—and the moment we stepped inside, the warmth of the kitchen wrapped around us, carrying the scent of slow-cooked roast and fresh bread.

Mom glanced up from where she was setting the table and smiled. "Oh, good. You're just in time."

Amber tensed slightly beside me, but I didn't let go of her hand. This was a statement—loud and bold to my family, that she was mine and I was hers, and that was that.

Across the room, Liam and Ethan were shoving each other playfully near the fridge, arguing over who got the last of the sweet tea.

Trent and Lauren sat at the table, deep in conversation, but when they looked up and saw us, Trent raised a brow.

His gaze flicked to our joined hands.

Then, slowly, a grin spread across his face. "Well, dad gum."

Amber stiffened, and I shot Trent a look. "Stop."

He chuckled and nudged Lauren. "Told you it was only a matter of time."

Lauren smiled warmly at Amber. "Welcome to the circus."

Amber shot me a look that very clearly said, *I will kill you if they make a big deal out of this.*

I squeezed her fingers in reassurance before turning to my mom. "You made plenty, right?"

Mom waved a hand. "Like I'd ever make a meal that wouldn't feed an army."

Amber hesitated.

I could feel it—the weight of her uncertainty, the way she was still getting used to this.

To not being an outsider looking in.

So I didn't give her a chance to overthink it.

I tugged her gently toward the table, nudging her into a chair before sitting down next to her.

Mom passed her the mashed potatoes without missing a beat. "Amber, sweetheart, you like butter, don't you?"

Amber blinked, clearly still catching up. "Uh... yeah?"

Mom smiled and pushed a dish of melted butter toward her. "Good. It would be a shame if you couldn't have dairy because I don't know any other way to make the best potatoes. Help yourself."

Amber hesitated for only a second before reaching for the spoon.

And just like that, she was part of the table.

Part of *us*.

The conversation flowed around us, easy and familiar, the kind of lively back-and-forth that came naturally in a big, close-knit family.

Ethan and Liam made fun of each other. Lauren and Trent kept up their endless debate over ranch logistics. My mom asked Amber how work had been lately.

And the more Amber relaxed, the more I saw something in her expression shift. Like maybe—for the first time—she was starting to realize she belonged here. With us.

With *me*.

I nudged her gently with my knee under the table, and when she glanced at me, I murmured, "Told you coming inside was a good idea."

She rolled her eyes but didn't argue.

And when I reached for her free hand under the table, lacing our fingers together, she didn't pull away.

Chapter Twenty-Seven

Amber

T HEY LOOKED... OKAY.

Too okay.

I studied the screen, taking in the image of my parents sitting side by side in their new apartment at the assisted living facility. The place was nice enough—bright, clean, well-furnished. There was even a painting of wildflowers on the wall behind them, the kind Mom would have picked out herself.

Dad was grinning as he launched into a story about some group outing they'd gone on, and Mom smiled along, nodding at the right moments. I tried to let it ease the knot in my stomach, tried to tell myself this was good. They were happy. They had people around them, things to do.

But something in my gut kept whispering that this wasn't right.

I wanted to believe them.

I just... didn't.

The conversation drifted, circling through the usual topics—work, the weather, Mom reminding me to eat more vegetables like I was still a kid. I answered on autopilot, nodding and responding when I was supposed to, but I barely heard myself.

Because I was thinking about something else.

Or more accurately, some*one*.

Gage.

I hadn't told them yet. Not because I was keeping it from them, but because—until now—it hadn't felt like something to tell. But after last night? After everything we'd finally admitted to each other?

This wasn't just some harmless flirting anymore.

It was real.

I hesitated.

Then, before I could talk myself out of it— "I wanted to tell you guys something."

Dad grinned like he already knew what was up.

Mom tilted her head curiously. "What is it, sweetheart?"

I exhaled, steadying myself. "Gage and I are... well, I don't know exactly how to define it. We're... together."

For a second, silence. Then Dad's grin exploded. "Took you long enough!"

Mom's eyebrows lifted slightly before her lips curled into a delighted smile. "Oh," she murmured, like she was savoring the idea. "I knew I liked that boy."

I blinked.

What?

This was... not the reaction I expected.

"You knew?" I repeated.

Dad chuckled. "I had a hunch."

Mom tilted her head. "The way he was always around? The way he looked at you? Amber, honey, it was obvious."

I frowned.

It had *not* been obvious.

Not to me.

I opened my mouth to argue—but then snapped it shut, because what was I even arguing?

That Gage *didn't* look at me like that? That he hadn't been around more than any reasonable cowboy should?

Yeah.

I had nothing.

I let out a slow breath, shaking my head as Dad chuckled like this was the best thing he'd heard all day.

"You really like him?" Mom asked gently.

I thought about that for all of half a second before nodding. My voice was shaking when I finally forced it out. "A whole lot more than *'like,'* Mom."

Mom's smile softened. "Good. That's all that matters."

But the way she said it made something twist in my chest. Like she wanted to believe it. Like she wanted to hold onto the idea that something was going right.

And that's when I knew for sure.

She was faking it.

Not the part about being happy for Gage and me. The rest—the smiles, the happy stories about her new friends at the facility, how "comfortable" their room was... It was all fake.

Dad had moved on to another story, this time about a guy he'd met at breakfast the other day. He was still smiling, still talking like this whole thing had been an adventure. But Mom...

Mom looked tired. The kind of tired you couldn't sleep off.

She was smiling, nodding in the right places, acting like she was adjusting just fine.

But it wasn't *her.*

I knew my mother. And my mother didn't pretend things were fine. She said it straight, whether you wanted to hear it or not.

I almost asked.

But before I could, she shifted in her chair and sighed lightly. "Well, this was nice."

I swallowed hard, nodding. "Yeah."

Mom hesitated, then gave me that familiar soft smile. "You're happy, sweetheart?"

The way she asked it—like my happiness was the most important thing—made my throat tighten.

I nodded. "I am." Mom's smile stayed in place, but it didn't quite reach her eyes.

I wanted to ask her.

I *should* have asked her.

But instead, I let it go. Because I knew—*I knew*—she would just tell me what I wanted to hear.

I wasn't sure what scared me more. That she was miserable.

Or that she was trying to convince herself she wasn't.

Gage

A MONTH AGO, I wouldn't have called myself the responsible one.

A month ago, I wouldn't have expected to be standing here, watching Liam climb onto a green-broke gelding, roping like he had something to prove.

A month ago, I wouldn't have expected to be settled.

But a month ago, I hadn't figured it out yet.

The sun was bright despite the lingering bite of early spring, casting long shadows over the pens. The bawling of calves echoed across the pasture as we worked through the branding line, the steady rhythm of roping, flanking, and sorting filling the space like clockwork. It was a good kind of busy—the kind that didn't let your brain wander too much.

Or at least, it was supposed to be.

Luke and Dusty had come over to help today, and I was glad of it. This was always a whopper of a job, and we never had enough time to get it done, so the more hands, the better. I swung my loop, letting it sail toward a sprinting calf. The rope landed clean around its hind legs, and I set my dally, letting Banner take the weight. Dusty was already moving in to flank it, but my head wasn't fully in it.

I kept thinking about Amber.

About how life had shifted so quietly, so easily, that I hardly realized how much had changed until I caught myself looking forward to things that weren't just ranch work.

Like seeing her at White Pines.

Like getting a text from her during the day, usually something dry and sarcastic that made me grin.

Like knowing, without a doubt, that at the end of a long day, she was the person I wanted to talk to.

"Langton, wake up," Luke called from across the pen, tipping his hat back. "You planning to stand there all day or actually work?"

I shook my head and loosened the rope, letting the calf go once the brand was set.

Trent laughed as he tossed the branding iron back into the fire. "Gage's got his head in the clouds."

"Yeah, that's new," Dusty added.

I ignored them, resetting my rope.

Luke rode up beside me, watching as Liam took his first practice swing from horseback. "Kid's got decent form."

I nodded. "Been working at it."

Luke smirked. "And look at you. All responsible and mentor-like."

I shot him a dry look. "Don't start."

He chuckled, reining his horse around. "Nah, just saying. You're not exactly the last man standing anymore."

I didn't reply.

Because I knew what he meant.

For years, it had just been me. Watching my brothers settle down, get married, take on new roles in the family. I hadn't thought much about it—figured my time would come when it came.

And now?

Now it had.

Luke shook his head, still grinning. "I'm happy for you, man."

I exhaled, rolling my shoulders. "Yeah?"

"Yeah." He tipped his hat. "Now stop standing around and rope something."

I grinned, kicking Banner forward as another calf broke loose.

A month ago, I wouldn't have known how to answer Luke's teasing.

T HE ROPE SNAPPED TAUT as I dallied off, the calf kicking up dust as Banner twisted to keep the rope tight. Across the pen, Dusty and Liam moved in, working fast and efficient, while the brand sizzled against hide, leaving behind the mark that would prove ownership. The air smelled like burnt hair and sweat, the familiar scent of branding season.

I was just about to swing for the next calf when my phone vibrated in my pocket.

I ignored it. My hands were full, and branding season didn't stop for phone calls. A minute later, the voicemail beeped.

I let the next calf go before pulling back and reaching for my phone. I wasn't the type to check messages right away, but something about this one sat wrong before I even saw the name on the screen.

Bob Morris.

Frowning, I pulled Banner out of the branding pen, still seated in the saddle as I tapped the screen. The voicemail wasn't really a message—just muffled noise, like maybe he hadn't hung up fast enough. A chair creaking, a quiet sigh, then nothing.

That wasn't normal.

Bob was the kind of guy who left short, to-the-point messages when he actually needed something. The kind of guy who didn't call just to chat.

I hesitated.

Then I dialed him back.

The phone rang twice before he picked up. "Hey, son."

His voice was that happy, casual tone. But not *real* casual. The kind of casual a man used when he didn't want to admit something was wrong.

I pulled my hat off, running a hand through my hair. "Hey, Bob. You called?"

A pause. Then, "Yeah. Yeah, I did."

Another pause.

Too long.

I swung my leg over Banner's back, letting him stand while I waited him out. Bob wasn't a man you pushed. He had to get there on his own.

Finally, he sighed. "I was thinking... might be time for Sherri and me to get out of town for a few days."

I straightened. "Yeah? Thinking about coming this way?"

"Maybe."

Another hesitation.

I frowned. "What's wrong?"

Bob chuckled, but there wasn't much humor in it. "Nothing's wrong, son. Just figured we could use a change of scenery."

That wasn't an answer.

I leaned forward, resting my forearm against the saddle horn. "You sure about that?"

Bob sighed again. "It's Sherri. She's..." He trailed off, then cleared his throat. "She's not settling in like we all hoped she would."

My grip tightened around the reins.

"And you?" I asked carefully.

Bob let out a breath. "I'm doing what needs doing."

I exhaled, glancing toward the branding pen where the others were still working. "Bob."

Silence.

Then—softly—"I don't have much choice, do I?"

The words hit hard.

I stared at the ground, jaw tight.

Because yeah, maybe in Bob's mind, he didn't have options. He'd made a decision. Picked a path. And now, he figured he had to live with it, whether he liked it or not.

But that wasn't true.

And I had a decision to make, too.

I lifted my head, looking around at the branding pen. The smell of cows and churned-up dirt filled the air, the crackling pop of the branding iron hissing through the dust. Liam and Ethan were on the sorting crew, moving calves into the chute, working in tandem like they'd been doing this their whole lives.

They weren't perfect, but they didn't need me to hold their hands, either.

Dusty was on a fresh horse now, roping clean and true, like he always did. Luke and Trent had a system going. The work was getting done.

And still—my gut twisted at the thought of leaving them to handle the rest without me.

This was my job. My place. The work needed doing.

But what was more important?

If I really was this so-called "leader" my mom and Amber seemed to think I was, then that meant making the call. Figuring out what mattered most.

And right now, the right thing—the thing that mattered—was Amber's family.

I could trust my brothers. I could trust the twins.

But Amber?

She needed me.

And Bob?

Bob needed someone to tell him that he did, in fact, have a choice.

I exhaled, setting my shoulders.

"Pack your suitcase, Bob," I said. "Amber and I will be there to-morrow."

Amber

I LOVED THIS JOB.

And for the first time in a while, I could feel that again.

The whole spring had been a blur—family stress, the wedding, Gage—all of it had pulled me in so many directions. And somewhere along the way, I'd started feeling like I was always behind, like I was constantly trying to catch up to my own life.

But lately?

Lately, I was here. In the moment. And it felt good.

Rocky walked steadily beside me, his hooves pressing soft prints into the sand as I kept my hand light on Ryan's knee. He sat tall in the saddle, his little hands wrapped firmly around the reins.

"Doing okay?" I asked, glancing up at him.

Ryan nodded, his lips pressing together in quiet determination. "I think so."

I smiled, watching as he guided Rocky—a steady, patient geld-ing—along the rail. His back stayed straight, his hands steady. No gripping the saddle horn like a lifeline. No tensing with every shift of the horse beneath him.

His mom had told me once that he didn't trust his own body. That cerebral palsy made him feel like he was fighting against himself all the time.

But right now?

Right now, he looked like he belonged here.

Kate leaned against the gate, arms folded, watching as he maneuvered Rocky through a set of cones. "Think he's ready to trot?"

Ryan's eyes widened, but he didn't immediately shake his head. Progress.

I squeezed his leg gently. "What do you think, bud? You up for it?"

He hesitated, flexing his fingers on the reins. Then—after a long, shaky breath—he nodded.

My heart swelled.

"Alright," I said. "We'll take it slow. You set the pace."

Ryan's grip tightened, but he sat a little straighter.

I gave Rocky a quiet cue, and he shifted into a smooth, easy trot, so slow it barely even counted as a trot. Ryan gasped faintly, his hands twitching toward the saddle horn—but then, he adjusted.

I watched the exact moment it clicked.

The moment his body moved *with* the horse instead of against him.

The moment he realized he could *do* this.

Kate grinned, leaning farther into the gate. "Well, look at that."

I swallowed the lump in my throat, warmth spreading through my chest. "Yeah."

Because for the first time, Ryan wasn't just sitting on a horse. He was *riding*. When he let himself trust it.

His laughter burst out, bright and unfiltered. "I'm doing it!"

Kate beamed. "You sure are."

I watched as Rocky carried him forward, moving steady beneath him, supporting him.

This was why I did this. This was what I'd been missing lately—the reason, the fulfillment.

Not the stress. Not the endless family drama. Just this.

The feeling of making a difference. And for the first time in weeks, I felt at peace.

Right up until my phone rang.

I never had my ringer on during therapy sessions. The only reason it was even on now was because I'd forgotten to switch it off after lunch.

I ignored it as it kept buzzing in my back pocket, my focus still on Ryan as he guided Rocky through another lap. But then Kate glanced up from the rail, brows knitting slightly.

"You gonna get that?"

I sighed, already reaching to silence it. "It's probably just—"

My fingers stilled when I saw the name on the screen.

Gage.

My heart did a weird little flip—the good kind. But right behind it, something else flickered in my mind. Gage never called me in the middle of the day. Ever. He knew I was working, and he respected that.

So why was he calling now?

A prickle of unease crept along my spine. I hesitated for half a second, then slid the phone from my pocket and answered.

"Hey," I said, tucking it between my ear and shoulder as I turned away from the arena. "What's up?"

His voice was comfortable. Familiar. Safe. "Hey." A pause. "You busy?"

I frowned slightly, glancing around the barn. "I'm at work. Something wrong?"

Another pause. "When do you wrap up?"

I stilled. Something in the way he said it made the hair on the back of my neck stand up. My fingers curled a little tighter around the phone.

"Gage, what's going on?"

He exhaled like he was bracing himself. Like he knew this wasn't something I wanted to hear. "Your dad called me."

My stomach dipped.

I turned, pressing my free hand against the fence post, my voice careful. "What now? And why does he always call you instead of me?"

"Amber... they're not happy."

The world around me kept moving—Kate talking softly to one of the horses, the rhythmic sound of Rocky's hooves as he carried Ryan through the last set of cones.

But I stopped.

"Well... I could have told you that. But why is he calling now?"

"They're struggling," Gage said simply. "Your dad said your mom is miserable."

I swallowed hard. "So, they're finally admitting it? All our phone calls lately have been full of nothing but sunshine and rainbows."

"They were pretending."

"Yeah, I got that. I still don't know why they had to pretend to me, but Dad tells you the truth."

"Because he's a dad. Because he doesn't want to worry his little girl. I don't know, probably lots of reasons. Bottom line, they've finally admitted it now."

Yeah. I sucked in some air and made myself calm down. A couple of months ago, I would've lost it over the fact that my parents had told Gage before they told me. I would've been furious. Hurt. Probably a little of both.

But right now? Right now, I wasn't mad. Because I knew Gage.

If Dad had called him, it wasn't because my dad didn't trust me. It was because Gage was the person he trusted to help fix it. The person he trusted to help *me*.

I let out a slow breath, turning toward the paddock. Ryan was still grinning, his shoulders relaxed, his confidence growing with each lap.

"What do we do?"

Gage didn't hesitate.

"Take tomorrow off. I'll pick you up at six with coffee for the road."

I closed my eyes for a second, my chest expanding on an inhale. No doubt. No second-guessing.

"We're going to get them?" I asked, already knowing the answer.

"Yeah."

Simple.

Final.

And for the first time in weeks, I didn't feel stuck.

Didn't feel like I was standing in the middle of something I couldn't fix.

I had Gage.

And together, we were just... fixing it.

Chapter Twenty-Eight

Amber

THE HOUSE FELT DIFFERENT already.

I carried my mom's overnight bag into the spare bedroom, setting it down by the dresser as she stood by the window, gazing out like she'd just stepped into another world.

"Oh, Amber," she murmured, pressing a hand to her heart. "Look at that view."

I turned, following her gaze. From this angle, you could see the fields stretching up the hillside, past my property line, rolling up toward the base of the mountains in the distance. The late afternoon light turned the peaks golden, casting long shadows across the land.

It was beautiful.

But it wasn't new.

Not to me.

I'd seen this view every day for years. But for my mom, it was different. A reminder of something she'd lost.

I swallowed. "It's pretty nice."

She exhaled softly, then turned toward the bed, smoothing a hand over the quilt like she was testing its softness. "This is lovely. I can't believe you're putting us up here."

I shot her a grin. "Mom, it's not like I had a choice."

She laughed—the first real laugh I'd heard from her for a while. "Oh? You're saying you were forced into this?"

I rolled my eyes, but it was teasing, not annoyed. "Gage wouldn't let me say no."

She let out a thoughtful hum, then settled onto the mattress. "That boy..." She trailed off, shaking her head. "He's something special."

I bit the inside of my cheek, ignoring the way my heart flipped at the casual way she said it.

Before I could respond, Gage strolled in, carrying my dad's duffel in one hand like it weighed nothing. He glanced between us, brow raised. "You two having a moment?"

Mom smiled. "Just admiring the view."

He nodded and ducked to peek out the window. "Yeah, it's nice here."

She shook her head. "No, I meant you, Gage. You're a good man."

To his credit, he didn't look fazed by the praise—just tipped his hat like he was accepting a business deal. "Well, thank you, ma'am."

I groaned. "Please don't encourage him."

Gage smirked at me, but my mom just laughed. "Oh, I like him."

I sighed, running a hand down my face. "This is already out of control."

My dad stepped into the doorway, arms crossed, watching the exchange with quiet amusement. "You ladies done fussing over the cowboy?"

Mom smiled up at him. "That depends. Are you jealous?"

Dad snorted. "Yeah, I'm a cowboy, too. I mean... I rode some horses in my day. Check this out." He stole Gage's hat with an audacity that made my jaw drop. Nobody, but *nobody* messed with a cowboy's hat!

But my dad did, apparently. He tapped it down on his head and spread his arms, grinning at my mom. "Whatcha think, darlin'?" he drawled.

Mom smothered a laugh. "Oh, honey. You don't need to impress me, you know."

I couldn't hold it back. I sputtered, covering my mouth with my hand. "Burn!"

Gage grinned and took his hat back. "I mean, I get it, Bob. I'm a lot to compete with."

I smacked his arm. "Out. Both of you. Let Mom rest."

Dad chuckled but gave my mom's shoulder a quick squeeze before stepping back into the hallway. Gage lingered for half a second longer, his gaze flicking to me, like he wanted to say something.

I lifted a brow. "What?"

He just shook his head slightly, the corner of his mouth tilting up. "Nothing. Just thinking."

And with that, he followed my dad out, leaving me alone with my mom.

She watched him go, then turned back to me with a knowing look.

I pointed at her. "No."

She blinked, all innocent. "No, what?"

"Whatever you're thinking. Stop it."

Her eyes twinkled. "I didn't say anything."

I exhaled, rubbing my forehead. "Mom."

She just hummed again, then leaned back on the pillows, letting out a satisfied sigh. "It really is beautiful here."

I let her have it.

Because for the first time in weeks, she actually sounded like she meant it.

Gage

B OB WAS TALKING WITH his mouth full again.

I leaned back in my chair, hiding a smirk as Amber's mom swatted at him.

"Bob, for heaven's sake, chew before you speak," she scolded, exasperated but fond.

Amber snorted. "That's a lost cause, Mom. He's been doing that since I was five."

Bob swallowed and pointed his fork at his daughter. "And yet, I'm still alive."

"Barely," Sherri muttered, shaking her head as she picked up her glass of iced tea.

Amber shot me a look across the table, and I grinned. I liked this. This comfortable, easy rhythm.

Their banter had a lifetime of history behind it, but it wasn't just that. It was the way Amber softened when her mom teased her, the way Bob pretended to be offended, the way the whole conversation bounced around like a well-worn routine.

I didn't just like it.

I wanted it.

Not just for tonight. Not just for a visit.

For good.

They belonged here.

Not here, in Amber's house. It was too small for them all to be on top of each other forever. But here, in this town, where Amber could stop worrying about them from hundreds of miles away. Where Bob could tinker and fix things to his heart's content. Where Sherri could wake up every morning to the sight of the mountains and her own kitchen.

It wasn't a new thought. It had nagged at me before, creeping in like something that wouldn't let go. But now?

Now, it felt like the only way.

The only thing that made sense.

Amber got up to clear the table, but I beat her to it, grabbing Bob's empty plate.

He scowled. "What are you doing?"

"Helping."

Bob started to get up. "I'll get my own plate."

Sherri reached over and patted his hand. "Honey, just let the boy be nice."

Bob muttered something under his breath but didn't argue when I took the dishes.

Amber giggled as I passed her on my way to the sink. "Making yourself useful?"

I shrugged. "It's the neighborly thing to do."

She rolled her eyes but didn't stop me.

Yeah.

I wanted this for good.

T HE PORCH WAS QUIET. Cool air rolled in from the fields, carrying the scent of damp earth and pine. Amber wrapped her arms around herself as she leaned against the railing, watching me.

"You're quiet," she said.

I turned my hat in my hands, my heart full to bursting with what I wanted to say.

Then, before I could talk myself out of it— "Marry me."

Amber blinked, shaking her head like she hadn't heard me right. "I—what?"

I grinned. "You heard me."

She let out a startled laugh, eyes searching mine. "Gage, are you serious?"

"Yeah," I said. "I'm serious."

She opened her mouth, then closed it, like she wasn't sure where to start.

I didn't give her the chance to overthink it. "Amber, I want this. I want you." I gestured toward the house, toward where her parents were settling in for the night. "And I want them. I want all of it."

Her lips parted slightly.

I pressed on. "I want to know that your mom and dad are safe, that they don't have to force themselves to be happy in some place that's not home. I want them here, where they belong. And you—" I exhaled, my voice softening. "I want you standing next to me while we figure it out."

She stared at me, something flickering in her eyes.

Then, finally, a teasing lilt slipped into her voice. "Are you proposing to me or my dad?"

I huffed a laugh, shaking my head. "Both."

Her eyebrows shot up.

I tightened my hands at her waist, firm but easy. "Marrying you means taking care of them, too. It means taking all of it. And I wouldn't want it any other way."

She gave a short, disbelieving laugh, running a hand through her hair. "Gage, we haven't even been together that long."

"So?"

"So," she repeated, shaking her head. "How do you know this is what you want?"

I stepped closer, reaching out to tuck a loose strand of hair behind her ear. "I was sure the moment I really saw you for the first time. The day you laughed at the idea of us ever being a couple."

Amber let out a soft, breathy laugh. "That's what did it?"

I shrugged. "What can I say? I liked your sass."

She lifted a brow.

I leaned in. "Still do."

Amber searched my face, her gaze softer now.

"You really think we can do this?" she asked.

"I'm not worried about my end of it. The question is for you. Think you can put up with *me?*"

Amber swallowed. "Please say it again."

I swallowed, resting a hand on her waist. "I want you, Amber. I want them, too. And I don't want to spend another second pretending like I don't know that for sure."

She let out a slow breath.

Then, so quietly I almost didn't hear it—

"Back at you, cowboy."

Amber

T HE MORNING AIR WAS starting to pick up the fragrances of
spring cherry blossoms as I stepped onto the porch, shrugging
into my coat. I was halfway through pulling my hair out from under
the collar when I heard the rumble of an engine. A familiar Ridgeview
truck rolled up the driveway, dust kicking up behind the tires.

I frowned. Gage hadn't mentioned coming by.

He pulled to a stop, hopped out, and strolled toward the house like
he'd done it a hundred times before. Like he belonged here.

"Morning," he greeted, flashing a grin as he tossed a set of keys
toward my dad.

Dad caught them on reflex, blinking down at his hand. "What's
this?"

Gage rested a boot on the bottom porch step, eyes gleaming with
mischief. "Figured you might need some wheels while you're here."
He jerked a thumb toward the truck. "Ridgeview loaner."

Dad's brows lifted. "You're just handing me a ranch truck?"

Gage shrugged. "Better than letting you get any ideas about renting
that red Mustang up the road."

Dad straightened, eyes lighting up. "What's this about a red Mustang?"

Gage chuckled. "Forget I said anything." Then, with a glance my
way, he added, "And if you don't, just make sure Amber doesn't hear
about it."

Dad smirked like he was already plotting, and Gage shook his head,
muttering something under his breath before turning to me.

"Hey, you heading up to White Pines?"

I nodded slowly, still watching him like he might pull out another surprise. "Yeah, why?"

"Chase is working on some fixtures up there. Thought I'd give him a hand." He tilted his head toward my truck. "Mind giving me a ride?"

I narrowed my eyes. "This was your plan all along, wasn't it?"

Gage grinned. "Can't prove it."

I rolled my eyes but motioned for him to hop in. He pulled the passenger door shut behind him, settling into the seat like he belonged there. I pulled out of the driveway, glancing at him from the corner of I glanced at him. "So, what's the deal?"

Gage stretched his legs out, rolling his shoulders like he was getting comfortable, but the way he rubbed the back of his neck told me he was sitting on something. "Been thinking about something."

I raised a brow. "That's dangerous."

His lips twitched, but he didn't take the bait. Instead, he tapped his fingers against his knee, quiet for a second before finally saying, "Ridgeview's got enough acreage. Zoning lets us put up three more dwellings." He turned his head toward me, his gaze steady. "I was thinking we could do with two."

I frowned, glancing at him before turning my eyes back to the road. "For what?"

"For us," he said simply. Then, softer, "And for them."

I sucked in a breath, my hands tightening around the wheel.

For us. And for them.

It hit all at once—what he was saying, what he was offering. A home. A place for my parents, close enough that I could look after them, but not so close that they'd feel like they were intruding.

If they'd go for it.

I let out a breath. "Gage..."

He didn't say anything, just kept watching me, giving me space to take it in.

I shook my head slightly, still trying to catch up. "You—this is—you've really thought this through?"

His mouth quirked. "Didn't just come up with it five minutes ago, if that's what you're asking."

I gave him a look. "Not what I meant."

"I know," he admitted, his voice softer now. "Yeah, I've thought about it. A lot. And the more I do, the more it just... makes sense."

I swallowed, heart knocking against my ribs. "You don't think it's too fast?"

Gage exhaled, like he'd already had this argument with himself. "Amber, I know what I want."

My throat tightened. "And you're sure you won't regret it?"

He turned fully in his seat, waiting until I met his gaze before he said, steady and sure, "Not a chance."

And just like that, something inside me settled.

Because this man—this infuriating, teasing, dependable man—wasn't just thinking about our future.

He was building it.

Gage

Bob pushed open his door before the truck had fully stopped, stepping out with the kind of energy that said he was itching to stretch his legs. He adjusted his hat, took a few steps forward, and let out a low whistle.

Amber's mom wasn't far behind. She moved more cautiously, one hand trailing along the truck door as she stepped down, but when she lifted her head, her breath hitched.

Amber sat beside me, her hands still folded tight in her lap. She hadn't moved yet, her eyes locked on her parents, waiting.

I reached for the door handle. "Come on, Baby."

She exhaled and followed.

The land stretched wide in front of us, the valley opening into rolling green pastures below, a distant river cutting through the fields like a ribbon of silver. The mountains stood tall against a clear blue sky, their peaks still dusted with the last remnants of spring snow. The afternoon sun was warm, the breeze just enough to carry the scent of fresh earth and wild sage.

Bob took it all in, nodding to himself, like he was already making calculations in his head.

Amber's mom just stared. Then, softly—so soft I almost missed it—she whispered, "Oh."

Amber turned to me, eyes questioning. "This is the spot?"

I nodded. "Right here."

She swallowed, looking back at her parents.

Bob shifted his weight, hands on his hips, eyes scanning the land. "Now, this..." He let out another low whistle. "This is somethin'."

Amber's mom finally looked at her husband. "It's beautiful," she said simply.

Amber let out a slow breath.

And I knew right then—this wasn't just a maybe anymore. They weren't just considering it. They were already picturing themselves here.

No one spoke.

Finally, Bob glanced around, his sharp, practical mind already kicking into gear. "So how does this work, son?"

I grinned. "Simple," I said. "We build you a home. Stick built on site—I happen to know a guy— or if you're in a real hurry we get a nice manufactured."

"They have great floorplans," he mused. "Sherri and I looked at one that had an ADA bathroom, standard. And all on one level, too."

"Well, there you go. Choice is yours."

A hush settled over us.

Then, after a long moment, Sherri looked at Bob. "We could really do this?" she asked softly.

Bob ran a hand over his jaw, thinking. Then, without hesitation, he nodded. "Yeah," he said. "Yeah, I think we could."

Sherri exhaled. Then—just barely—she smiled.

I looked at Amber.

She was watching them, her lips pressed together, her eyes bright, her fingers twisting absently in the sleeve of her coat. I nudged her gently with my elbow, just enough to get her to look up.

"This was their choice," I murmured.

She nodded. "Yeah," she whispered. "I know."

I wanted to tell her more. Wanted to say that I'd hoped for something like this all along—that this was where they belonged. But she already knew. I could see it in the way she watched her parents, her expression softening as her mom leaned into Bob's side, as her dad wrapped an arm around her shoulders.

Amber let out a slow breath, then turned to me fully. Her voice was steady when she spoke. "And you talked to your family about this?"

"Yeah. And I have their full blessing. Matter of fact, I haven't seen Mom that excited since the day a squirrel got into her pantry."

She laughed, then threaded her arms around my chest and leaned her face into my shoulder. "So Ridgeview..."

"Is home," I finished. "For all of us."

Epilogue

Amber

I HAD NEVER REALIZED how quiet the mountains could be.

The early morning light spilled over the ridge, turning the distant peaks a soft, hazy gold. The pastures below stretched wide and green, rolling toward the horizon, the faint outlines of cattle moving lazily in the distance. Ridgeview was waking up, the world easing into motion, but up here, on the porch of our house—the house I now shared with Gage—everything felt still.

Peaceful.

Home.

The screen door creaked open behind me, and a second later, Gage stepped out, his own coffee in hand. He was already dressed for the day, a Langton Ridgeview hoodie—one of Lauren's newest ideas—hanging loose over his shoulders, his jeans slung low on his hips. He bumped his shoulder against mine as he leaned against the railing.

"You gonna stare at the mountains all morning, or are you gonna help me finish your parents' deck?"

I exhaled a quiet laugh, following his gaze down the hill to where the newly built house stood, framed perfectly against the peaks. My dad had claimed the best view before the foundation was even poured.

Not that I blamed him.

"They don't even have all their furniture in there yet," I pointed out, taking a slow sip of coffee.

"Yeah, well." Gage took a drink from his own mug, his lips twitching. "Your dad's already got a grill. And I'd rather not be eating steaks in the dirt come dinnertime."

That earned him a full laugh. "That's a solid point."

He looked at me then, his smirk softening into something steadier. Something warmer.

For a man who had spent most of his life floating—never quite landing, never quite deciding where he belonged—Gage Langton had built something real. Something that mattered.

And not just for my parents.

For me.

For us.

By mid-morning, Ridgeview was in full motion.

With my parents' house nearly finished, today was a workday, which meant people were rolling in one after another, all ready to pitch in.

Luke and Audrey Walker pulled in with their kids—Lizzy, the teenager who still couldn't parallel park, and the two-year-old twins, Henry and Josie, who immediately bolted in opposite directions the second their feet hit the ground.

Lizzy sighed, crossing her arms as she watched her little brother and sister shriek-laugh their way around the yard. "I don't know why they won't let me drive yet, but *those* two are still allowed in public."

Audrey chuckled, tucking a strand of hair behind her ear. "Because we love you, sweetheart."

Luke smirked. "And because we need someone who can actually buckle them into their car seats."

Lizzy groaned. "Fantastic. A built-in babysitting gig."

Before she could say anything else, Ethan and Liam wandered over, both fresh off morning feeding chores. Liam leaned against the pickup, watching the twins wrestle each other to the ground. "Which one's winning?"

"Neither," Lizzy said dryly. "They just keep trading positions."

Josie shoved Henry over and scrambled on top of him. Henry cackled, then somehow flipped himself around and tackled Josie instead.

Liam snorted. "Well, at least they're evenly matched."

Morgan and Cody pulled in next, their daughter Nikki hopping out before the truck had fully stopped, her blonde ponytail swinging behind her. "Okay, but who brought dessert?"

Morgan sighed, shaking her head. "Everyone's happy to see you too, sweetheart."

Nikki waved her off. "Yeah, yeah, love you, Mom. Where's the cake?"

Nora stepped down from the Langton truck, hands on her hips as she surveyed the growing crowd. "Now, why does everyone always assume there's cake?"

Nikki turned to her with wide, innocent eyes. "Because you're a gramma."

Nora let out a laugh. "Not yet, I'm not, unless you know something I don't. You're a menace, you know that?"

Nikki just grinned. "So... is there cake?"

Cody chuckled. "Tell me you're the daughter of a horse trainer without telling me you're the daughter of a horse trainer. You're worse than a barn cat looking for treats."

Trent and Lauren pulled in next, Trent's truck loaded down with supplies. Lauren climbed out, stretching her arms overhead with a groan. "I cannot believe I married into a family where weekends mean free labor."

Trent grinned, looping an arm around her waist. "Welcome to ranch life, babe."

Cole and Emily arrived right behind them, Emily hopping out and waving before grinning in Gage's direction. "What's this I hear about steaks in the dirt? Gage's text got me all worried."

Gage shot a look at Amber. "See? I'm not the only one concerned."

Emily held up a plastic grocery bag. "Relax, cowboy. I brought paper plates and a picnic blanket."

Nora arched a brow. "And what makes you think I don't have real plates?"

Emily grinned. "Oh, I know you do. But let's be honest, by the time the kids are done, at least one of them is gonna use a plate as a frisbee."

Luke gave a low whistle. "That's... actually a good point."

Finally, Chase and Kate pulled up, Kate waving as she climbed out. "If this is a housewarming party, I assume there's coffee?"

Gage groaned. "Do none of you people actually plan to work?"

Trent clapped a hand on his shoulder. "Sure we do. But work is more fun with coffee and food."

Nora laughed, already heading toward the house. "Fine, fine, I'll go inside and help Sherri make a fresh pot. But if y'all want cake, you better hope she's got something in the freezer."

Nikki cheered. "Gramma Sherri!" And she raced up the porch, pigtails bouncing, calling my mom her new favorite nickname.

I chuckled, watching Gage shake his head. He was used to this by now. The Langtons might have been a busy ranch family, but when they showed up, they showed up. And that meant turning everything into a full-fledged gathering.

Through the morning, I watched my dad settle into his new place. Gage and my dad stood side by side, surveying the work in progress like two old cowboys overseeing their land.

"Well," Dad muttered, arms crossed. "Ain't bad."

Gage nodded. "Not bad at all."

My mom, meanwhile, was already deep in conversation with Nora Langton, pointing at the garden plot she was planning for the spring.

"It's been too long since I've had a proper vegetable garden," she said. "And these raised beds Gage built me will be perfect."

Nora nodded approvingly. "Just wait 'til you see the greenhouse we've got. You'll have tomatoes year-round."

I swallowed hard, the emotion sneaking up on me.

This was right.

They were happy.

And I had nothing left to fight.

Later, after the last deck nail was hammered and the final railings were set in place, the work slowed.

People sprawled in their lawn chairs, drinks in hand, steaks sizzling on the grill.

I stepped away for a second, looking out over the land.

The sun was low now, stretching the light over the mountains, painting everything in shades of gold and blue. Gage found me like he always did.

He leaned next to me, shoulder brushing mine, hands tucked in his pockets. "You okay?"

I let out a slow breath. "Yeah. Better than okay."

He turned slightly, watching me. "Really?"

I met his gaze. "Really."

Gage tilted his head toward the fire pit, where my parents were laughing with his family.

"C'mon, Mrs. Langton," he murmured. "Let's join them."

I smiled.

And took his hand.

C C *ATCH UP ON ALL the Ridgeview Brothers books!*

From our hearts to yours

THANK YOU FOR SPENDING a little time with the family at Ridgeview Ranch.

I hope you've enjoyed getting to know everyone. I'd love it if you would share this family with your friends so they can experience life on the ranch with these swoony cowboys and sassy cowgirls. As with all my books, I have enabled lending to make it easier to share. If you leave a review for *A Match for the Cowboy* on Amazon, Goodreads, Book Bub or your own blog, I would love to read it! Email me the link at **TheCowgirlWrites@TessThornton.com**

Would you like to read Blake Walker's romance? Dive into Blake and Meryl's story, and stay up to date on upcoming releases and sales by joining my newsletter: https://mailchi.mp/11ce46b43f43/join-the-family

And now, keep reading for a sneak preview of Cody and Morgan's love story!

A Home for the Cowboy

Chapter One

Cody

"Welcome, folks, to the National Reined Cowhorse Association Western Derby, here in beautiful Scottsdale, Arizona. We've had an exciting few days of competition with some of the best cow horses and cowboys in the country. We're back now with the fence work, so grab your seats and settle in for a terrific afternoon."

THE ANNOUNCER'S VOICE ECHOED from the arena, calling the audience back to their seats after an hour's break. A hot shiver of excitement ran through my chest, and I took a deep breath. I had a lot riding on this afternoon, but it wouldn't do me any good to get edgy now. I mopped the trickle of sweat off my temple and pushed my hat a little farther down on my forehead. Time to get to work.

Two of my horses had made the finals today. My top horse, a classy bay stud named Five Iron, had an excellent shot at taking home the win this year. Finally! I was still one of the youngest riders around, but I had already been trying to claim that buckle for eight years. Five Iron could be the horse to take me to the winner's circle at last, and I was itching to prove myself.

But Five Iron would have to wait, because the horse that came first in the draw was a sweet, dopey, overgrown buckskin gelding. He was ambitiously named Jewels N ShowBiz, but everyone just called him Biz. The only reason he was in the finals at all was that Tom Barker's horse had taken a fall in the prelims. Still, he was the boss's sentimental favorite, and more than anything, I wanted to make Blake Walker proud of both of his horses today.

Biz didn't have to mark a top score. We weren't even planning on campaigning him much longer. If I could just make today's run clean and strong, then maybe he could retire from showing and Blake or his son Evan would find another job for him. I checked my bridle and snugged up the cinch, then led the big gelding toward the waiting area. We were third in the draw. My horse was warmed up and as ready as he'd ever be, so I was in no hurry.

"Good luck, Cody!" my friend Ray Purvis called.

"You too, Ray!" I answered with a wave.

A couple more friends said the same, and I thanked them all as I stood there, idly slapping the rein end against my chaps. I'd take a few minutes to cool my jitters, then mount after the first horse went. No sense getting more worked up right before I went in, or letting my horse get wound up feeding off my anxiety—which wasn't likely to happen, anyway. Biz was asleep where he stood. I scratched his ears and shook my head when his lower lip drooped lazily. Some competitor.

Don't get me wrong. I was pretty fond of the big guy. You had to like him, really, because he didn't give you the option not to. But I'd also trained him since he was two, so I knew pretty well what he was and wasn't capable of. Biz had a big motor when he decided to use it, and he was a gorgeous mover, so he always scored well in the dry work. But he was all grace and no grit. He was about the prettiest thing in any barn anywhere, but pretty doesn't catch cows.

"Haskins, there you are. Gonna take home that reserve championship again?"

My neck prickled at a familiar voice, and out of nowhere, hate curled in my stomach. Sure enough, there was Jonas Weatherby, leading his chestnut mare up to the gate. She had wicked talent, and Jonas was last year's champion, so naturally, I wanted to beat him. But that wasn't why I despised him.

"Hey, Cody," purred the woman hanging on Jonas' arm. "Good luck out there."

A punch hit me right in the chest when I saw my ex-wife. Courtney Lowe. She'd even dropped my name like I never existed. That was the part that stung. I didn't miss her—hadn't for a long time. It was the betrayal, the lies, and just being discarded like worthless baggage after all I'd done for her.

But I kept my glance short and cool and shrugged like I didn't care. Like she hadn't stomped on my guts and thrown away five years of marriage for a blowhard with a bigger buckle and tighter jeans. Jonas was cowboy number six or seven since she'd left me. Not like I was keeping track or anything. She shot me that snide wink, the one I despised more than broccoli or traffic jams, and turned her syrupy attentions back to Jonas.

"Gimme a kiss for luck, darlin'," Jonas said as he mounted his horse. Loudly, of course. I didn't watch, but I could hear them, and I couldn't help but remember the last time she'd kissed me. The memory turned my stomach. Maybe her lips wouldn't make so much noise if she hadn't pumped them full of collagen. She used to be pretty good looking, but she was looking more and more plastic every time I saw her, and I could hardly recognize the girl I'd married anymore. And I sort of hated myself for ever seeing anything in her.

I closed my eyes and forced a calming sigh. Back to work... back to work. The first horse came out, posting a pretty stiff score. That would be tough to beat, but Jonas would do it. And, I decided as I swung up in the saddle, so would I. With both my horses, if I had anything to say about it. The second horse went, turning in a pretty respectable performance. Finally, the loudspeaker crackled, and it was my turn.

"Next up, we have Jewels 'n' ShowBiz, bred and owned by Blake Walker of Walker Ranch in beautiful Big River Valley, Idaho, and ridden by Cody Haskins. Haskins was our reserve champion in the Two Rein event last year, and he'd like to take home the win this year in the Bridle class. Give them a big welcome, folks. On deck, we have Jonas Weatherby, with...."

I blocked out the announcer's voice. I blocked everything out, except the feel of muscle and bone, my horse's heartbeat pounding through the saddle, and the electricity that I could always feel flowing up the reins. "All right, Biz. Do your stuff."

Biz pricked his ears right on cue and trotted into the center of the arena. He was eager—I could feel his pulse quicken, and he played with the bit as his eyes fastened on the gate at the far end of the arena. The crew had our cow ready, and they were only waiting for me to give them the nod.

I spared one glance at the edge of the arena where the boss was watching. I gave him a tight look, not quite a smile, and we both knew what it meant. Biz had once belonged to his granddaughter Emma, but... not anymore. But Emma had had big dreams for this horse, and now it was finally our chance to make them come true. Blake nodded back, and that was it. We were on. I signaled the gate crew, and a wild-eyed black baldy jumped out at us.

The fence work is my favorite of our three events. It's hands-down the most dangerous of them all, but it's also a hair-raising good time and just about the greatest thrill a body can have on horseback. It takes guts and speed, finesse and athleticism, and it will make a king or a fool of you faster than anything I know.

We boxed the cow at the gate end of the arena, learning the "feel" of the cow before we took off down the fence. Biz dropped impressively low to the ground with each block. Those turns would score well. Maybe the big guy was waking up to his job, after all. We made six turns, proving that we could hold the wild bovine, then I held Biz back and let the cow run down the fence.

My hair was on fire by this point. There's nothing like it: the feeling of power, speed, and perfect understanding between horse and rider. Five Iron would be even hotter, more tightly tuned, and more thrilling. But Biz was giving me everything he had, which was more than I'd ever seen from him before. And I was going to turn all that try into a top score if it was the last thing I did. I leaned forward and got more aggressive to show the judges how much horse I had under me. Jonas Weatherby would be licking his wounds until the fall futurities after I finished with him today.

We rode into the next turn hard. Biz responded willingly, and we were just about home. Every turn had been spot-on the money, every stop had been powerful and perfectly executed, and that cow had never once slipped out of our control.

That was until the black devil dodged, whirled, and jumped the wrong way.

There was nowhere to go. Biz was laid back and half a hand taller than the best cow horses, so it took more time for him to react. Already committed to the turn, he could never get his feet back under him in time.

I tried tugging on the rein, but it was too late. The cow tangled with my horse's legs, and all three of us balled up in one ugly nightmare. The last thing I remembered was seeing Biz's head slam hard into the wall.

Then I blacked out.

Morgan

Big River Valley, Idaho
One Month Later

I was beaten and I knew it. I screwed up my face, trying not to sob like a baby, and lifted my arms in defeat. My throat wasn't working right and I couldn't see through the tears. I knew the answer, but I asked anyway. "Isn't there anything else you can do for him?"

Doc Burns, the local veterinarian, and also my employer, rinsed his hands in the bucket. "I'm afraid not, Morgan. Even if we could get the poor guy all the way to the teaching hospital, and even if they could do an emergency colic surgery, with his age, his chances of survival are slim to none."

I closed my eyes and fought against the ugly cries. "I know. He'd never make it out of sedation."

The vet shook his head. "The trailer ride alone would be too much. It's the worst part of my job, but it's the kindest thing you can do for him."

I gulped down all my tears and anger and kneeled by Dodger's head to pet him one last time. I'd grown up with this horse. Had him since we were both nine years old. I'd shown him probably hundreds of times as a kid, and then, several years later, I'd pulled him out of the pasture to start up my horse therapy program. He'd done everything I'd ever asked, given all he had and then some, and now, there was nothing I could do in return but let him go.

He groaned again. His eyes were glassy and dull, and his lips pulled back from white, pasty gums. One last time, he tried to lift his head at my touch, and the tears broke free like a waterfall. I buried my face against his neck and stroked his long ears. "Oh, my boy. My good boy..."

Dodger's breathing was becoming more labored now. I scratched that dish above his eyes that testified to his twenty-five years and sniffed back a sob.

"You're the best old man," I choked into his neck. "All right. You win this one."

"Do you want to go to the house?" Dr. Burns asked gently. "You may not want to watch."

"No." I shook my head. I didn't want to see this, but I owed it to my old friend. "He was always there for me. I can be there for him one more time."

In a few moments, it was all over. I watched until the last flicker of life dimmed and cooled, the pain finally eased, but even then I could not force myself to look away.

"I'm not sure what to do now," I said at last, dazed and more than a little lost.

"Yes, I imagine he'll be hard to replace as a therapy horse," Dr. Burns agreed. "Everyone loved him."

I swiped a tear away. "No, it's not that. I mean, yeah. I don't know how I'll replace him, and it's not like I have offers for more horses pouring into my inbox. But I just... I don't know how I'll look out my window in the morning without seeing that big old friendly blaze of his."

The vet smiled sympathetically. "Every owner says something like that to me. They wonder why on earth they're out here doing this at all, if they're just going to lose them. Some even think about hanging it up, but then, some nice youngster will steal their heart and they'll dive in all over again."

"Oh, no. I might have to find a new horse for the program, but I won't fall in love with any horse like I did Dodger. He... he was special."

Burns put a hand on my shoulder. "I'm sorry, Morgan. If it's any comfort, we've all been there. Take the day off, alright?"

"Yeah. Thanks."

The veterinarian put his equipment away, and I wandered into the cool of the barn to think for a minute. It was a good thing none of the kids were here. I'd come out early to feed before going to work at the vet hospital, and that was when I'd found Dodger down.

It hit me then—I couldn't let the kids see him like this. I'd have to do... something. How and what? I had no idea. It wasn't like I could get out my garden spade and put him in the backyard like my cat. But at least I could give my old friend a bit of dignity, so I grabbed a couple of blankets to throw over him.

Doc Burns was on the phone when I came back out, so I gave him his privacy until he finished. "Yes," I heard him say. "Yes, I'll do that. What? Oh, excellent. Thank you, Blake. Yes, the old Baxter house, with the white fence on the left. You'll see a sign for the program out front. Right, see you soon."

I perked up. I lived in the old Baxter house, and that sign was mine.

"What was that?" I asked when he hung up.

"I called in some help. Thought you wouldn't mind. Blake Walker lives about a mile up the road. Heard of him?"

Had I heard of him? I'd only spent most of my life drooling over the beauties grazing the fields around Walker Ranch. "Ahm... yeah." I stuffed my hands in my pockets. "Why did you call him?"

"He's an old friend. And he has equipment. You know. He'll be right down to talk to you."

"Oh." Embarrassment flooded me. I wasn't even sure how I was going to pay for today. The non-profit should cover it, since Dodger was a program horse, but there weren't enough loose funds at the moment. The other horses had basic veterinary insurance, but Dodger's age had made it impossible for him. The vet fees would probably eat my entire check, since I only worked part time to make ends meet, and now I'd have to reimburse one of the best breeders in the country for his trouble. Or die of broke-girl humiliation.

Blake Walker arrived ten minutes later. He was a barrel-chested, iron-whiskered giant of a man—not that he was tall, but there was something about him that made me feel terribly intimidated as I watched him getting out of his truck. That feeling evaporated almost immediately when he came toward me with his hat doffed and his hand extended.

"Miss Westcott? It's a pleasure." He tipped his head toward Dodger under the blankets. "I'm awfully sorry, ma'am. I assume you'd like to bury him on your property here? I can have the boys bring down a backhoe."

I tried to smile, but I probably just looked like I was about to bawl. "Thanks for the offer. Ah, look, I appreciate you coming down and all, but I'm not sure…"

"You already have a truck coming?" Walker glanced between me and the vet.

"No, it's just… I can't afford much," I mumbled.

"Oh, think nothing of it. I've heard a bit about your program, Miss Westcott. I always meant to pop my head over here and see what it was all about, so I suppose now's my chance. You run on sponsors and volunteer help, right?"

"Yes. It's just enough to cover the usual expenses and labor." Well, it was almost enough.

Walker grinned. "I know all about that. 'Usual' ends up being 'unusual' pretty quickly. Let the boys take care of this for you, Miss. Consider it our volunteer service for a neighbor."

"That's… that's really nice of you." I crossed my arms and tried to release a breath, but I just shook instead. It was all too much to carry, and my shoulders were only so big. I wasn't about to turn down an offer like that. "I sure appreciate it, Mr. Walker."

Dr. Burns closed the back door of his truck and came over. "Well, thanks, Blake. I'm back to the hospital, but I'll see you tomorrow about that gelding."

A cloud darkened Walker's face, but he nodded and lifted a hand. "Tomorrow." He turned back to me. "I know this isn't a great time, but would you mind if I asked a bit about what you do, Miss Westcott? I've been curious for a while."

"Oh. Sure." I cleared my throat. Never in my wildest dreams could I have imagined that Blake Walker, practically a legend in the horse world, would stand in my driveway and ask about my little therapy program. I guess this was Dodger's last gift to me—bringing the kind of man who was rumored to be both ridiculously wealthy and good to his very bones to take an interest in the dream we'd started as a team. I hoped I could put two sentences together.

"We mostly work with troubled kids. The school counselors sometimes refer them, or they might get our name from a private therapist or pastor, something like that. We have a couple of kids with disabilities, but we don't have the facilities—yet, anyway—for a full physical therapy program. We have one dementia patient now and another with clinical depression, but we only have about thirty regular clients." My ears were hot, and I hurried to explain myself. "I'm hoping for more. Obviously, as soon as we can handle them."

Walker was turning about, his hands on his hips and his hat pushed back over a squinting brow. "What do you need?"

"A miracle or two would be nice."

Walker smiled faintly. "I don't know any angels, so give me something lower to aim at."

Hope brimmed up in my chest. He was interested in helping! I didn't dare expect much, but I was a professional, and I could hold myself together long enough to lay out our needs. I cleared my throat and put on my best tour guide voice.

"Our most pressing needs are listed on our website. I can send you a link if you'd like. We're raising funds this summer for a better fence. Our goal before winter is to start work on a safe indoor saddling area for multiple horses simultaneously. But our biggest need right now is a viewing area in the indoor therapy arena with a ramp and a hoist for mounting assistance. And I'm always on the lookout for volunteers, and two...." I stopped to take a breath. This was going to ache for a very long time. "Make that three more horses."

"And hay to feed them, no doubt."

I shoved my hands back in my pockets. "We usually get enough donated to get by, but it's never too much."

Walker nodded. "I'll have the boys bring down a ton of alfalfa. And I'll see if there's anything I can do for the other things."

"I appreciate it, sir, but are you sure? The hay would be amazing, but you don't need to put yourself out. Helping me with Dodger is already huge."

He shrugged. "Call it a tax writeoff. Hey—" he pointed at the corrals, where Duke and Badger were whisking flies from each other's faces. "What sort of horses do you look for to use in your program?"

I glanced between Walker and my corrals. My horses were nothing to what I'd seen gracing his fields. Mutts by comparison, but I was still proud of them because they did something good and noble. His horses might win big money at national events, draw industry attention for their quality, but my horses... they were the steeds that helped battle darkness.

"They're all rescued or donated. I'm not particular about a lot of things," I admitted. "Some of my horses aren't even ridable, but of course, we prize the ones that are because they can do more types of therapy. I don't care about age, but they have to be reasonably healthy. I wish I had a recovery facility for the serious rescue cases, but I don't have the space here for quarantines or medical treatment." I sighed at that. Someday... *someday*, I'd love to have the kind of place that rescued both horses and humans, but for now, I was lucky just to save a few humans.

"You can't risk getting the other horses sick, though," Blake observed, still scanning my corrals with a thoughtful eye.

"No," I admitted. "But I do have some horses that came from rescue organizations once they were ready to be re-homed. They have to be sound enough to be comfortable walking, but we don't care about beauty or papers. The most important thing is they have to be a people horse. Kind, soft, dog-gentle and willing to please, and responsive to the sensitive moods of the kids. And smart. The best therapy horses are like four-legged humans."

"Huh." Walker stuck his thumbs behind his buckle. He was looking over each of the animals with the experienced eye of a lifelong horseman. "Interesting. Well, I won't keep you. I'll have Marshall or Evan come down as soon as they can. You don't want those kids to arrive first."

I gave him the best smile I could, but I'm sure it was pretty thin. "Thank you again, Mr. Walker."

He lifted his hat as he got in his truck. "Nice to meet you, Miss."

Chapter Two

Cody

I HOPPED OFF THE two-year-old filly I had been working and gave her a pat of satisfaction. "Going to be a nice one," I said to Marshall, who was perched on a fence rail.

"You bet she is. Another daughter of Iron Ridge. Best stud we've ever had. What do you think about Dad selling him?"

Marshall Walker was technically my employer, being number three of the four Walker boys, but he was more like a brother to me. I'd never have amounted to much in life if it hadn't been for him bringing me home like a stray dog when we were kids, but he never held it over me. In fact, when it came to their performance horses, the Walkers all agreed that I was in charge.

We'd all grown up together, but while the sons of Walker Ranch had taken to cow doctoring and hay farming and the general business that kept the ranch afloat, I had struck out to make a name for myself. For twelve years, I followed the top trainers around, working my butt off and learning everything there was to know about shaping good colts into elite athletes. And three years ago, I had come home to the opportunity of a lifetime, managing the Walkers' show barn.

"Iron Ridge was great for the ranch while he was here, and you got top dollar for him when he sold. It was a good call," I grunted as I pulled my saddle. "You've got his babies coming out your ears, and Five Iron's going to fill his daddy's shoes someday. Time to get some fresh blood. Just as long as the boss picks a good outcross stallion this time."

Marshall grinned. "Not like the Stars N ShowBiz stud? His colts were always the prettiest."

"And the fattest and the slowest. There was a reason we sold most of them as two-year-olds."

"Yeah," Marshall echoed, though his voice was suddenly flat. "Most of them."

I threw my saddle over the rail and leaned on it. "Look, what happened in Arizona...."

"An accident," Marshall interrupted. "Nothing you could have done. No one blames you for it, so stop blaming yourself."

"I broke your dad's heart because I was stupid, and I thought I'd rub Jonas' nose in it. I should never have pushed that horse. Five Iron missed his shot in the finals, but what kills me is Biz...."

"He ain't the first, and he sure won't be the last horse ever to lose his eye in an accident."

"Yeah, but your dad's pet horse is washed up, all because I got greedy."

"Oh, I wouldn't say that. Evan's talking about using him for his ranch horse. Slower pace, steady work. He'll do well once he's all healed."

"It's not the same, and you know it. I think your dad would rather see Emma's horse grazing the front lawn like some ornament than put to work like all the others."

Marshall frowned and shrugged. "Well, it's Evan's call. She was his daughter, so I suppose the horse is actually his."

I fisted my hand on the horn of my saddle and gazed out over the rolling green-gold meadow beyond the barns. "Yeah."

Blake rolled up behind us in his new truck, and I went back to the filly, who was standing quietly like I'd trained her to do, and slipped off her bridle. I had my back turned when the boss walked up to the pen.

"Marshall, the neighbor up the road lost a horse this morning. Nice girl, needs a hand. I told her you'd be over with the backhoe to help her out."

"I've got to go set irrigation pipes today," Marshall groaned. "That kid we hired from town flaked out again. Not that I wouldn't prefer to go bury a horse, you know. My favorite thing to do, right next to an all-night calving."

Blake squinted. "Where's Evan?"

"Went to town for parts to fix the stack wagon. And Luke and Dusty are weaning calves on the south parcel this week."

"I can be free," I offered. "I only had five colts to work before lunch, and this was number four."

The boss nodded. "All right. It's White Pines Therapeutic Riding Center down on the highway. She's in the old Baxter place. Remember Gus and Nancy?"

"Good grief. I haven't heard of them in eons."

"That's because Gus passed eight years ago, and Nancy went into a home in Colorado right after. I think Morgan Westcott was their niece. Anyway, she's got the house now. She works part time for Doc Burns, and she's trying to get that new therapy program going on there. I told her we'd donate some hay. But the first problem is to get that horse out of her driveway before all her kids show up."

"I'm on it." I closed the gate and adjusted my hat. Anything to please the boss because I'd never get over how bad I'd let him down. And it killed me that he didn't even seem mad about it all.

"Thanks, Cody," he called after me. "Oh, and check out her program while you're there. Let me know your opinion."

I looked back at the boss. There was a slight edge to Blake's voice and more than the usual pinch around his eyes. I glanced briefly at Marshall, wondering if he had seen it, too.

"Right, boss."

Morgan

I WAS ON THE phone with my volunteer coordinator when the semi towing the equipment trailer rattled up to the gate. *Great.* I sighed, kneaded my eyes, and tried my empty coffee cup for the third time, but it was no use. This day really was happening, and it was just as rotten as it had been two hours ago.

"Kelli, I have to go," I said. "The truck is here."

"Really? Which one is it, Evan or Marshall?"

I made a face. "How should I know? I've never met any of them."

"But I thought you worked at Doc Burns's! They're tight."

"Yeah, in the back office. It's not like I see people. Look, I'm not really in the mood for ogling cowboys. I'll call you after, okay?"

"Okay. I'm really sorry, Morg. Dodger was one in a million. Italian on me tonight, and we can cry buckets and watch sappy old movies."

I smiled into the receiver. "That sounds great. Thanks, Kel."

I hung up and walked outside, just in time for the driver to slam the door of his truck and drive through the gate he'd had to open for himself. I bit my lip. *Tacky, Morgan.* A fine welcome for someone who was doing me a favor. I couldn't even get outside to get the gate.

I waved him into the turnaround and stood back, my stomach buzzing with a thousand butterflies. Despite what I'd told Kelli, there was a certain thrill in knowing it was one of the famous Walker brothers coming to help me. Every single woman within five hundred miles at least knew who they were. A pity I was in no shape to appreciate a tall, rich, single, and hot as August cowboy right now.

I brushed my hat and face self-consciously. I'd taken care of my smudged mascara, but last I'd looked, my eyes were still swollen, and I was still wearing that same grimy t-shirt from earlier. Oh, well. It wasn't like I had any chance of making an impression anyway, and I had an ugly job ahead of me.

The cowboy was looking down, so I couldn't see his face as he rolled to a stop and pulled the brake lever. Then he opened the door and stepped down from the truck. And strike me with a two-by-four. My jaw dropped, and I forgot to breathe until my head spun. *Oh, my stars.*

Yeah, that was worth coming out to see.

Chiseled features, hard from a life under the sun, but still clinging to a sensitive mouth and brow, brown eyes brighter than the sunrise, and a smile ringed by tan lines. He came toward me and doffed his hat, revealing wavy dark hair, cropped short around the temples. Just like I liked a man to look. I had to blink a few times, and my tongue was glued to the roof of my mouth.

"Are you Miss Westcott?"

I straightened and remembered to stick my hand out. "M-Morgan. You must be... Evan Walker?"

He grinned and shook my hand. Nice hands... "Nope, I'm afraid you'll have to do with the hired help. Cody Haskins."

My stomach dropped through my feet. And like an idiot, I just blurted out whatever came into my head. "Cody Haskins? You're like, a world champion trainer, aren't you?" Oh, for pity's sake, could I sound like a bigger goon?

"Not even close, but I can still hope. Hey, I'm sorry about your horse."

I died a little in mortification, but I managed a shaky smile. He must have thought I was funny in the head, but at least he was nice about it. "Thanks. It's been an awful day."

He nodded. "I bet." His chin tightened in sympathy, and he just stood there looking at me.

I glanced nervously to the side, then questioningly back at him. Was I supposed to say something? Or was it his turn? Neither of us seemed to know, so we just kept staring at each other.

Finally, he cleared his throat and chucked a thumb over his shoulder at the backhoe. "So, where should I...?"

"Oh. Right." If my face got any hotter, I'd have to take a dunk in the horse trough. I twisted away, hoping it would look like I'd meant to gesture somewhere else. "Ah... I was thinking about laying him under the white pine over there."

He shook his head. "A place under the tree. Must have been a special one."

"Why do you say that?"

"Because every ranch that's been around long enough has a few shrines in the field somewhere. The best horses get a spot under a tree or on a hill. Something that will be remembered."

"I guess it must be true, then." I sighed. "I'll never forget Dodger, I can tell you."

He peered down at me, and for a moment, he almost looked... like he got it. Like he didn't ride a hundred of the country's best horses every year and knew what it was to find just one special one. Then the softness faded, and he was all business again.

"I'll get started, then. It will take me half an hour or more, depending on your soil. Probably hard as a rock this time of year."

"Probably. I try to dig fence post holes in the spring because of that clay."

He stared at me. "By hand? You?"

I shrugged. "Some people don't have big equipment and lots of ranch hands."

His eyebrows jumped. "Got it." He pulled a pair of gloves out of his back pocket, dusted them off on his jeans before putting them on, and swung up on the equipment trailer to loosen the bindings. "Can you unhook that? Thanks. And that one there."

I ducked around the hitch and helped where I could. A moment later, he was backing the big tractor down the ramp. This time, I managed to open the gate out to the field for him.

"Thanks," he called as he drove through. "If you have other work, I don't need anything right now."

I *did* have other work. I always had work, but fat chance of being able to focus on it with him there. It was just my luck to meet a man that could make George Strait look frumpy on one of the worst days of my life.

Cody Haskins, showing up like a regular guy and running a backhoe for me. Everyone around here knew his name. Women flocked to expo events where he was demonstrating, all posing for selfies, begging autographs, and giggling like little girls. Local ranchers and small-time trainers either name-dropped him or acted like they were better than him. Even Doc Burns had pictures of Cody showing some of the Walker horses up in his clinic.

I'd never seen him on a horse, but he looked pretty good without one. And he seemed like a nice guy, too—the kind of guy who could understand how I felt about Dodger. I'd thought nothing could brighten this day, but he was a decent pick-me-up. If only I could keep from embarrassing myself in front of him again.

Oh, well. He was probably married or something, anyway. I left off standing at the rail and went back to say a last goodbye to Dodger.

G RAB YOUR COPY OF Cody and Morgan's love story!

A Winter Surprise for the Cowboy

Blake Walker has built a legacy in his family and his ranch. His five boys are starting to find love and build their own lives, and he's beginning to wonder what adventures are left for him.

Meryl Justice has raised everyone's kids but her own, and now she's looking forward to retirement from the job she's had for thirty years. She loves her home and her farm animals, but is that all there is?

Find out when these two hearts set out to discover if wintertime might not just be the best time of all to fall in love!

Click HERE to get your story.

More from Tess Thornton

<u>The Walker Ranch Series</u>

A Home for the Cowboy

Cody and Morgan's Story

A Second Chance for the Cowboy

Marshall and Kelli's Story

A Winter Surprise for the Cowboy

*Blake and Meryl's Story

An Angel for the Cowboy

Dusty and Jess's Story

Taming the Cowboy

Luke and Audrey's Story

A Heart for the Cowboy

Evan and Meg's Story

A Winter Surprise for the Cowboy is a Free Novella available only to newsletter subscribers

<u>The Ridgeview Brothers Ranch Series</u>

A Rival for the Cowboy

Cole and Emily's Story

A Crossroads for the Cowboy

Chase & Kate's Story

A Christmas Wish for the Cowboy

Trent & Lauren's Story

A Match for the Cowboy

Gage & Amber's Story